D1503405

GEMSIGNS

GEMSIGNS

®EVOLUTION BOOK 1

Stephanie Saulter

Jo Fletcher

New York • London

Jo Fletcher Books
An imprint of Quercus
New York • London

© 2013 by Stephanie Saulter
First published in the United States by Quercus in 2014

ISBN 978-1-62365-467-2

Library of Congress Control Number: 2013913476

Distributed in the United States and Canada by
Hachette Book Group
1290 Avenue of the Americas
New York, NY 10104

Manufactured in the United States

10 9 8 7 6 5 4 3 2 1

www.quercus.com

To the memory of my mother,
who started it all with a hobbit

Greer-Ann Saulter
1948–2006

0

WHEN DESCRIBING A CIRCLE ONE BEGINS ANYWHERE. EACH POINT PRE-cedes and succeeds with no greater or less meaning; the tale they tell remains unvaried. There is neither cause nor consequence, for every moment is both. It is curious the resignation with which we declare this pattern in human affairs, and the virtue with which we credit it in nature.

But beware illusions born of too still and centered a perspec-tive. A mere tilt of the head, a sideways step—and history unspools. The triumphs and tragedies, victories and defeats, dark and golden ages come and go and come again, each shaped by the revolution of which it is the final coordinate, shaping that for which it is the first. No two moments are exactly the same, for traveling the circuit con-veys a momentum that displaces the point of return from the point of departure. Life proceeds in a spiral, pushing outward and forward, expanding and accelerating as the players whirl through their evolu-tions, building a vortex.

Be careful. Stand in the middle and the maelstrom will pull you in.

But you must pick the right moment to join the dance. There are events that ripple down the helix, maiming and molding all the moments that follow. These are worth understanding.

Beginnings are important.

So our story begins, perhaps, with Dr. Eli Walker, tasked with the mapping of divisions, accosted, accused, and propositioned. Insulted, as he would have it, but then Dr. Walker is a principled man. To himself he is a player in a morality tale, unraveling dissimulations. He knows, or thinks he knows, what the choices are. His own righteousness is in no doubt. He has the conviction of a man who fights on the side of angels.

But Dr. Walker is a reactor to a reality, the effect of a cause. We might better begin with Gaela Provis Bel'Natur, struggling with corollaries as she makes her way across the city. They will lead her to a treasure beyond imagining, the discarded relic of a dismayed hegemony. Does our story flow from what she finds, or from the manner of her finding it? She could not tell you. Gaela is the very embodiment of unintended consequences. It is her boon and her doom, her grace and her gall. It exhausts her. Gaela could tell Eli a thing or two about the hard grind of duality. She would give a lot for a middle ground, some quiet gray in which to rest, and she may find it, for a while. But not for long. She has convictions of her own.

So Gaela, maybe Gaela is the starting point. Or maybe not. All beginnings are endings, after all, so perhaps we should commence with a departure. A long time ago, in a forest, a deep dark wood that would befit a fairy tale. A young girl, not much beyond childhood, flees between towering trunks, bearing an impossible burden, running for her life. She has emerged from earth, and the great silent spaces beneath the cathedral of trees frighten her. She pauses for breath, rests her hand against rough bark. She has never felt anything like it.

A moth flutters away from her fingers, brown-gray and mottled and invisible until it moves, finding a safer vantage higher up. The girl is transfixed. She is reaching up toward it, hoping to see it fly again, when a whisper of sound reaches her, sighing on a breeze through the forest. For a moment she has almost forgotten the pursuit. She wishes she shared the moth's gift of camouflage, or the possibility of escape in the trees. But even if she were to ascend into the canopy she knows they would find her, track her, burn the forest to retrieve or destroy her. There are men and dogs on her trail, and darker things as well. So she turns, slips away up the slope, running as fast as she can, making for the open ground she knows is there.

Knows? She does not know. She has seen a map. They did not think she would understand it and so did not trouble to hide it from her. She understands only too well that it may be old. The place she is making for may have changed. The trees may stop too soon, or not at all. There may be people, and not the ones she hopes to find. She had very little time, and has judged this her best chance. There is nothing to do now except struggle uphill, hearing more distinctly the whir of a helicopter in the distance, feeling the stitch burning fierce in her side, the low branches and brambles catching at her as the trees become smaller, newer, and the forest turns to scrub on the flat land of the plateau.

This is unexpected. The trees have been cleared, a hazard she had anticipated, but some time ago, and the new growth has not been managed. So she is not exposed as she had feared, but she is slowed down, reduced to walking pace as she pushes through the dense brush. Her pursuers are still moving rapidly, and she can hear the dogs now, and the shouts of the men.

Strangely it is the helicopter she fears most, and she scans the sky. Its endless unbordered space should panic her, but instead the blue immensity overhead fills her with a strange, wild joy. She marshals it. There is no time yet to explore this feeling, and if she is captured the time will never come again. No sight of the helicopter, and its sound has become distant: it must be at its apogee as it circles the forest. For a moment she marvels at her luck, and wonders that it is not tracking the movements of her pursuers, as they are tracking her. The others must not all have been rounded up yet, she thinks, and hope surges in her. Again, she damps the emotion down. She is the only one who has any real chance, and that will be dashed in minutes if the helicopter is called in before she reaches her destination.

Which it will be the moment they realize where she has led them. She can clearly hear the other sound she had been straining for. It was a distant murmur as she came out of the trees, then a growing grumble as she pushed through the dense growth, and now a rushing, tumbling roar as the bracken releases her and she stumbles out onto a narrow, grassy ledge.

She peers over the edge, down into the gorge that falls away a short stride from where she stands, then to the right and up to where the river pours out of the mountain far above her head, crashing into a valley as far again below her feet. White mist and water spray billow up to meet her. The cleft is narrow, a vein of softer rock scoured away over eons. On both sides the walls are nearly vertical, broken here and there by solitary trees that colonize the few ledges and point up at her like spears. As she leans over, the waterfall's turbulence buffets her, wetting her face as though with tears.

No one is there to meet her. A mountain climber with ropes and anchors might hope to rappel down the side of the cliff; she has neither the skill nor the equipment. White water boils at the base of the drop, and she feels panic rising up into her throat. She takes a deep breath, then another and another, and casts a last look up at the deepening blue of the evening sky. Then she fixes her eyes down the long plunge into the gorge.

A moment later the tracking team bursts out of the forest and into the sticky embrace of the scrubland. The leader hears the faint thunder of the waterfall, checks her map and swears. She screams into her earset.

Within seconds the roar of the helicopter rivals that of the river as it heaves into view. By the time the trackers and dogs force their way through the undergrowth and onto the ledge, it is hovering above the gorge, swaying a bit in the updrafts, staying high to avoid the steep walls and buffeting currents. Its rotors almost span the width of the crevice. Retrieval specialists in orange safety suits hang out of the door, sweeping the gap with binoculars. Even from a distance their body language signals disappointment.

The ground team leader spots her counterpart above as he pulls himself back inside the helicopter. She knows what he will say before her comlink crackles with the news.

The girl is gone.

1

THE HEADACHE BLOOMED BEFORE GAELA'S EYES, A VIOLENCE OF REDS AND violets. Her knees jellied as turbulent, aggressive colors pulsed in time to the pounding in her skull. She'd felt it coming on as she left the museum, had gulped some painkillers and hoped she'd caught it early enough to at least stave off the florid accompaniment. No such luck. The meds should kick in soon, but for now she felt buried under waves of pain and almost-purple.

She often wondered what norms—or even other gems—would call her colors, and knew she would never have the answer. Hyperspectral vision coupled with an unimpaired intellect was a rarity, and hyperspectral synesthesia was, as far as she knew, unique. She could have done without the distinction. She struggled endlessly to describe hues no one else could see.

Today they were intense enough to interfere with her carefully modulated perception of her surroundings, and she stumbled and stopped, eyes half-closed. The street was lined with old, faceless buildings hard up against the pavement and she leaned against one of them gratefully. The migraine was not exactly a surprise. She'd known the likely outcome of the day's task, a hurried evaluation of a massive private collection. The paintings were rumored to include old masters, even some Renaissance work, but the museum had had its doubts. It was only at the last moment that someone had thought to request Gaela's services.

Now they had a treasure trove of lost masterpieces, awaiting painstaking analysis of the ancient underdrawings, corrections, and layers of paint by highly trained specialists wielding delicate instruments that could reveal to norm eyes what Gaela had seen in an instant. After hours spent checking dozens of canvases, trying to describe her findings in terms the others could understand, she had a headache. And, she reminded herself, payment and the prospect of more work. It was still far better than other things she'd had to do for a living.

But it had been an exhausting day and the early winter evening had long since deepened into night. At least there was no one around; she always chose her route carefully, preferring quiet streets where there was less passive surveillance to avoid, where she was less likely to be accosted, and where the visual bombardment would be less severe. She should be able to wait, unmolested, for the double-barreled barrage to recede.

She tipped her head back to rest against the cool masonry and gazed up at the sky. Even to her it was largely blank, washed out by the city's glow. Peaceful. She picked out gentle rays of ultraviolet, followed them up until she could make out a few stars. She stood in the shadow of the wall and watched them wheel slowly overhead, letting her eyes rest in the invisible light, until the pain diminished to a spatter of lavender. Her earset buzzed.

"Where are you?" Bal, worried. She'd told him about the paintings and that she'd be late, and messaged him as she was leaving. Still, she should have been home long since. She could picture him resisting the urge to call, wanting to trust that the Declaration would keep her safe, finding things to do around the apartment to distract himself, and finally grabbing his tablet in an excess of anxiety. It gave her a warm feeling.

"Almost home." She swung away from the wall. "I had to stop for a while. Headache."

"You all right? Want me to come get you?"

"No, it's okay. I'm feeling a bit better. Should be there in fifteen minutes or so."

"Dinner's ready." The warm feeling spread. She could feel herself smiling, a huge happy grin that pushed the headache all the way back.

"Great. I'm starving."

She flicked off and picked up the pace, still smiling. Bal: what a treasure. A gem in the literal sense, a godsend if you believed in god. She remembered how they'd met, when she was still a runaway staying barely a step ahead of the Bel'Natur retrieval squads and he a newly arrived refugee from the Himalayan mines. He'd used the chaos of the transit camp to keep her safe, and she'd kept the cash coming in. Once the danger of forced repatriation and indenture had passed, they had ventured out into the city and found a new home in the Squats. For a long time their nascent community had been barely noticeable, a tiny tract of alien territory carved out of the heart of London. Now it was exploding, as gems flooded in on the back of the Declaration.

She crossed the broad, brightly lit avenue that separated the backstreets of the financial district from buzzier clubs and cafés, barely noticing herself twisting and angling to slip unregistered between infrared camera beams and traffic monitors. The Declaration might have brought with it a new sense of security, but with scarcely a week gone by it still felt too tenuous for her to give up the old habit. The strange, dancing gait drew a few puzzled looks, which Gaela ignored. Gems were expected to be weird. In an open, populated place like this, with her hair uncovered and no companion, a touch of harmlessly off-putting eccentricity was useful. She sidestepped between a couple waiting for a table—who politely, pointedly looked away— and the perimeter of the sweeper field in front of the neighboring jewelry shop and plunged into the network of alleys that ran down toward the river.

The boutiques and bistros ended abruptly. There was less surveillance now, and she walked more or less normally. Little light penetrated these narrow streets, but she was using night vision, seeing as a cat sees, navigating easily around obstacles, on the lookout for lurkers in the shadows. From a hundred yards away she spotted a couple grappling with each other, hands pulling at belts and britches as they crammed themselves into the angle of a doorway. Gaela blinked at the telltale glow, not unlike her own, as one of them fell to his knees. She looked for a similar glimmer from his partner, couldn't find it. She hesitated a moment, then turned off into an adjacent lane.

So one was a gem and the other not, unless his gemsign was well hidden. None of her business. Such liaisons—relationships even— weren't unheard of. Now that the Declaration had confirmed a universal humanity, there would inevitably be more. And if it was a business transaction, well, most gems had few choices. Still, it made her uncomfortable. This was not yet a safe place for a gem to linger, still less to leave himself so vulnerable.

The lane she was in ran directly toward the Squats, but she changed course again to avoid a motion sensor, the infrared beam as clear to her as a red rope stretched across her path. The authorities were evidently trying to monitor the numbers moving into the inner-city colony of the radically altered.

Worry sparked in her, coupled with a deep-seated resentment of the endless, obsessive data gathering. There were a lot of very good reasons for newly liberated, often baffled and disoriented gems to band together; but they were in effect corralling themselves, the more easily to be counted and cataloged. Social services had been at pains to reassure them that the information would only ever be used for their benefit. The department liaison was committed, kind and clearly believed what she said to be true. Gaela wished she shared her confidence.

She came out onto another main road, as broad as the avenue she'd crossed earlier but dim and deserted, its surface pitted with age. A damp, stickily cold mist rolled up from the quayside, diffusing the glow from a few ancient streetlamps. Blocky, rectilinear buildings rose in front of her, lights twinkling from very few windows. Still, more than there had been even last night.

She glanced farther up the road to where the old leisure center squatted, dark at this late hour. Bal would have been in there today, working with the others to welcome and settle the newcomers while around them the building was slowly brought back to life. It had been the hub of a desirable area once, a development of modern apartments and communal gardens running down to the river and a short walk from offices, shops, and entertainment. People had flocked to live one atop the other, competing to claim a place in the heart of the city.

Then the Syndrome rolled through like a decades-long tsunami and the survivors, disheartened by the echoing solitude of so many empty homes, dispersed into the more spacious suburbs that ringed the center. Plans had occasionally been floated to demolish the old apartment buildings, reclaim the riverside, but for so long there had been so little money, so few people, and so much else to salvage that it had become an endlessly deferred project.

Now the gems were moving in.

Gaela angled across the crumbling boulevard, aiming for the dark mouth of a side street that wound into the heart of the Squats. Even this close to home she was scanning through the electromagnetic spectra, her senses alert for any new intrusions.

Still, she might have missed the ragged bundle, tucked away as it was among the litter that had collected behind a grubby metal cable box poking up from the pavement, stuffed with live wires that made it glow brightly in her specialized sight. It was a sound that made her look around: a querulous little whimper. She noticed the bundle, focused on the heat signature within, and stopped dead.

The bundle stirred, the sounds becoming more urgent and distressed as it tried to sit up. Gaela moved over to crouch in front of it, shocked to the core. She reached out, thought she should say something, found herself almost unable to speak. Her voice shook.

"Hang . . . hang on, take it easy, let me help."

She pulled away the muffling layers as what was trapped inside them scrabbled frantically to get out, trying to be gentle and reassuring even as she caught the fringe of panic, even as a rage beyond anything she could remember rose like bile in her throat.

"Easy, easy . . . okay . . . there. You're all right, it's all right. Don't be scared. You're okay."

But it was not okay, and she knew it as well as the little boy who emerged from the windings of blanket and trash bags and looked around at the dismal street, the dirty crevice, and the strange woman with glowing red hair and began to cry.

DAY ONE

2

Eli sensed someone settle into the seat opposite but didn't immediately look up. The train was pulling away from the platform, gathering speed for the final leg of the journey, and he supposed this traveler had just boarded. Some hint of perfume or whiff of pheromone told him it was a woman. That she had chosen a seat at an occupied table when the car was largely empty was, to say the least, annoying.

Eli was juggling two tablets, rereading the Conference brief and his own draft analysis on one, writing notes on the other. He shifted his feet out of the intruder's way and glanced up, intending only a brief nod, just enough to convey a touch of irritation and forestall any attempt at fellow-passenger small talk.

The woman was staring at him.

Her face was striking. Black-dark eyes took him in over sharply angled cheekbones, red lips, and a cut-glass jaw. The hair was swept back, glossy and blond. She was tall; he thought that when she stood she would be almost his height. She lounged against the mass-transit upholstery with the easy, powerful poise of an athlete and was simply but expensively dressed. Her black coat would have set him back a month's salary at least; her tiny earset coil was crystalline and almost invisible. He could not have hazarded a guess at her age.

The woman regarded him without expression. He thought her appraisal was intended to discomfort, and had to suppress the urge to shuffle his feet under the table while he parsed his new companion's face. He was certain he'd never seen her before, would have remembered such harsh beauty, but he couldn't shake a sense of familiarity: as though he *ought* to know who she was.

Looking away was impossible. The woman had created an intimacy with her stare, had taken over his space and captured his attention without a word. Eli was unnerved. He felt a need to respond to this invasion, regain a sense of territory. He also felt, instinctively, that if he spoke first he would be at a disadvantage.

He took refuge in props, his left hand holding the tablet he'd been reading at an angle that ensured only he could see its surface. He flicked the other into standby, shielding his notes from view. He left it lying on the table, leaned back in his seat, and gazed at the woman with what he hoped was an air of composure.

She smiled for the first time, a crimson flicker that softened her jawline but went nowhere near her eyes.

"Good afternoon, Dr. Walker."

He let a few seconds tick by, assessing who she might be, making her wait. The voice was as expensive and cultured as the clothing. Her attitude remained relaxed, as though she had all the time in the world. He thought of simply not responding, forcing her to plow on unassisted, but somehow couldn't. He tried to muster an aura of scholarly dignity.

"You have the advantage of me, Miss . . . ?" He let it trail off, inviting her to supply a name. She smiled again at the gambit, then ignored it.

"I've been meaning to make your acquaintance. This seemed," she nodded at the tablets, "an opportune moment."

He thought he saw an opening. "You favor interruptions?" he asked, intending to sound irritated, wincing inwardly when it came out arch. She smiled widely at that, for an instant looking genuinely amused.

"Not as a rule, no." She shifted in her seat, crossing long legs. "I am in a position to contribute to your research, which, I believe, you are intending to present shortly."

"My research."

"Indeed."

"If you'll forgive me for saying so, you don't appear to be a gem."

That earned him a flash of annoyance. Her brows creased and lips twisted for a moment. Then the sculpted face smoothed out again.

"I am not. But it seems to me, Dr. Walker, that relying solely on gem-derived data fails to capture the entire picture. It will inevitably leave a gap in your findings; one might even say a flaw."

"I see." He felt surer of himself now; he thought he knew what this was about. "And you think you're able to fill this . . . gap?"

"I am." She folded her hands together on the table. They were long and strong, beautifully manicured and without adornment. It was interesting, Eli thought, how the *lack* of accessories could often be the signal of serious wealth. Something flickered at the back of his mind; a hint, an intimation of who this woman might be.

"However, I'm aware that you have had similar opportunities before," she went on, "and have failed to take them up. I'm less clear on why."

"I'm not sure what opportunities you're referring to."

"Oh come, Dr. Walker. You've had access to the genetype reports of all the major firms. It's well known that you've been selective in your focus."

"That's your view, is it?" The tablet he was holding had blanked to standby as well. He stacked it atop the other one, being careful to activate neither. "You're mistaken. My team and I have reviewed all of the data from, as you say, all of the gemtechs. That we've declined to adopt their interpretations is down to our commitment to objectivity. We have in fact been anti-selective."

"Not true. You've chosen to ignore the conclusions of those who have a lot more experience in the field."

"We found their conclusions to be predetermined and self-serving."

"Then you haven't been given sufficient information. I can remedy that."

"Who are you?"

The blunt question gave her pause. She regarded him for a moment before responding. He thought she wanted to make sure he understood the significance of the answer.

"My name," said the woman, "is Zavcka Klist."

He had already mentally floated a number of possibilities. This one had been the least likely, and the most impressive. Eli raised an eyebrow.

"From Bel'Natur. I assume I should be flattered."

"I'm not here to flatter you, Dr. Walker. I'm here to explain some things that you may be in danger of not considering fully, and to provide you with material that I think you will find compelling."

He felt his hackles rise. This was more and more like familiar territory. The condescension, the suggestion of deep matters beyond his comprehension, the hint of a bribe. He marshaled his anger. The fact that Zavcka Klist had come in person, to catch him alone and unawares, signaled that the gemtechs were really worried. Their efforts to get him on board had become increasingly frequent and unsubtle.

He had rejected the most recent just the evening before, a slick, smooth-talking "businessman" who'd set up a meeting on false pretenses and spent half an hour trying to convince him that his entire approach was misguided. The man had then gone on to speculate, hypothetically of course, just how damaging such an error might be to a prominent and distinguished career, and to point out how beneficial a less uncompromising attitude could prove, before being summarily ejected from Eli's office. It had been the third such approach in a month.

Word must have reached her. Since this most recent lobbyist had claimed to represent Recombin, it suggested that the industry's internal espionage apparatus was functioning well. Or, he thought sourly, that they had teamed up, an enemy-of-my-enemy alliance, and sent one of their biggest hitters to bring him to heel. It was not a comfortable prospect. He wondered if she would acknowledge the incident.

"That sounds remarkably like a proposition that was made to me yesterday."

"I know about the idiot from Recombin." She said it quickly, exasperated. "Your response to him was entirely understandable. What is not understandable is the notion of a new classification system for gems. There is already enough uncertainty around an appropriate, affordable social settlement. Suggesting that established designations should be revised at this point would be a mistake."

"My conclusions about gems are based on data, Miss Klist. Gained both from direct observation and court order. If, as you've suggested, you have new information I'd be happy to consider it."

This was tricky ground and they both knew it. The courts had long since ordered full disclosure of gemtech records, despite massive, costly, and protracted opposition. Her response was careful.

"I can provide a more detailed exploration of different behavior modalities, based on extensive Bel'Natur research and observation," she said. "I understand that the raw statistics you've been working with can be . . . troublesome . . . to interpret."

"I haven't found them that difficult."

"That's because you haven't understood what they represent," she snapped. The change of tone was startling. "You don't have a comprehensive understanding of what gems are capable of—both the advantages and the risks. There are thousands of those *people*"—she spat the word out as though it were bitter—"wandering around amongst ordinary human beings, whereabouts unknown half the time, with extraordinary capabilities and unclear intentions. They *cannot* simply be left alone to tuck themselves away in unmonitored enclaves as though they were all the same as each other, or the same as us. They're not."

"No," said Eli quietly. "They're not. You and your predecessors saw to that."

She leaned forward, lips compressed, nostrils flaring. "We fulfilled an urgent need at the time of greatest peril for our species. We kept the human race from becoming extinct, or reverting back to some sort of medieval existence. *We* are the only reason any of us are *here*."

"That is undeniable. And since"—he held up a hand to stop her from cutting in—"since we *are* still here despite all the odds against us, our imperative is to have regard for *all* members of our species."

He threw her a speculative look. "Or do you think that because you've changed some of them almost beyond recognition they should be removed from our consideration?"

"The solution needs to fit the problem. Don't misunderstand me, Dr. Walker." Her fingers drummed the table for emphasis. "I don't want their welfare to be disregarded, I don't want them treated badly. I regret that the conduct of our industry has on occasion been less than humane. But we are where we are, and you have to understand that many—most—of the gems are simply not capable of leading a normal life. They are best suited to the environments they were engineered for, and the work they've been designed to do. And the point is that they *can* work. The social services emphasis there's been since the Declaration is enfeebling, not empowering. Gems who are quite capable of earning a living are ending up in menial roles or becoming nonproductive wards of the state. What kind of sense does that make?"

Eli concealed his reaction with a deep breath and a thoughtful glance out the window. He was surprised to see buildings flash past instead of fields and forests. They were well within the borders of the city, would be arriving within moments. He needed to decide how to play the rest of the conversation.

He had pissed her off with his apparent disdain for the gemtechs. Despite this she was being remarkably candid. This was surprising. Zavcka Klist's business acumen was legendary: many observers considered her to be the real power at Bel'Natur, itself arguably the most powerful and sophisticated of the bioindustrialist conglomerates. She was not thoughtlessly having this conversation, with a man she did not yet have the measure of, in a public train car. It had to mean she was prepared, or preparing, to take the argument to a wider arena; testing it out on him before the Conference, inviting him to take sides, demonstrating by her presence and her boldness what he'd be up against if he made the wrong choice.

She was after something specific with this emphasis on classification and employability. He sensed a significance there. Time to dial down the antagonism, try to draw her out. He pulled his eyes back from the window, focused on her face, conjured a concerned frown onto his own.

"Their capabilities are limited to spec."

"For the most part, yes."

"And they therefore should be understood in such terms."

"Just so." She caught herself, backtracked. "I don't suggest they shouldn't have options. No more mandatory indentureships, we understand those days are over. But they need to be channeled into appropriate roles, with appropriate management and oversight. It makes absolutely no sense for a gem with high-res memory, say, or a gillung, or an organ regenerator, with all that potential, with all that *value*, to end up driving taxis or sweeping streets. Or on welfare, which is frankly more likely."

"Who's to decide what's appropriate? You're suggesting a system of . . . what? Support? Governance?"

"The details will have to wait for the Conference, but you've identified the most important points. Whether you flinch at the thought or not, Dr. Walker, the fact is we—the gemtechs—designed them, produced them, raised and trained them. For better or worse, we understand them. We've always known how to evaluate their abilities, and their needs. Our expertise should be used better than it has been for the past few years."

"Miss Klist." Eli rubbed his hands over his face. He felt weary suddenly, and dirty. The public-address system chimed softly. He needed to end this, but Zavcka Klist wasn't finished.

"Furthermore—and I cannot stress too greatly the importance of this—all gems are not equally competent. Many are simply incapable of proper socialization—you can provide all the therapy in the world, they just don't have the wiring for it. We know from experience that their behavior can be unpredictable. We used to be able to prevent those problems from impacting on society in general. Then it was decided we should no longer have that influence. Fine. But what have we been replaced with? So far, nothing."

She sat back, hands folded once more on the table, and fixed him again with that keenly observant gaze. He realized that his responses were being examined closely; as closely as if he were a gem in a testing chamber, pinned and probed and scanned for reactions, capabilities, endurance. She was waiting for something.

Eli considered his options. If he rejected her outright he'd lose the insider information she'd dangled and cauterize a potentially valuable link to the secretive gemtech hierarchy. If he appeared too ready to agree, she would suspect him of duplicity. He needed to find a response that was encouraging but noncommittal.

As he mentally reviewed the conversation it occurred to him that only half the pitch had been made.

"Miss Klist. With respect, you'll be aware that many of the concerns you raise have been raised before. I am not oblivious to them, and I appreciate your coming to discuss them with me personally. However, my findings must be substantiated. What can you share with me that is verifiable? And *quantifiable*?" He answered her keen look with one of his own.

She gave a satisfied little sigh and smiled that red smile again.

"Take this."

From nowhere a memtab had appeared on the tip of her finger. He reached over and she transferred it to his. He felt a slight tingle.

"It's keyed to you now. Once you've reviewed it we'll talk again."

"Password?"

"Same as your bank account."

That was blunter than anticipated. But then this woman wore confidence like a coat.

The train slid silently into the platform. There was nothing more to be said. The other passengers were on their feet, collecting coats and climbcases, chattering into earsets.

Zavcka Klist stood up. She was as tall as he'd expected. "Goodbye, Dr. Walker. No doubt we'll speak soon."

With that she turned and strode off the train.

Eli glared at the memtab, then pressed it to an intake port on one of the tablets. It slipped off his skin to bond with the machine. He slumped back against the seat and ran his hands through his hair. The tension Zavcka Klist had generated had snapped with her departure, leaving him completely drained. He looked around the car, wondering if anyone had noticed them. He was occasionally recognized. Even within the guarded gemtech world Zavcka Klist was notoriously publicity shy, but anyone who knew who he was and wanted to know who he'd been talking to could no doubt find the information with a quick scan.

Oh well. Too late to worry about that now.

He stood to pull his coat and battered climbcase from the overhead rack. There was one other person still in the car, a scruffy, tired-looking young man at the far end who'd boarded with him in Edinburgh. He carried an ancient backpack instead of a climbcase and was struggling to pull it on over an equally ancient jacket.

Student, Eli thought. *Too much work, too little money, future uncertain. I can relate.* He felt as worn out and vexed as the other man looked. He was muttering angrily, apparently to himself; Eli assumed an earset must be hidden under the shaggy brown hair. Terse notes of complaint in a thick brogue wafted up the car to where he was pulling on his own coat. As if suddenly aware of the attention, the passenger glanced up, caught Eli's eye. Eli flashed a sympathetic smile at the young man, who grimaced and turned away. Eli sighed and stepped onto the platform.

3

THERE WAS NO SIGN OF ZAVCKA KLIST AS HE HEADED FOR THE TURNSTILES. His car had been at the back of the train, and he found himself to the rear of a line of departing passengers shepherded by a crowd of climbcases. He stayed well back, out of their way, and kept a firm grip on his own. Climbcases might be keyed to their owner, programmed to roll independently along and sound an alarm if carried outside the preset radius, but thefts were not unknown. The tablets were tucked inside his now, and Zavcka Klist wasn't the only person who wouldn't mind an advance look at his report.

Several platforms had merged into an apron where departing passengers pushed past him to get to their trains as the arrivals lined up to go through the turnstiles. Eli, lost in thought as he waited his turn to shuffle forward and place his identity pass on the scanner, started at a harsh buzzing from one of the turnstiles. A petite, remarkably pretty woman stood on his side of the barrier, the rejected pass in her hand, as she stared at the flashing light on the machine.

She looked vaguely familiar, but unlike the sense of almost-recognition he'd had with Zavcka Klist, Eli knew that what he was identifying here was a type, not an individual. It was something about her littleness and delicacy of bone structure, her excessive prettiness and the shyness with which she carried it. She stood out in a way that had become rare since the Syndrome. Even Klist did not exceed the usual height-weight-attractiveness ratios nearly as much as this woman. Yet there was something incoherent about her, some subtle counteraction to her beauty. He was no follower of fashion, but he sensed that something about her appearance was wrong.

He was struck by her hair. It was shoulder length and stylishly cut, but the dull, matte-black color was at odds with her modish grooming and fashionable clothes. Eli felt a glimmer of satisfaction at identifying the disguise. He considered whether it was a wig or a dye job, decided on dye. A wig might slip, and besides, if this woman had decided to take such a risk she'd have chosen a better wig. No, she'd dyed her hair, poured on layers and layers of light-barring pigments and fixatives to block the telltale gem glow. He wondered what color it really was. A gentle rose pink maybe, or pale lilac.

For the briefest moment she raised her eyes to the man who was waiting for her on the other side of the barrier. He looked at least twenty years older, and better at hiding his discomfiture. His hair was receding and gray, and he wore the kind of well-cut, conservative suit that made Eli think of a banker. He had a confident, well-cared-for air. Someone used to money and privilege, universal rights and automatic respect. Definitely not a gem.

"Must be due for renewal," the man said, in a voice intended to carry. Although he was looking at the black-haired woman, Eli thought the comment was meant for the turnstile guards. The one on the bodyscanner was watching the woman keenly. Those adjacent to her in the crowd took in her looks and her unease and edged away. The woman bit her lip as she carefully lowered the pass onto the scanner again. This time a soft, welcoming tone accompanied a steady green light as the barrier gates hissed open. The woman stepped through and prodded her slim climbcase into the luggage scanner.

Intrigued, Eli sidestepped into the line for the same turnstile to watch what happened. He was certain the woman was a gem, traveling on a forged—or stolen—norm pass. It was a serious violation, and on the face of it an irrational one. Gem travel had not been restricted since the Declaration—not yet anyway—and she would have been allowed through on her own pass.

But then she would have been recorded as having arrived in London. He could think of two reasons she might wish to avoid that. One was common to any criminal, gem or norm, who wanted to cover their tracks as they moved from city to city. The other was specific to gems who simply wanted to disappear, fall off the index of the underclass and slip into norm society. If their appearance allowed them to pass, the cleanest break with their old life was to register in a new location under their new identity.

He thought the latter was more likely in this case. There was something about the woman that seemed inconsistent with a city-hopping professional crook. Her nervousness and her companion both suggested someone unused to this kind of endeavor. He wondered if the man was a lover, a well-heeled gent past his prime but with the means and charm to attract a beautiful companion who would be grateful for the life he could offer. Such cases were not unknown; were not even restricted to the rich. It was very much at odds, he thought, with Zavcka Klist's analysis.

The climbcase hissed swiftly through the automatic sensors and paused rather longer at the visualization monitor. Eli could see a guard bending down to peer at the screen. He knew this was a waste of time: the chemical sensors and hazard-recognition software were much more perceptive than human faculties. The same was true of the bodyscanners. The guards were really there to deal with the people and luggage that the machines flagged up, not to identify problems themselves. Until a year ago they had had very limited authority to intervene once the equipment had signaled acceptance, but this had been extended as part of the hodgepodge of post-Declaration protocols. Approval by the scanners of papers, person, and possessions no longer guaranteed swift passage.

Which was why Eli wanted to see what would happen if—as he suspected—the woman did not set off the bodyscanner. She stepped up to and through it with a bit more confidence and stood on the exit mat waiting for the light to turn green. No physical abnormalities then, no strange internal anatomy. The guard glanced at the monitor, then peered around it to give her a long look. Eli thought he was manually overriding the lights to keep her on the mat. He was focused on her hair. She stood perfectly still, barely breathing, still biting her lip, not lifting her eyes from the ground.

A mistake, that, thought Eli. *It would be more natural to glance over at him, see what's taking so long.* He found he was holding his breath too, waiting for the guard to press a button that would make the lights flash red, to stand up and ask the woman to step aside and follow me, please. She seemed resigned to it. He could see her companion draw himself up in readiness.

Then the lights flashed green and the guard said, "Congratulations, madam. Welcome to London." The woman did look over at him then, flashed a grateful smile as she stepped off the mat and went to collect her climbcase. She linked arms with the waiting man and they hurried for the exit, climbcase trundling along to keep up.

Eli was dumbfounded. Congratulations? What for? Sneaking in? It confirmed his conviction that the guard had figured her for a gem. If he had—if he even suspected that a traveler had presented a false identity—he was supposed to pull her out of the line for further checks. When it was his turn he watched the guard with interest as he slapped his pass down, put his case onto the belt and stepped through the scanner. The lights went green immediately. Eli stayed on the mat. The guard looked up and Eli caught his eye, raised a quizzical eyebrow. The guard looked puzzled, said, "Welcome to London, sir," as Eli stepped off.

"Thank you," said Eli. He paused, leaned confidentially toward the guard. "Um . . . that lady who went through a moment ago. The pretty one in the purple coat." The guard's gaze sharpened. "She took some time, didn't she? I thought the scanner was broken." Eli smiled pleasantly.

The guard looked at him thoughtfully. "It can take a little longer than it used to," he said. "The scanners have to check for so many things now. Can't be too careful." He gave Eli a bland, impersonal smile right back. "Sorry to keep you waiting."

"Not a problem." Eli grabbed his case and headed out, feeling none the wiser. Had the guard decided to overlook the woman because he felt sorry for gems in general? Or her in particular? She had the kind of vulnerable, fragile beauty that brought out the protective instinct in men. Or had he too clocked her companion and decided if she was being escorted by that kind of money it would be more trouble than it was worth to get in their way? Maybe he just didn't want to face the paperwork. Eli grinned at the thought.

Bureaucracy strikes again. Maybe. Or maybe he was paid off.

That was an equally plausible explanation. He had a mind to try to catch another glimpse of the couple and had almost reached the street when someone grabbed his sleeve and shouted.

"Eli! Eli! Bloody hell, man, have you gone deaf?"

He swung around, looked into a round, red face a bit below his own.

"Rob? Good lord. Sorry, I was miles away." He looked ahead to the doors. No chance of catching up, they'd be long gone by now. He looked back at Robert Trench: old friend, classmate, colleague. They shook hands. "Good to see you. What are you doing here? Not heading north surely?"

"The week of the Conference? No, I'm meeting you. Or trying to. Where were you tearing off to?"

"Nowhere. Thought I saw something interesting. Not important." Eli collected himself. "You're here for me? Thanks. I didn't know I was being met. Why?"

Rob was steering them away from the entrance to the Underground, which Eli would normally have taken, and toward the parking lot. He kept glancing around, a bit nervously, Eli thought.

"I couldn't get you on your 'set and you weren't responding to messages . . ."

"Oh, sorry. Forgot it was off." Eli flicked his earset back to standby. "Press calls have been driving me crazy, I wanted to get some work done. But then I had to let the tablets go down as well."

They were clear of the station crowd now, and he finally released the climbcase, letting it roll along beside him. Rob frowned at it.

"You been holding on to that for a reason?"

"I was approached. On the train," Eli said. "Made me nervous . . ." He stopped. Rob had rocked back on his heels, looking at the ceiling, sucking air in through his teeth. It was an old gesture, something he did when upset.

"On the train. Fucking figures. What happened—? Wait. Tell me in the car." He opened the storage hatch and Eli prodded the climb-case in. "I was trying to get hold of you to warn you, because we thought you were going to be met *here*, when you arrived."

Eli mulled this over as they got in. Once they had pulled away into traffic he asked, "Who did you think was going to meet me at the station? Because you won't believe who pitched up on public transport."

"Who?"

"You first."

"Well, word got around about the bloke you chucked out yesterday. Our head of events was at a Conference planning meeting this morning at which some of the gemtechs were also present, and she let it be known she didn't think much of them for constantly trying to pressure the one person whose job it is to provide a purely empirical analysis. Lots of snickers of course, but the Bel'Natur rep said he was sure that there'd be no more misunderstandings by the time Dr. Walker got to St. Pancras. Something about it bugged her, and then we couldn't reach you, so I thought someone might try to pull some sort of a stunt at the station."

Rob paused for breath. Eli grinned at him.

"So you came to rescue me? Thanks. I'm starting to feel properly important."

"Don't mention it, and for fuck's sake don't underestimate them, Eli. The shit is really hitting the fan this week. The gemtechs are petrified that your report might knock them back even harder than they've been knocked back already. Gempro are really hacked off they're not kings of the world anymore; they just haven't been able to stop fighting amongst themselves long enough to figure out what to do about it. Recombin were set to take the lead in human gemtech until a couple of years ago, and they still cannot believe that business is gone forever. And then there's Bel'Natur. They've played it quietest and cleverest so far, but the rumor is they're planning to present some sort of proposal, which they would no doubt like you to endorse. Don't ask me what, they're keeping their cards very close to their chest."

"Not anymore."

"They sent someone?"

"Zavcka Klist."

Rob stared at him. "No. No *way*."

"I'm telling you."

"That's . . . bloody hell. Are you serious? What did she say?"

Eli sighed, stretched his legs as far as he could in the compact passenger seat, and told him more or less how the conversation had gone. Rob listened intently.

"So they've got some kind of solution that gets the gems back to work."

Eli nodded.

"And cements the segregation between them and us."

"So it seems."

"Sounds like the good old days." Rob's voice dripped sarcasm.

"Doesn't it just. But it won't be anything that crude. That's what Recombin want, to erase the Declaration and just turn back the clock. It'll never happen. Bel'Natur are smarter." Eli paused. "*She's* smarter. She was all about moving forward. Gemtechs should work for the good of society, gemtechs understand gems best, gems need structure and guidance."

Rob had programmed in their destination and let the car go to autopilot. He was gazing out the window, pensive. "The thing is— and you know how much I hate to say this—but it's going to be tough to argue with that. A lot of gems do have jobs, of course— some businesses can hardly operate without them—and their labor is cheaper now that the gemtechs are out of the loop. But most of them are still completely dependent on the state or their friends for support. No one really understands how this brave new post-Declaration world is supposed to work. Norms are scared it's going to mean them paying a lot more taxes."

"You deal with both sides. What do people want? What do the politicians expect to get out of the Conference?"

"Well." Robert Trench took a moment to organize his thoughts. "Even those who weren't wild about the changes are resigned now to gems being designated an artificial subspecies with rights and protections and so forth, but everyone wants clarity on how the Declaration should be applied. Most are open to the idea of autonomous housing estates or even villages, but they're less sure about, shall we say, more personal mixing. The truth is a lot of norms, especially young people, get a kick out of being around gems. They've added a lot of color to daily life, no pun intended. But the rest want to know where they stand, how they're supposed to behave, what kinds of separations should be established. It's been twelve thousand years since there was more than one strand to the human race, and no one knows what the rules should be."

"And the gems?"

Rob looked at him, eyebrows raised. "You're asking me?"

"I'm an academic. I have reams of data and I know what it tells me, but I want to know what you think."

"I think the gems want clarity too. They've got used to this new way of life really quickly, but the ones who are most clued up realize that it's just a transitional stage, and they're worried about what happens next. Bracing themselves for the backlash, almost. One of the things that strikes me is how good they are at sticking together. Ninety percent of the gems in London live in the Squats, they take care of their own with some help from social services, and they don't come out any more than they have to. I don't think most norms appreciate how much resentment there is. The gems know now just how different their lives were to ours, and how much money the gemtechs used to make off them, and how long we stood by and let it happen, and it pisses them off. Understandably."

"So you don't think they want to integrate."

Rob turned bodily around in his seat and fixed Eli with a long, thoughtful look.

"I wouldn't say that. It varies. Some have assimilated really well—which not all norms, or gems for that matter, are happy about—and

I think many others would like to. But again, we don't always realize how alien we are to someone who's only ever known the inside of gemtech crèches and dorms. And the barriers are even greater on our side, because we find *them* too alien. We struggle with their diversity. Not everyone obviously." He waved vaguely at himself and Eli, then swept a hand to take in the world outside the car. "But many people. Most."

"So you've got a norm public who resent the cost of maintaining a nonworking gem population, gems who resent the fact that enormous wealth was generated off them with neither consent nor compensation, and people on both sides who find the other weird and scary."

"That's it in a nutshell. And the resentment is starting to boil over."

"I've seen the newstreams," said Eli quietly. "The harassment is increasing."

"It is. It's really picked up the past couple of weeks, and it's not just name-calling and a couple of shoves anymore. It's horrible because many of the gems are so passive, they've no idea what they've done wrong; half the time they haven't done *anything* wrong except cross the path of some hoodlum who thinks whatever problem he's got is their fault. For which they get the crap beaten out of them. But sometimes they fight back." Rob drew a deep breath. "Occasionally they even start it. And you know what *that* means."

Eli did, had been among the first to understand the correlation. A gem who was prepared to fight was one who hadn't had all aggressive tendencies engineered away. Combat capability was intrinsic to a number of core evolutionary characteristics, including the instinct for self-preservation and the stamina required for tough, dangerous physical activity. So gems who were up for a brawl were often strong and fast and pain resistant. But not always smart.

"What do the police think?"

"They're worried. They're particularly worried about this week and the Conference. They think things are escalating fast. They're dealing with a rise in incidents, but they tell me there's been an even bigger spike in chatter on the socialstreams. It suggests there are way more than the cops can verify."

Eli closed his eyes, swallowed past the knot in his stomach. He'd been commissioned to work quickly, in the hope of outrunning just this sort of backlash. But it was all happening too fast.

"That'll play right into Bel'Natur's hands. No wonder Klist was so sure of herself."

"They'll get more of a hearing than the public realizes, way more than they deserve. The economy's been flat for a couple of years now. The pension funds are getting desperate: if the gemtechs don't pick up soon a lot of them will go bust. We hear there's starting to be a black market, what with all the engineers and technicians who've been laid off. The political view is, the gemtechs need to be brought in from the cold."

"Do the gems understand that?"

"Most of them don't. They don't realize how long a year is in politics. But the ones who really engage with us do get it. There was an argument that the gemtechs shouldn't be allowed at the Conference at all, and they lost that early."

"So they know they're up against it." Eli sighed, thought about all the ramifications, all the problems. The gems versus the gemtechs in the coliseum of the Conference floor felt like a very unequal contest. "I was surprised by their choice of representative. I thought it would be someone with a familiar ability, or at least a less obvious . . ." He trailed off, feeling awkward and guilty.

"Disability?"

"Yes. We're so unused to difference—let alone weakness or illness—since the Syndrome. If it's a strategy, it may backfire."

"It isn't and it won't. Aryel Morningstar is extraordinary. You haven't met her?"

Eli shook his head, frowning. "No, I've just seen her profile on the streams. But that's one of the things that wasn't explained. One of *many* things. Morningstar. I've never heard of it."

"No one knows where she's from, I think not even the other gems. There is no Morningstar Corporation, not that that means much. The gems aren't keen on using their parent gemtech as a surname, as you know, and there's nothing now to stop them choosing another. But I asked her about the name once and she said it was given to her." Rob shrugged. "It doesn't really matter. The selection was never in doubt, Aryel's been their de facto leader ever since they began to colonize the Squats. And despite her appearance, she is the exception to what I was saying before. She's very easy to be around, she understands the issues incredibly well, she's smart, she's charming, she's *very* well educated—"

"Seriously?"

"Very seriously. She can quote Shakespeare by the sonnet, she'll go toe to toe with you on Darwin, and I wouldn't be surprised if she knew how to write computer code and wrangle particle physics. Someone gave her a proper classical education."

"For what?" Eli rolled his eyes. "You know what I mean. It makes for a nice change, but what's her ability?"

"I don't think she has one. There was a rumor making the rounds at one point that she wasn't a gem at all, that her deformity was faked, but that died away pretty quickly. Everyone started grabbing water glasses after meetings for DNA analysis and ended up proving themselves wrong. I heard her genome looks like nothing on earth, the technicians couldn't make head or tail of it." Rob sighed. "The prevailing theory now is that she must have come out of one of the black-ops bionics trials, and we know what a disaster *they* were. It would explain why she doesn't show up on any of the gemtech datastreams, and why she avoids bioscanners. She says they don't get along well with the way she's made up."

"She must have had to go through some."

"Not necessarily. The compulsory high-res scans are mostly at major transit points." He jerked a thumb back over his shoulder, roughly in the direction of the train station now far behind them. "She got issued her papers here in London, so presumably she's been here all along, or was brought in under gemtech license before the Declaration. There are the usual Remnant mutterings, of course, but I can't see it in her case. They're too far away, and you couldn't imagine her pulling off any kind of daring escape."

"What about within the city? She must have to travel around a lot. Meeting with you for one thing."

"Public buildings are low-res and optional, as long as you go through the hazmat sniffers. I'm told that whenever they've given her a hard time about skipping the visuals, neither the machines nor the people could make sense of what they were seeing anyway. Too much distortion."

"And she never uncovers herself?"

"Never ever. I mean, would you? Poor soul." Rob sighed again, heavily. "All she'll say is that she was a failed experiment."

"Well, she's got company there."

"Indeed." Rob was back to looking out the window. "I'm surprised she hasn't been in touch with you. The gems are as anxious about the report as the gemtechs."

"That's occurred to me too. But she hasn't."

"I know she'd like to meet you."

Eli stared at him.

"She mentioned it a week or so ago. I thought it was her way of letting me know in advance she was going to make contact—it's important to her that the gems aren't thought of as underhanded. But now I think—" Rob threw back his head and laughed. "Blimey, she's clever, she is. Now I think she said it so I'd repeat it, so in effect the only person it's coming from is me."

Eli chuckled appreciatively. "Very subtle. And your recommendation?"

"Is that you should do as you think best, of course. However, if I were asked to comment in my official capacity, I would have to say that given the grossly inappropriate overtures you've had from the gemtechs, it would only be fair for you to give equal time to the other side."

4

ZAVCKA KLIST WALKED THE PERIMETER OF BEL'NATUR CORPORATE HEAD-quarters, footsteps echoing between hard floors and high ceilings. To her left a gently curving glass wall allowed a panoramic view of the city below, five centuries' worth of architectural styles punctuated here and there by clumps of green and, in the middle distance, the gray glint of the river. On her right the wall consisted of a massive, intricately grained wooden panel that precisely paralleled the arc of glass. There were no breaks or joints in the wood except at the four doors, spaced evenly around the circular tower, that gave access to the heart of the executive suite.

She could have gone directly there, along a plushly carpeted corridor that ran from the elevator to the boardroom, but she preferred this route with all its reminders. She had a theory that their current challenges might have been avoided had her associates made a habit of pacing out the circumference of their citadel.

She paused by one of the doors, looking south toward the river. Her view was interrupted by another skyscraper, a steel-colored splinter that sprang up from a traffic-encircled plinth to which several roads ran. She could see tiny figures congregating on a terrace near the top of the structure, shielded from the wind by huge fins that projected out along the lines of the building. Beyond it and at the very limits of her vision, there was a fingerlike smudge of green where a century of human abandonment had allowed trees to march down one of the tributaries of the Thames, terminating in an encampment where the smaller river emptied into the large one. Closer but partly obscured, the brown lumps of the Squats clustered like carbuncles on the riverbank.

Zavcka headed inside, bypassing her own office. She stopped at another door, pressed a forefinger to an identipad set into more unbroken wood paneling, spoke her name, and stepped through the door as it hissed open.

The man in the room was standing at an antique glass-and-chrome bar cabinet, pouring amber liquid into a goblet. He raised the bottle at her with a questioning look. She shook her head, seated herself in one of the baby-soft leather armchairs arranged around a small conference table. The man joined her and she cocked an eyebrow at the glass.

"Bit early."

"I'll take a scrubber later." Felix Carrington sipped his drink and regarded her over the rim of the glass. "I hope your morning went better than mine."

"It went as expected. I've given him the report."

"He'll have seen similar stuff before."

"Not quite like this."

Felix nodded, let it go. He always felt just slightly off balance around Zavcka Klist. He knew that she could have maneuvered her way into the top job several times over the past few years, and for reasons known only to herself had chosen not to. Instead she had supported him, first to get the post and then to keep it in the face of the bitter recriminations that had surrounded the Declaration.

She had been among the first to see, several years ago now, where the growing calls for review of the industry could lead. When her warnings went unheeded she had declined to wage the internal war that would have forced the issue and probably delivered her his job, and instead had changed tactics, knocking heads and twisting arms to get more resources pumped into the agricultural and forestry divisions. Those who had derided her for doomsaying joked that she had become more interested in making paste than mining diamonds, even as her profits soared.

Then the bottom had fallen out of human gemtech, and no one was laughing anymore. Bel'Natur had long-term contracts in cows, corn, and coppices, and better cash flow than any of its rivals. In that moment she had become the authority on how to predict, survive, and recover from disaster. Now when she proposed a course of action, no one argued. Felix was uncomfortably aware that to a great extent the future of the firm—both its reputation and its riches—depended on the success of her scheme.

She was looking at him with a smile somewhere between affinity and amusement.

"What's got you so cross?"

"Conference details. You won't believe how many gems they're letting in. I'm going to have to sit on a panel with that . . . troll."

Zavcka had gotten hold of a draft and committed the delegates and program to memory days before. She had also briefed Felix repeatedly on the threat posed by Aryel Morningstar. She mentally counted to ten.

"Felix, you have got to start taking her seriously. She's not there as a token and she's not a lightweight. They like her. She arouses their sympathy. You have to appear to share that, or this isn't going to work."

"I still think it would be simpler if you were the one up there. It's your proposal after all, you know it inside out. You're better at dealing with them than I am. And"—with a burst of hearty generosity—"if it works you should get the credit."

And the blame if it doesn't.

But she was shaking her head. "We've been over this. It has to come from the most senior source, the CEO of Bel'Natur. Anything else will look less than fully committed. I'll be there to back you up, you can throw anything difficult to me and I'll handle it. But it has to be fronted by you."

He glared at her and nodded sharply, tossing back the last of the drink and swallowing down a surge of anger with it. *You can throw anything difficult to me, I'll handle it.* As though he would be less capable than her. Even though he had just suggested as much himself, it piqued him that she should so easily assume a greater level of competence.

"It's going to be a tough sell if the damn gems don't cooperate."

"They will."

"So the rest of the plan is . . . ?"

"Already under way."

"You're sure it's necessary?"

"The correct incentives need to be in place, Felix."

He nodded again, his stomach sinking as it always did when he tried to trip her up in some detail of her meticulous planning. The woman was infuriatingly efficient. He ran through a mental list of projects and priorities that she was responsible for, noting with irritation that it was both long and remarkably well in hand. Near the bottom he found something.

"While we're on the subject—sort of—any word on that prototype?"

"No. We're still looking for Henderson, along with the police, NSPCC, and every investigative journalist in Europe."

"If the press get wind of it . . ."

"There's a good chance Henderson's sold or cached it by now. The question is where."

"I can't believe we had our hands on something like that and just let it slip away."

"The priority then was crisis management; we had to cauterize all links to Henderson and the lab. The timing was just bad luck. Nobody knew the Declaration was coming. And you have to remember, Felix, that if we'd been associated with Henderson the reputational damage would have been catastrophic."

He nodded, knowing this was true. Henderson's methods were questionable, even though his results were excellent. Still, the media had made an inordinate amount of fuss.

"And we still have no idea where it came from?"

She frowned. "Oh, I wouldn't say we have *no* idea. Henderson's report suggested two possibilities; it's just that, as he noted himself, neither of them is particularly plausible. Either some obscure firm, which we haven't been able to identify, managed to generate a supposedly impossible ability *and* disguise the engineering *and* lose the sample—"

"That's what the quote-unquote parents said, isn't it? Before they scarpered."

"Yes, although they had no satisfactory explanation for how they came to be implanted with it. But the other possibility is even less likely. Henderson dismissed it out of hand."

"Wasn't worth mentioning, then or now. But they must have known more than they said, seeing as they were the donors. Maybe they had a deal with one of the smaller firms that went out of business early."

Zavcka refrained from pointing out the holes in this theory. "As I said, neither explanation is satisfactory, but it doesn't really matter at this point. The priority is locating the prototype. If Henderson's sold it on, I should pick up some industry chatter eventually. But he wouldn't have got top value for it, not then. I think it's more likely he's taken it underground."

"Well, we've got to find it. The potential is huge, especially if this plan of yours works."

Yes, she thought. *The potential for complete fucking disaster is monumental.*

Aloud she said, "I know. I've got searches running on the streams as well as in the field."

"Is anyone else looking?"

"Doesn't seem so. Which is comforting, means they haven't got wind of it."

He nodded a grudging acknowledgment and suppressed the urge to pour another drink. The one he'd just finished was hitting nicely, smoothing off the edges. He remembered something that just might come as a surprise to Zavcka Klist.

"Back to the Conference. The United Churches are in."

They hadn't been on her draft list, and given her recent forays into the sector she was surprised not to have heard. All Felix got was a raised eyebrow. "That's odd."

"I'll tell you what's even odder." He allowed himself a little smirk of satisfaction at finally knowing something she didn't. "That Morningstar monster asked for them."

On the public terrace of Newhope Tower two men stood hunched against the cold, gazing toward the black glass of the Bel'Natur building. Behind them the meeting was breaking up, the cleric shaking hands and issuing last-minute exhortations to his departing flock. Those who worked in the building headed inside, making for the interior elevators that would redistribute them along the thousand-foot rise of the tower. Others lined up for the pair of glass pods that ran down its gray surface to street level. A few wandered over to stand with the waiting men. By the time the cleric joined them, around a dozen men and women stood in a ring. The chatter hushed as he stepped into the circle, pulling on gloves and looking expectantly from face to face.

One of the initial pair was the first to speak. "Thanks for that, Preacher. Inspirational."

His companion added, "It's clearer and clearer. No doubt what's required."

A third: "Yeah, there's been a lot of talk, not enough action."

Murmurs of agreement sounded around the circle. Another speaker chimed in, "No more standing on the sidelines. They need to hear from us, loud and clear."

The murmurs grew louder. A few people clapped. Others joined in. It grew and ran around the circle. The preacher stood nodding his head, letting the applause build, before he raised his hands to quiet them.

"Brothers and sisters, you are the hope and the promise of this cursed age we're living through. We've been given an opportunity here, an opportunity to let our voices be heard, to lift this blight from the lives of decent men and women. The day is almost at hand, my friends, for the instruments of the Lord to reveal His will to the unbelievers and the misbelievers, and the abominations most of all. We must cast out the evil among us, as evil was cast down from Heaven itself. I pray you have the strength and the courage to do what must be done. I will come amongst you again when it is time."

He returned their applause with his gloved hands, stepped back from the circle, bowed his head, then turned and walked briskly toward the elevators.

Gabriel was playing with his blocks, selecting carefully from the brightly colored shapes spread out around him on the living room floor. If he got the balance just right, the static charge built into the toys held the pieces together and he could branch off his original structure, build twigs and flowers and tendrils. His current creation stretched above his head as he sat on the floor. He chose a blue polygon and added it to a knobby, multicolored frond that bobbed just at eye level.

He felt Papa look in on him from the kitchen, nod approvingly, and step back to check on something in the oven. He didn't look up. Papa was really good about letting him be, making sure Gabriel knew he was there but not interfering. They were relaxed with each other. Mama would always ask if he wanted something, get down on the floor to play with him or ruffle his hair as she passed. She worried he might not feel right if she didn't, but really it was more for her than him. He could feel how happy she got when she held him in her arms, gave him a bath, or read him a story. They both took care of him, but her need for it was more urgent and anxious than Papa's.

Gabriel didn't mind. Mama's fierce love could be overwhelming, but it made him tingle with happiness. She was home a lot less so most of the time it was just him and Papa, in whose calm, steady affection it was easy to feel safe.

He knew they both worried about him, but they didn't get scared the way his old parents had. He had a vague memory of the way the people he used to call Mommy and Daddy had flinched and tightened up their minds when he came into the room.

Everything else about them had almost completely faded away. He thought there might have been another place between that long-ago past and the bright present with Mama and Papa, but he wasn't sure. There was a black space in his head, a yawning gulf of nothingness that lapped right up to the edge of his awareness, and everything on the far side of it was faint and fading. He couldn't remember much from before Mama had pulled him out of the rubbish and brought him home.

He was certain, though, that the apartment was unlike wherever he'd lived before. It felt smaller and warmer, full of mismatched pieces and gentle colors. From the beginning, no one had minded if he stretched out on the rug to play, or crawled under a table and just sat for a while. No one minded that he knew things he hadn't been told; no one was afraid of him, or wanted him to be afraid of them.

He guessed it was because being different was so ordinary here. Sometimes he got Mama to talk about all the invisible stuff around them so he could understand what was going on behind her eyes, and he would sit on her lap while they made up names for things, and she laughed and laughed. When she had a headache it made him feel a bit ill too, and they would go and lie down on her and Papa's big bed, and when they woke up everything was fine.

He liked it when Aunty Aryel came to visit, although she was so busy now she didn't drop by as much as she used to. He could recall the very first time he saw her, even though he was so scared he couldn't remember how to talk, and he felt thirsty and sick and aching, and the waves of outrage and bafflement from Mama and Papa kept making it worse. She had come back to see him again and again. She said he had something called trauma, and that was why he couldn't remember his name or what had happened, even days later when he had worked out how to talk again. She had calmed them down, and him too, because she was so different he forgot to be afraid, so he could focus.

They had figured each other out pretty quickly in the end. He remembered the look she got when she was kneeling in front of him, staring at him with so much concern, wondering why he was frowning back at her and if she was frightening him. Then she saw him understand, his eyes widening as the picture of her came clear in his head. The huge wash of anxiety that flooded out of her, about the bad things that could happen if he said anything, made him put a finger to his lips and shake his head so she knew not to worry.

She had smiled and hugged him and told Mama and Papa that she thought he was going to be okay, but he was very special and it would be better if the people looking for him didn't find him. They could keep him, and be a family, and their friends would help make sure that as far as the world was concerned, nothing had changed.

"If," she said, looking down at him and stroking his strange hair, "that's what you want, little one. Is it?"

Gabriel was fairly sure that no one in his four years of life had ever asked him what he wanted. He nodded so hard that all the grown-ups laughed, and Mama had picked him up and hugged him so tight he could barely breathe, and Papa had put his arms around them both. He still felt the pulses of worry coming from Aryel even as she smiled at them, but she was thinking of how to take care of him, not what to do about him.

After a while his old name had drifted back to him across the void, but he didn't tell them. He liked the new one better.

5

How We Got Here:

THE SYNDROME, THE FIGHT FOR SURVIVAL
AND THE RISE OF GEMTECH

This is the first in a series of articles examining the impact of human genetic modification ahead of next month's European Conference

Register for ongoing coverage and analysis
Autofeed @Observer.eu/features/GMH_Conf_bkgd_1of3/3011131AS

The Syndrome arrived in the first decades of the twenty-first century, slipping unnoticed into virtually every human community on the planet. It revealed itself gradually, via a slow increase in neurological disease among the young. In the West it was generally diagnosed as a particularly pernicious and difficult form of epilepsy, presenting shortly after puberty, refusing to be outgrown and causing more and more damage until the patient was wheelchairbound and catatonic, usually before their thirtieth birthday.

In rapidly developing countries it was variously identified as brain damage due to high pollution levels, a neurological reaction to industrial poison, or mental illness caused by parental absence as families creaked under the strain of upward mobility. It was slowest to take hold in the most deprived regions of Africa, but even where cell webtech was only just beginning to shift populations out of abject poverty neighbors saw it strike down the children of the most successful, and ascribed the new madness to the jealous application of witchcraft. The variation in presumed causes and apparent characteristics, and errors in prognosis and estimates of prevalence, delayed its identification as a unique, globally distributed disorder for almost twenty years.

The first researchers to aggregate the data identified a number of commonalities. It struck boys and girls equally, generally between the ages of twelve and fifteen. Initial symptoms ranged from a momentary neural freeze, during which all cognitive functions appeared to shut down, through to violent seizures. In some individuals these episodes happened often and in some they were rare, but regardless of their nature and frequency the condition of each patient gradually deteriorated.

When the number of people in their early twenties seeking treatment for the first time shot up, rising by orders of magnitude in every country year on year, the authorities realized that the true extent of the illness had been hugely underestimated. Most children had had the mild and infrequent combination; it had neither been reported nor recognized as a problem, since all their friends had it too.

No single cause could be identified. For some time scientists in the developing world insisted that affluence had to be a factor, since it manifested almost exclusively among the better-off, better educated. The Americans, Europeans and Australians disagreed, noting that while the wealthy were more likely to seek early treatment, they saw less of a correlation between actual illness and household income. The Africans and Asians replied that by their standards, even the developed world's poorest patients were rich.

As the search grew ever more frantic and fractious, neural damage accumulated. The most severely affected began dying fifteen to twenty years after they had first become ill, and needed constant care during the last years of their lives. Those who had appeared to have a more mild form of the Syndrome got at most another five to ten years. The rate of new cases continued to increase exponentially. The statisticians crunched the numbers and reported that the human race was likely to be within a few decades of extinction.

The breakthrough came later that same year as mass suicides, quack cures and religious revivals swept the globe. A crossdisciplinary team from the medical, academic and business sectors had left the search for a smoking gun to others, and concentrated on the patterns left by the bullets. They analyzed terabytes of data about the victims, their friends, families, homes, lifestyles, and the recent history of their communities. The conclusion they arrived at had been mooted early and dismissed. This time the evidence, though technically circumstantial, was irrefutable.

The incidence of the Syndrome mapped perfectly onto the worldwide growth of what the previous century had dubbed information technology. It occurred where children had, from infancy, been exposed not only to a plethora of computing and communications devices, but to the immense load of interactions, analysis and responses they demanded, and the radio frequencies over which they traveled. Its distribution through the socioeconomic strata of every nation-state matched the degree not just of exposure but of immersion.

There was an outcry. Previous studies to examine whether wireless communications could damage the human nervous system had reported no danger. Cognitive and behavioral tests had indicated that too much time dedicated to gaming and social media could cause eye strain, carpal tunnel syndrome and a lack of attention to personal hygiene, but did no other harm. Nevertheless the correlations were clear. The final proof lay in the evidence that it was only those groups who had had no exposure to the full weight of the technologies—such as the American Amish, some monastic communities and the remaining Amazonian hunter-gatherer tribes—who had no cases of the Syndrome.

For a week the world turned itself off. Hundreds of millions of devices were destroyed. Server banks were blown up, corporate headquarters were burned down, ministers of technology and captains of industry were assassinated. The global economy crashed. Nothing moved. Food ran out in the shops, water stopped flowing from taps. Those who still used vehicles powered by petroleum traveled on empty roads, only to discover that the pumps they needed to refuel for the return journey were inoperable.

The few who stayed plugged in pleaded for calm, pointing out that a calamity that had been half a century in the making was unlikely to be exacerbated by a few more weeks or months while the findings were tested and the planet worked out what to do. Governments dug out ancient public-address systems and repeated the message, begging their populations to log in at least enough to receive instructions; and to stop throwing their computers into the sea lest they poison the oceans too.

Gradually the hysteria abated and people drifted back, denouncing the addiction even as they indulged it. Digital networks had become the most essential component of normal life, the default means of communication. They needed the systems that were killing them, so they could tell each other how scared they were to die.

The scientists got to work and quickly confirmed the findings. No one aspect of the networked world was responsible, but all of them, all together, all of the time, amounted to a greater cognitive load than human beings had evolved to process. The Syndrome was believed to begin at the sub-molecular, perhaps even quantum level, at the very earliest stages of cell division. As the child grew, structural damage built up in the delicate neural pathways. It accelerated as they acquired language and literacy and began to interact with the digital interfaces that surrounded them.

It had long been held, and hailed as a triumph, that the explosion both in artificial processing power and in the content it enabled had facilitated a massive and frictionless increase in intellectual productivity. The machines did the work of transmission, organization and storage, and humans were free to be creative with the inputs and clever with the outputs; to connect, communicate and multitask across a vast array of platforms.

Now the researchers understood that the burden on the primary biological processing device—the human brain—had been exploding at virtually the same rate, but without any corresponding increase in capacity. The elasticity of human cognitive potential, the vast redundancies built into the neural architecture, had appeared able to keep up. But a tipping point had been reached.

There were, observed the then President of the United States, three options: to give up all of the technologies and interactions that were the connective tissue of the modern world and return to a pre-networked state, never again allowing development down this particular path; to continue as they were, mitigating the damage where possible and trying to ensure there would be at least some survivors, but essentially accepting lengthy illness, early death and the twilight of the human race; or to find a cure.

Those who did not believe one could be found in time, or feared its consequences more than the Syndrome itself, left cities and civilization behind and became those relics of a bygone age that we know today as the Remnants. While they slipped away into the last wild places of the world, medical research facilities shelved whatever else they were working on, or found a way to redirect it. Every country committed its financial resources and political will to the problem. Any remaining restrictions on research methodologies or avenues of inquiry were lifted. Most religions found they were able to incorporate whatever adjustments their credos required in order to support the mission. Those that didn't were told to shut up, and their congregations deserted them in droves.

Without a cooperative global effort the solution might never have been found. As the children of the world sickened and died, a genetics team in Canada identified a series of complex sequence adjustments that conferred resistance to the initial destabilization. A lab in India figured out how to incorporate them into the genome at the zygote stage. The British established a process for retaining the viability of the engineered embryo, and the Chinese government ordered accelerated testing on a massive scale. While they were busy confirming that the technique did indeed result in immunity, which appeared to be heritable and to have no negative side effects, the Brazilians found a way of scaling up in-vitro fertilization facilities to industrial levels.

The genetic modification technique worked only if applied at the pre-embryonic stage. Within ten years natural conception was almost unheard of; several countries outlawed it. A cure for those who already had the Syndrome was never found. The death toll mounted, and the cost of caring for the sick soared. Young women were encouraged—or required—to start early and bear as many Syndrome-safe children as possible.

The burden of caring for those children as their parents became incapacitated formed yet another component of the continuing crisis. Multigenerational households in which grandparents cared for their sick children and healthy grandchildren became commonplace. This exacerbated the already severe labor shortage and ongoing economic decline.

A way had to be found to get people back to work. As children grew up they began to take on the care of their parents, and the last generation of healthy adults—the grandparents—could become economically active again. But they were much older now, and governments stared into the yawning productivity gap and shuddered. It looked as though the depression might last a century or more.

So they did not intervene as businesses turned to surrogacy. Parentless girls in particular were offered payment for undergoing more implantations, enticed by the prospect that their children would become their caregivers, and would lead happy and healthy lives after they were gone.

The practice, once established, became endemic and was broadened to the gestation of more extensively engineered embryos. The techniques that had been perfected in order to respond to the initial emergency were being applied to a far wider range of characteristics, creating humans uniquely suited to the under-served needs of the market. That these babies were removed from their surrogate mothers at birth, in many cases leaving her cradling a Syndrome-safe but otherwise normal sibling with whom they had shared her womb, caused no complaint. In the uncompromising calculus of care, One for You— One for Us was a bargain.

In fact experimentation on a vast scale was being conducted on human genetic material. The conferring of immunity against other afflictions, physical and mental, was just the start and was included with Syndrome protection as a matter of course. Quite apart from any humanitarian considerations, there were no resources available to deal with frailty; the new generations of humanity needed to start and stay healthy.

There were other priorities as well. Food production had crashed along with population levels, and needed to be restored quickly lest starvation replace the Syndrome as the new scourge of humanity. Away from the cities, unharvested grain and other food crops had naturalized, livestock had escaped and proliferated and fish stocks were flourishing. The challenge was getting them out of the wild and into the mouths of hungry children. Workers who had the strength and stamina for hard labor, could tolerate heat, cold and hunger and were unconcerned with compensation, career prospects or indeed any considerations of personal safety or comfort were desperately needed.

That formed the brief for the first generation of genetically modified humans—GMHs, or gems as they quickly came to be known. Raised in crèches, they were put to work very young, housed separately from the populations they served and remained functionally illiterate. Intelligence levels were generally low, as much due to upbringing as engineering, and of little consequence. Gems were a necessary measure, a stopgap until there were enough normals to take over. Encountering gems in the wild lands they were sent to reclaim, Remnant communities were among the first to criticize the two-tier society they saw developing back in the civilized world; but as outcasts themselves, they commanded little attention and were lightly regarded. That they were suspected of encouraging and harboring runaways did not help.

Children grew up, the labor swap progressed, and the original gemtypes were reassigned. There were huge numbers of abandoned, crumbling buildings which needed to be made safe; there were trees to be felled, reservoirs to be repaired, mines to be reopened. The gems took on the menial work of demolition, clearance and waste disposal.

As society stabilized and slowly began to recover, genetic engineering objectives became more focused. After over half a century of crisis, natural procreation could resume. The vast scientific and technical capacity that had rescued the human race found itself in danger of becoming redundant. Those bright minds looked out on a landscape of need and saw opportunity. They redeployed to commercial production.

The original gems had been crude, brute-force laborers, but their impact on both science and society had been immense. The bioengineering conglomerates, the gemtechs, had learned more from the unconstrained experimentation of their manufacture than they ever could have from the focused fight against the Syndrome. The public were accustomed to gems being the default resource for work deemed difficult or dangerous; indeed, having grown up with the arrangement, the Syndrome orphans found it in no way strange.

The way was clear for specialist gems to be created: gems with hyper-developed senses of smell and taste for toxic waste detection, gems with the strength, lung capacity and altitude tolerance for mountaintop mining, gems who could breathe underwater, gems with paranormal speed and dexterity for the new consumer-product assembly lines, gems whose bodies synthesized drugs or grew organs and tissue for transplant. Gem females became the new surrogate mothers, often having no other purpose.

From the beginning many gems had been marked by unmistakable anatomic differences: a contrast made more sharp by the complete absence from post-Syndrome norm populations of deformity, disability or even the traditional variations in body size. While ever more extreme and outlandish experiments continued to alter the human form, the engineering of a clear visual identifier for the gems who had no other obvious physical modification quickly became a rigidly observed industry standard. These alternative gemsigns have most often been in the form of brightly colored, phosphorescent hair. Some gemtechs have even become known for signature hues: Recombin Blue, Gempro Green, Bel'Natur Red.

The recovery turned into a boom. Gemtech fired a renaissance in industrial processes, scientific discovery and artistic expression. New players entered the market, exploiting the entire spectrum of living matter; flora, fauna and bacteria quickly outstripped human gems both in scale and economic significance. But the oldest, richest and most prestigious companies were those that still practiced their art on the human double helix, turning out ever more exotic and expensive products.

It was the very uniqueness, the individuality, of those products that began to trouble the norms. A growing sense of affinity was augmented by the fact that, because their extraordinary abilities increasingly had a sensory or cognitive basis, they could not be dissociated from intellectual capacity. Even those whose special characteristics were physical rather than mental were now working in environments which required sophisticated interactions with equipment, norms and each other. Simply put, gems had to be smart to be useful.

Being smart meant they were able to assess their own circumstances, note the discrepancies between themselves and the rest of humanity, and demand redress. Being smart made it much more difficult to dismiss them as subnormals incapable of appreciating the full richness of human experience. Being smart made it easier for normals to empathize with them, and for gems to understand the importance of encouraging that empathy to develop.

Gems began to work collectively, withholding labor and forcing confrontations. The ability to learn, analyze and communicate that had made them marketable now enabled them to form alliances, identify sympathizers and smuggle their stories onto the socialstream networks. Some escaped entirely, using their specialized skills and senses to circumvent gemtech security, and found outside the sealed factories and locked dormitories a society growing increasingly uneasy with itself.

A steady stream of revelations about the true conditions to which gems were subjected horrified the public. Pressure groups sprang up. Governments demanded access and explanation. Gemtech reports on errors, accidents and deaths were reviewed and found to be finely detailed with respect to the implications for bioengineering, but otherwise cursory. In the newly resurgent universities, students compared them to eighteenth-century insurance reports of Middle Passage losses, put their heads in their hands and wept.

Supporters of the status quo, led by the gemtechs, pointed out that since gems had not evolved naturally but had been created for a specific purpose, they could have no reasonable objection to the uses to which their creators intended they should be put. The gems and their allies reacted with fury. The religions woke up, recollected their core dogma, and indignantly reminded faithful and faithless alike that whatever else they might believe, they were in error if they presumed to possess the authority of God.

Eli thumbed the tablet off and squeezed his eyes shut. Zavcka Klist's "different behavior modalities" replayed in the darkness behind his lids. He found he was shaking.

He wondered for a moment if the vids embedded in the otherwise drily academic language of the report had been tampered with, the horrific scenes artificially generated, but knew it was a false hope. She was much too smart to make such an easily detectable mistake. Likewise she would not now have given him information that should have been turned over a year ago. He was certain he would find that what he had just witnessed had been neatly tabulated and included in some obscurely indexed datastream. Without the video, of course.

He could give her a very hard time for that, report it to the courts, accuse Bel'Natur of burying a potential risk to public safety when it would have counted against them and revealing it only when they thought they could turn it to advantage. It was perfectly true and maybe he would. But the stone was back in his stomach again, and he knew that he was having these thoughts to distract himself.

Ruthless though she might be, Zavcka Klist wasn't really the problem. What she had shown him was.

He paced the hotel room, trying to think while he ran a diagnostic on the vids. It confirmed what he already knew. He needed a way to work through the material, an explanation, some context. As if in response, his earset buzzed. Some instinct for caution made him walk over to look at the tablet instead of simply flicking his 'set to receive. The memtab had included her personal comcode, which now flashed to identify the incoming transmission.

He stared at it in disbelief for a moment, then resumed his pacing, letting the earset buzz away into silence. So she'd built an alert into the report, intending to tackle him again as soon as he'd viewed it. While the images were fresh in his mind.

The manipulation was so blatant it gave him purchase. He'd speak to Zavcka Klist, but not now and not first.

He picked up his other tablet and called Robert Trench's comcode. It buzzed twice before Rob's slightly sleepy face filled the screen.

"Rob. Sorry, I know it's late."

"Not very. You look terrible."

"Yeah. Just finished going through the Klist stuff."

"And?"

"I want to meet with Aryel Morningstar."

DAY TWO

6

HE WAS TAKEN TO HER IN THE MORNING, DRIVEN BACK AMONG THE GLEAM-
ing towers of the city's bustling heart, winding through the newly
revived cultural quarter to reach an older, unrepaired road that ran
down to the river. A gray winter drizzle barely ruffled the surface of
the water. The driver stopped outside a building that looked as if it
might once have housed a gymnasium, or maybe an old-fashioned
library.

He was on his own. Rob had been ready, eager even, to rearrange
his packed schedule and accompany him, but Eli had said no.

"This is likely to be a difficult conversation," he'd pointed out.
"You already have a good relationship—I don't want it tainted if
things get unpleasant. Besides, you've already spent enough time
babysitting me."

Rob had sighed and conceded, and now Eli was shaking his head
at the driver as she made to get out of the car with him.

"It's fine, thanks. I'm expected," nodding at a man with a shock
of vivid green hair who had emerged through the double doors and
was walking down the steps. "No need for you to stay."

The driver was explaining that Dr. Trench had told her to wait as the green-haired man arrived to greet them. His name was Horace, and he surprised Eli by endorsing Rob's instruction.

"Hardly ever any taxis down here," he explained, "and very few private cars. We could arrange to get you back, of course, but it might take a while."

Eli left the driver waiting by the curb and followed Horace back up the steps and into a spacious entry foyer. It was bisected by a display counter, across which a succession of gem-related announcements flickered. Eli noted a community meeting on the upcoming Conference, a list of skills and jobs available, and a theatrical performance in that very building in a few days' time.

The man sitting behind the counter glanced up from his tablet, then rose as Horace walked Eli over. He was tall, powerfully built, and olive-skinned, with vaguely Asian features under close-cropped indigo hair. As Horace introduced them, Eli stuck out his hand and the big man shook it. There was none of the momentary hesitation Horace had shown at the same gesture, a sign of a gem unused to the courtesy; but the same glint of appreciation showed in the brown eyes. The little boy flipping pages on a child-size tablet on the floor behind him looked up.

Eli was immediately curious. It was unusual to see children in a gem community; most gems had been given contraceptive implants at puberty, and few so far had had the means or the conviction to have them removed. Whether they should be aided, encouraged, or even allowed to do so continued to be one of the most contentious issues in the ongoing debate about gem entitlements, and one which, despite norm discomfort around the subject, he sensed the Conference would have to grapple with.

One of the things that many norms found disturbing was that there was no guarantee there would be gemsign to identify naturally conceived offspring. The few such babies who had been carried to term and born healthy generally had a normal, nonradiant hair color, and indeed this child's head was covered in a completely ordinary sandy-brown tangle. But the children he knew of were all infants and toddlers, much younger than this boy.

"Dr. Walker, meet Bal. He's one of our volunteers, been here since the beginning. And that," following Eli's gaze and sounding, he thought, just a touch uncertain, "is his boy, Gabe."

"Good to meet you, Bal. Hi, Gabe." The boy smiled at him and Eli smiled back. He glanced back at Bal and noted that the eyes had gone just a little bit hard.

Horace led him through a side door and along a corridor lined with vidpaintings. He was friendly and chatty, full of tidbits about the history of the building and the way it had been repurposed.

"It must have taken a long time."

"Most of the past year to get it to this point, but there's plenty more to do. We've worked so hard on all the buildings in the Squats. I hope we get to stay."

Eli swallowed a sigh and wondered if the green-haired gem really thought it was up to him. They were going through another door, and up a flight of stairs.

"The lobby felt like a proper neighborhood place," he offered. "Nice that kids can hang out there as well." There was a long pause.

"Yes ... of course we don't have very many. Bal and Gaela, though, she's his partner, they're great parents." He pushed open another door. "Here we are." Eli thought he said it with relief.

The room they stepped into was large, chilly, and dim. It had far fewer of the trappings of modernity than the areas they'd walked through before. Eli suspected that the dark, heavy curtains that lined the walls were covering up patches of damp and peeling paint. The ceiling looked to have inset lights, original to the building and probably defunct; a couple of power panels had been set up, casting a paltry glow over the large wooden table in the center.

The people sitting and standing around it looked up as they entered. There were three: an ordinary-looking young man who scowled at him, a rotund woman with big hips, big breasts, and tousled turquoise hair, and a seated figure on the far side of the table. He picked up something familiar about the youth and a distinctly aggressive aura from the large woman as he followed Horace over, but his attention stayed fixed on their companion. There was no question who was in charge of that room.

The first thing that struck him was how small she was; the vidclip attached to her profile had given no sense of scale. In the low light he could make out little besides a delicate face and slender hands, lightly clasped where they rested on the massive table. She seemed to emerge, ghostlike, from the shadows. Dark hair smoothed back from a high, clear brow, appearing to dissolve into the indistinctness of clothing and curtains. As he grew closer he could see that she was wearing some kind of enveloping garment that blended into the charcoal grayness of the background fabric. Against it her skin shone a pale, smooth bronze. Her eyes were large and clear, a blue the color of a summer sky.

But she looks fine now, he thought, and knew it for a ridiculous understatement. Against the decay of the room and the animosity of its occupants, she was a revelation.

She sat perfectly still and watched him approach. The man and woman stepped back, ensuring that she would be introduced first. The instinctive deference also had the effect of turning them into an honor guard, flanking and framing her as he was presented. Horace bowed ever so slightly from the waist, extending a hand toward her as they stopped at the table. Even though Eli understood the subtle psychological cues at work, he still felt their effect, a sense of being exalted by her presence. It was made more powerful by his conviction that it was unconscious and unplanned.

And then she rose to greet him, and the wall moved with her.

Or so it seemed for a shocking instant as she broke away from the illusory continuum of curtains and clothing. She bore a lump on her back wider than her shoulders, a triangular swelling that appeared to start at the nape of the neck and carry on down the length of her spine. It looked to be more than half again the size of her torso. She stood straight and appeared to carry it easily enough, but he shuddered inside at the thought of the extra weight on her diminutive frame, the pain she must suffer if it really was made up of embedded hardware. She was barely five feet tall.

The true size and shape of whatever grotesquerie had been visited upon her was covered by a voluminous cloak that fastened close about her throat and fell to her feet. Her hands emerged from tight-fitting sleeves set into the garment. She was holding one of them out to him now, finely shaped lips twitching into a wry smile. She did not seem angry at his discomfiture, or pleased or satisfied. Just mildly amused.

He shook her hand. It was tiny but surprisingly strong.

"Dr. Walker, it's good to meet you. I'm Aryel."

"Eli, please."

"Eli. Welcome to the Squats."

"Thank you." He released her hand, made a helpless gesture. "I'm sorry, I didn't mean . . ."

He trailed off as she laughed. Her voice was low and beautifully modulated, almost musical. It sounded strange coming from so small and misshapen a body. "Don't worry about it. Happens all the time. Let me introduce you."

The turquoise woman was Wenda and the young man Donal. Wenda shook his hand with an air that said if Aryel thought it was okay she supposed she'd have to go along. When Eli turned to Donal the scowl deepened. Eli was sure he'd seen that look before. When Donal shrugged away from the handshake, instead deliberately using his right hand to tuck shaggy, mousy brown hair behind his ear, Eli got it.

"The train!" he said. "You were on the train with me yesterday. You—Oh," as a prodigiously overlarge, sharply pointed and funneled ear became visible from behind the mass of hair. "Oh, I see." He looked at Aryel.

"Yes," she said simply. "We knew you were being targeted and it seemed to me that a long, unaccompanied train journey was an opportunity unlikely to be missed. Your work is crucial to the future of our people and I needed to know what we're up against. Donal was traveling down anyway so I asked him to keep an ear on you." She fixed him with a very direct look. "What he overheard was . . . distressing."

"I can understand that." Somehow, strangely, he found that he was not angry about being spied on. The lack of subterfuge, the candor with which she told him what she'd done, the provision of reasons but not excuses, and the way she took responsibility were completely disarming. They had every reason to wonder, and worry, whether he would succumb to pressure from the gemtechs. The conversation with Zavcka Klist would not have reassured them.

He looked from her to Donal, hands now shoved deep in his pockets; Wenda, arms folded and nostrils flaring; Horace, standing one foot atop the other, cringing with embarrassment; and back to Aryel. She stood calm and unhurried, waiting for him to explain himself, move them past this moment, make it acceptable to the others for her to talk to him. He understood that exactly how he did so was important. And that he could expect no help.

He kept his eyes on Donal but addressed himself to all of them. "What you have to understand . . . please . . . is that I have to listen to everybody. My job is to consider all of the information and come to some kind of balanced conclusion. I can't just cut people off, but I do want to hear from everyone." He spread his hands. "It's been less than twenty-four hours and here I am. I've got a lot of questions, and I'm hoping you can help me with the answers."

He left it unspoken but obvious that they had not come to him; he had sought them out in order to achieve just that balance. They all glanced at Aryel. She looked pointedly at Donal.

"So you're no' jus' for them then?" he finally said, with a kind of grudging disbelief. "Tha's wha' you're sayin'?"

"That's why I'm here."

The silence stretched out. Donal's fists clenched and unclenched in his pockets. Finally he tore his eyes away from the floor, met Eli's gaze for a moment, then looked at Aryel and nodded.

"Soun's like he's tellin' the truth."

Eli offered his hand again and this time Donal shook it reluctantly. "You can tell whether someone's lying?" Eli asked. He told himself it was an opportunity to change the subject, but he could feel his endless fascination with gems, with the breadth and depth of the permutations the human envelope was capable of, threatening to take over. "That's one I hadn't heard of. I imagine," he looked Donal in the eye again, "it's difficult as well as useful."

Donal grimaced an acknowledgment, even as he shook his head. "Yeah, but it's no' a sure thing. Depends if it comes easy. I c'n usually hear if it doan't."

"And you don't think it comes easy to me."

"No, but tha' doan't make you one o' the good guys."

"No, I suppose it doesn't." Eli looked around at them. "I hope you'll decide I am, but I can't promise."

Aryel nodded, and took over with an ease that made him blink. He had apparently passed whatever test had just been set. For the next hour, as they sat around the big table, she deftly routed his questions between herself and the other three. He realized with a mixture of surprise and appreciation that he was not getting any sort of prepared party line: Wenda, Donal, and Horace all had markedly different personalities, and a range of opinions to match. But they would each, he thought, have happily accepted a role as witness, and allowed Aryel to answer every question without complaint.

She was having none of it. She had clearly decided it was important for him to hear the full range of views on every issue he raised and had set herself the task of managing the conversation to ensure that every split and nuance was on display. It was a shockingly brave strategy, and part of his mind was busy trying to figure out why she would run the risk of allowing her people to appear fragmented, even as he admired the way she drew them all out.

She was gentlest with Wenda, which he initially found odd. The big woman appeared menacing, her powerful form taut with anger. But her belligerence was belied not only by a speech impediment but by a desperate shyness and a bewilderment at finding herself consequential enough to be asked important questions. Eli could see her eyes widen and her brows crease in concentration as she struggled to organize her thoughts. As she grew embarrassed and self-conscious, Aryel stepped in, absorbing the attention while keeping Wenda focused, leading the discussion back to her when she was ready to have her say.

Donal needed no such support. He was clever, quick-witted, and convinced that gems faced a complicated web of norm conspiracies designed to deceive and subjugate. Aryel let him have his head. Eli wondered why she wanted him to hear Donal's series of increasingly far-fetched theories; then observed how intently Wenda listened, and how Horace rolled his eyes when he thought no one was looking.

Horace lacked Wenda's hesitation, Donal's acerbic certitude, or Aryel's calm rationality. He spoke easily but seemed, Eli thought, to have the least to say. He had an almost childish conviction that everything would turn out all right in the end, as long as they didn't make too much of a fuss. It was Donal's turn to snicker, which he did with far less concern about being noticed. Privately, Eli agreed. Horace, for all his polish, bore the hallmarks of long servitude in a sheltered environment. That background and the acquiescence that often accompanied it were not atypical, but neither were they well adapted to the current circumstances.

He thought he understood what Aryel was doing, showing him the range of their differences and disagreements. In responding to the questions he posed she was putting the diversity of the gem community on display. It was a complicated, counterintuitive maneuver, and he wondered what she hoped to achieve. Maybe she simply wanted to counteract the perception of gems as homogeneous and simplistic, but he sensed there was more to it than that. She seemed too astute to be taking such a risk simply to set the record straight. Behind her poised handling of the meeting, the deep respect with which the others treated her, and her own clearly articulated responses, he sensed layers and layers of meaning. A ferocious intelligence was at work, guiding a complex series of calculations that might give even Zavcka Klist pause.

7

HE WAS EVEN SURER OF IT LATER, AS THEY WALKED ALONG A PASSAGE AT THE
back of the building. It was lined with windows that let in the weak
winter sunlight and a panoramic view of the Squats, all the way down
to the gillung lodges on the quayside. Aryel pointed out the solar col-
lectors and described the rooftop garden plots and water capture and
waste reclamation facilities.

"When this estate was built there was a real fad for sustainable
living," she explained. "We were able to repair and build on what
was already here. It's given the community something useful to do,
developed new skills and a sense of independence. I know people
think we cost more than we contribute, but that's not what we want.
We'd much prefer to be fully normalized, employed, tax-paying citizens. In the meantime we're living in as self-sufficient a way as we
possibly can."

"It's very impressive. I imagine it must rankle when norms think
gems don't have that kind of aspiration. Or ability. Zavcka Klist certainly doesn't think so. Or does she? I should ask Donal."

"I already have. He says, and I quote, that she believes her own
bullshit."

The rain had intensified into a gray curtain that blurred and washed the buildings together. It reminded him of his earlier jolt when she had come into focus in the dark meeting room, and he tried once again to apologize. She waved it away as a moment of no consequence but then cocked her head to look up at him as they walked side by side.

"I confess I was a little surprised by your surprise," she said. "You didn't search out any pictures? Most do."

"Just the vidclip that was attached to your profile. It wasn't very clear." *It doesn't do you justice.* "Beyond that, no. I just . . . I always sort of think that's cheating."

She nodded approval. "I agree. Presumably you wouldn't do so when meeting another norm, so why a gem? I would rather," she said, as they reached the end of the corridor and turned to pace back, "deal with a moment of genuine discomfort than the contrived not-noticing I often get."

He wondered which she had gotten from Rob. He was a true egalitarian, but so much at pains to make sure he treated everyone the same it could sometimes stray into farce. He was glad he had insisted on coming alone. Rob would have tried too hard to smooth out the awkward moments.

"I'm not sure all the others feel the same way. Horace for instance."

She shook her head. "Horace hates conflict. He was contracted out to a company who, by his reckoning, treated him well—as long as things were going well. When they weren't, a bit of snideness crept in. The condescension started to show. So he tries very hard to avoid any sort of friction because that, in his experience, is when people start to be mean."

"And Donal?"

"Donal is like me in that he dislikes hypocrisy—and he's far more aware of it than most of us. He's unlike me—and Horace—in that he tends to assume the worst in people. You're guilty until proved innocent with Don."

"He was treated badly."

"He was treated badly, both in crèche and out in the world. The welfare inspections started when he was still too young to have been sent to work, so he got a full-on demonstration of how deceitful the system could be—concerned citizens coming in and being shown around this happy home for extraordinary children, which turned back into a hellhole once they'd left. But he could hear the doubt in their voices, he knew they'd talked themselves into believing the lie, and he never forgave that. Then when he was indentured he got an earful of the lies norms tell each other."

Eli winced. "So his cynicism is justified."

"He certainly thinks so."

He hesitated for a moment, then said, "And Wenda?"

They had reached the far end of the corridor again, and she turned and stopped, resting her bulging back against the wall as though for support and looking at him over folded arms. The watery light washed her face and throat.

"You've been studying us for a long time," she said. "You're the expert. What do you think Wenda's story is?"

"I . . ." He stopped, ran a hand through his hair. He felt gauche and uncertain, as if he were probing into family secrets best left buried. "Is it all right for us to be talking about them? I mean, are you sure they wouldn't mind?"

"If they did I wouldn't do it."

"Right. Well then." He thought about Wenda: the physicality of the woman, the combination of bashfulness and ferocity, the difficulty she had expressing herself, and the sense of inarticulate despair that surrounded her like a fog. "I think she was a surrogate."

Aryel nodded. "Yes. And how many babies do you suppose she carried?"

"She's in her forties, I'd guess . . . and maybe some multiples, so . . . around ten?"

"Try fifteen."

Eli swallowed hard, watching her face as she spoke.

"That's live births. More if you count the failed embryos, the miscarriages and abortions."

"So they kept her pregnant for . . ." He shook his head at the enormity of it. "What, twenty-five years? And the children?"

"Left with her to nurse for three to six months. Then removed so they could start another cycle."

Eli closed his eyes and leaned his forehead against the glass. He couldn't look at her. She spoke without anger, the violation quietly recounted as though to a visitor from a land so foreign they might not comprehend such barbarity. The compassion in her voice was more searing than a denunciation.

"Wenda could be any of our mothers. Practically speaking most of us can be certain she's not, because of our ages and where we were and where she was. But the point is she *could* be—most of us will have started life inside someone just like her—and for some of us, she actually might be. You've got the gemtech datastreams, you must realize that she's one of the more competent, well-adjusted surrogates. Most of the others are far more broken than she is."

He knew this, but it had never struck him to the quick before. "I'm so sorry," he said.

"What for, Eli? It wasn't your fault."

"I know. I'm still sorry."

He straightened up, meeting her eyes, readying himself to pose the next question. She waited for it, but he found himself unable to speak or even to move, caught like an insect between the gray glass behind him and that piercing blue gaze. He ran his tongue over dry lips.

"I'd like to ask about you, but I'm told you don't speak about your past."

"I don't."

"That seems pretty inconsistent with how freely you discuss the others."

"The others understand my reasons. Their entire lives, from the moment of conception to their leaving indenture, have been recorded in detail. That's useful to someone like you, and depending on what people like you do with the information it may end up being useful to us; but that doesn't make it less intrusive. They'll allow me to talk about things that you'd be able to determine anyway, knowing that I will at least put a human face on the data. But as for me—" She paused, gazing out at the rain. "I am lucky enough to have something most gems can only dream of, and that is an element of privacy. It's rare and precious and they are happy for me to hang on to it for as long as I can."

"How long will that be? You're a public figure in a way few others are. And you're about to become even more so. Don't you think that sharing your own story—which I can only imagine must be exceptional—would win you support?"

"I don't want superficial sympathy. We already have a lot of that and I'm not convinced anything tangible will come of it. We all have our tragedies, our personal histories of grief. Mine is no more or less profound than anyone else's."

"You're a living example of how well a gem who hasn't been through the indenture system can function."

He'd meant it as a counterpoint, a way of reminding her that the little that was known only emphasized her difference from other gems. It was a distinction he imagined she would wish to avoid. She took his clever riposte and flipped it on its head.

"Exactly."

She stepped away from the wall and they moved back along the row of windows again. She seemed to think she might have been too abrupt, because when she spoke again she was gentle.

"For what it's worth," she said, "the fact that you can have such sorrow for Wenda leads me to suspect that you may indeed be one of the good guys."

He barked out a harsh laugh. "Don't be too sure." He stared straight ahead, feeling her look up but not wanting to meet her eyes. He had been putting it off for hours, so intrigued by this magnetic, malformed woman that he was loath to do anything that might disrupt this strange simpatico they were developing. He reminded himself sternly that he had a job to do.

"I was given something, on the train," he said finally. "You haven't asked about it."

"It's the reason you're here. I assumed you'd get to it eventually."

"It's not the only reason. I would have wanted to meet you anyway, see for myself how the community is functioning, but it made it . . . imperative." He sighed. "At least to my way of thinking. Bel'Natur would probably not agree."

She understood immediately. "So the redoubtable Zavcka Klist doesn't expect you to share with me what she shared with you."

"I can't imagine she would. And I wish I didn't have to." He looked down at her, reluctantly. "She's shown me something. I can't ignore it, and I don't think it's fair for it to be sprung on you without warning somewhere down the line. But at the same time, I'm not sure how significant it really is. So I want to show it to you—assuming it'll play again—and ask what you think it means." He drew a deep breath. "But it's . . . gruesome."

They had reached the end of the corridor again, next to the door that led back into the heart of the building. Aryel was regarding him thoughtfully.

"I imagined you were still making up your mind about us," she said. "That's not it, is it? You were sure of yourself, and now this is making you doubt."

She had captured all of his anxieties in a sentence. It was unsettling. "It's making me afraid."

"I get the feeling this isn't something you want to share with the others at this point."

"I'd rather not. If that's all right."

He watched the back of her head, dark hair nodding over the swaying mass of the cloak as she led the way down a flight of stairs. "It's fine. I'll explain that it's sensitive. I won't promise"—she turned onto a landing and glanced back up—"not to tell them about it later."

She had a quick word with Donal, cup of tea in his hand as he leaned against the meeting-room door, while Eli retrieved his tablet. It occurred to him that for all his paranoia about security the day before, he had trusted her completely when she had said he could leave his stuff behind while they went for a walk on the upper floor. The Klist report could not be accessed by anyone but him, but there was lots of other information that a clever hacker could break into without much difficulty. He had ignored his own careful protocols, hadn't worried about it, wasn't worried now. He could see that his bag had not been moved, the various flaps and catches positioned exactly as he had left them, and found to his surprise that this was just what he'd expected. She had said that no one would touch his stuff, and he had not doubted her for an instant.

She rejoined him at the table while Donal went to tell the others they wouldn't be needed for a while. He thumbed the tablet on, angled it for shared viewing, and activated the memtab port, leaning forward for the retinal scan that would unlock the file. As he sat back he caught Aryel's raised eyebrow and sighed.

"No, I don't know how they got my print. I should run a security check, I suppose." He shrugged. "Unless they've left an obvious trail, it puts me in an awkward position. Potentially."

"I doubt you'll find anything. Bel'Natur know how to cover their tracks." She settled herself more comfortably in the chair. "Are you familiar with the Provis line?"

"Specialized eyesight? Some can see UV wavelengths, some into the infrared?"

"And a very few range across both, including one of our residents here. True hyperspectral vision. She tells me they also developed a variant with the ability to scan and record individual retinal prints."

He was shocked. "What? *Why?* And how could they ever transcribe that kind of information?"

"That part's quite easy, apparently. There's a software template. The gems are pretty far down on the autistic spectrum, with a lot of the cerebral cortex given over to visual processing. Transference of the data onto the template isn't a problem. As for the *why*," she fixed him with that direct look again, "use your imagination. Bribery? Blackmail?"

"They've not offered me anything"—*not yet anyway*—"or threatened me." *Yet.*

"If they do we may be able to help. Gaela can fill you in on the gems she knows and knows about, maybe help identify who you met. I assume you have records of all your interviews."

"Yes, but I meet gems casually too, especially these days. People come up to me."

"I doubt any of the Provis retscanners would be able to engage you in conversation over a coffee. The adults are severely developmentally disabled, and functionally blind beyond a few feet. If the engineers did figure out how to avoid those side effects, the results would still be small children."

Her voice was even and matter-of-fact, another litany of exploitation calmly narrated. It was a not uncommon mannerism; a shield against the emotional weight of events, a way of parsing the unspeakable. Somehow it did not make her seem cold, as it often could with gems.

He wondered if she would be able to maintain it.

He suspected that whatever her reaction, he was now deeply, personally enmeshed in its consequences. The implications of this apparently casual tangent about his compromised retinal identification were significant. Zavcka Klist had given him one piece of information the gemtechs had buried; Aryel Morningstar had just countered with another, and a way out if Klist dumped a million credits into his account and tried to frame him.

She had also neatly boxed him into a corner. He could now never say that he was being blackmailed and had no choice. She had sensed he was about to put her in an invidious position, and, depending on what his own intentions were, she had either extended the hand of friendship despite this—or had put him there first.

The file image pulsed on the screen. He tapped it and text rolled up, scarred with color-coded links to vids, statistical analyses, and genome data. "You should read the report itself," he said quietly. "The vids are what I really want you to see, I'm afraid, but the context in which they're presented is important."

For the next forty-five minutes he watched as she read, followed the links, came back ashen faced to the text, and went on to the next section. She skipped nothing. When she was finished he made to speak but she raised a finger to silence him and went back to the report. She replayed some of the vids, slowing or pausing them so that she could scan every detail. He did not know whether her fortitude was admirable or appalling.

After a while she pulled her own tablet out of a pocket of her voluminous cloak, glanced up at him briefly, and said, "May I?" as she thumbed it on. He nodded and then, unable to bear it any longer, said, "The vids are genuine. I've checked."

She was making notes, eyes flicking between the tablet and one of the endless genome tables. "I don't doubt that they are." Her voice was terse.

"Aryel." She continued to write one-handed, while her other hand flicked through the reams of data on the screen. "Aryel, please. Tell me what you're thinking."

She looked up then, and he thought he saw tears in the blue depths of her eyes.

"What do you want me to say, Eli? That this is an atrocity? That nothing like this should ever *ever* have happened?" She squeezed her eyes closed, as if trying too late to shut out the images. "You know that already."

"What I'm asking," he said, feeling the stone in his belly and the hollowness in his throat, "is if you think it could ever happen *again*."

8

Declaration of the Principles of Human Fraternity

AGREED TO BE THE SHARED AND UNIVERSAL BASIS
FOR NATIONAL LAWS PERTAINING TO ALL INDIVIDUALS,
GROUPS, CIVILIZATIONS AND CULTURES

Issued by the United Nations, Tokyo, 21 December 130AS

The Peoples of the World, having passed through great calamity, and having secured the survival of our Species only by dint of certain manipulations and interventions, executed under direst emergency and with the willing participation and to the mutual benefit of all nations and races, now hereby declare and affirm these several Principles which all human beings, regardless of origin, nation, heritage, circumstance, condition, capability, conviction or disposition shall rightly and reasonably expect to form the foundation of the laws that shall govern our Societies and the rules, regulations and restrictions to which we shall in fellowship submit.

That it shall be the right of every human being:

First: To be at liberty from incarceration, except as properly and lawfully required for the detention of suspects, the punishment of the guilty and the protection of the public.

Second: To be free and protected from unwarranted oppression, indignity, negligence or harm.

Third: Not to be required to provide labor or perform services without compensation.

Fourth: That movement, expression, association and employment shall not be unreasonably restricted.

Fifth: That property and possessions rightfully and lawfully acquired shall not be arbitrarily removed or reduced; but shall be subject to the reasonable and ordinary contributions required by the state, or as agreed under contract or for the settlement of accounts.

Sixth: That alterations, manipulations, procreation or reproduction of any individual, or utilization of the cellular or genetic material of any individual, shall be subject always to the consent of said individual.

Zavcka Klist's face filled the screen. She was not amused. Eli had continued to ignore her calls until he was back in his hotel. He was still not entirely sure what she was expecting, but clearly it wasn't this.

"What do you mean by *corroboration*?"

"I'm not suggesting that the vids were fabricated . . ."

"I should hope not."

". . . because I checked." That shut her up momentarily. "I'm now checking the databases of the other gemtechs."

"You're *what*?"

"Your report said it may not have been an isolated incident."

"It said we couldn't rule that out."

"Fair enough. Maybe I can. Or maybe I'll learn that your competitors have been just as negligent as you have."

She was seething. "The only reason we're having this conversation is because I *gave* you that material."

"Yes, you did. A year after all gems were released from the *appropriate oversight* you're so concerned about, and more than a year after you were required to deliver up all relevant genotype records. So tell me, Miss Klist: if what you showed me reflects a present danger to ordinary people, why have you only decided to worry about it now?"

"It wasn't brought to my attention—"

"An assault, a *violation* like that wasn't reported immediately, all the way up the chain of command? Please."

"Hear me out. The tragedy was recorded, obviously, and reported to the relevant authorities, and investigated immediately. But our full analysis, which you now have, wasn't completed until *after* the handover. And in the confusion, with all the redundancies and reorganization that we had to undergo at that time, it got overlooked." She stared up at him from the tablet, lips compressed into a thin line. "I make no excuses. We should have stayed on top of it, and we didn't. Eventually it was sent to me. As soon as I understood the implications I handed it over to you."

You mean as soon as you found a way to use it. Eli slapped at the thought, trying to curb his own cynicism. "And I am now working to independently confirm whether your assessment is correct."

He could see her mastering her temper, selecting an appropriately measured response.

"With all due respect, Dr. Walker, even if you don't turn up any comparable episodes it doesn't mean there's nothing to worry about. Frankly I'd be surprised if there'd been similar incidents. For the rules to have been broken in exactly the same way elsewhere, *and* in the presence of a susceptible genotype, seems very unlikely."

"But you don't think such an . . . episode . . . is unlikely now?"

"There are no rules now. They're out in the world. An equivalent situation could arise very easily."

"Exactly how *many* are out in the world, Miss Klist?"

"Gems?" she blinked at him. "You must have better population data than I do. Hundreds of thousands, maybe millions."

"How many *with this flaw*?"

"We don't know. We weren't aware of it until . . ." She waved an aristocratic hand. "What you saw. We'd never have implanted or allowed it to come to term if we had been."

"And what caused it?"

"Unclear. Prior to the incident the subject's behavior was not what you'd call exemplary, but it wasn't particularly threatening. Although the circumstances represented a complete breach of protocol, there's no way anyone could have predicted that reaction."

"Then what do you mean by a susceptible genetype?"

"Well clearly he had a predisposition to violence, but I can assure you it wasn't intentional on our part. We haven't been able to identify the error that encoded that kind of aggression into the genome. If we had a lot of cases to study we could probably find it, but of course," she looked earnestly out at him, "our priority has to be to ensure that there aren't any more."

"If you don't even know what the error was, what makes you so sure it wasn't isolated to this individual?"

"Are you prepared to take that chance?" He was silent. She went on. "The fact that there was nothing particularly unusual about this gem's engineering is precisely the point. Whatever was hiding in his genetype could be hiding in any number of others."

Eli sighed, rubbed his face. The satisfaction he'd felt at putting her on the defensive was evaporating quickly. The gem had been one of many engineered for segregated, often solitary work in closed-shop industries. It had never been anticipated that they would interact with norms other than their specially trained supervisors and caregivers. They were among the ones Rob Trench had talked about yesterday in the car, floundering in a world they did not understand, constantly confronted by situations and stimuli of which they had no experience. His meeting that morning at the Squats had confirmed that they were the ones about whom other gems worried most.

He could not disregard the possibility that Zavcka Klist might be right.

"What happened to him?"

"Who?"

"The gem, Miss Klist. The gem who committed the assault."

"He was taken down by the security team ..."

"I saw that. Unavoidably shot in the head, I believe. Killed?"

"No. Severe brain damage. He was left in a vegetative state in one of our hospital wards."

"Now under state control?"

"Of course."

"And the victim? Her mother?"

"The young girl's injuries weren't survivable. Our staff member, the one who ignored proper procedure in the first place, was also very badly hurt. I understand she was suicidal for some time. Given the situation there was no question of any disciplinary action. We did everything we could to assist the family. They've asked for their privacy to be respected."

So the child had died and they'd paid off the parents. The mother would have to live with the memory of what had happened to her daughter and the knowledge of her own culpability, which Bel'Natur would not have attempted to minimize. The killer was in no position to be questioned about what had triggered his cravings and his rage, about whether he'd had such urges before, or whether what he had done was as much of a surprise to him as to everyone else.

As calamities went, it was remarkably tidy.

"I have one more question. For now."

"Yes?" Zavcka Klist's tone was icy. Their follow-up discussion had not gone, Eli thought, quite as well as she'd expected.

"Why have you only given this to me, and directly instead of through channels? If you really think there are gems out there who are ticking time bombs, why haven't you gone to the police or the press?" He raised an eyebrow. "Or are you planning to do that next?"

"We considered it, of course. I don't see what it would accomplish, other than creating panic and making all gems a target. That wouldn't be good for them any more than for us. We've no way of knowing when one of these time bombs, as you put it, might go off. We don't want to inadvertently create a situation that might make that even *more* likely."

"Why would it?"

"Gems have tablets now, they read the streams. I worry that if the details of this start being passed around, that in itself might be a trigger."

She had moved from frigid to frank, almost conspiratorial. They were back on track. "Let's be honest," she continued. "It's not going to do Bel'Natur's reputation any favors if and when this information breaks, but it would be even worse if we hadn't at least *tried* to protect the public. You're in charge of the analysis that will underpin whatever settlement comes out of this Conference. I think you understand now why I felt so strongly that this was something you needed to know. My preference is for it to be addressed in context, as part of a broad review, but," she threw her hands in the air, "if you think the right thing to do is to send it to the newstreams and the security services, I won't argue. It's in your hands, Dr. Walker."

And there it was: maneuvered into another corner by another clever, calculating woman. At least he'd seen this one coming.

"I'll be in touch," he said, and winked out.

Zavcka Klist glared down, fists clenched on either side of the blank screen. *How dare he,* she thought. *I wasn't finished with him yet.* She had been prepared to make another oblique reference to the potential rewards that might flow from a suitable settlement, albeit through gritted teeth. Dr. Eli Walker was living up to his reputation for recalcitrance.

She flicked the tablet back on, manually entered a comcode, and sent a string of unintelligible alphanumerics. She took calls and responded to messages until the tablet pinged softly. She glanced at the screen, grabbed it and her coat, and headed out.

Fifteen minutes later she was buying a coffee over the counter of a bustling café. She took it through to a small courtyard at the back, out of the wind but nevertheless deserted in the winter chill, sat on a damp metal chair, and sipped.

The coffee was half-finished when the door opened again and a man stepped outside, glanced around, and sat at the next table. She noted with irritation that he had not troubled to buy anything. His gloved hands rested on his knees. He did not look at her.

She raised the cup to her lips, said, "Proceed," and sipped. The man looked down at his hands.

"Immediately?"

"Yes."

"How extensive—?"

"Don't hold back."

The man nodded. She caught his eye as he made to rise, and he sank back into his chair. She drained her cup and left it on the table.

The man waited for three minutes. While he waited he pulled out a tablet and composed a series of messages. As he sent the final one the tablet started pinging. He scanned the first few responses, nodding in satisfaction. Then he pulled his gloves back on and left.

When his earset buzzed a few minutes after he'd hung up on her, Eli braced himself for another round with Zavcka Klist. A glance at the comcode flashing in the corner of the tablet filled him with relief, immediately chased away by a flicker of embarrassment. He tapped to receive.

"Dr. Walker? Sally Trieve here. Sorry I wasn't around earlier."

The face on his screen was reassuringly plain, the voice pleasantly professional. He wasn't sure if she was apologizing for not having been available to take the call he'd made as he was being driven away from the Squats, or for not meeting him there in person.

"Not a problem, Sally. Thanks for getting back so quickly." He adjusted the earset while he thought about how to put what now seemed like a ludicrous question. Sally Trieve was responsible for coordinating all of the social service support for gems in the Squats. It was complicated, pioneering work and after his visit that day he was even more inclined to think that she did it remarkably well. He decided it would be simplest to just come clean.

"I'm not sure I really need to be bothering you after all," he said. "It was just that at the Squats this morning I met a family I hadn't been aware of. Little boy and his father."

He thought he saw her tense.

"Was anything wrong?"

"No, not at all. Just that the child seemed too old to have been born into the community, and I couldn't remember any references to a family joining the settlement who already had a son that age." He sighed. "I rang you too soon, to be honest, because when I went back and checked the datastream archives, there they were. I can't quite believe I never picked up on it when we first started studying the Squats, but there you go. I'm sorry to trouble you."

Her expression was carefully unreadable.

"You met Bal and Gabriel."

"Yes."

"And you also didn't remember there being any families registered in the initial survey."

"No, like I said I must have—Wait. What do you mean, 'also'?"

She grimaced at the question, then said, "Well I'm glad we were able to clear that one up. Oh and yes, I've got time to meet while you're in town."

He gaped. "I don't—"

"I agree, it's always better to get a live review of the trickier cases. Of course if you think you've got the full picture from the datastreams, there's no need."

For several long moments Eli was too baffled to speak. Sally was staring at him with a squinting intensity.

"You'd like us to speak in person?" he finally said, slowly. Either that was what she was trying to get at with this bizarrely off-course line of dialogue, or the woman had gone insane. Her eyes were sharp and clear and trying hard to communicate something. She nodded vigorously.

"Only if you still think it would be helpful."

He had made no such request. He felt another mystery coil itself around him.

"Let's meet tomorrow."

9

A GUST OF WIND PUSHED HARD AT GAELA'S BACK AS SHE STOOD, COLD FIN-
gers pressed against the Maryam House identipad, waiting for the door
to open. The weather had turned blustery, bitter air from the north
whistling down the narrow streets of the Squats. When the thick glass
panel slid back into its housing she practically fell over the threshold.

She pushed the closer, the door hissing shut behind her as she
headed for the ground-floor lounge. The apartments that had once
occupied the space had been knocked through to create a big communal room with satellite kitchens, toilets, and utility areas. She
slipped inside, nodding greetings to the gems who glanced around
as she entered. There were almost a dozen people in the room, most
of whom did not look up. Heads glowed orange, blue, emerald, and
canary yellow as the more sociable clustered around tables. Others sat solitary, rocking back and forth, some staring into space and
some into tablets. She pulled her hat off as she headed for a back
room that served as an office, her own fire-bright hair tumbling past
her shoulders.

She tapped on the door frame. The man behind the desk looked
up. His face was almost at her eye level, halfway between the desktop

and the ceiling; giving the momentary impression of a short man standing up instead of an extremely tall one sitting down.

"Hey, Gaela. What's the word?"

"Crappy, I'm afraid." She flopped down into a chair. "How're you doing, Mikal?"

"Today," he said solemnly, "is no better than yesterday, and with any luck will be no better than tomorrow."

She laughed. Mikal had a fondness for constructing aphorisms, the more mind-bending the better. She thought about it for a moment and decided he was, on the whole, being optimistic. "Sorry I can't be more help."

"Work drying up?"

"Yes. I think it's partly the time of year, but also . . ." She stopped, shook her head. "The clients are skittish. It's almost like they're not sure whether it's still cool to hire gems."

"I'm hearing that from everyone." Mikal blinked. His eyelids slid up from the bottom as well as down from the top, meeting in the middle.

"We'll keep on giving whatever we can, but it's going to be less than I thought. Can you cope?"

"We'll manage." He glanced down at the screen inset into the desk. "Energy production is steady, even with not much solar. We're still getting a lot of food from up top. And the United Churches have just upped their pledge."

"They have?" She frowned. "Why?"

"Don't sound so cross, dear. We need the credits."

"I know, I know. But they must want *something*."

"No doubt they'd like more of us to join their congregations, but they're not making it conditional. I think they're pretty sure kindness and charity will get us there in the end."

Gaela snorted, but she felt a twinge of guilt. Members of the religious confederation had been among the loudest voices calling for gem protection. She'd eaten many a meal in their soup kitchens, clothed herself with their donations. When the high-altitude mining operations started to produce more dead bodies than minerals, it was they who'd fought for and funded the evacuation that had brought Bal to London.

"They also," Mikal said thoughtfully, "have been invited to attend the Conference."

"Bit late in the day. How'd that happen?"

"We made it happen."

Gaela stared, then rolled her eyes. "Oh, Aryel."

"One step ahead, as usual."

"She thinks they'll be able to help?"

"You think they won't?"

"It's getting rough out there, Mikal." Gaela looked down at her hands. They were still cold, a sensation she could see as well as feel. She rubbed them together. "Mostly it's little things: people don't look you in the eye, you sort of pick up the vibe as you walk past. But sometimes it's . . . Today, for instance. There's this young guy, plays a guitharp in Covent Garden. He's always there, and he's very good. This afternoon I'm passing by, hear the music, but instead of applause there's shouting. When I look there's a group of norms yelling at him to stop, saying it's a disgrace. Most of the others who were standing around listening are just dissolving away without a word. The kid says what's wrong with my music, they tell him if God had wanted people to play like that everyone would have fourteen fingers."

She paused. Mikal softly drummed his own fingers on the desk. He had three, bracketed by two opposing thumbs on either side of his palm. "What happened?"

"One of them shoved him, another tried to grab the guitharp. I waded in, shouted back, got between them. I was wearing this," she flicked at the hat resting on her lap, "so they probably thought I was a norm. Then a couple of the shopkeepers piled out and yelled at them, and a couple of the bystanders started sticking up for him, and a cop showed up, so they backed down and headed off. He was in tears—you can imagine." Gaela sighed, twisting the hat in her hands.

"Did the cop do anything?"

"Said no actual crime had been committed but he'd keep an eye out, have a word if he saw them again. He kept telling the kid to be careful, which is reasonable enough except it made it sound like it was his fault." Gaela shook her head. "I got him a coffee, and his name and comcode, and I'll message him when I get home to make sure he's okay."

"Where does he live?"

"West End. I said he should consider moving here. Although I sometimes think we just make a bigger target."

"That's occurred to me too. Concentrations concentrate contentions."

She threw the hat at him. He caught and returned it.

"You'll write this up?" he asked. "Make sure he's on the database?"

"Yep."

"Thanks." The look he gave her was warm with admiration, and sympathy. "That was brave of you, Gaela. And not surprising. Just remember that the people who most need your protection are already here."

Gabriel was at the door to greet her before she could get it all the way open. She swept him up, burying her face in the little-boy smell of play and sweets. He patted the back of her head with grubby hands, sing-shouting, "Papa, Mama's home! Mama's hooome!"

"Whatever happened," she said, lowering him to the ground, "to the quiet boy who used to live here? The one who used to whisper when he talked?"

"He's GONE!" Gabriel collapsed in giggles as she tickled him. She straightened up into Bal's embrace, was thoroughly kissed as he helped her off with her coat.

"Eew!"

"Eew yourself." Bal looked down at the grinning child. "Finish your lesson?"

"Almost."

"Almost sounds like you can get it done before dinner."

"I want to play with Mama."

"Mama wants to play with you," Gaela said, "as soon as you've finished. What are you working on?"

"Adding stuff up."

"You'll be done in no time. I'm going to go and talk to Papa for a bit."

They left him sticking his tongue out at his tablet. Bal handed her a mug of tea and dropped dumplings into a stew while she told him about the young musician. He'd been hearing similar tales over the counter at the leisure center.

"I think," he said quietly, "that when you have a job now, I should go with you."

"Sweetie, I don't need an escort. I'm fine."

"So far. I don't like this, Gaela. Have you looked at any of the socialstreams recently?" She shook her head. "Gems are trending—nothing new there—but the last few days there've been all these new posts. From silly stuff like gems staring at norms or their kids"—they both glanced, involuntarily, toward the living room, where Gabriel was—"to more serious things."

"Like what?"

"Assaults. Robbery. Kidnappings."

"That's ridiculous. If that was happening we'd have heard, and the newstreams would have picked it up."

"That's the thing. It's all very," he waved a big, floury hand in the air, "amorphous. My best friend's aunt's neighbor got mugged by a gem. Someone who works in my mate's office heard that someone in the building next door got beaten up by a gem. My girlfriend's cousin is a teacher and she said a gem tried to pick up some kids from the school."

She stared. "All of that?"

"That's just a sample. And of course they all get reposted umpteen times. But I cross-checked against the newstreams and the police posts. There's been the odd incident, there always is, but there's no correlation with the socialstream gossip. When that gets pointed out on the streams, the response is that the police and the media must be conspiring with the gems."

She looked down at the mug, watched its heat transferring into her hands.

"Have you told Aryel?"

"Sent her a message with the links. She was in meetings all day."

They continued to fret over it while Bal set the table and Gaela pulled out her tablet. He had just sent Gabriel to wash his hands when there was a knock at the door. Gaela glanced at it, blinking to refocus into infrared. "It's Aryel," she said, and Bal opened the door.

"We were just talking about you."

"Really? Oh dear." She looked tired and worried. Bal was puzzled. "You didn't get my note?"

"I did, thanks. I've been monitoring those streams myself. I passed your findings and mine on to the police, I'm seeing them tomorrow." She perched on a stool, looking precariously top-heavy in her lumbering cloak, and accepted a cup of tea gratefully.

Gabriel skipped back into the room, grinned at the new arrival. "Hey, you."

"Hi, Aunty Aryel."

She spotted the stillness of concentration settling over his face and shook her head sternly. "Don't look," she said. The little boy pouted. "I mean it, Gabe. Aunty Aryel's mind is not a good place to be today."

He sighed theatrically and flounced onto his seat, piled high with cushions, as Bal put a fourth bowl on the table. Aryel opened her mouth to protest, and Bal wagged a finger at her.

"No argument. We have plenty and I know for a fact you didn't eat today. So unless you have a hot date waiting somewhere . . ."

She laughed at that, and acquiesced. For a while there was no sound but the clinking of cutlery and light chatter about the weather. Finally Gabriel swallowed a massive mouthful, burped, and looked around.

"Are you all *really* going to wait till I've gone to bed before you talk about stuff?"

They stopped eating to look at him. Gaela mastered the smile that was trying to twitch its way onto her lips and put her spoon down firmly.

"Gabe."

"But Mama, I *know* already. I could tell *you*."

Bal cleared his throat. "Tell us what, exactly?" Aryel was staring anxiously at Gabriel.

"Well," he said, reconsidering solemnly. "I don't know *exactly*. Aunty Aryel wants to talk to you about me but it's all kind of complicated. That's not," he held a small, stew-stained finger up for emphasis, "the really bad thing that's making her upset. That's something different."

"Thought I told you not to look."

"I haven't. I'm scared of it."

"Good." Aryel sat back, relieved.

"Gabe, honey." Gaela combed her hands through her hair in frustration. "There are things that grown-ups just aren't supposed to talk about in front of kids."

"But those kids don't know stuff."

"You may be an extraordinary kid," Bal tried, "but give us a break. We're just ordinary grown-ups."

Gabriel chortled. "No you're not."

Three adults opened their mouths for a comeback, glanced at each other, and dissolved into slightly hysterical laughter. Gabriel glared at them and went back to his stew while they pulled themselves together. Bal was the first to recover.

"Right. Aunt Aryel," he said with exaggerated politeness, dabbing at his eyes with a napkin, "did you want to talk to us about Gabe?" He looked across the table at Gaela. They exchanged elaborate shrugs. Gabriel rolled his eyes.

"As a matter of fact, Bal, I did." Aryel was vastly amused. They had had endless conversations about the futility of trying to hide things from Gabriel, but the instinctive diffidence of the mature toward the very young was turning out to be a hard habit to break.

"I wanted to tell you that I've got the final set of results. They confirm our earlier tests, and Gaela's suspicions."

The laughter bled out of the room. Bal and Gaela locked eyes on each other, then on Aryel.

"What," demanded Gabriel, "does that mean?"

"You remember what we talked about before? About how come you can do what you do, and why your hair is different from Mama and Papa's?"

He nodded.

"Well it turns out that what we thought is true."

He looked doubtful. "Are you sure?"

"I'm sure."

His mouth turned down. "Does that mean I have to go away?" He looked anxiously at Gaela and Bal.

"No." Gaela leaned over to cup his little face in her hands and look into his eyes. "*No.* This is your home. You do not *ever* need to go *anywhere.* Hear me?"

"Yes, Mama." He slipped off his chair and wriggled onto her lap. She wrapped her arms around him and looked fierce. Bal reached over and rested his hand on the boy's head for a moment.

"Mama's right," he said. "It doesn't matter where you came from and what happened before. You and us are a family now. Okay?"

"Promise?"

"I promise."

"Okay."

They finished the meal quietly. Gaela went to get Gabriel ready for bed while Aryel helped Bal with the dishes.

"What it does mean," she said, "is that we need to make him understand how important he is, without scaring him. He's got to learn to be careful. Which isn't going to be easy."

Bal nodded. "He's not a shy kid anymore."

"I've noticed."

"When Gaela found him, I was so sure whoever did it must have had a plan—either he was being traded, or they wanted him to turn up dead on the doorstep of the Squats so it looked bad on us."

"I think the latter's more likely, since no one's ever shown up to collect. Henderson certainly wouldn't have wanted him found alive. Considering the way he was wrapped up, the plan may simply have been to take him down to the river. We might have the gillungs to thank for that not happening. They were arriving en masse that week."

"If Henderson's ever found . . ."

"I'm pretty certain," Aryel said evenly, "that he won't be." Bal looked at her. There was something in her face and voice that told him the matter was neither in doubt nor open for further discussion.

They were quiet for a while, Bal washing and Aryel drying. Finally he cleared his throat.

"But you don't think the danger's passed."

"I think we can never forget that others are looking for him. They just don't know to look *here*, it's the last place they'd expect. If they did know, we'd have a fight on our hands that . . ." Her voice trailed away and she sighed. "We'd have to do things none of us wants to do."

A shadow passed over his face, of anger mixed with revulsion, and fear. "They're going to use this Conference to try and get us back."

"Yes, they are."

"The scientist you met today. Eli Walker."

"Yes?"

"He a bagman?"

"No, but they're leaning on him. Why?"

"Gabe was with me in reception. He noticed."

"Damn." She chewed her lip in thought. Finally she shrugged, the movement exaggerated and made ponderous by the ungainly bulk of her cloak.

"Let's not worry about it too much. He's got other things on his mind, and the datastreams are solid. I'll ask Herran to keep an eye on it. Did he say anything?"

"Just hello. Very civil."

"What did Gabe think?"

"That he was smart. And nice, but a bit mixed up."

Aryel grimaced. "That would be exactly my assessment. Dr. Walker is in a very difficult place right now. I don't envy him." She sighed, staring into the distance, thinking.

"He did something quite brave today," she said. "It makes me think he could be a friend. We're going to see a lot of him over the next few days—he's going to want to talk to Gaela, and you too, probably. There's no point trying to hide Gabe. It could even be dangerous. We'll have to play it the same with him as with everyone else, and see how far he can be trusted."

Hail drummed on the roof of the stairwell as Aryel climbed up to her apartment some time later, moving with a weariness she rarely let others see. It hammered against the picture windows of Eli Walker's hotel room, rousing him from the chair where he sat with a tablet, working on the final draft of his report. He walked over and looked out at the storm sweeping in. A blanket of ice and bitter cold was falling across the city. Eli pulled the curtains closed and went back to work.

A young man with glowing orange-red hair and the pale, pouty features of a Pre-Raphaelite painting emerged, along with a blast of music, from a club on one of the roads that ran toward the Squats. He swore as the sleet slapped at his face, blinding him as he stumbled around a corner to get out of the wind. He bumped into someone and looked up, blinking and shaking the water and hair out of his eyes.

"Sorry, didn't see—" he began, and stopped.

Six people clustered in the shelter of the alley. They were dressed for the weather, collars turned up on heavy coats and hats pulled low. Some had even pulled scarves right across their faces. There was nothing to recognize them by except the current of threat, intangible and unmistakable.

He stepped back and found that the way was blocked. "Where d'you think you're going?" someone said. The group closed in around him.

"Heading home," he replied, feeling fear clamp cold and hard around his intestines. "I'm not looking for any trouble. Sorry to get in your way." He held up his hands, turning slowly, thinking if there was only one behind maybe he could dodge past and make a run for it. There were two.

"The Lord permits no home for such as you," came a voice at his back.

"Abomination," muttered another.

"I don't know what you mean," he said. He could feel his knees starting to go.

A hand fell on his shoulder, swung him around.

"You think we can't see what you are?" The speaker was a man with the heavy build of a boxer, swinging a fist into a gloved hand. "What you're doing in that place? You think we don't know?"

The young man understood, with a conviction buried too deep in genetic memory for any clever tampering to touch, what was coming. He thought of pleading and knew with the same sinking certainty that it would do no good.

He summoned bravado, a last hope. Maybe sheer impudence would win him a way out. "That what you're looking for, pops? You should've said. One at a time now."

The curse and the fist hit him at the same time. He crashed back into the two blocking the mouth of the alley. They broke his fall with fists and feet. He went down, and the gang and the night closed over him.

$=$ DAY THREE $=$

10

GEM PATRON LEFT FOR DEAD

Police are investigating a violent attack outside a nightclub that has left a young gem fighting for his life. The attack occurred at around midnight near the Sparklers club on Cable Street, a venue known to be frequented by both genetically modified and normal patrons. The victim, a gem known as Callan, appears to have been targeted because of his genetic status.

Witnesses say that Callan, formerly of the Bel'Natur conglomerate, left the club shortly before midnight. He was found several hours later in a nearby alleyway as Sparklers was closing down for the night. He was unconscious and appeared to have sustained both knife wounds and a severe beating, most likely committed by multiple assailants. He was taken to the Royal London Hospital where he remains in a critical condition with what are said to be particularly horrific injuries. Police confirm that anti-gem graffiti was found in the alley where he was assaulted.

Staff members describe Callan as a frequent and popular visitor to Sparklers, and were not aware of any disputes or enemies he may have had. Stunned revelers spoke of a fun-loving and attractive young man with many admirers. Callan is thought to reside in the city's primary gem enclave, the area known as the Squats in East London. Residents there are said to be deeply shocked. The attack is the most serious in a recent string of incidents involving gems.

Initial reviews of surveillance vids from the vicinity of the attack have so far proved inconclusive. Police are asking anyone who may have information, or who may have been in the area between 11:30 p.m. and 3:30 a.m., to come forward. The authorities are unable to say whether the European Conference on the Status of Genetically Modified Humans, which begins in London this week, is a factor in the growing tensions. Dr. Robert Trench, the Acting Commissioner for Gem Affairs, has condemned the attack and appealed for calm.

Eli gulped his coffee, found it had gone cold as he read. He fumbled his earset into place as he pulled up Aryel Morningstar's comcode. It buzzed twice before she answered.

"Eli. Morning. Sorry, I haven't got visual." He could hear the wind whistling in the background and wondered where she was. It was still dark outside, the predawn gloom of a short winter day.

"Just as well for your sake. I wouldn't have called so early, but I'm reading the news."

"I've been up since they found him."

"How is he?"

"Very bad. They don't know if he's going to make it. He looks more like a piece of meat than a human being."

"You've seen him?"

"I've just left the hospital."

There was a pause. He could imagine her struggling down steps and around corners, fighting the wind that would catch her oversize coat like a sail and try to sweep her off her feet. The buffeting sound stopped abruptly, with a click that sounded like a door closing.

"What do the police think?"

"That it was a godgang. They've got them on the area vids, wrapped in layers of camouflage so ID will be next to impossible. They left signs—an inverted cross, hate messages—on and around his body." Her voice was bitter. "They used his own blood."

"Dear lord."

"Do you believe in god, Eli?"

For a moment he could not understand why she would ask such a question. Then he replayed his own muttered imprecation. "No, I don't. Just one of those expressions the language can't seem to shake. A substitute for not knowing what to say." He rubbed his hands over his face, resenting the gritty feel of not enough sleep. "Look, what can I do? Seriously."

"Come tonight."

"You still think that's a good idea?"

"I think it's even more so. You said you were after balance. Well, we need some of that ourselves."

He had already decided to say yes, had called in part to see if she wanted to rescind the invitation under the circumstances. He was unaccountably pleased that she had not.

"Rob told me"—When had it been? The ride from the train station felt like ages ago—"that animosities were growing. He was worried about gems being victimized, but also that they wouldn't *just* be victims."

"He's right. A lot of us would have no trouble at all fighting back, especially after what's happened to Callan."

"The attack on him will shock a lot of people—norms—into greater sympathy for the gem position. It always happens: people don't really think about it, they sit on the fence, until there's an . . . event."

"Have you checked the socialstreams this morning?"

Another apparently unrelated question. This time he could not discern the connection. "No, I don't spend much time on them. Why?"

"You should, especially this week. Look at any of them. MyNews or Bushgram, something like that."

"Hang on."

He pulled up the links on his tablet, flipping from one stream to another, cold sweat gathering on his spine. The story was everywhere, reposts and commentary flickering into life as he watched. Many linked to pictures of the alley, even of the victim in situ, taken before the paramedics and police had arrived and secured the scene.

He scrolled back through the timeline. The initial posts were dominated by the combination of outraged condemnation and horrified fascination he expected. That theme was continuing. But as the hours had rolled on a different note had crept in: first excusing and then justifying. Now the streams were alive with posts registering satisfaction, gratification, even encouragement. Disapproval of the permissiveness that now allowed gems not only to live as freely as norms but to go partying with them as well ranged from unease to fury. Rumors were circulating of Callan's supposed proclivities, and those of other gems. Tales were offered up in vindication of what the soft-minded might unfairly view as harsh treatment. The competing trends vied for supremacy on every stream he checked.

"Aryel?" he said, hearing his own voice soft with shock. "I don't believe this."

"When people get off the fence," she said, "they tend to come down on both sides."

Zavcka Klist read the streams with considerably greater equanimity. She wondered whether it would be inappropriate to send flowers, decided that a simple bouquet of medicinal blooms and a handwritten note expressing deep concern would be just the right touch. She ordered them for delivery that morning and was rewarded by an aggravated call from Felix when she arrived at the office a couple of hours later.

"There's a news team asking for a comment. Something about a get-well card. PR routed it to *me*."

"I know. I told them if there were any inquiries to send it up here. Didn't you get my message?"

He mumbled something about not having checked yet. "I don't know what the hell you're doing. *I* don't intend to talk to them."

"No problem." Her voice was crisp. "I'll do it."

She would have preferred to handle it via message, but there was a reporter with a vidcam waiting. She went down to meet them.

"We're all shocked and deeply upset," she told the woman from the BBC. "We remain very concerned about all of our former associates. Obviously we're no longer able to protect them from this kind of violence and hatred," she shook her head sorrowfully, "but we do monitor what's going on. It's very distressing."

"Do you worry about them?"

"Very much so."

"Do you think there will be more incidents like this?"

"I sincerely hope not. It's hard to imagine such a thing happening even once in a civilized society, but," she spread her hands, "here we are. Poor Callan has paid the price. We can only pray no one else has to suffer like that."

"We understand his condition remains critical."

"So I gather, but I don't know any more than that. The health service doesn't regard us as family. We do have Callan's genetype of course, as well as his health records up to the point he left our care, and we've offered to share them with the hospital in case they might be helpful to his recovery. Beyond that I'm afraid we just have to wait and hope he's able to pull through."

The reporter was looking perplexed.

"I must say, Miss Klist, that your concern for this young man is . . . well, not what most people would expect."

"I think there's been a real misunderstanding of our position with respect to people like Callan. I know," as the reporter tried to interrupt, "that there have been some serious errors and abuses in the past, and unfortunately the public has formed the impression that those incidents are representative. I think you and I both know that they're not. You don't spend a lifetime creating and caring for people without caring *about* them as well."

"Do you wish he'd stayed within Bel'Natur?"

Zavcka stared over the reporter's shoulder for a moment, as if deeply considering the question.

"At the risk of being politically incorrect . . . ," she said slowly. "Under the circumstances? Given what's happened to him? Yes, I wish he had. He'd have been safe."

"Thank you very much for your time."

The interview was uploaded almost immediately with virtually no editing. She was thoroughly satisfied with it. She sent the link to everyone who was working on preparations for the Conference. Felix responded with an almost-chastened reply to her earlier message that simply said, "Oh, I see. Well done."

A few more press inquiries came in and she repeated the best lines. By lunchtime the deep and sincere concern of Bel'Natur formed part of the background to the story. She was pleased to note that some of the other gemtechs were following their lead. The assistant to the managing director of Gempro messaged to ask when she would be free for lunch.

At around mid-morning a call came in on her private comcode. The knife-thin face peering up from the tablet ran an unregistered company out of a nondescript address. She was quite sure no one else at Bel'Natur knew he existed.

"I see you're Our Lady of Charity now. Not sure I should even be calling."

"I do what I gotta do, just like you. You have something for me?"

"Maybe. Sample came in, matched the one you provided."

She was completely, tensely alert. "Came in from where?"

"That's what's weird. My guy in the lab is pretty sure it was a gem."

"The sample or . . ."

"We couldn't find any engineering markers on it either, but we knew to expect that. No, I meant the person who brought it in. No obvious gemsign, but my source was in the biz long enough to tell."

She sat back and thought about that. "Very curious. Do you have a location?"

"My bet is it's going to turn out to be fake, along with the name. We've got some ideas, though."

"Send me everything."

Eli watched the interview in silence. Rob was sputtering indignation at the screen.

"*Some* serious abuses? *Some*? *SOME*?" He turned to Eli. "Do you believe this shit?"

"I believe she wishes he'd been locked up in a dorm somewhere. As for the rest of it . . ." He considered the conversations he'd had with Zavcka Klist. "Her attitude on the train was proprietary, yes, but also very paternalistic, so it sort of fits. There was less of that yesterday, but under the circumstances . . ." He shrugged. "What strikes me is how much more concern she's showing for this victim than for the ones in the report she gave me."

"You didn't have a vidcam and a worldwide audience."

"This is true."

Eli had gone to Whitehall early so he could talk over the social-stream trends with Rob. Many posts included the link, along with their own sympathies and best wishes. Opposing views ranged from vitriolic denunciations of gems and gemtechs alike to assertions that political correctness was indeed to blame for turning a manageable situation into a crisis and there ought to be a great deal less of it. Those posts linked to the interview as well. He found neither association encouraging.

Rob was doing his teeth-sucking thing. "She's laying the groundwork for something. She's trying to make it look like they want to help the gems."

"That's not the only angle. She wouldn't have volunteered that vid without a reason."

Eli watched the posts crawl up the screen: pro-gem, anti-gem, pro-gem, anti-gem. "Either she knows about a real threat for which Bel'Natur would be liable, and dumping responsibility on me is a damage-limitation exercise—or she's planning to leak the vid and sweep in with a plan to keep gems and norms safe from each other." He leaned back in the chair and stretched out his legs, an extended hypotenuse to its right angle, as he stared at the ceiling. "Or both."

"That's a hell of a conspiracy theory."

"Doesn't mean it's not true."

"What are you going to do?"

Eli followed the almost invisible lines where power panels had been inset into the plaster, reached the window, and gazed unseeing out at the freezing gray of a London winter.

"What if the threat is real?" he said. "The fact that we're being manipulated, that she's doing it for her own ends, still doesn't prove the world isn't full of gems who are latent psychopaths. And sure, it's not their fault, but is that going to make it any better if even one turns out to be another sexual sadist? Or a serial killer? Or a pedophile?"

He looked at his friend. "What's my obligation here, Rob? Do I say all gems should be treated equally, and take that risk? Or do I find that the evidence supports some kind of typing, a categorization that lets us control the ones we're not sure about? Because it could. That interpretation wouldn't be much of a stretch."

"It would make a lot of politicians happy." Rob was struggling to contain his upset. "You know what I think. Dealing with gems every day, seeing the wreckage, the trauma, all the fallout from the gemtechs . . . *They're* the ones responsible for this. The gems didn't ask to be created, they didn't ask to be different, they didn't ask to be saddled with all this crap. For them to get the blame . . ." He shook his head. "It's just *wrong*."

"I know. But it's not going to do any good if the damage they've suffered keeps generating more damage." He folded himself back into the chair. "What if Bel'Natur's proposal takes responsibility? What if it really does help? If it's the right thing does it matter if they do it for the wrong reason?"

"Eli, I hope to hell you're just being devil's advocate."

"Somebody needs to be. Would you prefer me or Zavcka Klist?"

Guilt pricked at him as he thought of Aryel Morningstar: her dignity, her compassion, her insight. "We need an agreement. Or an alternative."

He was still wrestling with uncertainties as he made his way along the icy sidewalk to his rendezvous with Sally Trieve, a bit surprised that she hadn't canceled given the events of the morning. He had replayed their conversation over and over in his head. He was sure

there had been a little nod of satisfaction, as though she had confirmed something to herself, when she said that he *also* had not
remembered Gabriel. But her insinuation that it was he who had
requested the meeting, that there was more to discuss, was completely baffling. The slippery surface underfoot felt like the mental
landscape he was trying to navigate.

She had suggested they meet in one of the ancient pubs that dotted the backstreets of Westminster. He found the place and stepped
into its warmth with relief. It was too early for lunch and therefore
not crowded. He spotted her sitting in an alcove next to an antique
fireplace, at a table too big for just the two of them but too small to
share with another party. It was the only one in the space, and as he
made his way across he picked up the irritated glances of other early
arrivals who, he thought, had been denied their usual spot.

They shook hands and he settled into a chair. He wondered if she
was waiting for him to begin, until several other patrons who had
followed him in wandered over to a table some distance away and sat
down. Then she leaned forward and launched in without preamble.

"Dr. Walker, I apologize for the way I set up this meeting. All that
nonsense I was spouting was just that, nonsense. But I promise you
I'm not crazy." Her voice was low and intense. "I needed to speak
with you directly and I couldn't explain why via tablet." She shook
her head. "I mean, I didn't think I should. It might not have mat-
tered, but I can't be sure."

"Can't be sure of what?"

"Whether the transmission might have been monitored, or
recorded, or could have been tampered with . . ." She took in his
disbelieving stare. "I don't know exactly what is and isn't possible,
especially now. What I do know is this."

She leaned even farther forward, dropped her voice even lower.
"When you first started looking at the datastreams on the Squats,
well over a year ago now, there was no mention of a family with
a young child. You would have noticed if there was. Well, me too.
I studied the pre-Declaration community survey when I commissioned the follow-up and started assembling services. I even remember the particular entry on Gaela and Bal, because when I saw the

note of her ability I was surprised she didn't need any specialist support. I am absolutely certain there was no mention of a child."

"You mean the entry was corrected later? He was missed the first time around?"

"I don't think so, and *corrected* is not the term I would use. For one thing there would be a record of the change, and believe me when I tell you there isn't. I have looked in every way that it's possible to look. And for another, any such update should have been done by me or someone on my team. It would have been brought to my attention and I, like you, would have remembered."

"I don't understand."

"Gaela and Bal were among the very first gems to move into the Squats. Maybe *the* first. We don't know exactly when they arrived, but it couldn't have been while the retrieval squads were active. Whenever it was, I do not believe they had a child then, and I do not believe one has been born to them since."

She held up a hand to forestall Eli's interruption. "And Gabriel is too old to have been born there anyway, I know. I think he came to the Squats—from where I don't know—and was unofficially adopted by Gaela and Bal around the beginning of the year. It would have been at the same time that hundreds upon hundreds of gems were arriving after the Declaration, and I can only assume he arrived with one of them and was handed over. Which would be strange enough, although it's possible that someone who couldn't care for their child might want him fostered by a couple who could. But that doesn't explain how a gem just released from a lifetime of lockdown could have had a natural-born four-year-old, or how or why our records were altered. Because that is the *most* bizarre thing."

She paused, looking at him as though anticipating his reaction to her next words.

"I think that somehow, someone has been able to get into the datastream of that initial survey and alter it, and alter at least the first-generation reports, which included that data—and maybe second and third generation as well, since everything links back—to make it look as though he's been with Gaela and Bal all along."

Eli stared at her. What she was suggesting was completely irrational, but she was deadly serious. She obviously believed it was possible.

"Sally, that's—Forgive me, but what you're saying makes no sense. A completely untraceable security breach? How could that have been done? And if it was, why are we whispering about it in the pub?"

"This is complicated and it's going to sound nuts, but bear with me." She glanced around again to make sure no one was in earshot. Eli looked around himself, thinking suddenly of Donal.

"I first became aware of Gabriel's existence a few weeks after the Declaration. It was at a meeting at the Squats to introduce the social workers I'd assigned and to set up protocols for how we were going to support the community, assess ongoing needs, all of that early-intervention managerial stuff. Aryel Morningstar was there, and a Recombin gem named Mikal, who was another pre-Declaration arrival, and Bal and a bunch of others, mostly newcomers. And someone just happened to mention Gabriel, very casually, as though anyone who knew anything about the Squats would know who they were talking about. I was baffled, but I didn't say anything at the time because I didn't know what was going on or how to deal with it. And honestly, I still don't.

"As soon as that meeting was over I did exactly what you did yesterday. I checked the datastreams. And I saw what you saw: an entry that showed him living in the Squats with his parents at least six months earlier."

She paused for breath and a sip of water, and leaned forward again.

"But I'd *been* there when the community was still quite small. When the Declaration was issued and we realized what would happen, I was at the Squats a lot. And yes, almost a thousand flooded into the area within a month, but I never saw or heard anything about a child. The surveys were being updated daily and I referred to them constantly. There were a few pregnant women and a couple of babies but no record of an older child, either present or arriving. But if you log on to those archives now, he's there. If you look at the statistical summaries aggregated from the data, he's in them. And if you check the edit logs there is no indication that any of that information has ever been changed."

Eli was staring open-mouthed. "That's not possible."

"It's not supposed to be. I've never heard of such a thing happening, but think about it." She spread her hands. "If it *did* happen, how would we know? Everything is logged and uploaded and linked. We rely absolutely on the robustness of the data systems. If someone did have a way of changing the base data, how would you contradict it? All you'd have to go on is your own memory versus the machine's. Unless you had lots of people all prepared to swear that the information had once been different, or like in old times when it was recorded on paper or stone or something, how would you prove it? Who would the authorities believe? Who would *you* believe, nine times out of ten?"

She sighed. "You don't know what a relief it was to me when you said what you said yesterday. I have been close to certain I was stark, staring mad a couple of times. I even went and got memory and psych checkups. Listening to myself today, I know I sound completely paranoid." She stared back across the table at him, something pleading in her eyes. "But I'm not, Dr. Walker. This isn't a figment of my imagination. I can be absolutely sure of that now."

"Because," he said slowly, "you and I both remember a different version of that early survey."

"Yes."

"But you're saying that version no longer exists, and there's no proof it ever did."

"Yes."

"And the whole point of this change . . . this deception . . . is to disguise the fact that the child did not arrive at the same time as the parents? And the community is colluding with it?"

"Yes. As far as I can tell that's the only piece of information that's been tampered with. I've gone over and over the reports and everything else is just as I remember it. As for collusion, it would only need to be a handful of people, the original members of the community. Who are all very good friends."

He felt suddenly, absolutely certain that Aryel must know the truth. He felt a pang of hurt at the thought. He had already discovered she could be nonchalant about withholding information, but somehow he had not thought her capable of active deceit.

"But how could they pull off the datastream hack? And why?" He had a vision of the little sandy-haired boy, the big, protective father. "What's so special about this kid? If he's not theirs, where did he come from?"

"The answer to all of that is, I don't know. He's a very empathic child, but I'm not aware of his having an ability as such." She was frowning at the table, doodling in the water that had condensed and run down the sides of her glass. "I thought if he was being hidden in the Squats for some reason then he must be *missing* from somewhere, and surely they couldn't hide that. A kid disappears, there'd be an uproar. So I checked on all the gem families we have on record, which as you know aren't many. And I checked every crèche and care home in the country. And before you ask, I didn't just look at their datastreams, I got in touch with them. I even checked, don't ask me why, if there were any *norm* missing kids of around the right age. There aren't. No one has reported losing this child."

"Then maybe he *is* theirs. Maybe they left him in someone else's care while they got themselves settled and then they took him back."

"Then why not just say so? I don't think Bal and Gaela could have been together long enough to have a kid that age, but even if I'm wrong about that or he's from a previous relationship, why the deception?"

"I don't know." The picture of the smiling child playing at his father's feet was replaced suddenly by an image from the Bel'Natur vid: another child, bloody, brutalized, and dying. "You don't think he's being . . . harmed in any way?"

"No." The response was quick and firm. "That is one thing I'm sure of. I've kept as close an eye on them as I can, and if I thought anything untoward was happening in that household, or if the child wasn't thriving, I'd say evidence be damned and be in there like a shot. But Gabriel is just about the healthiest, sunniest kid I can think of. He seemed a bit withdrawn at first—which would make sense, settling into a new place—but not anymore. His parents adore him—see, even I think of them as that. Their friends dote on him, he calls them aunty and uncle. He's been set up on a home-school program and he's in the top percentile. I suggested he do some general cognition and social awareness tests as well, just so we could benchmark his progress. I have a feeling Gaela knew exactly what I was after, but they went along with it. We did it under controlled conditions and he aced every test."

"So he's a bright, happy, well-adjusted kid who loves his mom and dad. Even though he probably also knows they're not."

"*Exactly*. He's obviously not pining for wherever he was before."

Her hands opened and closed in the air, as though she were trying to capture something ephemeral. "I've been doing this kind of work for a long time, Dr. Walker, and it doesn't *feel* like abuse or abduction to me. You know, they're taking a big risk. It feels like they're protecting this boy, and doing a damn good job raising him while they're at it."

Eli did not think Sally Trieve sounded paranoid at all, despite her improbable story. She seemed in person just what he would have expected from her reputation and meticulous reporting: committed, competent, and sensible. She had spent many months unable to decide what to do, her seasoned social worker's instinct loudly warning that a by-the-book reaction would not deliver the best outcome for the child. Her relief at finally being able to share the burden was palpable.

They agreed he would quietly pursue some avenues of his own. He did not specify what they were. She seemed content, like Zavcka Klist the day before, to put the entire matter into his hands and abide by whatever decision he made.

He wondered how he had found himself in a position of such power over other people's lives. His ambition had been to observe, understand and advise; he had never sought to sit in judgment. The mountain of things he did not know loomed over him, and he felt ill equipped to serve as arbiter.

They spoke about the attack outside the nightclub. Sally had sent crisis counselors into the Squats as soon as she'd heard, and would be there herself that evening. She only knew Callan by sight.

"He was another one who didn't need any help from us," she explained. "I gather he spent a lot of time outside the Squats, had no trouble making friends with norms. His looks would have helped—he is, was, a beautiful young man—but I suspect his ability did as well."

"What is it? No one's actually said."

"He's a linguist. Multiple languages and the ability to learn more really fast. Bel'Natur in particular seems to have been experimenting with those kinds of very specific mental gifts. I've met a number of children in crèche who were part of the same line, and the thing you notice about them is how well they socialize. Really high levels of emotional intelligence. My guess is Callan was a prototype."

He told her what Zavcka Klist had said on the train. "It strikes me as odd that she would go on about how gems can't be independent or interact normally if her own company was turning out people who prove just the opposite."

Sally considered this.

"I would say," she said finally, "that what she told you is about half right, and I guess that's the half she wants you to focus on. You know that over forty percent of the gems in this city either are or should be in the social services system, and nationally the percentage is even higher. They are," she ticked off on her fingers, "children in crèche who are mostly going to be okay when they grow up, adults who are too badly damaged to manage outside of an institution, and those who can live in gem communities as long as they have the right kind of support."

"That's a lot of people who need to be taken care of. Especially since, unlike the gemtechs, we don't find ways to force them to work."

"True, but the numbers in care are going to drop. Hugely. Even the kids who have problems are generally doing much better now that they're being raised as children and not commodities." She kept her voice even but Eli could hear the anger in it. "The way they were conditioned for fast learning and adaptation means that most of them absorb the benefits of therapy really well. If we can keep the quality of care high until they're grown up I think very few will require long-term support. And given time and resources I believe some of the adults can become more independent as well." She was thoughtful. "Some of them . . . the autistics . . . also have some of the most extraordinary abilities. I've wondered if it isn't one of them who was able to change the datastreams."

"I'm not a techhead, but I always thought that kind of manipu-lation could only be done by someone who doesn't need a binary interface, who can work with raw code. The gemtechs say they never achieved a true digital savant."

"The gemtechs say a lot of things. But I wonder if they would even know. The world has opened up so much for these people, they're not limited in what they're allowed to do anymore. I think there are gems out there discovering talents the gemtechs haven't even guessed at."

11

GAELA CRANED TO KEEP TRACK OF GABRIEL, WISHING SHE'D BEEN ABLE TO leave him at home, or at any rate keep him away from the chaos of the community room. Not, she had to admit, that it would have done much good. The reaction to the attack on Callan was almost palpable, a fog of anger and fear that the boy had felt from the moment he woke up. He'd picked threads of meaning out of the jumble, woven them into a fairly accurate understanding of what had happened, and appeared in the kitchen, barefoot and pajamaed, demanding to know who Callan was and why bad people had hurt him.

It was a mercy, she thought, that Callan wasn't one of the gems he'd met in his time at the Squats. As he wormed his way through the minds of others he seemed able to process the details and distress of the crime from enough of a remove to allow him to maintain his own equilibrium. She was sure he would have struggled to separate his responses from theirs if the victim had been someone he knew, like Aryel or Mikal or Wenda. Or Bal or herself.

She blinked her vision into ultraviolet for a moment and spotted him, half-hidden behind two gems who sat huddled with one of the counselors from social services. He was standing next to Mikal, barely knee-high to the towering gem. She saw him look up and say something. Mikal glanced around until he spotted Gaela, nodded at her and rested a hand on the boy's head in a don't-worry-he's-with-me gesture. She could almost have heard Gabe tell him that Mama was looking, and could he please let her know that he was all right.

She turned her attention back to the gem she was trying to comfort, a pitiably shy teenager named Jora who turned out to have a huge, and hitherto unguessed-at, crush on Callan. Jora was doubled over on Gaela's lap, sobbing uncontrollably. Gaela patted her back, thinking that poor Jora's dreams would inevitably have been dashed one way or another. She was engineered for tissue regeneration and as such was dumpy and lumpy with various odd duplications of features and organs; had poor social skills and limited intellectual potential; and moreover was female. She had clearly been unable to grasp the obstacle that this last fact presented to any hope of attracting Callan's amorous attention.

Gabriel frowned at her across the room. Gaela understood. Once you got used to his ability you didn't actually need to share it to communicate without speaking. *Of course I won't say anything*, she thought at him. *I would never hurt her feelings like that. Mama's done this kind of thing before, you know.* He looked momentarily chastened, then slipped from under Mikal's hand over to the kitchen, where Horace was bringing plates of sandwiches out.

The green-haired gem was uncharacteristically subdued. Gabriel silently helped him transfer baskets of crisps to the big refectory table. When everything had been delivered, Horace fished out a crisp and crunched it absently. Gabriel did the same.

"Horace?"

"Yes?"

"How come you're so confused?"

Horace pushed a stack of plates closer to the edge of the table. "Everyone is a bit mixed up today, Gabe."

Gabriel munched another crisp. "Everybody's really sad and scared," he declared. "And angry."

"Well, me too."

Gabriel frowned. "Yes," he agreed, "but you're . . . not sure about stuff."

"I just keep wondering . . . did Callan say something, did he provoke them in any way . . ."

"Why would he do that?"

"He wouldn't have meant to. Sometimes you can make a mistake and not even know you made it."

"What kind of mistake?"

"I don't know, Gabe. Maybe if he'd kept a lower profile, hadn't been where he was . . ."

He looked up, suddenly noticing the silence falling around them as people came up for food. Mikal stood at the periphery of the quiet, glaring. Horace dropped his head and busied himself pouring tea, muttering, "It's just, if he hadn't been there, he couldn't have got hurt."

He jumped back an instant later as two fists crashed down, sending scalding tea splashing up at him. Sandwiches levitated with the force of the blow; plates and cups rattled and tilted. Everyone jerked away from Wenda, who stood across the table from Horace, her clenched hands rigid in the spreading puddle on the tablecloth, teeth bared, veins distended, the tendons in her neck tensed almost to breaking point. Her mouth worked as she struggled to speak. Only a prolonged, tortured grunt came out. Her teeth gnashed.

Horace backed up, palms raised in startled placation. From beside him Gabriel stepped forward, head cocked to one side as he leaned on the table, staring at Wenda. Across the room, Gaela struggled to shove Jora off her lap.

The tableau held for an agonizing moment. Wenda looked poised to leap over the table and strangle Horace, an acceptable substitute for being unable to scream at him.

Gabriel reached his small hand out to her.

"Aunty Wenda?" he whispered. "Horace didn't mean it like that."

She did not look at him. All her attention remained focused on Horace.

"Aunty Wenda? Aunty Wenda, I can tell them for you." He looked around at Horace. "She doesn't like what you said," he explained unnecessarily.

Wenda slapped a hand down hard on the table, the sound rever-
berating around the room along with the howl that finally ripped
itself out of her. Mikal pushed through the crowd, but she shoved
him away as he tried to lay his hands on her shoulders and spun back
to face Horace.

"*N-n-n-not!*" she shrieked. The word seemed a paltry contraction
of a whole spate of meaning and emotion that she was desperate to
convey. Her jaw contorted with effort. "Not h-h-h-him! Them!"

"It wasn't his fault, and you shouldn't say it was," Gabriel translated. "It was their fault. They were bad people. He didn't do anything wrong."

He turned from Horace to Gaela, as his mother finally dropped
to her knees next to him.

"*Gabe.*"

"I know, Mama, but Aunty Wenda feels so bad and she can't
explain and I need to help."

Horace was shaking, his face mirroring the green of his hair,
mumbling denials and apologies as he flattened himself against the
wall. Wenda blazed daggers at him, but she finally allowed Mikal to
pull her gently away. He guided her to an armchair and she slumped
into it, burying her face in her hands. Gabriel tried to pull away from
Gaela.

"Gabe, that's enough."

"No, Mama, you don't *understand.*"

Wenda looked up, peering at Gabriel through her tumbled turquoise mane. She turned to Gaela. It looked as though she were trying to speak again, but all she could manage was "P-p-please" before
her face fell back into her hands.

Gabriel wriggled free and went over to her. He slid a hand under
her arm and tugged with all his strength to pull it away from her face,
twisting around to peer up at her from under the waterfall of hair.

"It's not your fault," he said. She pulled her arm back, nodding
sharply into the closed cage of her hands. Her thoughts were loud in
his head. *It is, it is. I should have protected him.*

"You couldn't. 'Cos you tried, when they took him away, you
tried so hard."

She was keening now, a soft wailing grief that ripped at Gaela's heart as she stood transfixed with the others. A mantra of guilt pulsed into Gabriel's mind, echoing over the morass of anguished memories that he was pushing through. *I should have stopped them. I should have kept him.*

"When they took him away?" Mikal stared from one to the other. "Gabe, what are you talking about? He wasn't taken away, he went out on his own."

Gabriel looked up at him, puzzled for a moment, then said, "No, not now. A long time ago." He patted Wenda's arm and she enveloped his small hand in her large one, holding on to it as to a lifeline. Gabriel took a deep breath.

"When Aunty Wenda was having babies she used to have them for different companies," he explained, "and one of them was the same one you came from, Mama, and Callan, and she had a baby boy with red hair that looked just like Callan so she thinks that was him. And one day the people came and took him away, and she tried to stop them 'cos she wanted to keep him and be his mama, but there were a lot of them and they took him away anyway. And so she feels bad, like she wasn't a good mama, but, Aunty Wenda," he turned back to the sobbing woman, "it's not your fault. Nobody thinks so. I bet Callan wouldn't think so, even if he is the same baby."

Gaela found herself across the room, moving through a shocked silence. She brushed at her face as she knelt beside the chair, wondering why her vision was blurring, and found it wet.

"Wenda," she whispered. "Wenda. Oh sweetie." She wrapped her right arm around the older woman's shaking shoulders and gathered Gabriel firmly into her left. He was glancing around the room, eyes flitting from face to face along, she was sure, with his mind. He seemed finally to have gotten the message to *Shut up.*

"Gabe's right," she murmured. "He's right, love, you know he is. It's not your fault. Callan's a grown-up, there's not one thing you could have done. And," she glared across the room at Horace, "it wasn't his fault either. There's nothing any of us could've done."

"Of-of course not," Horace stammered. He looked stricken. "That's not what . . . of *course* not."

Mikal met Gaela's eyes over the back of the chair. She relinquished her grip on Wenda, letting him take over, and stood up, holding Gabriel. The tension started to slacken a little, replaced by a stunned whispering hum. The most disconnected gems, the ones who sat and rocked and spoke little, took refuge in a faint echo of Wenda's moaning grief. Friends and counselors converged on them, trying to damp down the distress before someone else flared into crisis. Soothing murmurs washed around the room.

One of the counselors appeared in front of Gaela. She was a regular, a speech therapist named Rachel who worked with Wenda and others. She was blinking back tears, but her jaw was set and her mouth firm. Gabriel whispered, "She wants to help."

Rachel glanced at him, then gestured past them to Wenda, mutely requesting permission to approach. Gaela nodded and stepped aside. Rachel replaced her, kneeling at Wenda's feet, and Gaela slipped out.

On her way to the door she noticed a newcomer, a man Mikal had said was a United Churches volunteer. He was staring at them, an expression of wonderment on his face. She double-checked for infrared as she strode past, Gabriel clutched in her arms. There was none. Somehow it comforted her not at all.

Gabriel wanted to know if she was cross with him.

"Can't you tell?" she snapped. He flinched, and a tear rolled down his cheek.

"No," he snuffled. He had turned into a mouse, meek and barely audible. "Your head is all muddled up."

She fell onto the sofa and pulled him into her lap. It was still damp from Jora's weeping. He added another wet patch to her chest while she cuddled and comforted him, kicking herself as she considered how scary the journey through Wenda's scarred mind must have been.

"What you did for Wenda was very kind and very brave," she said finally. "And I am very proud of you for being a kind, brave boy. But it was also very dangerous. We don't want a lot of people to know

what you can do, especially ones who don't live here. And you just
showed the whole room. So I'm upset with you for that." She sighed.
"It turns out, Gabe, that I can be proud of you and cross with you
at the same time."

"Am I in trouble?"

"I hope not."

He tipped his head back to look up at her. "I mean am I in
trouble with *you*."

"Oh, baby . . ." She shrugged helplessly. "No, you're not in trouble
with me. Or Papa."

He snuggled into her arms, a relief she could almost see washing
through him. She knew he could feel her other thoughts, the anxieties that knifed through her rippling against his mind like waves on
a beach.

But he was getting better at focusing only where he wished, and
she realized, with a strange coupling of frustration and approval, that
safe in the cocoon that she and Bal had woven around him he could
simply choose to disregard anything else.

A powerfully built man stepped out of an interview booth and
rejoined three more gems—two other men and a woman—in the
employment office waiting room. All four of them were tall and
strong, hair ranging from dusty violet to deep blue. They sat apart
from the other hopefuls, more than a dozen norms who clustered
closer to the ancient wall heaters or peered again and again at the jobs
flickering across notice screens. They looked askance at the gems, a
furtive, embarrassed squinting that the four noted and ignored with
the ease of long familiarity.

One name was called, and then another and another. The summoned went into booths and emerged either with the cheerful
demeanor of the newly employed, departing immediately to share
the good news, or downcast and anxious, returning to peruse the
jobscreens once again. None of the gems had been called.

The number of vacancies gradually dwindled. There was particular interest around one of the remaining listings, an advertisement for
reconstruction engineers to work high up in the city's skyscrapers. It

was specialized, difficult work, and consequently well paid. Several of the remaining norms had applied. It was unclear exactly how many posts were available.

Eight norms remained when first one and then another of the gem men were called in. The first to emerge went back to the remaining pair, nodding in affirmation. They murmured congratulations. The second returned after a couple of minutes, also successful. The norm applicants started being called in quick succession, coming rapidly out again with disappointment stamped on their faces.

"That it?" asked the gem woman.

"'Spect so," muttered one of the men. "Don't really need more, far as I can see."

As if in agreement the notice rolled up on the screen, slipping its place in the rotation. The four gathered up their jackets, which had been shed despite the chill of the room.

One of the norms stormed over to them, others trailing in his wake.

"You." He was a pudgy, middle-aged man a full head shorter than the purple-haired gem he was pointing at. "You got that job?"

The gem looked at him without expression, flicked a glance at the screen on which the position no longer appeared. "Yeah."

"How?" The pudgy man was spitting with fury. "How the hell d'you get a job like that?"

"Got a head for heights." The gem grinned without humor. The four were shrugging into coats. The pudgy man grabbed at the purple-haired gem as he turned away, spinning him back around.

"I'm *talking* to you!" he shouted. "I got my certificates, I been working in this business twenty-five years, so you tell me how you people just come in here and take our jobs!"

The other norms crowded behind him, muttering disgruntled agreement.

"Fucking favoritism," said one. He was strapping and younger, a match in size for the gems. They looked at him in astonishment.

The woman said, "What?"

"Yeah!" he yelled. "Some pansy glowhead gets beat up and they figure, 'Oh, poor gems,'"—his voice rose into a little-girl parody—"'we better give 'em a job! It ain't right!'"

The purple-haired man stared at him. "You are out of your fucking mind."

The center's staff was peering out of booths, mouths agape. The manager, a matronly woman, came briskly forward.

"Everyone please just calm down."

"What? What the fuck do you mean calm down? You gave them our jobs!"

She heaved a sigh and spoke to the pudgy man as though to an errant child.

"Sir, I'm sorry you weren't successful today, but there were only two positions to fill and the client has made their selection. If you'd just come back tomorrow . . ."

The muttering rose to a roar. "What d'you mean two? There were four!" someone shouted. "That's why they want them, 'cos they only have to hire half!"

"That's not—"

"They took our fucking jobs!"

The brawny norm squared up to the gem closest to him, chest to chest. The gem did not move. The pudgy man shoved the one he had first accosted. The gem rocked back for a moment, off balance. Then he grabbed the pudgy man by the shirt and threw him across the room.

As the melee unfolded, the manager found herself grasped by the shoulders and steered firmly aside. She was guided to the relative safety of a wall, and turned to see the gem woman duck a roundhouse punch and return a lightning-fast jab that dropped her attacker like a stone. She landed a kick in his kidneys to make sure and waded back in. Ninety seconds after the first push, seven norms lay broken and bleeding on the floor. The eighth had backed as far into a corner as possible and stood in a puddle, shaking.

The gems surveyed the battlefield, straightening clothing and checking for tablets and earsets. The manager noticed a bruised knuckle on one, a ripped sleeve on another. They appeared to be otherwise unhurt. The woman glanced over at her.

"You okay?"

She nodded mutely. The gems stepped over the fallen and walked out.

12

Aryel Morningstar knocked on a door on the first floor of Maryam House. It was a special knock, a succession of quick taps interspersed with pauses of specific and varying duration. She could discern no meaning in the pattern, but Herran had said that it was, for him, the equivalent of hearing her name.

The door slid open and she slipped inside. She did not really have time for this visit, not with the Klist interview leading the lunchtime viewing, Callan still critical, and reports of violent confrontations coming in from all over the city. But the security of Gabriel could not be allowed to fall down the list of her priorities. Especially after what had just happened in the community room.

"Hello, Herran." She spoke to a small gem, not much taller than herself. He sat with his back to the door, hunched forward, a tablet balanced on his knees. As she approached she could see he had it configured for input only, his eyes darting across the semicircular bank of oversize screens in front of him. He had socialstream and newstream feeds scrolling slowly down one. Next to it program code rolled a bit faster down another screen, and next to that a third was covered with binary text zipping past almost too fast to register.

He appeared not to have noticed her enter. She knew better. He was using the fourth screen to work while he monitored the feeds on the others, and she could see a tiny graphic of the apartment pulsing in one corner. The red dot that represented the door turned back into a black line of wall as it clicked shut behind her.

She sat, maneuvering the bulk of her back and cloak into a chair placed at right angles to Herran's workstation. Its too-tight arms pressed in on her. It was desperately uncomfortable but she remained still, leaning forward with her forearms resting on her thighs, hands loosely clasped together in front of her knees.

After a while Herran glanced at her, a quick sideways flicker before his eyes went back to the screens in front of him. In response she turned her hands out, palms open toward the ceiling. In a few moments he glanced again, and then a couple of seconds later swiveled to face her. He tucked the tablet farther up on his lap and placed his hands on hers.

"Aryel." His voice came out soft, almost muffled, with a hint of a lisp. His face between nose and mouth was marked by the line of a cleft palate, indifferently repaired. His hair was a mass of fine, glowing, red-orange curls, covering a head that seemed too large for his diminutive frame. She closed her fingers around his hands, felt the answering pressure, and immediately let go. That was as much human contact as Herran could manage. He withdrew his hands and turned back to the screens.

"Hello, Herran," she said again. "Are you well?"

He nodded, a rhythmic, exaggerated motion that involved his upper body as well as his head. "Okay." The nodding now was directed toward the screens. "Don't like streams today."

"No. It's a very bad day."

"Could fix."

"You couldn't, love. They'd still think what they think, they'd just find other ways to say it. What's more, they'd find *you*."

"Come for me."

"Maybe."

Herran's thin shoulders shook for a moment, as though he was wrestling with what she'd just said. Aryel knew it was less a visceral fear for his own safety and more his disdain for the concept of "maybe." Herran preferred clear alternatives: yes and no, open and closed, gem and norm. He disliked noncommittals.

"Something just happened, with Gabriel and Wenda and Horace," she said. "Anyone been posting about it?"

"Yes. Don't understand. Callan Wenda's baby?"

This time Aryel remembered to say "I don't know" instead of "maybe." The structural logic of the phrase met with Herran's approval. As she told him what had happened, his fingers danced over the tablet, reorganizing the screens to highlight the internal gemstream that they all posted to, as well as picking up any posts to external streams sent from a local hub. So far nothing about the incident had gone outside. She had no doubt that would change.

The gemstream posts were excited about the possible link between Callan and Wenda. There was only passing mention of Gabriel's role. However, Herran, despite his fascination with the prospect of Callan actually having a mother, understood the implications.

"Trouble for Gabe?"

"If the norms start asking questions about him then yes. Are there any new searches?"

His fingers sped across the tablet. The work screen changed, reams of code she couldn't decipher flying past. Herran's eyes scanned rapidly across the screen.

"Not today. Yesterday, late." He paused as he translated a name from the coded feed. "Eli Walker."

So Bal was right. He had noticed, and checked the archive, and hopefully been satisfied.

"Anything else?"

"Not new. Others still looking for Henderson." He shuddered. "No problem. This was good check, but quick." His fingers slipped across the tablet and he frowned. "Sally called."

"What?" She was nonplussed for a moment, then she got it. "Sally called him?"

"Yes. He first. Voice message, then he made search, then she called back."

"*Herran*—" Aryel found herself struggling between the impulse to scold him for so casually accessing Eli's tablet transmission records, and a mounting sense of alarm.

"Problem?"

"I don't know. I don't think Sally was ever convinced by the datastreams."

"Was perfect." He sounded injured.

"Oh, I know that. What you did was amazing, Herran. We'd have been in deep trouble a long time ago without you. But you remember how she searched and searched and searched? She knows something was wrong. We can't rewrite her memory."

"Not wrong." He frowned at her. "Right."

"Yes. Sorry. Not wrong in that sense. She knows something was different."

They were quiet for a time. Aryel was still leaning forward in the too-small chair, thinking hard, when a couple of direct messages flashed up. One was from a counselor letting Sally Trieve know about the additional trauma generated by a possible family connection. Another was from one of the volunteers to a fellow member of the church. He called Gabriel a "blessed child." Aryel's lips twisted as she read.

"Herran, I think there are going to be more searches very soon."

"Won't see anything different. Nothing different to see."

"That's just going to send them in another direction. There are people who will take a look at Gaela's genetype, and Bal's, and think that it just doesn't make sense. They'll check the dates for how long they could possibly have been together, and that's going to raise a whole load of other questions."

"I fix." His fingers were poised to get to work.

"You can't. It's too big. Too many pieces of information are in too many places. There are too many people who would remember it differently. It's not something we can take care of onstream." She sighed. "We've just got to hope we can keep on top of it at least until after the Conference. Will you monitor anything that's said and searched about Gabe? I don't want you to change anything, just watch. And let me know."

"Okay."

Her earset buzzed with an incoming message. She looked at her tablet and pushed herself up out of the chair. Herran turned to her, hands out, ignoring the sudden urgency of her movements.

His face and voice were filled with wonder.

"Callan might be Wenda's baby?"

Across town from where police and paramedics swarmed over the employment center, a community-service team moved through a warren of small plazas, the connecting passageways meandering between seating areas and around towering sculptures. Some guided cell vacuum trolleys, the compactor units compressing the detritus of the city as they went. Others came behind on washers that scrubbed the sidewalks and laid down a coat of antifreeze. Flanking them were the wall and glass cleaners, men and women with backpack-mounted sprayers attached to long wands who tackled the vertical surfaces of the city canyons.

One of them was a man of average height, but with extraordinarily long arms and a slightly stooped posture. His features were heavy and slack under a dirty thatch of glowing, shocking-pink hair, turning gray and dull at the temples. He hummed to himself as he worked, a faint atonal drone almost on the edge of hearing. The sound had a nails-on-blackboard quality that set the teeth of his fellow workers on edge.

The gem worked quickly, leaving a gleaming strip almost three yards high behind him as he sidestepped along the building. When his rapid progress brought him closer to other members of the team they shifted away, noses wrinkling at an odor that contradicted the detergent freshness of the cleaning fluids. What with the smell and the droning, the man occupied a bubble several yards in diameter. He appeared not to notice, operating undisturbed within his own exclusion zone.

Except for when another man walked behind him, which he seemed to find occasion to do every few minutes. He carried his wand low and flicked it at the back of the gem's legs. A spray of liquid flashed across, taking a few seconds to soak through the greasy, heavy fabric of his overalls. The norm picked his moments: when the gem was angling into a difficult corner or reaching up for a particularly troublesome patch of grime and everyone else was preoccupied with their own tasks. He would step quickly away, slipping behind one of the cell units or addressing his attention to some other feature of the urban landscape, so that when the gem felt the cold and looked ponderously around, he was neither the closest nor the most obvious suspect.

The first couple of times it happened the gem was distracted for only a moment before returning to work. The third time he grunted angrily at his nearest neighbor, a woman who shook her head and shrugged in bafflement as he waved and mumbled. The fourth time the woman noticed the culprit as he slipped past her, but her attention was diverted by the gem's offended roar as the water soaked quickly through already damp cloth. Others stopped and turned, moving to stand and stare and mutter to each other from the edge of the stench horizon as the gem gestured and growled.

It took a minute or more for him to calm down and everyone to return to work. The anonymous taunter waited almost ten before applying another dose of freezing irritant. This time the woman saw him do it. She opened her mouth for a challenge, inhaling a lungful of stink as a hand on the end of an extraordinarily long arm closed around her throat.

Another newstream alert started flashing in the corner of his tablet. Eli killed it, scanned the latest on-the-scene report of a gem–norm flare-up that had ended badly, and disciplined himself back to work. There was nothing to be gained by obsessing over each new incident or plotting the track of rising hysteria on the streams. He had assigned someone else to that. He was determined to spend the time before he departed for the Squats tackling problems that he might have some hope of solving.

He had decided, deliberately and purposefully, to ignore the possibility that every piece of information he accessed, cross-checked, ran statistical analyses on, and sent to colleagues for expert opinions might have been manipulated to ensure that just the right conclusions were reached. He told himself it was impossible for there to be such widespread infiltration into all the various avenues of inquiry he was undertaking. Changes on that scale, however subtle, would have been noticed and reacted to. If the gemtechs had had such power at their disposal, the revelations that had cost them so dearly would have been altered in the telling. Nevertheless, the thought now lurked in the back of his mind every time he picked up his tablet.

He had said nothing of the day's events to his research team when they had conferenced in with results earlier. They had confirmed that, as Zavcka Klist had predicted, there were no other records of gems maiming, raping, or killing norms or their children while under gemtech control. Toward the end, when public opinion had turned against the gemtechs to such a degree that gems could escape curfew by simply walking away from their keepers while out on assignment, more attention had begun to be paid to those held in secure quarters; stories of unauthorized visits by intrepid journalists on fact-finding missions formed part of the pre-Declaration mythology. Not all had escaped unscathed, but none had been killed or seriously injured. The stories of the twisted, terrified, terrifying creatures kept under lock and key that they had come back with had fueled the demand for the modification of humans to stop.

Eli had shared the report and embedded vidstreams with his team the day before. The salient facts had now been verified: the mother had occasionally taken her daughter to work, against all regulations and unbeknownst to her superiors, when unable to arrange child care. Her colleagues had turned a blind eye; having never had any real problems with their charges, they were untroubled by the breaking of rules that seemed to them excessively cautious. She had made the girl stay out of the vidcam fields, which was easy enough since they were programmed only to follow the movements of the gems. She had told her simply to stay away from them, and them to stay away from her, as the small group she was responsible for minding moved around their living area.

The gem had attacked at a time when all the others had been removed, to work or for whatever other purpose the day's roster decreed. While the mother was escorting the last of his companions away he had begun his assault on the child. The soundproof walls that had kept any conflict among their regular occupants from spreading, coupled with lackluster vidcam security, meant that no one knew what was happening until the mother returned. He had casually incapacitated and tossed her aside and gone back to the girl, who by now was mercifully unconscious. But the woman's scream before the door had been slammed shut was heard. It had taken ten minutes to determine what was going on, assemble and arm the security team, and get inside the dormitory apartment. In the aftermath, the police had apparently agreed that the only thing that news coverage of the incident would achieve would be further trauma to the family by publicizing the mother's negligence.

The review of incidents of unheralded violence—sexual, serial, or otherwise—since the Declaration was rather less straightforward. The team had spent a lot of time discussing the findings, and the implications. Eli set out several very specific analyses that needed to be done in order to confirm their conclusions before the start of the Conference. It would require intensive work overnight. He thought the prospect had come as a welcome relief to them after the minutiae of the Bel'Natur report.

He had uncovered some other interesting facts on his own. These he kept to himself.

A few hours and several new reports later, Zavcka Klist watched, jaw clenched, as Aryel Morningstar spoke live to an assemblage of journalists from the major newstreams. The vidcams lingered over every detail of the small, terribly misshapen gem with the sweet face, unmistakable intelligence, and unaccountable charisma. What she had to say was simple and eloquent. The gigantic lump on her back was a silent testament to the wrongs of which she spoke. Zavcka could see her own morning's efforts being, if not wiped out, severely diminished.

She wasted five furious minutes haranguing her covert sources for their continuing failure to find anything at all on Aryel Morningstar, even to determine the nature of the deformity she hid beneath her cloak. The garment continued to repel their most sophisticated scanners.

Then she calmed herself down and sent another string of coded symbols to another comcode. At the meeting, standing in front of the displays in an obscure art gallery, she issued new instructions.

@L8ERGENIUS Fckg gems on rampage killing folks in LDN.

@FRAKKK gems kicking off all ovr twn, 12pple in hsptl.

@S3GW8 @FRAKKK I heard 30 but govt trying to keep quiet

@GOGEM dont beleve it! sumthing mustve happend, gems r gr8!

@PLI5T whats up with gem got beat up yestday?

@S3GW8 retard on dolework went crazy 5 hurt lifes tuff enuff

@H8GEMS @PLI5T deserved it

@S3GW8 crazy letting them mix with us, need separation back!

@CTYBEE @S3GW8 Did you see what happened after w/ hunchback?

@FRAKKK @GOGEM ur crazy, theyre a menace

@GMCUCKOO @PLI5T @H8GEMS heard it was all faked for conference.

@L8ERGENIUS fckg politicians let them out never shouldve happened

@LDNLVR @GOGEM Heard gems WERE provoked, overeacted, no deaths tho.

@GMCUCKOO not surprised weve been beating gems up for decades now its war.

@PLI5T felt sorry for gems before, not anymore, conf better come up w smthg

@CTYBEE thought she was amazing: urbannews.ldn/headlines/current/morningstar

@LDNLVR @GOGEM shudve just backed down, kept thr place

@GOGEM gems r oppressd, not ther fault

@CTYBEE shes awesome

@GMEVIL10 this is just the beginning, 1 of them can take out 10 of us, need a plan

@FRAKKK urbnews sayng gems thrtned kids on way to skl

@NOTOGEMS been saying 4 years ths wd happen! shoodve cxld them all.

@H8GEMS @NOTOGEMS @GEMEVIL10 agree, are you of the Faith?

@GOGEM gems need help not hate check out morningstar link

@GMEVIL10 @GMCUCKOO @PLI5T no excuses for evil, gems shd not exist

@S3GW8 @GMEVIL10 gems do lots of things we don't want to / cant

@LDNLVR @GOGEM @GEMEVIL10 gems v useful but not same as us

@FRAKKK @GOGEM so what FUCK OFF

@GMEVIL10 @S3GW8 if humans cant do it then shudnt be done

@NOTOGEMS politishans need to no wont stand for bein wiped out

@LDNLVR whtevr, cant go on like this, system needs to deal

@NOTOGEMS @H8GEMS yes, more evry day

@GMCUCKOO Another one! Gems robbed shop beat up woman.

@H8GEMS @NOTOGEMS Im NHT grp shd meet

@GMEVIL10 GEMLOVERS DIE 2 NO MERCY

@H8GEMS Im ready

13

THE ROOM WAS FILLING UP. THEY WERE IN A LARGE HALL LOCATED ON THE ground floor of the former leisure center. It was the sort of space that had been intended to be multifunctional, accommodating everything from performances and parties to lessons and lectures, and as a result fulfilled many purposes adequately but none of them well. This evening it was set up for a meeting of the entire Squats community. Hundreds of chairs faced a raised stage, a little too high off the floor for comfort, not quite high enough to afford those at the back a clear view. The problem had been solved by a vidcam suspended from the ceiling, which Rob said would beam a closed link to gems unable to attend as well as to the tablets of those in the room.

Eli had expected there to be several more chairs waiting on the stage, but it was empty except for a spindly metal lectern. He stood next to it with Rob, Commander Masoud of the Metropolitan Police, and Sally Trieve. He felt uncomfortable in the little cluster of norms, banked together at the front of the room as if to emphasize their distinction. Or rather their lack. Gems of every shape, size, and color crowded in through the two entry doors. Not all of the looks they sent his way were friendly. The room hummed with traded reports of the day's events, updates from those who had been to the hospital and from others who had been visited by the police.

This had mostly been as part of the authorities' attempts to investigate allegations circulating on the socialstreams. The supposed incidents had, as expected, proved largely fictitious, and the police had put out a statement to that effect. Still, he thought, it would not have endeared them to the gems to know that while they were being questioned in their homes over nonexistent offenses, others were being set upon all over the city.

Rob was getting a terse assessment of the situation out of the commander while they waited. There had been twelve known cases of physical assault on gems by norms over the past twenty-four hours, including the attack on Callan. Another gem had been accosted by a godgang during the day, but the attack had been interrupted before it got into full savage stride. The others were apparently random, and ranged from shoves to muggings to beatings. Two more gems had joined Callan in the hospital.

By contrast, there had been only three confirmed assaults on norms by gems. One of these, the fight in the employment office, could be construed as self-defense: security vids and the eyewitness accounts of the staff confirmed that the norms had landed the first blow. The manager had been at pains to explain to the police how the gem woman had acted to ensure she was not harmed, and noted that several of the norm applicants had, in the course of their interviews, appeared surprisingly unfamiliar with some of the basic requirements of the post. Four were in the hospital awaiting police questioning. The gems involved did not reside in the Squats and had not been seen since. The police were appealing to them to come forward. Eli thought this unlikely given the prevailing mood, but the commander muttered something about Miss Morningstar maybe being able to help.

Vid footage had been retrieved that suggested that another fight, which had resulted in two more norms being hospitalized, had been deliberately provoked. The full details of what had taken place

seemed always to be just out of frame, but a member of the cleaning crew said that a fellow worker had whispered, in the minutes
before it kicked off, that she thought one of their number might be
teasing their gem coworker, and wasn't it just another reason why
community-service teams should be segregated. The woman was
comatose and had therefore been unable to expand on her views
and suspicions; the man thought responsible had not been on the
welfare office's roster and had since disappeared, and so, initially, had
the gem.

It had been Aryel Morningstar, arriving into the boil of press,
police, and paramedics, who had managed first to find him and then
to coax him into custody. She had tracked him to the mouth of a
drain culvert and made the officers who trailed grumbling behind
her shut up long enough for them all to hear the grunted sobs coming from somewhere within. While their leader was busy describing
search-or-siege options to a dozen armed commandos, she had had
a quiet word with the medics, picked up an emergency blanket, and
walked in alone. When she emerged twenty minutes later it was with
the pink-haired, blanket-wrapped gem. He limped along beside her,
weeping quietly and apparently passive.

The vidcams caught all of it, following them as she warned the
officers off with a look and guided him instead to the medical van,
where she held a cup to his lips and persuaded him to drink. The
sedative took hold a minute later, and he sank back onto the gurney.
While the paramedics fastened the restraints and the police shuffled
their feet and looked sheepish, the press scrambled for an interview.
Despite his tone of official disapproval, Commander Masoud was
clearly impressed.

"The third incident," he said now, "was, as far as we can tell,
completely unprovoked. Three young gems went into a shop and
started destroying goods and roughing up staff. They haven't offered
any explanation, beyond telling us that the business had it coming."
He shrugged. "We'd heard anecdotal reports that the shop owner
wasn't very friendly to gem patrons or job applicants. No formal
complaints though."

"Did they live here?" Eli interjected.

"No. In a gem hostel south of the river, close to where it happened."

So none of the gems who had taken the fight to the norms were residents of the Squats. He wondered if that was significant and turned his attention back to the gathering audience. A large group of gillungs had come in together and commandeered a bank of several dozen seats. He used to think that the distinctive physique of the water-breathers was such obvious gemsign that it made their lime-green hair a bit redundant, until an interviewee had explained to him how they used it to keep track of each other in murky waters. Now a field of phosphorescent heads nodded and tossed like seaweed over to his left.

He noticed several gems he thought must be autistics dotted throughout the crowd, distinguishable less by appearance than manner. They were the ones who came in alone, finding seats right away and burying themselves in tablets. They responded to the noise and movement that surrounded them little or not at all.

There would, he knew, be many savants in the room—gems with prodigious powers of memory and calculation, sensory perception, and cognitive processing. He wondered if whoever was responsible for changing the datastreams was among them. Most of those old enough to be here still paid for their gifts with impairments to social intuition and emotional intelligence. The gemtechs had not initially considered this a problem worth solving. However, as the market for their abilities had expanded, clients had requested gems who could integrate more seamlessly with the rest of the workforce. Sally Trieve had spoken the simple truth—there was far less disability among the youngsters. The reports from the now government-run crèches, where the new generations of genius children were being raised, glowed with the health of their charges.

As if in response to his musings, Bal appeared at one of the doors. He was with Wenda and another woman, a Bel'Natur redhead whom Eli recognized from his earlier research. She held Gabriel by the hand, and Eli wondered if they were bringing him to the meeting. There were things he would not say in front of a child. But then Gaela crouched and kissed him, and he transferred his handhold to

Wenda. Her face was red and puffy under the turquoise hair. Bal squeezed her shoulders and patted the boy's head. As they departed the hall Eli had to blink away an illusion of reversal: the impression that it was the child who guarded and guided the woman.

Bal and Gaela were making for seats near the front. Eli muttered to Rob, still deep in conversation with the policeman, and headed in their direction.

On the way he spotted Donal on the far side of the room, next to a gem who looked to be about eight feet tall. He said, "Hi Don, good to see you," in a normal voice, prompted by some imp of mischief and curiosity to test both the young gem's range and whether the thaw from the day before had held. Nearby gems shot him puzzled looks. Donal turned around immediately, and Eli raised a hand in greeting. Donal flashed him a startled smirk and waved back.

Bal had apparently taken the exchange in. His grim expression lightened somewhat, but an aura of alert reserve remained around him and Gaela. "Hello, Dr. Walker. I see we haven't scared you away."

"It'd take a lot more than a few made-up stories on the streams," he said, and watched carefully. This time he was sure he sensed a slight increase in tension, as from a sentry hearing a noise in the night. He stuck out his hand. "Please, call me Eli. Dr. Walker's reserved for people I think I can impress."

It seemed to be the right touch, although the wariness remained. They shook hands and Bal introduced him to Gaela. "Aryel mentioned you," he told her. "As did Horace, if I remember right." He glanced around, looking for the green-haired gem. "Is he coming tonight?"

She and Bal exchanged glances. "No," she said. "Horace isn't that well today."

He had seemed in the peak of health yesterday. "Nothing's happened to him?"

Gaela smiled, a little stonily he thought. "No, not like that. He'll probably come in on tablet."

"Good. Only," he shrugged, "it's been a hell of a day, and I thought Wenda looked a bit upset." He gestured toward the door. "I noticed her just now with your son."

"She . . . knows one of the people who's been hurt and it's got to her a bit. She didn't feel up to the meeting, and we didn't want Gabe here for this one, so they're going to go and watch a nice relaxing vid together." She threw him a musing look and changed the subject. "It was good of you to come tonight, with everything that's going on."

"I was really pleased to be asked. Hopefully I can help explain a few things, and I expect I'll learn a lot."

"Will you really?" That was from Bal, abrupt and edgy. "I mean, haven't you already done all your studies and reports and whatever? Figured out what to do with us, for the powers that be?"

"What ends up being done isn't up to me," Eli said quietly. "And there's no such thing as being finished in my line of work." He suddenly, urgently, wanted them to understand this. "A year has been very, very little time to do what I've been asked to do. It's as complete as it can be, but there's still a lot that I—we—don't know." He gestured to the room around them. "There's a lot we *can't* know because communities like this have existed for such a short time. At the moment, we're trying to understand the present and predict the future based on not a lot of data."

He hesitated, worried that it was too soon to turn the conversation back. But people were starting to sit down all over the room, and he might not get another chance.

"I realize this might be an intrusive request and I'll understand if you say no," he began. "But I wonder . . . would you be willing to talk to me a bit about how you find family life? As people who didn't grow up with parents, what's come easily and what you find most challenging?" He spread his hands. "You're pioneers, you know. There are so few gem families that it's difficult to know what the issues are."

Gaela's eyes were boring into him. "You think we have particular issues?"

"I'm not assuming that at all." He was scrambling instinctively for a prevarication when it occurred to him that Donal might be listening. He fell back on a slightly edited version of the truth. "In fact I was talking with Sally earlier and she mentioned that you and your son were doing really well, no special needs. That's great of course, but I don't know if you realize how unusual it is."

He decided on a final gambit, offering up a genuine concern that they might find persuasive. "There's a danger sometimes that the only gems someone like me talks to are those who have, as you say, particular issues. That really would skew the findings, and I'm anxious to make sure it doesn't happen."

Gaela and Bal looked at each other, apparently stumped. There was a rustle in the room behind him, a new focus to the murmured conversations. "Aryel's here," Bal said. The relief was clear in his voice. "Let us think about it and let you know after, okay?"

He nodded assent and turned. He didn't see her at first, her diminutive figure hidden behind the crowd of taller, broader gems as she paused for hellos and handclasps, kisses on the cheek and whispered conferences. Eli watched her make her way down the room. As she moved in and out of view behind and between the crowding gems, he had the strange sensation that he was watching her take on the hopes and fears, the desires, disasters, and desperation of everyone she met. He had a sudden image of them as a physical mass, a sack of cares hidden under her cloak.

She reached them and smiled. "No need for introductions, I see. Sorry I'm late." Together they drifted toward the front. Behind her, those who had been standing quickly found seats. Eli noticed that Bal was one of them, keeping a chair free beside him, while Gaela strolled forward to the stage. Rob beamed at Aryel with undisguised affection, then guided Eli and the others to chairs left vacant in the front row, whispering, "She'll get us up when we're needed."

Aryel lifted the cloak clear of her feet to climb the steps, paced to the front of the stage, and stood quiet, waiting. An expectant murmur swept the hall.

"Are we ready to start? Gaela?"

The flame-haired woman was leaning nonchalantly against the stage, apparently gazing idly around the room. Eli had supposed she was just being slow to settle in for the meeting and found her insouciance very much at odds with the tone of their earlier conversation. For a moment he thought Aryel was suggesting she take her seat.

But Gaela was gazing intently into a rear corner where a couple of people with unremarkable hair were sitting.

"Hello, Tobias," she drawled. "Who's your friend?"

One of the men blinked at her, then rose. "He's . . . this is George." He gestured at the man next to him, who looked first startled, then flustered. He seemed reluctant to stand, but did so when Tobias prodded him in the shoulder. "He's a member of my congregation, he's volunteered to spend his holiday working in the community. He . . . we . . . thought this evening would be a good introduction?" He turned to George, who was looking increasingly uncomfortable. "George, do you want to say something about yourself?"

"Do, George," Gaela called. "Especially say why you have a vidcam and sound mic stitched into your shirt."

The room went graveyard quiet. George gaped. Tobias spun to stare at Gaela, then back at George, then back at Gaela. "He doesn't! What are you . . ." He turned back to George. "What? What is she talking about?"

A muttering started, angry but with a tinge, Eli thought, of amusement. Everyone had turned to peer at the hapless George, who looked too stunned to speak. He finally managed to mumble, "I don't know what you mean." Then, trying for a bit more conviction, "I'm a volunteer like he said, I just wanted to—"

"Two top buttons," Gaela interrupted. "Connected to . . . would you turn around please, George?" He stood as if paralyzed. Eli thought his clothes looked perfectly normal, the shirt a fashionably retro piece in a rather loud pattern. Tobias was bending away now, as though George might be infectious. He seemed to re-collect a sense of responsibility, leaned forward with distaste, and poked George into a shuffling turn.

"Connected," said Gaela, as his gray-coated back came into view, "to a power pack. Five or six hours' juice by the looks of it. Goodness me, George, how long do you think our meetings last?"

Now sardonic laughter punctuated the muttering. Eli found himself grinning. Gaela was milking humor out of a potentially explosive situation, keeping the crowd entertained. He noted the look of intense interest with which Masoud of the Met was regarding her,

Rob's furious face and balled fists as he glared at George, and Sally Trieve's seen-it-all-before impassivity.

"Thank you, Gaela," said Aryel. "George, would you like to explain what you're doing here, or would you rather just leave?"

George seemed not to realize for a moment that he had been given a choice. Then he stumbled for the exit. Donal was on his feet.

"Blooady hell, Aryel, doan' you think we should fin' out who the hell he is?"

"I thought," she said peaceably, "that you might like to show him out, Don. Perhaps he might mention it once he gets over the stage fright."

More laughter. Donal rolled his eyes and followed the interloper out. Tobias was falling over himself to apologize to the assembly. Gaela made a final scan of the room and took her seat while Aryel was accepting his protestations of ignorance and settling him down. She had just finished when Donal came back.

"Newsbeat," he reported. "On his 'set before he was even down the stairs. Silly bugger's goan' have a long walk back to civilization. An' it's rainin'." He grinned. "He doan' like you much, Gaela."

She waved indifference. "Not the first, won't be the last."

"Right," said Aryel. "Let's get started."

It was indeed raining. It was raining hard, and the nearest station was at least half an hour's walk away. George flicked his earset back to standby, pulled the hood of his coat as far forward as he could, and cursed every gem that had ever been born.

He could tell he would get no credit for all the work he had done to get himself inside the meeting in the first place: the tedious hours of Sunday services, the spare time spent volunteering in soup kitchens and care homes, the invented interest in civil rights. His editor had made it clear that all that counted was what he had *not* done. His ears were still ringing. He had not gotten an exposé from the innermost gem sanctum. He had not gotten evidence of pro-gem bias on the part of the police. He could confirm their distaste for intrusion, but he was not bringing back words and images to counter the growing perception of Aryel Morningstar as honest, heroic, and honorable.

He realized he had made a mistake in not responding to her invitation to explain himself; if he had, and had still been thrown out, he could have claimed it as proof of there being something to hide, something to which certain norms in high places were privy. But he had been so taken aback by the way the redheaded woman had homed in on him, the shocking ease with which she had literally seen through his disguise. Worse yet, he thought she might be the mother of the child who was being spoken of with something close to awe among the UC faithful.

There might be an angle there, though. The only recording he had managed to get was of his own humiliation at Gaela's hands. The story could be of a secretive group of grotesques in the heart of the city, harboring unknown powers, protected by those who rightly ought to be concerned with the defense of their own kind . . .

The piece was practically writing itself. He fumbled inside his coat, switched the power pack back on. If he started now he could convert the dictation into text and have a rough draft by the time he got back to the Newsbeat office.

So it was that, between the pounding of the rain on his barely shielded head and his own muttering into the top button of his shirt, he heard nothing until the step, so close behind him as to almost share the same space, so close that as he turned to look the movement spun him into the short club clenched in his attacker's fist. In the split second before it connected he caught a flash of purple hair, plastered and dripping. He dropped, boneless, staring up from the pavement at a vision that swam in and out of focus as his consciousness wavered and the rain beat down on his face.

Two men, both topped with glowing purple, standing over him. Even through the waves of pain and fear he thought it strange they had not covered their heads.

"Looks like a good one," floated down to him from above. "Let's get it done."

14

COMMANDER MASOUD SLIPPED BACK INTO HIS SEAT ON THE OTHER SIDE of Rob. Aryel had begun by reviewing the events of the past several days and had invited him up to confirm the details of interviews, assaults, and arrests. He had essentially repeated what he'd told Eli and the others before the meeting started, adding an exhortation that his audience not respond to the increasing provocation from the streets and the streams by taking matters into their own hands.

"I know sitting tight can be a tough ask," he'd said. "And this is probably going to get worse before it gets better. We'll do everything we can to protect you, but for the next few days it would be a good idea to stay close to home if you can."

That had prompted an uproar. Aryel had quieted them down and picked out a few representative voices. They all had the same point to make: it was more than a bit unfair for people who had done nothing wrong to be imprisoned in their own homes while their aggressors roamed the streets. Those who wished them to be once more isolated from the rest of humanity, if not eliminated altogether, would be getting what they wanted by default. Masoud agreed in principle, but in practice he feared for their safety in the current climate. He had, in what Eli thought was a commendable display of candor, spoken directly to the crowd.

"Aryel and I began this conversation at the Royal London at five o'clock this morning while a member of this community was still in surgery. I understand how you all feel, but you need to weigh up the risks that next time it might be you. Callan is very, very lucky to be alive. I don't want to have to come back here to tell your friends that one of you was less lucky."

There were serious faces and nods of grim acknowledgment around the room. Aryel thanked him and updated them on the condition of Callan, the other gems, and interestingly, the norm casualties as well, while the commander stepped down.

Eli understood the format now and was impressed by how well it worked. He had expected a series of presentations, punctuated by a few questions from the floor, but instead it really was a meeting in which all were encouraged to participate. Aryel had propped her tablet on the lectern and was using it to receive messages from those outside the hall and those present but unwilling to draw attention to themselves. This allowed the autistics and the shy to take part on an equal footing with the rest, since she checked the tablet frequently. She would read the messages aloud and, as with questions voiced from the crowd, would either respond herself or direct them to where they could best be answered.

Bal's hand was up. "I appreciate that the police may be doing the best they can for us at the moment," he said when Aryel gave him the floor. "But the simple fact is they follow orders, and the orders could change. If I understand correctly, the Conference that we're here to talk about is going to decide whether we have the same rights as norms, or not." A murmur started at that. Bal raised his voice and kept talking over it.

"If it decides we do, then things might be rough for a while, but the commander and his colleagues, and Sally and her team," he nodded to the social services director, who shifted uncomfortably next to Eli, "and the health services and all the rest of it, will keep on supporting us just like they do everybody else. But if it decides we don't, then all of that changes."

The murmur rose to a growl and then stopped as Aryel raised her hand for quiet. Bal's words fell loud into the sudden silence. "If it decides we don't, then all of those institutions could be told not to *protect* us from discrimination but to *enforce* it. We've been in this neutral zone for a year, and we all like to think that when we come out of it it'll be as full citizens, different but equal to the norms. But it's up to them, and they could decide to kick us right back where we came from."

The entire room seemed to have been inhaling, like a free diver preparing for descent. Now it erupted. Most of the shouts were of disbelief, even derision, but Eli heard more than a few who thought Bal had gotten it exactly right. The prevailing view, though, seemed to be that Aryel should tell him to stop exaggerating. He sat impassive, Gaela's hand in his, and Eli thought a flicker of acknowledgment passed between him and Aryel.

She raised her hands and they quieted down again, more slowly this time. "Bal is essentially correct," she said, and waited for the words to hit home. "That possibility had, until very recently, seemed remote. But the timing of this campaign against us is not a coincidence. It's clear to me that there is a move ahead of the Conference to try and make us seem as dangerous and unpredictable as possible. And the obvious reason for that is to be able to justify restricting our rights as much as possible."

There was another outburst. The Declaration was repeatedly invoked. Aryel nodded acknowledgment while she stepped over to glance at the tablet. She looked up.

"The number one question, from the floor as well, is how could they do that," she said. "I think everyone needs to understand the purpose and powers of the Conference. Dr. Trench, would you please come up?"

Rob climbed onto the stage and launched into a long explanation of who had organized the Conference, what authority they had, and what processes would have to be gone through before anything they recommended had any practical impact. Eli could see him trying to find more to throw in before he was forced to get to the point. He glanced around, taking in the growing bewilderment in the room.

Rob was a vocal advocate for gem equality and consequently very well liked, but he was starting to sound evasive and look desperate. When he paused for breath, Eli raised his hand.

"Dr. Walker," said Aryel. Eli stood up and turned around to face the room.

"There's a very widespread misunderstanding about the rights gems now enjoy." Behind him he could hear the air go out of Rob. He cringed inwardly at the thought of how hard this must be for his friend.

"The fact is you exist in a sort of legal limbo," he went on. "What the UN acknowledged a year ago was that on the back of the Syndrome society had drifted into allowing certain categories of human beings to be treated as property. That had been illegal in every country of the world for centuries, but when the various governments allowed embryos to be genetically modified beyond what was necessary to avert the Syndrome and other illnesses, they neglected to define the legal status of the resulting people. They just let the gemtechs get on with it."

Another roar erupted, the bitter flotsam of generations of hurt washing furiously around the room. Aryel let it go on. She raised an eyebrow at Eli when he glanced at her. He raised his own hands for quiet instead. When the noise dropped to a manageable level he pitched his voice over it as Bal had done.

"I think you have every right to be angry, and we could have a very long discussion about whether they were being collusive or just incompetent, but it was a hundred years ago and I'm not sure it would serve much purpose right now." The growl fell back to a murmur. "The thing you need to know about the Conference is that it will finally recommend—for Europe at least—what that legal status should be, and what rights gems should have. The expectation is that the various governments within the Union will ratify its recommendations and turn them into law within, say, another year. Since we're the first to get our act together on this, and assuming it doesn't all dissolve into chaos, it's likely that the other continental federations will follow our lead."

He looked around again and Aryel beckoned him up. She nodded acknowledgment of the shouted questions and checked her tablet while he was mounting the steps. Rob was still there, eyes on the ceiling, sucking air in between his teeth. "Sorry, mate," Eli muttered. "They were starting to think you were avoiding the subject."

"I was."

"It was making you look bad. They've been through worse than straight talk from you and me. And they might have to again."

He faced the crowd. Aryel looked up.

"The question everyone seems to be asking is, what about the Declaration?"

Eli looked pointedly at Rob. The acting commissioner took a deep breath and stepped up.

"The Declaration doesn't actually grant you any unequivocal rights, except for one. It doesn't grant me any more either. What it sets out are six principles on which it says all laws should be based. All of them, except the sixth, are just restatements of legal tradition, and all of them, except the sixth, allow for exceptions. So the second, for example, says everyone should be free from *unwarranted* oppression, which implies there might be some form of oppression that is warranted. The third says no one can be forced to work without compensation, but it doesn't say that the compensation has to be to your liking. And so on. Only the sixth is absolute."

The giant gem next to Donal raised an astonishingly long arm topped by an astonishingly shaped hand. Aryel picked him out.

"Mikal."

"Thank you, Dr. Trench," he said politely. "Why then are we all under the impression that it was the Declaration that freed us from service to the gemtechs?"

"Because it did, by reaffirming the *negative* rights that underpin our legal system—the right *not* to be locked up, *not* to have your property taken away, *not* to be denied a job—*unless it is legal to do so*. It's the *law* which then says under what circumstances those things *can* be done. And because the legal status of gems had never been defined, setting out those principles was a way of telling governments to stop assuming the same rules didn't apply to you. It allowed them—*obligated* them—to stand up to the gemtechs. And *that* was what got you away."

Mikal blinked. "So you're saying it's still possible for laws to be created that would exclude us from having the same rights as normal humans."

"Yes."

Surprisingly the room stayed quiet. The gems were hanging on every word. Eli noted Sally Trieve's furrowed brow, the sea of white-lipped faces under jewel-colored hair, and the clasped hands of the priest, Tobias, as he bowed his head.

Rob had obviously decided that having gotten this far into it he needed to be thorough.

"All the Declaration does is confirm the default position. Some clever lawyers in Tokyo came up with it as a sort of emergency escape route to break the global power of the gemtechs, a way of quickly extending some degree of legal protection to gems. But it was just a stopgap until they could figure out what the new laws for the new people ought to be."

"So," said Aryel, "once gems are formally defined as an artificial subspecies, new laws *will* be created. Just for us."

"That's the expectation, yes."

"And the purpose of the Conference is to confirm us as a subspecies, and to set out this legal structure."

"Yes."

Distressed muttering from the floor. Rob held up his hands. "Please, folks, don't assume that the only possibilities are bad ones. Anyone here ever try to register to vote? No? Why not? Because the Declaration doesn't state that everyone shall be allowed to participate in a representative democracy. That's a *positive* right, and there are at least a few politicians who would like at least some of you to have it."

Mikal didn't bother to raise his hand. "The opportunity for advantage is the advantage of opportunity."

Rob blinked back at him, parsing the aphorism. "Quite."

Aryel was checking her tablet.

"A point of clarification," she said. "Franko, Aster, Horace, and a few others want to know why the sixth principle is different."

"Because it's new. It wasn't until the Syndrome hit that they really discovered how to do the things that the sixth protects against. So the lawyers didn't have to come up with language to accommodate exceptions, because there wasn't an existing body of law to dance around."

Aryel stepped forward, standing still at the front of the stage until she had their full attention.

"And now we come to the main point," she said quietly. "The importance of this moment for all gems—not just here in the Squats or in London, but all over this country, this continent, and this planet. In less than two days, around two hundred people are going to arrive in this city, and they're going to decide our future for us. They're going to decide whether we're too different to be allowed to live the same kind of lives that they do. They're going to decide whether our equality is worth the money it will cost. They're going to decide not only whether we should have the same rights as them, but whether all gems should have the same rights as each other. They are going to listen to what we have to say about it, but they are also going to listen to the gemtechs. They're going to tell themselves that they won't be swayed by what's happening on the streets and streams, but they are going to find it very difficult to remain detached.

"They're going to need to navigate through these issues, and they will want to feel that they have an objective, independent, factual basis for the decisions that they make—not least so they'll have some cover if things go wrong.

"Which doesn't put the person they've entrusted to provide them with that evidence in a particularly comfortable position. Whatever his conclusions, I think he deserves a fair bit of credit for being prepared to come here and talk to us at all. Dr. Walker."

It was a good introduction, he had to admit. None of the usual effusiveness about background and qualifications; she hadn't even said what he was supposed to be basing his findings on. She had set out the political context and added a note of sympathy but was once again leaving it up to him to explain himself and make the right impression.

He stepped forward.

"Good evening, everyone. My name's Eli Walker, and I'm a genetic anthropologist. That means I try to identify connections between human genotypes and behavior. About a year ago, when the Declaration was issued and you all found yourselves entering the neutral zone Bal spoke about, the European Federation asked me to undertake an analysis of what distinguishes gems from norms. I'm not concerned with genetic modification as such. What I look at are the ways people interact and relate to each other—comparing the range of gem behavior with the range of norm behavior. The outcome is a report which I'm going to be presenting to the Conference."

"What's it say?" The shout came from Donal, to a smattering of tense laughter.

Eli shrugged and spread his hands. "I can't actually tell you that, because I'm obliged to reveal the findings to them first. What I can tell you is it focuses on differences that are *solely* due to genotype. A big part of the work has been correcting for the fact that most gems have—up to now—had a different upbringing and education to most norms, and obviously that has an impact. In other words, the question I've been asked to answer is not just whether gem behavior varies, but what variations are purely down to the engineering. And whether it falls outside the normal range."

There was confused muttering from the crowd. A few tentative hands were raised. Aryel glanced at her tablet, then up at him. "Can you summarize? What exactly is it that you're trying to work out?"

"It comes down to three things, I think." He held up a hand, hooking his fingers up as he went through them. "One—what do we mean by normal? Two—what differences are solely due to having an engineered genotype? And Three—what do we know? Is there enough information about gems to even answer these questions?"

Gaela's hand shot up.

"The answer to number three's going to be yes, isn't it? I mean we know you've got all the gemtech records, and they were always testing and compiling data."

"That is an excellent point." Eli wondered if it was another setup with Aryel. "The answer is that the gemtechs, not having wanted us to get their records in the first place, now take the position that there's more than enough there to show a clear distinction between gems and norms. What they tend to overlook is how much of that is due to circumstances—"

"The circumstances being them keeping us as slaves?" This came, with no small amount of sarcasm, from a gillung man sitting in the front of their contingent. There was a murmur of loud and angry agreement.

"They would no doubt object to that label," Eli replied drily. "But essentially, yes. They assigned every gem to a category, based on how marketable your engineered abilities were and whether you were capable of functioning well enough to exercise those abilities. Then they ran the scores through a matrix to come up with a commercial value. It's a classification system that ignores the impact of upbringing and quality of life. They think their approach is practical and sensible. I think it's appalling and perverse. If it makes you feel any better, I am not exactly popular in gemtech circles."

A smattering of applause began. It built until the whole hall was clapping. A couple of people were on their feet. It was not what he'd expected. Eli looked at Rob, who was grinning hugely, and over to Aryel. She was studying her tablet, a small smile playing over her lips. She glanced up and met his eyes. She nodded briefly, her face back to serious. He returned his attention to the room and raised his hands.

"Please, folks, don't relax just yet. Remember that I still have to provide an objective analysis, whether the results are to my liking or not, and there are two issues which I am frankly still struggling to resolve. The first is that not all gems are the same in terms of intelligence, empathy, social ability. Take this meeting, for example. Everyone who's here will have those qualities, but we all know that many gems don't. Aryel was involved in an incident earlier today with someone who I suspect would be an example of that. The expectation is that gems will continue to be categorized on this basis, if nothing else.

"The second issue is that we still don't know the full impact of all this engineering, physically, mentally, or emotionally. And a concern has been raised that some gems may carry a latent psychopathy, something they may not even know they have, that could have devastating consequences."

Aryel stepped forward. The sea of faces looked back at them, puzzled and worried. He heard *What does that mean?* muttered back and forth, like a chorus sung in the round.

"This," she said quietly, "is what we really need to talk about."

Something had changed. It wasn't the pain, pulsing through kicked kidneys, stamped hands, and cracked ribs. It wasn't the way he kept flickering in and out of consciousness, or the taste of blood in his mouth, or the sound of a faint, animal moaning. Something else was different. Maybe he should look. George tried opening his eyes and found it was harder than anything else he'd ever attempted. Above him he heard voices, and cringed.

"Look, he's wakin' up. Can you hear us? 'S okay, don't move."

These voices were new. He forced his eyes open, squinting against the rain, and discovered another difference: it was no longer falling on his face. Someone was leaning over him.

"What happened? Can you tell us what happened?"

"Don't even know what he is." That was a different voice, more distant, less concerned. He had a sense of being surrounded, although he could see only the man who crouched next to him, shielding him from the rain.

"He looks fine, don't he?"

George did not think he could look fine. He was finding it hard to breathe. He heard someone whisper, "Help. Please help me." It sounded like him.

"What happened, mate? Who did this?"

He coughed, turned his head painfully to the side to spit out blood and a piece of tooth.

"Gems," he mumbled. "Please. Help."

The man started and leaned closer, grabbing his battered face. It hurt.

"What did you say? Did you say gems did this?"

He nodded, whispered "gems" and "help me" again, but the man seemed to have lost interest. He sprang to his feet.

"D'you hear that? I told you. God led us here for a reason. He's one of us. They did this to him! Look at him!"

"Right you are then, Mac."

Mac had moved out of his line of sight, and through the rain falling again on his face George could see the shadowy outline of the speaker. He was pulling a glove off with his teeth so he could manipulate the tablet clipped inside his coat.

"I'll use a ghost code to get him some help. We can't stay here." His manner was businesslike, matter-of-fact. "We've got work to do."

A train pulled into the Underground station that George had failed to reach, and a slender gem with luminescent lemon-yellow hair got off. He looked around nervously as he made his way up to street level, hoping to see someone else heading for the Squats. There were few other passengers, none of whom were gems. He supposed that everyone who could would have stayed at home and gone to the meeting. He was sorry to have missed it, would have liked to leave work early, but there was a lot to do and, with so few opportunities around, the job had to come first.

He pulled a hat on, pushing as much of his hair up under it as he could, and hunkered into his coat. He didn't like having to walk alone with everything that was going on, but waiting around the station in the hope that someone else might turn up wasn't a good plan either. He'd stick to the main road and walk fast. It wasn't that late, plus the weather was terrible. He wasn't likely to run into trouble.

The conversation went on and on. Eli was astounded. There was none of the furious rejection or weeping fear he had anticipated. Aryel had explained, succinctly but accurately, what the Bel'Natur report contained and what it might signify. They had quickly under-stood the implications, and the position in which Eli had been placed.

"You, sir," observed Mikal, "are over a barrel."

The questions they raised were probing, the comments insightful. They were seriously examining the possibility that what Zavcka Klist had suggested might be true.

"We don't know everything that's been engineered into—or out of—us either," explained a gillung woman. "It's a question we live with every day. Generally the worry is for our own health, and whether it's okay to try and have children. This just," she spread webbed hands apart, "expands the fear."

Sally and Masoud were asked their opinions. "You deal with norms who hurt people, right?" Aryel read the question off her tablet. "What makes *them* do it?"

Someone asked Tobias what the church's view was of someone who hadn't done anything wrong but one day might. "That," he replied, "could describe any one of us."

The questioner was not satisfied. "But what if it's someone who's more likely than most?"

"We believe everyone should have the right to prove they can live a good life, and will be judged on their actions at the end of it. A person with the additional burden we're talking about needs to be vigilant, and so do their friends. I believe that their best course is to be aware of the danger and get the help they need to overcome it."

Sally Trieve was nodding. Masoud looked less sanguine. Eli interjected.

"What if they can't?" he asked. "The two issues I mentioned are related. What if the people this flaw occurs in are the very ones who are least able to guard against it?"

Hands went up all over the room. Aryel started picking them out. If George had remained, Eli thought, he might have needed the entire power pack after all.

George was still conscious, barely. They had dragged him aside and propped him up against a building. It still hurt to breathe, but at least he was partly shielded from the rain.

He had begged them not to leave him there alone. Mac had assured him that help was on the way. "We can't stay till they get here, mate. They don't understand what we're about. We're doing the Lord's work in a time of iniquity. They'll take care of you, mate, but casting down the evil ones is up to us."

"Cover your face," came a growl from behind him. "We got to get movin'."

Mac had pulled a scarf up to cover his nose and mouth.

"You won't say anything, will you, mate? All will be revealed in time, but for now don't say nothing."

Then they were gone.

He went away again himself for a while. When he came back it was to flashes of blue light that rhythmically illuminated the falling rain. The blue light got brighter and brighter, and then there was a steady white light, and then two vehicles slid to a stop in front of him.

And then, finally, there was something on his face helping him breathe, and gentle hands were lifting him onto a stretcher, and the rain was off him completely as he was slid into the back of the ambulance.

"Can he speak?"

"He's in pretty bad shape, officer."

He could feel the power pack pressing into his back. It reminded him there was something he needed to do. He fumbled to push the mask aside with a damaged hand.

"Look, he's trying to say something. Let him talk, if he can."

The mask was pulled away, but he had to rest for a bit.

"Can you tell us what happened, sir? Who did this to you?"

"Told them already," he mumbled. "They're gone. To cast down. Evil ones."

"Cast what? Who did you tell? What's your name, sir?"

He said his name and plucked at the pocket of his coat where his tablet still resided. He felt someone take it out.

"Wasn't a robbery."

"Who did you say you told, George? Was someone else with you?"

He shook his head.

"Did you call anyone?"

He hadn't. That was what he needed to do. He needed to make a call.

"Shit," he heard. "Look at this. He's press."

"Never mind that. He needs treatment." Fingers were at his throat, then moving down his chest as his shirt was opened. "What the hell is this?"

He looked up at the eyes of the paramedics and the policewoman looking down at the wire that trailed away around his waist.

"Need to call," he muttered. "Editor. Newsbeat. Feature story. Need to call."

Less than half a mile away, the godgang was close to being finished. Glowing hanks of lemon-yellow hair, with shreds of bloody scalp still attached, swam in the red-tinged puddles at their feet. Mac once again knelt over an unconscious body. This time he held a knife in his hand.

He was ready to complete the holy work, but the rain kept washing away their marks. This was distressing. Justice must not only be done but must be seen to be done. If he left it like this, people would know, sure, but they wouldn't *understand*. He sat back on his heels, looked up at the water falling from the Lord's heaven. His eyes traveled to the buildings surrounding them.

The others were milling around, mostly still riding the euphoria of retribution. Kicks regularly landed on the limp body at his feet. A few had stepped away, looking out for movement on the wide road from which they had dragged the skinny brute. They were shielded by a building that fronted it, in a rear courtyard accessed by a driveway along the side. A narrow alley at the back led away from the road, and some of his companions were starting to edge toward it.

The gloved preacher, in particular, seemed anxious to be off. He was a good leader, Mac thought, he had opened their eyes and shown them the way, but he didn't seem to have the stomach to truly walk it himself. Well, no matter. Everyone had their strengths and their weaknesses. To criticize would be uncharitable. The test was to recognize when a fellow pilgrim had reached his limit and accept

the responsibility for taking their mission to the next level. He had
known in his bones they were wrong to leave the filth alive the night
before, should have made sure of him before they left, but he had not
then felt it was his place to insist.

Now he felt differently. He straightened up as another kick
landed.

"You're not gonna finish him?" The kicker was flushed with
effort, and excitement. "Want me to do it?"

"No. This isn't how it's supposed to go. The Lord is sending the
rain for a reason. He wants us to leave His sign some other way."

Those strongest in faith clustered around him. The others
drifted back more slowly. He caught the eye of the preacher, who
looked as though he might be about to speak. But he seemed to
catch the mood in the group and nodded at Mac as if to say, *Over
to you, son.*

Mac looked up at the building again, and at the double doors that
opened onto the courtyard.

"We need to leave more than the marks. People need to understand the judgment that waits for those who scale the pinnacles of
sin. We need to take him up on high."

He must have woken up while they were breaking down the
doors, from the way he twitched and moaned when they grabbed
him. He even tried to struggle as they hauled him into the elevator
and then up the access stairs to the roof.

George was finally being driven away, warm and sleepy with
painkillers, when he heard the scream.

Eli felt drained. The meeting was finally over. His assurance to Bal
and Gaela that he would learn a lot had turned out to be truer than
he could have imagined.

He saw them now, on the far side of the stage, speaking to Aryel.
The hall was clearing slowly, much of the crowd still hanging around
to talk. He was surrounded by gems eager to share anecdotes and
insights, or simply to tell him how much they appreciated his frank-
ness. He was reminded once again that a free and open society was
still a novel experience for most of them.

Rob was similarly mobbed, by a group that included Tobias the UC priest and the giant Mikal. Sally Trieve had slipped away and Commander Masoud had stepped to the side, frowning as he listened to messages on his earset.

Eli finished chatting with a couple of gillungs and saw with relief that the rest had become immersed in other conversations and drifted away. He turned to find Gaela at his elbow.

"You look worn out."

He rubbed his hands over his face. "Do I? Sorry. I am tired. But this," he gestured to the still-full hall, "this was amazing. I didn't expect people to try and be so *helpful*."

She tilted her head to look at him. She had an interesting face: full lips, slightly asymmetrical features, and huge pale-green eyes under the blazing hair. It lacked the exquisite delicacy of Aryel's bone structure or the classic lines of Zavcka Klist's, but in her own way she was just as beautiful. In three days, he thought, he had encountered three of the most attractive, enigmatic, and dangerous women he had ever met.

"We like knowing where we stand, even if we don't like the place," she said now. "And we appreciate actually being asked what we think about ourselves. Most norms seem to assume we don't have an opinion."

"They don't know what they're missing. This is as opinionated a group of people as I've ever met."

"I hope you'll remember that when you go to present your report."

It seemed an odd thing to say, but the more he thought about it, the more it made sense. A lot of things were starting to come together in his head: meanings and interpretations, solutions and resolutions. His comment, and Gaela's quiet response, somehow captured their essence. All he needed now were the results to confirm that his instinct about the murder was correct, and an answer to the mystery of the child.

They were meandering back over to where Aryel and Bal still stood in conversation with several other gems. From the far end of the hall, where it was quietest, Eli saw Masoud heading toward them rapidly.

"Bal and I wanted to let you know we'd be happy to talk to you. We understand you must have questions," Gaela said. Again that sharp look. "We could do it tomorrow if you like, or whenever's convenient."

The last piece of the puzzle, just in time. "Tomorrow sounds great."

They were still making the arrangements when Masoud arrived next to Aryel. She was in mid-sentence, saying something to Donal, but there was an urgency in his face that made her stop and turn to him. Donal simultaneously turned toward one of the big doors leading into the hall, a quizzical look on his face.

"Something's happened," Masoud said. "Not far from here."

As he spoke the door crashed open. Horace appeared in it, wild-eyed, stumbling into chairs and people in his haste.

"Aryel. *Aryel.*" He was shouting and running, the panic clear in his voice. Everyone still in the hall was staring at him. Eli saw the way Masoud looked from Horace to Aryel, lips compressed, and thought *Oh shit.*

The green-haired gem slid to a stop. For a moment, between the panting and the shock, he couldn't get it out.

"Aryel, it's Nelson. They've thrown him off a building. Aryel, he's *dead.*"

15

Zavcka Klist felt a bead of cold sweat gather on her spine as she watched the live feed. It was all blue lights and barriers and tearstained faces under damp, shimmering hair. The vidcams followed Aryel Morningstar as the police let her through. The view was of her swollen, swaying back as they escorted her over to the gurney that stood before a cordoned and tented patch of pavement. Nothing of what it carried could be seen as an officer raised one end of the white sheet, but the way that she started in shock as she bent forward to look, turning into profile as she buried her face in her hands, told enough of the story. The tall policeman with commander's bars on his uniform placed a hand on her arm. She looked up, white-lipped and dry-eyed, nodded, and said something to him.

We can't actually hear what's being said, but Aryel Morningstar appears to have confirmed the victim's identity . . .

Zavcka killed the sound and continued to watch as Aryel glanced toward the top of the building and then over to the side. She was still silhouetted beside the gurney, her ponderously overlarge body and small, somber face clearly illuminated in the bright lights surrounding the tent. She appeared to be listening as the commander spoke

to the scene investigators, their backs all firmly toward the vidcams.
As the attendants moved to push the gurney away, she placed her
hand on the sheet and looked down at it for a moment, a gesture of
benediction and sorrowful farewell. There was an iconic quality to
the image, as though one might have seen it before in stained glass or
ancient tempera. Zavcka knew it would be replayed over and over.

The commander walked Aryel back to the barriers. As the vidcam
swung to follow them, Zavcka saw Eli Walker and Robert Trench
standing amid a group of gems. There was a gigantic Recombin
assembly-line model, a Gempro Green-top who shivered and sniv-
eled, an indigo-haired, broad-shouldered, grim-faced specimen who
looked vaguely familiar, and next to him a Bel'Natur Provis redhead
whom she recognized from the file she had reviewed earlier in the
day. There were others, many others, clustered around them. A priest
stood to one side, collared and ashen-faced, a crucifix clutched in
his hands.

Aryel had stepped back through the barrier and was speaking, not
to the vidcams but to the group. Zavcka flicked the sound back on.
The press crew must have been filtering out the background noise,
because her voice came low but clear.

". . . it is Nelson. He'd posted that he had to work late tonight.
The police say it looks like he was grabbed on the way home."

The sound of weeping. Someone off-camera called, "Is it the
same as Callan, Aryel? Does it look like the same ones as got Callan?"

"The police will have to say for sure, but it looks so to me."

Through the muttering and muffled sobs there came another low
murmuring sound. The priest had begun to pray quietly, eyes closed,
crucifix raised to his lips. A mousy-haired young man without any
gemsign Zavcka could see swung around to confront him. The vidcam angled and pulled out to capture the scene as he shouted at the
priest.

"Wha' the hell're you doin' here anyway? They're jus' th' same as
you! Same god, same prophets, same savior, you all b'lieve th' same
crap! What're you cryin' for? Why're you here?"

The priest recoiled, blinking over damp cheeks at the furious
gem, and tried to compose himself for a response. "Nelson was my

friend too . . . My God has nothing to do with the people who did this to him. We're not the same as them . . . They are a complete perversion . . ."

"You are! You're all the fuckin' same!"

"No they are not." Aryel Morningstar stepped between the two men, her voice firm. "Donal, you know better. Even if they claim similar beliefs, there's no connection between the United Churches and the godgangs. The UC have supported us, they've defended us, and Tobias here has been a very good friend. Nelson went to some of his services."

"He did," Tobias said behind her. He was still struggling to pull himself together. "He came the last few Sundays, he—" He heaved a huge, shuddering sigh and shook his head. The vidcams drank it in as he glanced away, biting his lip, and then looked back at Donal.

"I understand your anger, I understand your grief, I share it. Please believe me."

He seemed to notice the vidcams, which must, Zavcka thought, have been edging closer, and spoke to them as well, as he gestured to the scene behind him.

"This . . . this is an atrocity. This is an act God condemns, and whether you are a believer or not it, is something we should all condemn. This kind of violence, hatred . . ." His voice broke. "We should have left this behind by now. We should be better than this."

The screaming fury seemed to have gone out of Donal. The priest stepped closer to him, speaking too quietly for the sound pickup. Aryel turned toward the vidcams.

Excuse me, UrbanNews, we're streaming live right now. Aryel Morningstar, can you tell us any more about what happened here tonight?

"I understand that the police will be briefing the press shortly. It would be inappropriate for me to discuss it ahead of that."

We've heard that the victim was a gem named Nelson, can you confirm that?

"I can."

We've also heard that the attack on him might have been in retaliation for an earlier attack, as a result of which a journalist is now in hospital. Do you know anything about that?

"I too have heard that this was not the only assault in the area this evening. I don't know much more than that at the moment, but I can assure you we will be cooperating fully with any police investigations."

We're aware that there have been more than twenty violent encounters between gems and norms just in the past twenty-four hours. Aryel, are we at a crisis point?

She had been about to turn away but paused at that, frowning into the camera.

"Are we in crisis? Yes, I think we are. I think it is not only a crisis of violence, but more fundamentally a crisis of conscience. I think all of the people out there," she gestured toward the vidcam, speaking directly to Zavcka and the thousands more who would no doubt see the clip, "need to decide whether they are going to allow the people who did this," waving now at the police, the point of impact, the mortuary van, "to determine what kind of world they live in."

Isn't that overstating the situation? How could they possibly do that?

"As you're no doubt aware, the European Conference to determine the future status of gems begins the day after tomorrow. It does appear that an attempt is being made to provoke a conflict ahead of it."

You think this murder is part of an effort to influence the outcome of the Conference?

"As I said, I'll leave it to the police to comment on this particular atrocity. But if you consider the campaign of hate that is being waged on the socialstreams, coupled with the upswing in violence you mentioned, the timing is very suspicious."

You seem to be suggesting that these events are being orchestrated. Who do you think is responsible?

"If I could be absolutely certain, I'd name names. I can't, so I won't. There is, however, an old adage about following the money which I would commend to your viewers."

I believe I understand what you're referring to. But the obvious suspects, if I can put it like that, would not appear to be natural bedfellows with the type of group suspected in last night's assault.

"No they would not. But we are approaching a moment of great symbolic as well as political significance. I do not think the conjunction should be overlooked."

That appeared to flummox the reporter. The bitch had probably planned it that way, leaving the interview hanging with the kind of cryptic inference that would guarantee it would be linked, reposted, and discussed for days. She nodded a crisp termination and turned away, the grotesque bulk of her cloak for an instant filling the screen. The reporter began speaking to the priest as the vidcam watched her depart, Trench and Walker flanking her on one side, the red and indigo heads of Gaela and Bal on the other.

Zavcka fell back against the opulent sofa, trembling with fury. *Dr. Eli fucking Walker. So that's where you are tonight.*

The twisted little bitch had figured out the plan, pointed the finger, and appeared to have suborned her ace in the hole. On top of which the fake fucking priest had gone well beyond his instructions.

They did not fucking understand who they were dealing with. She had not gotten where she was without knowing how to outmaneuver, outmanipulate, and out-fucking-last all opposition.

So Eli Walker did not appear to be on board. No matter.

There was still the child.

They stood next to Rob's car, parked behind a succession of police vehicles. Eli had driven it to the scene with Gaela, Bal, and Donal while Masoud transported and briefed Rob and Aryel. How the others had gotten there so quickly he did not know, until he noticed a large transport with the United Churches logo farther down the street.

No one seemed to know what to say, until Bal, arm wrapped protectively around Gaela, looked over at Aryel. "Do you think they'll do it?"

She shook herself out of a reverie. "Do I think who will do what?"

"What you just said about conscience. You were asking people—norms—to stand up. You really think they will? For us?"

"I think some will. Some already are; things would have been even worse today if bystanders hadn't jumped in. The UC will, and I think . . . I hope . . . that tomorrow there will be people calling their MPs and ward counselors and posting more rebuttals on the streams . . ." She sighed and shrugged. "If you want to know whether it'll be enough, I don't know, Bal. I just don't." She glanced at Gaela. "That reporter from earlier. He got mugged after he left."

"Oh shit. George." Gaela squeezed her eyes tight shut for a moment. "They thought he was a gem?"

"No. Apparently it was gems who did it. A reprisal for Callan. Beat him up pretty badly. He was found by the godgang."

"No. Oh no. Oh *shit*."

"I'm afraid so. Seems he told them what happened, they put a ghost call in to emergency services with his location, and then went hunting."

"No. Oh god. *Nelson*." Gaela was crying now, face buried in Bal's broad chest. Her shoulders shook. "Oh god, what have I done?"

"You've done nothing. Gaela. Gaela, listen to me." Aryel's voice was as close to harsh as Eli had heard it. He and Rob stood side by side, awkwardly silent, as Aryel reached between Bal's arms to place a firm hand on Gaela's shoulder.

"If anyone is at fault, it's me. You only identified him, I dealt with him. I could have sicced Masoud on him, or offered him transport back to the Underground. And you know what? This might have happened anyway. The godgang wasn't prowling around the Squats because they were feeling friendly."

Gaela was still shaking, but the sobs subsided as she nodded into Bal's chest. Aryel withdrew her hand.

"Have they found them?" Bal asked. "The gems?"

"No, but we might just be in luck there. The recorder that Gaela spotted was running. Masoud said it seems George was working up a piece to publish in place of the scoop he didn't get. He was furious at the police for taking it off him. Anyway, there should be video."

"They haven't looked at it?"

"Not yet. George told them it was two men, purple hair."

Bal winced.

"Masoud's asked me to look at it, see if I can identify them. At least if I—or any of us—can, it'll help offset the damage the idiots have done."

Rob interjected. "No one can hold their actions against you, Aryel, whoever they are. You've rejected violence from the beginning."

"Yes I have, which means if there's much more from our side I'm going to start to look pretty ineffectual."

"I'll look," said Bal quietly. "If you think it might help."

She nodded. Figures were starting to drift toward them, black shadows outlined against the arc lights of the crime scene. In the vanguard was Masoud, next to a uniformed policewoman and a white-suited technician.

He beckoned Aryel over to a crime scene van as the technician unlocked it. The others trailed after her. Masoud cocked his head at Bal, Gaela, and Eli and looked at Aryel, eyebrows raised.

"I've told them," she said. "It'll be all over the streams in no time anyway. I thought the more help with identification, the better."

Masoud looked surprised but pleased. As the technician fitted the recorder's memtab to a tablet, the policewoman briefly recounted what George had said.

"He wasn't very coherent," she explained. "They worked him over pretty thoroughly. He kept talking about his editor. When we found this, we realized he might have images both of the people who beat him up and the ones he said found him. But we didn't have time to look at it before the ... this ... before we became aware of this incident." She bit her lip. "I am so very sorry."

"Thank you." Aryel frowned. "How did you become aware of it? Did someone call it in?"

"In a manner of speaking. The ambulance that was transporting this victim," she nodded at the tablet the technician was working with, "reported hearing screams. We were on the scene in minutes, but ..."

"We're ready."

The technician stepped back, and Masoud and Aryel leaned in. There were several minutes of milling around in the community hall. Tobias had done a good job of introducing George to as many people as he could. Nevertheless, the image returned often to the distant figures of Masoud, Rob, Eli, and Sally where they waited at the front of the room. Then there was the scramble for seats and the exchange with Gaela. The policewoman turned to look at her in astonishment. Then Aryel, and bouncy images of the hall doors, the foyer, and George's feet as he scrambled down the front steps.

The video and sound cut out a few seconds into a tongue-lashing from his editor and came back on to a different view of the street unfolding in front of George. Masoud shook his head in puzzlement at the muttered monologue that accompanied it. Eli couldn't hear it clearly, nor see Aryel's face, but he noted the stillness that settled over her, and Gaela, and Bal.

Then a jerk and the flash of the club, so sudden and violent that they all reared back, and the shift in perspective as George landed on the pavement. They saw the purple heads, heard the approval of victim.

Then it got very hard to watch. Rob turned away first. Eli quickly found he needed to check on his friend. As he looked around he saw that Aryel was watching steadily, with the same intent gaze she had had for the Bel'Natur vid, and the same sick, drawn expression. Bal was a picture of grim impassivity. But Gaela was leaning in, frowning in disbelief.

"Stop it. Stop. *Stop.*" Gaela spoke over the grunted references to Callan and George's desperate pleas. Masoud looked at her.

"I'm sorry, you shouldn't watch. I know this is hard . . ."

"It's not that. It isn't *real*. Stop the vid. Now."

Masoud nodded to the technician, who paused the play. The policewoman turned to Gaela. "I know this must be difficult, but I saw the victim. And his injuries."

"That's not what I mean. That part's real enough. It's the others." She drew a deep breath. "They're not gems."

They all stared at her. Masoud's frown matched her own. "What do you mean? Do you know them?"

"Never saw them before in my life. But they're not gems. Their hair, it isn't genuine. I know it looks all right to you, but it's not." She pointed to the image on the screen, of the two attackers looming over George. "Our hair has a specific UV signature, it glows in a particular way. These guys are wrong. They're dye jobs. They're fake."

The policewoman was staring at her, open-mouthed. "But you . . . how could you know that? It would take a special scanner to—" She stopped. "Oh."

Gaela's lips twisted. "Oh yes. I am a special scanner."

She turned to Masoud. "You'll need to get it verified using a spectrometer. If you just took my word for it there'd be hell to pay, I understand that. But do it quickly, please, because this poor bastard thinks he's had the crap beat out of him by a couple of gems, and that's what he's going to be telling everyone, and that's the story Newsbeat is probably already running . . ."

His hands were up. "I get it, I get it. I understand." He glanced back at the screen. "Jesus, Mohammed, and all the prophets. Who the fuck are these people? Right." He was speaking now to the technician. "Get started doing whatever you need to do to get this image independently verified. Sergeant Varsi," to the policewoman, "please let your colleagues—and anyone else who might have heard about this—know that there is grave doubt about the genetic status of the assailants. We do not want to inadvertently assist in the spreading of a malicious and inflammatory falsehood. Feel free to quote me."

"Yes, sir."

"Aryel, you saw the vids from the employment center. These guys don't look the same to me, do they to you?"

"No. But since I don't share Gaela's ability I think it would be worth asking her to take a look at those vids as well."

He looked at Gaela. She said, "Happy to help."

"Okay." The tablet was still frozen on the impostors, false gem-signs glowing over snarls and fists and a boot raised for a kick. "I'm afraid I need to watch the rest of this."

Eli and Rob declined to rejoin them. Gaela and Bal also turned away. They stood together, close enough to hear the beating end and the footfalls of the attackers as they departed.

"We don't know how long he was there before they found him," said the technician, and speeded the vid up. They turned back when it was slowed to normal play. They heard more than George had, from the moments before he recovered consciousness—the concerns of some, the doubts of others, then the interrogation and the departure. There was a good view of Mac, and a partial of the man with the glove and the tablet. Everyone else was in shadow.

Aryel said, "Gaela?" Her voice was steady and soft. Eli ached with the knowledge that they had just watched men depart on a mission to murder their friend. Beside him Rob stood, chin tucked into his chest as though he might bury it there, quietly sucking air in through his teeth.

Gaela was wiping away tears, but her voice was also steady. "I got a bit more than you would. Enough to identify a couple of others."

═══ DAY FOUR ═══

16

ON ANOTHER COLD, GRAY MORNING, IN A CROWDED CAFÉ NEXT TO VICTO-
ria Station, customers spoke of little else.

"That's rich, innit, people pretendin' to be gems. Like there's not
enough of 'em already."

"Shameful. Beating up our own kind, just to make them look bad."

"Kinda works for them though, don't it? Between that and the
one got killed, everyone's feelin' sorry for them. Makes you wonder."

"Come on. You don't seriously think . . ."

"No, no, well I dunno. Like all the stuff's been on the streams,
then the cops say it's fake, now all these folks postin' sayin' hey I'm
no fake, mean what I said . . . I'm not sayin' I agree with them, you
unnerstand. It's just hard to know what to believe."

"I think it's horrible. Just terrible. The poor creatures."

"Yeah, well, they may be creatures but they ain't all poor!"

"True enough."

"Yeah."

"I hear some of 'em make a mint."

"Still, don't exactly make up for gettin' kicked off a roof."

"Kind of thing never used to happen. Say what you like about the gemtechs, no one was gettin' thrown off buildings back then."

"Yeah. Wasn't a paradise, but fuck me. I hear they scalped the poor fucker."

"Language, please." That from the barista.

"Sorry, Joe. But seriously. Some of 'em have got to be wishin' things'd stayed the way they were."

"I can't imagine they would ever wish that. We were supposed to make their lives better."

"I don't have a problem with that, ma'am, s'long as it don't make my life worse."

On the screen above the counter, set to a trending algorithm, the UrbanNews interview with Aryel Morningstar flashed up yet again. The conversation in the café dropped to a murmur, and the ambient noise sensor scaled the volume up.

. . . a crisis of conscience. I think all of the people out there need to decide . . .

"She's something else, this one. Wonder where they found her."

"Bit mysterious, apparently."

"Someone said mebbe she was with them Remnants."

"How'd they get hold of somethin' like her? They've not got a pot to piss in, nor a window to throw it out of."

"I heard that rumor, that ain't right. No, mate of mine told me she came out of one a' them weapons programs. Y'know, the ones that went wrong."

"Seriously?"

"S'truth. That's why it's all so hush-hush. You know." The speaker tapped the side of his nose meaningfully.

"She's so pretty, ain't she, you'd never guess. I mean she would be if the rest of her wasn't so fucked up. An' she wasn't so little."

"Good thing she *is* fucked up. At least she ain't got any powers."

"She can talk, though, can't she? Way with words for sure."

"She's got a point, too. I mean okay, so she's a gem, but these godgangs are fu—'scuse me . . . they're outta control."

"What's she mean by this part?"

. . . an old adage about following the money . . .

"She's talkin' about the gemtechs, I s'pose."

"The only place I want to follow any money is back into my pension where it belongs. It's worth half what they told me when I signed up. Half!"

"That's bad, mate, but money isn't everything."

"No, I mean the last part. That whole 'moment of significance' bit."

"Big date comin' up, isn't it? For all those religious types."

Tobias's interview had less prominence on the streams but was still generating a very respectable hit rate. The bishop had called early to register her approval, and the old brick church near the Squats hummed with somber congratulations. Volunteers had turned out in force. Many were not even people of faith but knew about the UC's involvement with the gem community and under the circumstances had no reservations about channeling secular support via an ecclesiastical route.

"None of this god stuff makes sense to me," a woman told Tobias, "but if it's what people want to believe I want them listening to you, not those racist maniacs."

"I understand. I'm very glad you've come. Our gem friends need everyone's help. And maybe after a while, the god stuff might start to make sense too."

The fact that Nelson had been coming to church was a subject of much discussion among the parishioners.

"That it would be a believer who fell in the way of those monsters . . . what he must have been thinking in his last moments . . ."

"At least he knew they were not really representative of our faith. At least he knew that. It would be so terrible if he'd died thinking that's what we're about."

"It finally shows the godgangs in their true light. People who only *claim* to be true to our beliefs killing someone who really *is*. It proves how illegitimate they are. We need to all keep making that point."

"This *cannot* happen again. It just can't. We have to find a way to get through to them. A cousin of mine sometimes goes to a godgang meeting. I don't approve but at least I know that not everyone there is this kind of person."

Tobias had in mind a more direct approach to preventing further attacks.

"Not many of our gem brothers and sisters are venturing out today," he said. "But for those who must, we should offer to escort them. Any volunteers?"

A forest of hands went up.

"How about tonight?"

People shuffled their feet and looked at each other. Two, then three, then four hands went up around the room. "Thank you, brothers. Thank you, sister. We'll work out the details in a minute."

Aryel dropped in early. People looked and whispered behind their hands. "Inspirational," was murmured over and over. "Able to do what she does. The pain she must be in, and she doesn't let it show. Just amazing."

Several of the new volunteers, including two who had put themselves on night duty, went over to tell her that they were there because of what she'd said. She looked tired, but her smile was as warm as her words.

"Thank you so much," she said. "You've just made a bad day a lot better. There's an old-fashioned notion about moral courage that I hoped . . . I trusted . . . would still be alive today. I can see I was right. Thank you."

Though her voice was not loud, it carried. Several more volunteers made their way over to Tobias and signed up to provide after-dark protection.

"I'm just stopping by to say thanks, for last night as well as everything else," she said when she got to him. "And I thought you'd like to know that Callan's out of danger. I've just come from the hospital."

"Thank God. Does he know . . . ?"

"He's still heavily sedated. I spoke to him for a while, but I don't think he understood much."

"That may be for the best."

"Indeed. The others do know, of course. They're coming home today. Also we're hearing from gems who live elsewhere in the city, who'd like to come stay in the Squats. Safety in numbers."

"Under the circumstances that sounds wise. We can help with transport, make sure they get here safely. Can't we?" He looked around. There was a chorus of assent, met by another brilliant smile from Aryel. "Will Mikal have the details?"

"He will. With the Conference starting tomorrow I'm afraid I'm all over the place."

"You need to get some rest, Aryel."

"In a few days. One way or another."

Once again Mac stood hunched against the cold, gazing across to the top of the Bel'Natur building. This time he didn't really see it. He was thinking about what to say to his flock.

They were sipping coffees and checking tablets, exclaiming at the various trends and posts. The news that George had been attacked by "fake gems" had been met first by confusion, then doubt, then derision. Mac was a little annoyed that it had taken them so long to come to terms with this turn of events, although in truth it had been just a few minutes. But it was such an obvious lie. They should know by now that the enemies of the Lord would stop at nothing to deceive, that the so-called police were deep in the pockets of the Beast.

He caught the edge of sound from one of the tablets, faint but enough to tell him that someone was watching the interview with the hunchback succubus again. He looked around sharply, stopped himself before he barked at the guilty party to change streams. Let them get it out of their systems, watch it enough for their own rage at the lies to build and boil over, as his had done after just one viewing. Still. She was the one he'd most like to get his hands on. Aryel Morningstar. Calling herself two names as though she were a proper person, hiding her mark away as if that could disguise what she was. But the Beast had slipped in his pride, branding his offspring with a sign that the faithful could recognize. The preacher had whispered its meaning to him before he departed, with the dawn.

Now the burden of leadership was his. The preacher had understood perfectly, had felt the shift and bowed to the inevitability of God's plan.

"You are an active man, Mac," he'd said. "An active man, and this is a time for action. Cometh the hour. You don't need me anymore."

"Where will you go, Preacher?"

"To another group whose eyes are not yet fully opened. To where the Lord can put me to use. My work here is done."

Mac had bowed his head in humility. It was a big responsibility, but he felt up to it. He had been anointed; kneeling in the rain on the blood-soaked pavement with the weapon of God in his strong right hand, he had been granted a divine inspiration and they had all sensed it.

He looked around and saw more members emerging from the elevators. Two of his stalwarts were checking them in, and two more were stationed at the doors that led into the building to guard against entry from that quarter. Although the streams they used were private, you couldn't be too careful. He was relieved to rec- ognize all the faces. It was much earlier than the regular meeting, too early for the police to send any spies or for random passersby to think of wandering up to eat a frozen lunch in the bitter wind of the terrace. Only the most dedicated had been granted word of this gathering: ones he knew already were, or were ready to become, warriors of faith.

The crowd was building. It looked like there would be two or three dozen in all. More than he'd dared hope. He knew he would have to start by putting right some of the lies, the Beast-witch's poison whisper of an alliance with the very cultivators of evil. It was such a ridiculous, such an *offensive* idea. It was hard to believe anyone could actually take it seriously. Proof, as if any were needed, that the Beast was insidious, and powerful. But there had to be a weakness, a chink in the armor, somewhere; and he would find it, the inspiration would fall on him again, and on that day the whole world would see the Truth, and the Light.

He had his sermon. The Lord had once more blessed his newest lieutenant, and he muttered a prayer of thanks before he turned to go. He would stand in the spot where the preacher had always stood. His gaze swept across the icy viewing platform with its clear glass barrier and metal railings, the city spreading away beneath, the gray sky and the black tower. This was a good place, high and clear and close to God. A place for faith to be transformed into action. A place for miracles.

The call from Eli Walker came in while she was with Felix.

"Dr. Walker. I'm surprised to hear from you this early, given the lateness of your night."

"Miss Klist. I gather my professional conduct continues to meet with your disapproval."

"You were conducting research at a murder scene?"

"I'm an anthropologist. The study of humanity is my business, including, sadly, where it is most lacking."

She pursed her lips. "A truly terrible event. We're all very shocked. It does appear that a backlash is taking hold."

"It's certainly being encouraged."

"That is an astonishing development. Difficult to credit."

"Strange that you would think so. Given that the discovery was made by a gem formerly of Bel'Natur."

"It does point to the unquestionable value of our research and engineering divisions," she said smoothly. "Although I am no less conscious of our failings. Have your further inquiries been fruitful?"

"In a manner of speaking. I've been advised, as you suspected, that no other gemtechs reported incidents of a similar nature. And the independent review I've had done also can find no genetic basis to explain what happened."

"So you agree with our risk assessment."

"Not entirely, although it has led me to revise some of the final text of our report. I have obviously shared the material with various collaborators, on whose expertise I rely. And I've raised your concerns with the police and social service departments. I thought you'd like to know."

She fought to keep a smile away. "I'm very relieved. As I said to you before, we are committed to doing whatever is necessary to eliminate any danger to the public."

"I suspect that will prove beyond your powers, and mine as well. If the events of the past two days demonstrate anything, it's that gems do not have a monopoly on senseless acts of appalling violence."

"Of course." The infuriating man. Even as he conceded, he was unable to resist a counterpoint. She no longer felt like smiling. "I meant to the extent that we *can*."

He nodded. "Until tomorrow then. The report will be part of the delegate links when you register your tablet on arrival."

"I look forward to it."

She killed the connection and turned back to Felix. "Well, that was a lot of worry for nothing."

"Zavcka, you don't actually know what he's going to say. And as for a backlash, it's happening in the wrong direction. Have you *seen* the streams today?"

"Yes, I have. And you are being far too pessimistic. People haven't become rabidly pro-gem, they're just saying they don't like the idea of gangs of savages roaming the streets. Which is exactly what we want. They want gems to be safe, but they are equally worried about having to pay for it. Again, what we want."

"I thought we wanted—no, *expected*—a lot more of them in handcuffs by now. Some serious, undeniable threat verification. What happened to that part of the plan? Because instead what I see is two clowns with dyed hair being rumbled by one of our own products! Who the hell thought that up?"

Me, she thought. *Fuck off, Felix. Who could have known they'd grab the one guy in the whole city with a hidden vidcam? Or that the runaway Provis bitch would see it before broadcast? And be able to tell the hair was wrong? I'm not a bloody fortune-teller.*

She said, "The reason we haven't seen retaliation on the scale we expected is down to Aryel Morningstar. She's been drumming it into them—for a while now—not to do anything that could erode public support. The message is to run away if they can, defend themselves if they have to, but stop as soon as they're safe. She's allied herself with the UC, who both reinforce the message and provide logistical support. Which reduces the opportunities for friction, shall we say. I will admit I didn't expect it to be so effective, but it just proves the point I keep making to you. Don't ignore her."

"I should be so lucky. She's all over the streams."

"That is because she knows how to work the media. It's not an accident, Felix. She's got her own campaign going. You notice how she never mentions being deformed? She doesn't have to. She works it without saying a word. She keeps her gemsign covered up so no one can actually see anything to be disgusted by, under this black shroud-thing which makes it look bigger than it probably is. And makes you notice her face more than you would otherwise. You think any of that is coincidence? It's not. It's about generating sympathy."

For once Felix did not respond with a stock dismissal of gem capability. He seemed to be actually considering what she'd said. Then he sighed.

"I don't suppose we could just get rid of her?"

"No we could not." Honestly. He was worse than Eli Walker. "Can you *imagine* what the reaction would be if anything happened to Aryel Morningstar? *Now*? No, Felix. We have to be cleverer than that.

"And we can be. I've got some more news for you, Felix. Something you'll like." She did smile, finally. "I've found the prototype."

17

Gaela was adamant that Gabriel was not to go near the Maryam House community room, the leisure center, or anywhere else that people were likely to be gathered. Nor were any of them to leave the Squats. The police had set up a command post next to reception and stationed two officers on site. One was out on patrol with a couple of residents, checking outlying buildings in particular for new and unregistered occupants. The other officer was on hand to help with coordination and reassurance, communicate with his colleague out in the field, and cast awestruck looks in Gaela's direction.

She doubted that the impostors who had attacked George would have risked actually staying in the area, especially now that their pictures had been enhanced and distributed to the streams. They would likely be far away, their heads recolored or shaved, lying as low as they possibly could. Still, it was worth confirming whether anyone had slipped inside the Squats unnoticed, for safety or more nefarious purposes.

The checks also served to ensure that Mikal's list of available, secure, and clean accommodation was up to date. One of her tasks was to casually glance at the city's refugees as they arrived and were assigned a place to stay. So far all of the jewel-colored hair had been genuine, and she expected it to stay that way. Whoever was behind the botched deception would not make the same mistake again.

She was relieved that no one had asked her if it was a disguise she'd seen before.

Her main assignment at the moment was to review the police database of known godgang members to see if she could spot the two that she alone had been able to make out from George's vid. The dim images had proved impossible to enhance enough for a machine scan. Even for her it was difficult. The database itself was disappointingly thin, and many of its images were of not much better quality.

Mac had, however, been identified: delusional loner with his own god complex, Christian fundamentalist, no family or steady job. He was anti-gem and anti-gemtech, and had a history of harassment against both. His current apartment had been raided and his accounts frozen. Neither showed signs of recent activity. Masoud thought he might have gone underground several days before, which would imply that the others had probably done the same. Of the gloved man with the tablet there was no trace.

"It doesn't mean he's not a regular," Masoud had said. "It's very difficult to get a handle on groups like this. The cells trade members and ideology but there's no real central structure. The meeting places change; they're promoted on private streams and by word of mouth so it's hard to follow a trail. And even when we do find a location, a lot of them are very savvy about camouflage. Lots of hats and scarves and reflective sun visors go into those meetings. I've even heard of masks and prosthetic makeup."

"So, no leads then." They'd been speaking via tablet, early in the morning. Masoud was bleary-eyed; she suspected he had not been to bed. She and Bal had, eventually, but the night had been just as sleepless for them.

"I wouldn't say that. We started questioning the ringleaders we have on file yesterday in connection with the attack on Callan, and we've been hauling them in again overnight. No one's admitted to knowing anything but the detectives tell me there's definitely a vibe. At least some of them knew something was up."

"No regrets, I suppose."

"No. Although we're not sure they anticipated quite this level of violence. But there's no sense they want it to stop—or that they expect it to."

"Commander, I hope you weren't calling to offer comfort and reassurance."

He had managed a smile that was mostly grimace. "I wanted to ask if you'd be available to work with us over the next few days."

"On what?"

"Suspect identification, threat assessment, Conference security. The list of things you could help us with is enormous." He shook his head. "Please don't be offended, but I'm surprised the gemtechs never marketed your ability to us. Didn't they see the applications to police work?"

"I'm sure they did. I worked security at a number of private events. Since we're being blunt, I suspect they might not have wanted someone like you to be fully aware of what someone like me is capable of. The other reason you wouldn't have heard is because I was a prototype. A not entirely successful one."

"You seem pretty successful to me."

"That's because you haven't met me when I have a headache." She sighed. "Look, there's something you should know before you decide whether you really want me assisting the police. You seem like a decent guy, so I'm going to trust that you'll take it on board without expecting me to go into details. Which I won't."

A pause. "I'm listening."

"I escaped and went underground several years before the Declaration. This was when the retrieval squads were still active, so finding work was difficult. I sometimes engaged in activities which you would not, as a police officer, approve of. I tell you this now so you can decide whether you're prepared to risk being embarrassed by it later."

"I see." He thought. "Were you ever arrested?"

"No."

"Did anyone get hurt?"

"No."

"These activities. I assume your knowledge of security systems from your prior assignments would have been . . . helpful?"

"That's a fair assumption."

"And since the Declaration?"

"All clear from before then. Once forced retrieval was banned I had other choices."

"Well, you sound rehabilitated to me, and no one can spot crime like a criminal. Welcome to the Met."

It sounded like a job offer. She decided not to pursue specifics just then. If she proved her worth over the next few days—and her family managed to safely negotiate the meeting with Eli Walker, and the Conference did not go against them—then it would be time enough to find out exactly what Masoud had in mind.

Eli had also called early, again expecting to be told that it was not, after all, a good time. He was again surprised, and pleased, when Gaela said that it was still fine for him to come if he was prepared for a few adjustments.

"It's going to be a very tense day around here. We're trying to keep Gabe away from the turmoil as much as we can, and frankly having a visitor will help distract him. As long as you don't mind him being around while we talk."

"Not at all. I'd love to be able to chat with him."

She chuckled. "You say that now. You may well wish he'd shut up."

He hung up, almost convinced that he and Sally Trieve had gotten it completely wrong. He put a call in to her, and to Aryel, and again studied the results that his team in Edinburgh and elsewhere had sent through in the wee hours. Then he called Rob to tell him that the final version of the report would not be ready for secure upload to the Conference datastream until late that night. Then he had spoken to Zavcka Klist, wondering all the while what Donal would have made of his end of the conversation.

* * *

He arrived at the Squats a little before noon, to find the young gem himself helping Mikal in reception.

"Blooady hell. Three days in a row. Mik," making a show of checking the list on the tablet in front of him, "we should fin' him an apartment."

Eli laughed. "You know, I think I would like that. If I end up spending a lot of time in London I might take you up on it. Assuming it'd be allowed."

"It wouldn't be us who had a problem with it, but would you really want to?" asked Mikal, as they executed a complicated triple-thumbed handshake. "Live in the middle of a bunch of gems?"

"Why not? The meeting last night was a remarkable experience. As was the day before," nodding to Donal, "with yourself and the others."

"Well, we could do wi' havin' a less remarkable day fer a change. If you doan' mind. It's a good thing we're no' a superstitious bunch, we migh' think you're bad luck."

"Be hard to blame you. How's the community coping?"

"Coping's something gems know how to do," replied Mikal quietly. "But pretty devastated all the same. People can't help wondering who'll be next."

"The police are putting a ring of steel around this place. I spoke to Rob—Dr. Trench—earlier, he reckons the Squats will be just about the safest place in the city tonight."

"We'll see," said Donal skeptically. "Who's blowin' yer mind today then?"

"Me." That was Gaela, emerging from a door off the foyer. "Not just yet though. Sorry, I heard you come in but I was on a call."

"Not a problem. Shall I wait?"

"I was going to suggest you go ahead. Bal and Gabe are on the top of our building scrounging some stuff for lunch. If Don doesn't mind letting you in, I should be done here in fifteen, twenty minutes."

So it was that he found himself escorted into the heart of the Squats by one of its most acerbic residents. The events of the past forty-eight hours had reinforced Donal's belief in widespread and interlocking conspiracies. Eli wished he felt able to calm some of the other man's wilder suspicions, but given all that had happened since Zavcka Klist had sat down opposite him on the train three days before, he was beginning to think Don might not be so far off the mark after all.

The spine of the Squats was a small main street that ran behind the leisure center, parallel to the boulevard. A series of narrow alleys and side roads connected the two. On the other side of the main street these byways became irregular in width, frequency, and direction. They would suddenly narrow, turn sharp corners, and dead-end, or curve around on themselves to dump the unwary visitor back onto the main street, a confused couple of blocks away from where they had just left it. Although he had seen plans of the area, Eli was grateful to have a guide.

They had exited the leisure center through a rear door that dropped them onto a small open plaza. It was almost deserted in the December chill, and after last night's rain the shaded patches were still icy underfoot. A few gems were out, mostly gillungs and heavy-labor types like Bal who were less troubled by the cold. He recognized faces from the night before, exchanged nods as they crossed the street. Most of the storefronts along it were boarded, but three or four had been repaired and opened up. One was a pub, another appeared to be a shop of some kind. The UC transport was parked in front of a third. Eli looked at it and raised an eyebrow at Donal.

"Yeh," he said. "Outreach center, tha's wha' they call it."

"I thought they had a church near here."

"They do, up a' the end o' the street." Donal nodded up the main street, away from the river. "Bu' I guess they reckoned they'd ge' more contac' wi' us if we didn' have to go there, an' there's lots o' empty space, so . . ." He shrugged.

"You were pretty down on them last night."

"Yeh. Los' my rag. I jus' think this whole fairytale o' theirs is such obvious crap. An' I've talked to enough of 'em to know they mos'ly don' really believe it themselves. Bu' they want it to be true so they keep the story goin', an' then th' godgangs crop up an' invent a version tha' they really *do* b'lieve. An' then we en' up wi' Nelson dead on the pavement, an' Callan close as dammit, an' the priest wailin' like it doan' have nothin' to do with them."

"He probably doesn't see the connection the way you do."

"He kind o' does, actually. He an' I talked a bit las' night after I calmed down. I doan' know if he's the best or th' worst of 'em, because he's a true believer as well, even though he's a decent guy. So he thinks he has a duty to keep the whole malarkey goin', even if th' godgangs are a consequence. Makes me crazy. But," he said, as they stopped at the entrance to a six-story block of apartments, "Aryel's point is that the UC, for all their flaws of logic—her term not mine—end up mos'ly tryin' to do right by us. Which is true, I can' argue with that. They're big on causes, an' right now we're it. So we need to be polite, even if mos' of us think they're a bit daft."

The identipad beeped approval and the door slid back. Donal stepped aside to let Eli go through. "Anyway, I ended up apologizin' an' agreein' to disagree, an' they're providin' transport an' all sorts for th' folks comin' in today, an' Tobias an' his bishop are goin' to be a' the Conference remindin' the faithful an' everyone else that they've got a moral duty to treat us as they would wish to be treated themselves. So really, it would be churlish to complain."

"Is that another line from Aryel?"

Donal chuckled. "Yeh. You've got her well spotted."

"She's eloquent in a way that feels like it's from another time, almost. It's a rare gift, being able to communicate the way she does."

They crossed the entrance hall to a pair of elevators. A hum of anxious conversation emanated from behind a set of double doors to their left. Donal waved at them.

"Tha's the community room for this buildin'. Been a bit fraught in there since yesterday. Mos' o' the larger blocks have one so people can hang out. Mikal's generally back there."

"This is Maryam House, isn't it? Does he live here?"

"Yeh. So does Aryel, an' Bal and Gaela o' course. I think this was the firs' one people moved into."

"Are you here as well?"

"No, I'm in a block closer to the river. Quieter."

They entered the elevator. Donal punched for the top floor and leaned back against the wall, arms folded. "You're quite taken wi' her, aren't you?"

"Who?"

"Our Aryel."

Eli took his time replying. "She fascinates me," he said finally. "I've never met anyone like her, gem or norm. I keep thinking she shouldn't be able to do what she does. It takes instinct and experience and a really broad understanding of what makes human beings tick, in addition to having the right kind of personality, to be able to—I don't want to say manipulate, that's the wrong word—to *manage* situations the way I've seen her do these past two days."

"Bein' pretty an' charmin' don't hurt."

"No. But that's another thing. Beauty affects people, it's part of our chemistry and there's no getting away from it. It's a difficult thing to measure, but everything I know, as a scientist and as a man, tells me Aryel shouldn't be beautiful. She just shouldn't. In fact she should be repellent. She's so tiny and her gemsign—whatever it is—is so huge, so warped, it should more than offset her face and her voice and all the rest of it. But it doesn't. She's lovely." He shrugged, perplexed. "Why is she lovely, Donal? How does she do it?"

Donal smirked. The doors pinged open and he led the way along a corridor. "You could ask her yoursel' if she was home, bu' I doubt you'd ge' anywhere." He nodded at a door off the corridor ahead of them. "I could tell you, but then, as the old sayin' goes, I'd have to kill you."

"You know about her."

"A few of us know a few things. I think the only person who knows everythin' abou' Aryel is Aryel." He looked thoughtfully at the locked door as they walked past it. "All I'll say is, she's no' nearly as helpless as she looks. An' what you're sensin' is part o' that."

They had reached the end of the corridor. Donal pushed open an access door, swinging it back to clamp against the wall, mounted a few metal steps and opened another door. Beyond it Eli could see gray sky. Donal cocked his head to listen. "They're there." He stepped back, letting the older man go past him. "See you later."

Eli watched him walk back toward the elevators. As he passed Aryel Morningstar's door he reached out, without pausing in his stride, and brushed the tips of his fingers along it as though touching something sacred.

He stepped out onto the roof and experienced another of the moments of dislocation that seemed to be part of the Squats experience. He was standing in an orchard. Row upon row of gnarled fruit trees marched away, rooted in deep inset troughs and espaliered along taut parallel wires that started down near his knees and ran to an arm's length above his head. A few cankered apples still clung on near him. He could have been in a garden in Kent were it not for the gravel instead of grass beneath his feet and, between the trees, glimpses of city rooftops in place of hedged fields.

Ahead he could see splashes of green low to the ground. As he wandered forward through the trees a series of raised growing beds came into view, some turned over and brown, some still covered in foliage. He heard a child's piping voice say, "He's here, Papa. I'll go and get him."

Gabriel appeared between two of the beds and ran toward him. They met where the rows of trees ended at a wide graveled pathway. The vegetable beds began on the other side of it. To his right, an area bordering the edge of the roof was enclosed by a fruit cage; ahead of him the muted sounds of machinery could be heard from a small, solidly built hut at the far end of the building; and to his left a long, narrow greenhouse shielded the beds in the middle from the wind that knifed at him where he stood on the path. Bal appeared in the doorway, his hands full of some sort of vegetable, nodded at him, and stepped back inside.

Gabriel stopped in front of him. "Hello, Dr. Walker. Do you like our garden?"

"It's amazing. I didn't expect it to be this big." He smiled down at the child. "Yes, I like it very much, Gabe. Do you?"

The boy nodded emphatically. "Yes. Papa and I come up here all the time. It's even better in the summer though, 'cos there's raspberries." He pointed over to the fruit cage. "In there."

"Mm, I love raspberries. We grow a lot of them in Scotland, where I live." He followed the child back toward the greenhouse. "What else is up here?"

"Well, not much right now. There's parsnips, and leeks, and spinach"—he was pointing them out as he went—"and there's some stuff in here." They turned the corner of a growing bed to approach the greenhouse entrance. "Papa's getting it."

"What's that?" Eli pointed at the hut with the mechanical noises.

"That's where all the water and poo and stuff gets recycled." He wrinkled his nose. "It's smelly." They stepped into the greenhouse. Bal looked up from a sink where he was rinsing soil off his hands.

"You know what else was smelly? What happened when a certain boy decided to eat every apple that fell off the trees, whether they were any good or not. Hi there." This to Eli.

"Oh yeah." Gabriel grinned. "There's apples, and pears, and plums. Too much makes you sick."

Eli grinned back. He could feel any pretense at scholarly detachment slipping away fast. The child was effortlessly charming. Gaela and Bal treated him with the relaxed, amused forbearance of parents of mischievous children the world over. The ease of it was completely seductive.

Until you recalled their histories, and realized that even without the memory of that original survey of the first residents of the Squats, something was very strange about that very naturalness. These people should not be able to have a child; he would not be this old if they had; and they should not know how to do this as well as they did.

Gabriel was shaking his head at him. "They read a lot," he said, and wandered off to peer through the plastic lid of a propagator.

"What?" Eli was sure Gabriel had just answered a question he hadn't asked. Bal walked over, drying his hands on a towel.

"Gabe, please don't do that."

"Do what? Oh," glancing at Eli, "sorry, Dr. Walker." He looked momentarily abashed. "I keep forgetting."

Eli shook his head sharply to clear it and looked at Bal. "I have a feeling I'm missing something."

The big man sighed. "Well, we might as well get this over with. We weren't sure whether to just tell you or see if you'd spot it on your own, but since Gabe is incapable of being discreet—" He shook his head, an irritated echo of Eli's confusion, and called to the boy, "Come here, you." Gabriel skipped over. "Who reads a lot?"

"You and Mama."

"And why did you tell Dr. Walker that?"

"Because he wondered."

"He wondered if we could read?"

"No, Papa." Gabriel rolled his eyes. "He wondered how come you knew how to be good parents since you didn't have any. And before that, he was looking at the garden and wondering how come we knew how to grow all the different stuff and make it so nice. He was thinking all sorts of things that were wrong."

Bal was looking at him over folded arms, a smile twitching at the corners of his mouth. "What d'you mean *we*?"

"I meant you and Aunty Wenda and Uncle Mikal and Franko and the others." He frowned at Bal. "I *do* help though, Papa."

Bal nodded amused agreement and Gabriel looked back at Eli. "There's lots and lots and *lots* of old books and vids about gardening and plumbing and having kids and all that stuff you were thinking it was strange for Mama and Papa and everyone to know about. They're always reading stuff like that."

Eli felt as though his knees were about to give way. Bal pointed wordlessly to a stool by the sink. Eli tottered over and sank onto it. Gabriel looked at him, head cocked to one side, then over at his father.

"Why does everyone think I'm impossible?"

"You're supposed to be. And you bloody well are, too, just not in the way they imagine. Now please go and pull me a couple of leeks while I make sure Dr. Walker isn't having a heart attack. Nice fat ones, and don't get covered in mud."

"Yes, Papa."

He slipped out. Bal filled a glass from an old-fashioned filter tap at the sink and handed it to Eli.

"Here."

Eli took it, gulped, and clutched it with both hands. He stared at the door through which the child had disappeared.

Bal said quietly, "Are you all right?"

Eli closed his eyes, opened them again, shook his head, and took a sip of water. His brain felt numb. Finally he looked at the other man.

"Gabriel can read minds."

Bal nodded.

"That's not possible."

Bal raised an eyebrow at him. "Really?"

"How . . . how is it possible?" He sipped again, out of nerves and shock rather than thirst. The water was ice cold. It helped him focus. "I've . . . I've never heard of such an ability, not in real life. The gem-techs said it was impossible."

"The gemtechs aren't responsible for Gabe. He's a natural child. As for how it works, we have some ideas but we're not entirely sure."

"I . . ." The questions flooded into Eli's brain. "I don't even know where to start. When did you know he could do this?"

"We were certain when he began to talk. We started to suspect from before." Bal shrugged. "He'd point at something that Gaela or I were thinking about, or he'd go and get something that one of us had moved and the other was looking for. Stuff like that."

"Does everyone here know? I mean, I hadn't heard . . . but for someone to actually have a psychic ability, it would be a sensation . . ."

"We really do *not* want that to happen." Bal spoke sharply. "Yes, people know. At first it was just close friends. More have been find-ing out recently because of stuff like what just happened with you. We're trying to get Gabe to understand there is a big difference between someone asking a question out loud and just thinking it. But unless he's paying attention he can't always tell whether he's heard a question or heard a thought."

He sighed again, gazing out the door. "Being gems, I suppose it's easier for us to take it in our stride than it is for you lot. We've been hoping people around here would just find out gradually and it wouldn't be a big deal. But he did something yesterday that a bunch of norms saw, which is partly why we decided there wasn't much point trying to hide it from you. That reporter last night had already got wind of it."

They were quiet for a while, Bal looking out at the rooftop vegetable garden and Eli staring into the water in the glass while his mind slowly reorganized itself. Finally he looked up.

"Shouldn't he be back by now?"

"I thought at him to give us a minute. You looked pretty ropy."

"I feel pretty ropy. There are things in my head he shouldn't . . . no child should . . . and in yours, and . . ."

"Don't think them," said Bal quickly. "He doesn't have access to all the contents of your brain, thankfully. He can only tell what you're actively thinking or remembering, and only if he's close by."

"Can he *send* thoughts?"

"No. It's a gift of perception, not projection. Our guess is that if he ever met someone else with the same ability they probably would be able to communicate telepathically, but until then . . ." He let it trail away, and shrugged.

"Have you ever heard of anyone else with this ability?"

"In real life? No."

"So he's unique."

"As far as we know."

"The gemtechs . . ."

"The gemtechs would love to get their hands on him." He looked over at Eli. "How're you doing? Got your head straight?"

Eli nodded, and a moment later Gabriel appeared in the doorway, three huge leeks held away from his body. Clods of earth still clung to the roots. He was scowling. "It's *cold*."

"Come on in then." Bal took the vegetables from the child and rinsed them. "Gabe, I said two."

"But you're going to ask Dr. Walker to stay for lunch."

"I still only needed two." Bal tapped the boy lightly on his sandy-brown head with the heel of the unwanted leek. "Eli, would you like to stay for lunch?"

18

THE MORE MAC THOUGHT ABOUT THE PLAN THE BETTER HE LIKED IT. IT FELT right, as though the angel of the Lord moved among them, touching his comrades with the same vision and boldness that had first been vouchsafed to him. It had been John's inspiration this time, and he was confident, certain. He knew the ways of the misbelievers well, and he had been the lookout when they had found the gembashed reporter with the hidden vidcam. So John could not have been identified, and he had come up with a way to turn his past mistakes to advantage. No one knew where he had gone when he left them; he should have no trouble being accepted again among the misbelievers.

His own face stared out at him from every newstream they checked. So did that of the preacher, although his was an enhanced still from the vid and not nearly as recognizable as the police mug shot of Mac. Still, he worried about the preacher far more than he did about himself. It would be difficult to do God's work, finding and fortifying the faithful, if he was not free to travel.

Mac's task, on the other hand, was to lead the battle. He did not need to move until it was time to strike. They had found a safe place to hide in the meantime, an empty suite of offices to which one of their number had access. But strike they must, which meant continuing to find ways to hurt and expose the enemy. The tactics of the past two nights, hunting for stragglers in the late-night streets around the Squats, would be anticipated now. Even without the constant streamed assurances from the police, Mac knew enough about their ways to know they would focus their efforts on preventing any more of the same type of attack.

But they were notoriously bad at anticipating anything new. That was why this could work. The streams were full of praise for the misbelievers, full of the mealymouthed priest promising safe passage and solace, full of images of their gem-ferrying vehicles and unconsecrated churches and sap-faced volunteers. Aryel Morningstar had been back on again, full of thanks for the staunch friendship of the misbelievers and those they attracted. They had made the mistake of thinking they were secure in their Squats, protected by authorities both profane and divine. All they had done was point the way to an open back door.

To use a route made by those who had strayed from the true path, invade the sanctuary of the evil ones, bait the Beast in his own den—that, they would not expect.

Aryel met him as he came into the leisure center from the plaza that faced the main street. She was escorting a pair of new arrivals back from reception, along with the gillung woman Eli had spoken to the night before. With her preternaturally long torso and preposterously short legs wrapped in an ankle-length oilskin coat, the woman appeared to glide rather than walk.

One of the newcomers was a handsome, willowy youth with a bruise under one eye, ordinary black hair pulled back in a ponytail, and long, elegant, seven-fingered hands. His companion was a blond girl who clung to one of them, with no gemsign that Eli could see. A battered guitharp case hung from the boy's back. They looked scared, tired, and not a day older than eighteen.

"Don't worry about it. Honestly. You're both very welcome," Aryel was saying. She caught Eli's eye and asked him to wait with a flick of her own. "Gaela wondered why you were reluctant to come before." This to the boy. "I wish we'd known, we could have told you it wouldn't be a problem. Just relax, get settled in, and get some rest. Lapsa will show you the way."

She nodded to the gillung woman and smiled at the boy and girl as Lapsa pushed open the door to the plaza. The girl still looked anxious. Aryel said, "It'll be *fine*. I promise," and she finally sent a timid smile back. Aryel waved good-bye to them through the door and turned back to Eli with a sigh.

"New neighbors?"

"Yes. He's been getting roughed up for a while, apparently, but they didn't think it would be okay for them to come here."

"Why not?"

"His girlfriend's a norm." She waited for his reaction. He raised an eyebrow.

"Blimey. They're pretty young to be that controversial."

"I think they're so young all they know how to be is in love. They didn't understand how difficult it would be, but they've been learning fast. He's definitely not welcome in her family—I'm not sure they're even speaking to her anymore—and they were certain we wouldn't want her here. Things were getting desperate, they had to barricade themselves into their apartment last night with people shouting and crashing things against the door all night long. We heard about it and got in touch and he finally let us know what the problem was. We sent for them straightaway, but they've spent so much time convinced it would be an issue wherever they went they still can't quite believe it's not."

"And it really isn't?"

"Not here. I know some groups feel differently, but when we made the Squats our home we made a commitment not to exclude anyone." She looked up at Eli with smiling eyes. "I hear you've just enjoyed one of our seminal experiences."

Eli glanced around to make sure no one was in earshot. "What, having my mind read by a five-year-old?"

"Gabriel needs to learn to be a bit less generous with his talent. No, I meant Bal's cooking."

"Oh." He smiled back. "That was one of the best meals I've had. Ever."

It had been, too. Gaela had met them at the entrance to the roof, taken the situation in with a glance, rolled her eyes in exasperation, and relieved Bal of the leeks and the final few minutes of scolding. Gabriel's apologies were so funny that by the time they got to the apartment Eli's amusement had outrun his shock. They had sat in the kitchen and talked about the garden, the library, and most of all how they had trained themselves to parenthood and worked out how to adapt what they learned to accommodate Gabriel's ability. Eli noticed, because he was looking for it, that the conversation managed not to include any indication of when this had happened.

All the while Bal was peeling, chopping, and assembling various ingredients in various pans. Gabriel sat on the floor, building an elaborate, branching tower from colored blocks, and from time to time interrupting the grown-ups with observations that Eli thought were as trenchant as they were hilarious. In what seemed like no time at all the rooftop forage had been transformed into steaming platters, delicately scented and delicious. Eli was dumbstruck.

"You *cannot* have learned to cook like this from books. Can you?"

Bal chuckled. "Not entirely. Back in Bhutan we used to take turns, and I always liked it. We didn't have much variety but they were letting us access pre-Syndrome archives by then, so I got into the habit of looking up whether any of the stuff in the mountains around us was edible and what you could do with it. That got me into databases of recipes, and they link to lots of old television programs about food and cooking. So I ended up doing more and more of it. When I came to London and met Gaela and we finally found this place, I used the same resources to figure out how to restore the garden."

He shrugged. "Gabriel's right, you know." He dropped his voice to a stage whisper. "But don't tell him I said so." The boy giggled.

"Almost anything you need to know about anything is in a book or a vid archive somewhere. So what if it's mostly pre-Syndrome? So are these buildings, so is all of our nonorganic technology."

"What's nonorganic?" piped Gabriel.

Gaela explained. Bal pitched in with examples. Gabriel fired questions at them until he was satisfied. They weathered the onslaught with practiced fortitude as Eli thought back to the pre-Syndrome family vids he had seen. It was not, perhaps, so surprising that this household was the very picture of loving, engaged, tolerant parents and precocious, inquisitive, confident childhood.

Now Aryel was looking at him, all sky-blue eyes over a knowing smile.

"So what's the verdict? Happy, healthy, well-fed family with just a bit of an interesting twist?" The blue gaze turned penetrating. "Or do you still think there's something there you need to worry about?"

"I think there's a lot to worry about," he said carefully. "Bal and Gaela are already concerned about the impact of Gabriel's ability. They're trying to both ensure he's properly socialized *and* shield him from notice by the outside world. That's not a sustainable situation."

"We know."

"I really like them. And I realize now that they—and you—must trust me to have allowed me to learn what I have about Gabe. I'm flattered by that. I'm touched. But I have to wonder why. When we first met you stressed to me how much gems value whatever privacy they can get. Gaela and Bal have just relinquished theirs, and their son's. I don't believe they would have done that—I don't think you would have advised them to do it—without a very good reason."

The smile had slowly faded as he spoke. Now the lips were a firm line, and the blue eyes were serious.

"What might that reason be, do you think?"

"I think you are concerned you might someday need someone like me to vouch for the health, the *normalcy*, of that family. And as I said, I wonder why."

She sighed. "He did say you were smart."

"Who did?"

"Gabe. When he first saw you, at reception a couple of days ago. That was his immediate impression."

"Again, I'm flattered."

"What did you think when you first saw him?"

"That he must have joined the Squats community recently. Otherwise I would have been aware of the family."

"And then?"

"And then I checked the datastreams and discovered that he and his parents have in fact lived in the Squats for at least a year and a half. Very odd. I thought I had a better memory."

"I believe Sally Trieve had a similar experience."

"I believe she did."

"And what do you think now that you've spent time with him?"

"That he doesn't seem to have many points of reference that predate the Declaration. That he learned to speak after he was already living here, which would suggest he started quite late. And that he's a bright, sweet kid with great parents."

They had wandered away from the entrance, Eli had thought quite randomly, to avoid being overheard. But now Aryel pushed open a door and led the way into a small office. She pulled her tablet out of her cloak and slid it into a dock. The larger screen on the desk lit up. She dropped onto a knee-seat that appeared to have been specially adapted for her and waved him to a regular chair. She sat there for a moment, elbows on desk and chin on hands, thinking, before she looked up at Eli again.

"Well, this is a week for conundrums, so let me pose you another one. Do you think the end can justify the means? That it's acceptable to do something that would otherwise be wrong, in order to achieve a greater good?"

He had asked virtually the same question the day before, in relation to Zavcka Klist and her rumored proposal. Once again Aryel Morningstar seemed to see right through him and pull his confusions to the surface.

"I think we would all say there are circumstances where that could be true."

"Would the protection of a child be among those circumstances?"

"Aryel, you're leading me into a trap. If I don't have any more information then of course the answer has to be yes." He spread his hands. "But it's not enough. What is the child being protected from? The authorities wouldn't just stand by and allow a gem child to be harmed, not anymore. So why this elaborate subterfuge?"

"You shared something very disturbing with me when you showed me the Bel'Natur report. You trusted me to understand what a difficult position it put you in, and the difficult decisions it might require you to make. Now I'm afraid I'm going to do much the same to you."

She tapped the tablet, entered a code, and leaned forward for a retinal scan. Eli's eyebrows shot up.

"Yes, another high-security vid documenting the abuse of a child. Not as gruesome as yours, and you already know the story has a happier ending. Or perhaps I should say a happy middle. We don't know the ending yet."

The image came on blurred and tilted, with Aryel's voice in the background. *Gaela, we need to record this. Before you clean him up any more, we'll need to be able to prove how he was when you found him.*

The vidcam righted and focused, with Bal's voice now. *She's right, honey. I'm just going to set it here, out of the way.*

Then the blur that must have been Bal moved aside and Eli started. A thin, naked boy-child, half-covered in a wrapping of blankets and what looked like black plastic, sat on an ottoman that Eli recognized from Bal and Gaela's apartment. Instead of sandy brown, his hair was a glowing royal blue. He was shaking, bruised, and dirty, and his eyes darted from one adult to another like an animal caught in a cage. There were tearstains on his cheeks, and he huddled toward Gaela. She knelt behind him, holding him in her arms, with an expression on her face that Eli thought would make an army throw down its weapons and beg for mercy on the spot. She held a cloth in one hand, and a basin of what looked like water rested on the floor beside her.

Are you still thirsty? Do you want some more to drink?

The child who barely resembled the Gabriel he knew was nodding dumbly and she held a cup to his lips. He drank thirstily. *Bal, he's going to need some more.*

Bal moved to get it.

The boy began nodding again a moment before Gaela asked, *Are you hungry, sweetie?*

Okay, we'll get you something to eat right away. Can you talk to us, sweetie? Can you tell us your name?

The boy was already shaking his head. On the vid, Aryel's frown deepened. Eli glanced over at her. There was an echo of the same frown on her face now.

Gaela fed another cup of whatever Bal had concocted to the child, whispering soothingly all the while. *Don't be scared, sweetheart. We won't hurt you. No one here will hurt you. You're safe now. You're safe, it's going to be all right.*

Gaela? Aryel spoke very quietly. *Stop speaking. Just think it.*

Gaela looked up. *What?*

Just for a few minutes.

Why? Gaela looked to Bal, but he was looking at Aryel and nodding. *Let's all just think it.*

The vid went quiet then, Gaela holding and rocking the child while she gently sponged dirt and tears off his face, Bal and Aryel watching intently. In her office, in the present, Aryel sighed and explained how Gaela had found him.

"She called Bal and he called me. It was late at night, so no one saw them bringing him inside."

"Why didn't you call the police? Take him to hospital?"

"Because of this next bit. I'll explain as we go."

The child had stopped shivering and sank into Gaela's arms, eyes half-closed. He kept squinting at her hair, and his fingers reached up and twined around it. Bal said quietly, *He seems to have got the message.* He looked at Gaela. *He's hearing things we're not saying.*

Her eyes went wide for a moment. Then she looked down at him, her brows creasing in concentration. The boy pushed down on the stuff that still entangled his legs. Gaela helped as he kicked himself clear. She looked up at Bal and Aryel. *I thought it was time to get him out of that stuff.*

Aryel nodded. *Very good.*

But his hair, Aryel. It's wrong. It's not real. And I don't see any other gemsign, do you?

No. Hang on. Her face on the vid went still for a moment. The boy looked over at her, a puzzled expression flitting across his own. It was the first hint Eli had seen of the curious child he had just spent a couple of hours with.

I don't think he knows what a gem is.

Eli's jaw dropped. Next to him Aryel began a quiet commentary as on the vid the child they would decide to call Gabriel was gently sponge-bathed, wrapped in a clean, soft blanket, and fed. Along the way the vidcam was moved in to capture the marks they found on his body: tiny burns at the temples, strap lines at the wrists and ankles, needle marks inside the elbows and on the buttocks. There were larger bruises on his upper arms that looked like fingerprints, and one on his cheek that looked like a slap. Eli felt sick to the stomach. The rape and murder of the young girl on the Bel'Natur vid had been infinitely more horrific, but this was heart-wrenching in a different way. This was a child he knew.

"He couldn't speak for days," Aryel said. "Dehydration, shock, and drugs too we think, to keep him quiet. Language came back to him, but no memory of who he was or what had happened to him. Which I think is a mercy."

"Does he actually believe he's Gaela and Bal's child? Doesn't he remember being found?"

"It's the oldest proper memory he has. Anything before that is just an impression, very vague. And he doesn't like trying to remember. It really upsets him. He knows that his life didn't start last winter in a happy home in the Squats with Mama Gaela and Papa Bal, but as far as he's concerned that's the only part he wants to think about. He's recovered extremely well, as you've seen. I think that's partly due to extraordinary resilience—we're seeing that again now, in the way he deals with the things he's picking up from the minds around him—but also because he hasn't been forced to try to recollect his past."

"I still don't understand why you didn't call the police. Find who did this to him. Get him professional help."

"Because we did find out who did it to him. We found out that very night. This was right after the Declaration, remember, and we didn't yet know whether the authorities would properly investigate the abuse of gem children. But we knew *we* would. And there were things about him that just didn't fit, that we wanted to understand."

"Such as?"

"Such as that despite his astonishing ability, he looks and acts just like a norm child. His hair had been dyed, and he had no other identifiers."

"So, he's unengineered and therefore lacks gemsign. A natural child." Which was what Bal had said.

"Yes, but. A naturally conceived gem child would have gem parents, and as you saw, he didn't seem to be familiar with gems at all. He was fascinated by Gaela's hair, and Bal's, and—" She jerked a thumb over her shoulder to indicate the swollen structure of her back. "When he caught sight of himself in a mirror you could see he was baffled, and scared. He didn't know who was looking back at him. We think he was sedated when they dyed his hair. Now a gemtech would have had no qualms about removing him from his parents as an infant, but where could they have kept him that he never saw or learned about other gems? And why?

"So we asked a friend who has a particular gift for navigating the streams to help us work out where an unmarked gem child who'd never seen another gem might have come from. Our plan at that point was just to try to get a bit of information ahead of reporting it because we knew that once we did, it would be very hard to do our own kind of digging. Gaela and Bal had already decided they were going to ask if they could foster him, which in the chaos of the Declaration and the government having to take over the crèches might well have been approved. But what we discovered changed our minds, Eli. And it brings us right back to your old friends at Bel'Natur."

19

One Year On: Whatever happened to Henderson?

"ONE YEAR ON" IS A SERIES OF RETROSPECTIVES TO
MARK THE FIRST ANNIVERSARY OF THE DECLARATION
OF THE PRINCIPLES OF HUMAN FRATERNITY

Register for expert opinion and analysis
Autofeed @Observer.eu/commentary/Declaration_GenPhen_Henderson/
2212131AS

For all the scandalous tales that emerged from within the gem-techs' GMH laboratories, dormitories, and indenture pools prior to the suspension of those institutions, it is worth remembering that many of the most egregious abuses were not uncovered until after the Declaration. The case of Nicholas Henderson and the GenPhen Laboratory in Essex is a sobering example, and should give pause to those pundits who advocate a return to reduced governmental regulation and oversight of bio-industrialist practices.

GenPhen was an ostensibly independent facility which conducted specialist research, testing and genome analysis. That the Bel'Natur conglomerate was by far its largest client has led to speculation that GenPhen was in fact a secret subsidiary of Bel'Natur, useful for keeping some of its more unsavory practices at arm's length while at the same time gathering confidential information on competitors' projects. Bel'Natur has always strongly denied this, pointing to the wide range of services offered by GenPhen, including gene scans for private clients unconnected with the human modification industry.

They claim that GenPhen was repeatedly selected by middle managers at Bel'Natur because of its exemplary track record in the early verification of highly engineered sensory and cognitive abilities, and have acknowledged only a failure on the part of these relatively low-ranking department heads to ensure that corporate welfare standards were adhered to. It was well known that lab director Dr. Nick Henderson had a seemingly unparalleled ability to accurately identify the expression of supernormal capacities in even very young children. It was something for which GenPhen was known and admired within the human gemtech industry, and gem children as young as three were sent to Henderson for testing.

The details of how he achieved such stellar results emerged shortly after the Declaration. Henderson and most of his staff had already disappeared by then; while several staff members have since been located and arrested, Henderson himself has never been found.

Contrary to popular belief, genetype alone cannot predict with 100 percent accuracy the degree to which the supernormal abilities engineered into a genome will actually be expressed. Time and extensive testing is required to determine what the engineered individual is truly capable of. This period of a gem's life was one of investigative and commercial dormancy for gemtechs, while they waited for the natural progression from infancy through early and into middle childhood. Obviously the sooner they could determine the success—or otherwise—of their efforts, the shorter the research cycle and the more cost-effective the end products.

It is only fair to recall at this point that the rampant abuse and neglect that had formerly characterized gemtech crèches had been addressed and significantly reduced by the time of the Declaration. For the most part what the health and social services were confronted with when they finally took full control of the crèches was less the fallout from overt physical and psychological damage than the passivity, depression and emotional isolation of children who had never been shown affection or given individual attention for their own sakes. However, a significant cohort of children who did exhibit signs of psychological, and in some cases physical, trauma were discovered to have one thing in common— they had undergone testing at GenPhen.

As the children's histories were collated and studied, a pattern of systematic abuse emerged. Photographic records compiled at intake documented fading evidence of physical restraint and injury, including in some cases what appeared to be electrode burns. The accompanying medical records indicated the use of pharmaceuticals both to facilitate testing and, apparently, to induce memory loss of the testing process itself—chemical cleansing as a substitute for parental care or professional therapy. Full or partial amnesia was the most ubiquitous characteristic of the GenPhen test subjects, and the one which initially caught the attention of the authorities.

When faced with this evidence Bel'Natur and other gemtech clients denied all knowledge of GenPhen's practices and joined the chorus of condemnation of Nicholas Henderson. While there appears to have been a widespread conviction among GenPhen employees that Henderson took orders from somewhere "higher up," no one knows who this ultimate boss may have been. Any evidence of links to a parent entity is protected by Dubai corporate registration. When police raided the lab three weeks after the Declaration, they found it deserted. Both on-site and remote datastream archives had been wiped. A year-long, worldwide manhunt for Henderson has failed to turn up a single lead.

Ultimate culpability has therefore never been established. The only records of what Nicholas Henderson did to helpless children, and why, reside in incomplete crèche intake files, the fractured memories of the children themselves, and the reluctant testimony of former associates. They claim that Henderson personally oversaw the care and medication of the children, and conducted the more extreme testing without assistance and in secrecy. While undoubtedly self-serving, without Henderson himself this assertion cannot be disproved.

To those who protest that such behavior, while regrettable, simply reflected the zeitgeist of the time, it should be made clear that it continued until at least a month prior to the Declaration. By then public and political opinion had turned firmly against the excesses of the gemtech industry, which claimed, loudly and falsely, that it had listened and learned. Indeed, one of the most disturbing aspects of the GenPhen scandal was the rumor circulating among several of the lab's employees that there may have been a child undergoing testing right up to the date of the Declaration.

A police investigation concluded that this rumor was unlikely to be true. As soon as the correlation was made between the amnesiac, abused children in crèche and the GenPhen facility, the inventories of GenPhen's clients were cross-checked against crèche rosters, and the whereabouts of all children were verified. The police are therefore inclined to discount the tale as an invention by those under scrutiny themselves, in order to appear cooperative or to deflect attention from their own abuses. One must hope most fervently that they are correct. If not, then the mystery child disappeared along with Nick Henderson. If he existed, his fate does not bear imagining.

The GenPhen scandal is just one of many that came to light only when the autonomy of the gemtechs was finally and fully rescinded. It was neither the first nor the worst example of their callous disregard for the safety, health or welfare of their human products, but it is a signal reminder to the rest of us of the dangers of an unregulated, arrogant, greedy industry.

Unless and until Henderson is captured, the full, dreadful extent of GenPhen's institutionalized child abuse may never be known. However, if those who call for a repeal or restriction of the Declaration have their way, it might be repeated.

Zavcka Klist read the *Observer* article with bone-cracking anger. The GenPhen affair had been little more than a wavelet in the flood of scandals that had accompanied the Declaration. She had worked hard to keep it that way, her own hunt for Henderson as much about finding him first to prevent him from being found by others as finding out what he had done with the child. She no longer needed him for that. But now their ability to reclaim the boy had been fatally compromised.

The rumor had never been made public before. She was sure of it, had made sure of it. In fact there was a lot in the piece that had not made it into previous newstream coverage. It was no secret where the *Observer*'s editorial team stood on the gem issue, but they rather pompously refused to engage in the often questionable tactics that led to scoops and exposés, tending instead to opine with righteous indignation on the findings of others. But this commentary was based on more than year-old snippets from public police briefings. Someone must have passed them a file.

She considered the options and concluded that it did not, after all, have much immediate significance, beyond the obvious negative publicity. Unless and until her proposal formed the basis for future legislation on gem rights, they would not be able to make use of the boy anyway. It would therefore not be worth the trouble of trying to claim him publicly, or the risk of attempting a retrieval. Not with him safely sequestered in the heart of the Squats. No, the best course would be to wait until the new, more regulated, more transparent, more humane, and infinitely more profitable indenture infrastructure was put in place.

Then she would do a deal with Biomin to acquire Bal's contract, a goodwill gesture demonstrating their commitment to keeping couples and families together. Maybe buy them all up, this little knot of rebels that appeared to have formed a pseudo-family around the boy. Forget the rights that had been signed over by his birth parents a year ago, before they abandoned him and fled. Rely instead on the ones she was creating for the future.

She would have to explain this to Felix. Rewrite his notes. Make sure he understood the significance of this development.

She messaged public relations with instructions not to respond to the piece beyond a reiteration, if necessary, of their previous denials. Then she turned her attention to the core business of ensuring the optimum environment for the proposal itself.

Despite her assurances to Felix, she was not at all sanguine about sailing through on the back of Eli Walker's report. Bel'Natur's proposition would, she was sure, go far beyond anything he would be prepared to support. He had said he'd shared their analysis and vids of the murder with the authorities, but she thought he would have done so cagily, mitigating the immediate, visceral response. She needed to bring that back, use the raw, shrieking horror of it to slam home the necessity for segregation and control until they could be absolutely, completely sure of each and every gem.

Such a commercially damaging revelation, delivered with their own breast-baring mea culpas, would position Bel'Natur as the ultimate honest brokers. Reformed characters. A giant brought low, humbled and contrite and ready to serve.

As long as none of the rogue elements came home to roost. There were too many, and she put down another surge of anger, this time at herself for having allowed so many plates to simultaneously spin. Still, the risks were minimal. No one save Henderson and the parents knew of their connection to the child, and it suited neither to surface. The fake gems had been shaved, equipped with facial prosthetics and dispatched to a comfortable retirement abroad. Their handler also would never have to work again.

The preacher had disappeared, and she could only hope he had the sense to stay that way.

They had to wait at reception for another set of refugees to be registered, assigned housing, and introduced to an escort who could guide them to it. John could not quite believe that even among the misbelievers and the abominations this was considered acceptable, that actual humans should have to cool their heels while a giant-size, lizard-eyed, demon-clawed monstrosity fussed over a pair of puce-haired goblins. But Tobias only smiled and nodded and stood back, for all the world as though it were normal behavior, and John could do nothing but follow suit.

It was an opportunity to learn, he told himself, and tried to listen in. But his confidence was shaken by the sense he had of being the alien, a lone and vulnerable intruder into hostile territory. It was the overwhelming ratio of gems to norms, and the easy way they inhabited the space. As another volunteer had walked him from the church to the outreach center, he had seen more and more of them, bustling about as if they owned the place. They had set up shops, they were milling around the entrances of buildings, they were strolling down to the river in a brief spell of weak winter sunshine. Some of them glanced at the two norms in their midst, even nodding in a familiar way to his companion, but most ignored them completely.

The lack of deference, even of notice, was like a slap in the face. It was as though they really imagined, actually *believed*, that they had some sort of rights here, some kind of status. If anyone out there in the sheltered, unthinking, let's-all-get-along world needed a reality check, he thought, this was it. He and his comrades were being denounced by every politician, priest, media channel and social-stream philosopher, but they all needed to get wise to what it was they were really fighting against. The possibility—no, probability—that if matters were allowed to proceed unchecked, one day *everywhere* would be like this.

Another vexation was the name he heard over and over as he delved deeper into the Squats. *Nelson.* It whispered and echoed from the snatches of conversation he caught among the gems on the street. His guide had intoned it, going on and on about the sweet, gentle nature of the victim, the cruel irony of his having been one of the first true converts from the Squats and how that made the murder a double tragedy. It had been the first thing Tobias referred to when they were introduced. He assumed Nelson was the inspiration that had sent John back to the arms of the UC. Which was not entirely incorrect, but it was still sickening to hear the mewling, lemon-headed coward spoken of in such glowing terms. Like he was actually important. And now there was the name again, flickering across the public-notice surface of the reception desk. A funeral, three days hence, on the quayside. Tobias would officiate at some sentimental parody of a true Christian burial.

I did it, John thought. *It was me and Mac and Simon that tipped him over the edge. I'm here to tip you over a bigger one. Stupid, unnatural bastards. If you only knew.* The thought gave him strength and renewed his sense of conviction, and he clung to it like a mantra.

The two at the desk retrieved their tablets, now linked to the local network, and waddled off behind another freak, a female gillung who looked like one of the gray seals John remembered from childhood trips to the seaside. He swallowed hard to keep the bile down as Tobias stepped forward, and steeled himself to look at the giant gem as he was introduced.

"John used to be a member of one of our sister parishes, over in Ealing," Tobias was explaining, polite as you please. "He's been away for a while but recent events have brought him back to us." He smiled benevolently at John, who nodded and tried to smile back. "He's made himself available over the next few days and we've put him on the rotation, but I thought I'd bring him over to meet you since he's new and I won't be here tomorrow."

Mikal eyed him thoughtfully. For one panicked moment John thought he was going to stick out that twisted travesty of a hand and knew that he would be unable to bring himself to shake it. But Mikal merely thanked him and glanced back down at his tablet.

"We may get a few more arrivals tomorrow, but it won't be anything like today," he said. His voice was deep and sonorous and a bit nasal, as though it had traveled miles up from the seat of his chest but been caught in a bottleneck on the way out. "And we've got a good system set up for that now. We'll still need to make sure anyone who has to travel is safe, but I think the main thing will be to help people settle in and make sure they have what they need. We'll be getting supplies distributed to the main residential blocks, so if you could help us with that?"

"Of . . . of course," John managed. "Sure. Whatever." He swallowed again. It was hard to actually speak to it, harder still to feel he was accepting instructions, almost impossible to request them. But he had volunteered for this and he had to make it work. "Where should I go, what time?"

"Come here, whenever's convenient for you. Someone's always around, and the police are based in there." He nodded at a door and raised his voice slightly. "Gaela?"

A flame-haired woman stuck her head around the door. "Yeah? Hey, Tobias."

Tobias raised a hand in greeting as Mikal said, "This is John. New volunteer, he'll be helping out tomorrow." He blinked that toe-curling, double-lidded blink.

"Oh," she said. "Great. Hi, John. Thanks. Welcome aboard." She looked him up and down, nodded to Mikal, and disappeared back into the room.

John knew who this was. She was the one who could see like an animal, who had sent the poor guy from last night out into the storm to be set upon by her kindred, and then lied about it. And been believed. The credulity of his own kind was sometimes hard to fathom.

Beside him, Tobias winced. Mikal chuckled. "Don't take it personally. Previous errors make future mirrors."

"Oh, I know. Quite right," Tobias returned. John realized with a start that the woman had just scanned him.

He almost lost it then, mouth opening for an instinctive protest. But Mikal was looking over his head, and Tobias turned, and John caught himself in time and turned as well.

Aryel Morningstar was coming toward them, her massive black cloak swaying as she moved. Beside her walked a tallish man with slightly graying hair who looked rumpled and a bit tired and altogether ordinary. John thought he had seen him somewhere, recently, might even know his name. But he had a sense that the setting had been very different, and he could not think who the man was.

They appeared to be nearing the end of a deep, quiet conversation. The man was nodding earnestly. John caught the words "Don't worry," and then Aryel looked up, saw Tobias and him, and changed the direction of what had been a stroll toward the exit. There was a flurry of greetings, Tobias murmuring, "John, new volunteer," again, him nodding dumbly again, and then the man was saying good-bye.

Gaela's head reappeared around the door. "You off?"

"Yes. Thanks again. I didn't realize you'd be back at work."

"Not for long. Just finishing up a couple of things before tomorrow."

Mikal looked up from his tablet. "Driver's out front, Eli."

"Thanks. You're sure it isn't a problem?"

"*No.*" It came out as a chorus from Mikal, Tobias, and Aryel Morningstar. She laughed. It was, John thought vaguely, through the dread that pressed in on him, a strangely appealing sound.

"It absolutely is not. We've got the most efficient transit service in the city at the moment." She slipped her hand under the man's arm to walk him to the door and cocked her head at Gaela. "Got a minute?"

"Sure."

As the double doors swung closed behind the three of them, John had to muster all his self-control to prevent a fit of trembling. He rubbed sweaty palms inside the pockets of his coat. Here was further proof, as if he needed it, of how deceitful the system was, how degenerate those it appointed. Mac would be glad to know this, but not surprised.

Eli Walker. He had been in the background of the newscast last night, would be in the spotlight at the Conference tomorrow. He was the one who had been entrusted to convey the truth, but instead, like all the others, would choose to lie.

They stood on the dank sidewalk and watched the car drive away up the decrepit old avenue. Gaela shivered a little in a keen wind that whipped up from the river and cut right through her coat. Aryel stood still, impassive and apparently warm enough in her cloak.

"You told him," Gaela said.

"Yes."

"All of it?"

"Almost all."

They turned, walking slowly down toward the water. Gaela drummed her fingers softly as they passed the stubby cable box behind which she had found her son, a year ago on another cold winter's evening.

"Was that necessary?"

"It was a lesser risk than leaving him with only what he already knew."

"What did he . . . ?"

"He was shocked. Horrified. He's still not convinced that we shouldn't have gone straight to the police, but he understands now why we didn't. He made the connection to Henderson before I got there, by the way."

"Speaking of which."

Aryel raised an eyebrow at her.

"Interesting piece on the *Observer* stream today."

"Ah, yes. Timely, don't you think?"

"Aryel, you know how much we trust you but this is getting fucking scary."

"Herran laid a few breadcrumbs. They didn't even know they were following them."

"Did you tell Eli about Herran as well?"

"No, and he didn't ask. Doesn't need to, really. He's bright enough to figure out that if we found something no one else did, we must have a capability no one else has. And he and Sally already knew the archives were fixed."

Gaela squeezed her eyes shut. Even on the quiet, quickly darkening street it felt as if she were trying to process too many inputs; as if every facet that danced off the river in front of them was a weakness, another way into the refuge they had built for themselves. She blinked back tears and thought a headache might be coming on.

"So yet another of the things we were trying to prevent is compromised. Knowing about Gabe is a straight line to knowing about Herran. Know about Herran, and you know that we poor, defenseless, coded, cataloged gems might have a dangerous talent or two that didn't make it into the brochure. Know that and you might decide the answer is more control, not less. Make *that* mistake—"

"Gaela, calm down."

"I'm sorry." She wiped a hand across her face and sniffed. "It just feels like it's all so close to unraveling. I like Eli. Gabe says we can trust him. If it was all up to him I think we'd be okay. But it isn't, Aryel. He's just one man. What can he do in the end?"

"One man can make an army. And Eli Walker is not the only weapon in our arsenal." They had reached the river and stood side by side on the quay, gazing at the ripples that spread and clashed and merged in the coal-gray water.

Aryel reached for Gaela's hand, clasped and held it tight.

"I know you're scared for Gabe. So am I. And I'm scared for you, and for Herran, and for the rest of us. I don't have the luxury of worrying only about one extraordinary child. There are compromises I might have to make in order to protect us all. But no matter what happens, I promise you, Gaela—I swear on my life—that I will keep him safe."

—— = DAY FIVE = ——

20

ELI WOKE TO AN INCESSANT, UNPLEASANT BUZZING. THE ROOM WAS STILL dark. He had been in a sleep of such deep and complete exhaustion that as he floundered blearily for the surface he could not for several long seconds recall who or where he was, or what the sound was that hummed repeatedly through the room. A fire alarm? Wake-up call? But then the lights would have come on. Lights. He fumbled for the button beside his bed. The blackness receded into gray, and his disorientation resolved.

He did remember, for the most fleeting of moments, that he had been dreaming about forgetfulness. Then the memory of the dream slipped away and he reached over and grabbed his tablet. It was flashing Rob's comcode. He flicked to receive, noting from the timestamp that he should have had at least another hour's sleep.

"What's the matter? Didn't it upload?" The last thing he had done was send his report to the Conference datastream.

"What? Oh god, I don't know. There's been another one." Rob looked as if he had been woken up only slightly less recently and stopped being sick just long enough to call.

"Another . . . ?" Then Eli got it. "Oh no. Oh *shit. How?* Someone went out?"

Every gem registered in London had been contacted and advised to stay indoors after dark. Employers had been asked to accommodate changes in schedule, and escorts had been offered to those for whom evening travel could not be avoided. Eli had nervously monitored the streams until the early hours of the morning and fallen asleep relieved that tonight, at least, appeared to be quiet.

"Someone *was* out. Looks like it was one of the gems from the employment center brawl."

"Where?" And then, with a sinking certainty of the answer, "Is he—or she—"

"He. In the financial district. They threw him off a thirty-story tower."

"Oh *god.*" Eli fumbled for his pants. "When? Does Aryel . . . ?"

"She knows, she's on her way. I'm heading there too. No need for you to come, but I thought I should let you know before some journo called up looking for a comment."

"Thanks." Eli slumped back onto the bed, tablet resting on his knees. "Did it just happen?"

"About half an hour ago. Security vidcams caught part of it, seems like it was a hell of a fight. They jumped two of them. The other one—the woman—got away, but not before they'd fought back hard enough to kill two of the godgang."

"Oh. Fuck." Eli dropped his head in his hands and let the import of that crash against him. "The rest?"

"Gone. They broke into an office building with one of those viewing terraces, chucked the one they'd caught off it, and were back down and out before the police arrived. Left their dead behind."

"Two norms. Not that many tears will be shed for them, but holy shit."

"Yeah. Self-defense and all that, just like before, but there were two gems with no weapons as far as we know, and maybe fifteen norms with clubs and knives, so . . ." Rob trailed off.

"That ratio's going to get a lot of attention."

"Probably." On the tablet's screen Rob finished contorting himself into a jacket. "Listen, I've got to go. I'd say turn your alerts off and get some more sleep but that's not bloody likely, is it? Sorry."

"Can I help?"

"Just be ready for the Conference. Four hours from now you're going to be starring as the voice of reason, and I think you're going to have to shout pretty loud."

Masoud and Gaela walked the route of the battle, sidestepping splashes of blood, discarded weapons, and sheeted bodies. White-suited technicians swarmed over the crime scene. The building was lit up inside and out. They could see tiny figures moving on the terrace that wrapped around the roof.

"I should have worked it out," he said. "Christ. What an idiot. Shit always happens where you're not looking for it."

"How could you have guessed they'd be here? Either of them?"

"Because this is one of the few places in the city that's deserted after dark. No one lives here. Perfect place to hide out." He gestured to the towering buildings around them. "We discounted it because of all the activity during the day. But there's lots of empty offices, even whole pre-Syndrome buildings that haven't been brought back into use."

He nodded at a discarded bag of provisions, contents spilling out, stamped and smashed into the dirty rime of frost on the pavement. "Looks like one or the other went out to get supplies. My guess is the gems, since there were only the two of them."

"The group could've split up."

"True. But the godgang were out in force, which doesn't seem like a grocery run. Which raises the question, where were they all going at that hour? Not to the Squats."

"What about the meeting place you located yesterday? It's close by."

"Newhope Tower," Masoud said, and frowned. "Over there. Very close." He pointed at the steel-colored shard, a darker gray against the lightening sky. "But that's a hell of a risk to take. I mean they were all together anyway, why go to a public place?"

"New recruits?" Aryel suggested. "Supporters? Suppliers?" They had returned to where she waited, shrouded in her cloak, next to a police transport.

"Maybe. But if they're using a private stream to coordinate movements they could have arranged to meet somewhere with no history. Less chance we'd have it under surveillance."

"Places can be important," she observed. "Symbolic. The UC have their churches, from which the godgangs are excluded. Maybe their meeting places assume a similar significance."

"They've definitely got some fixation on heights," Masoud said thoughtfully. "The Newhope terrace is eight hundred feet up. You might have something there." He sighed and gestured toward the transport. "This is turning into a habit, but Gaela, if you can recognize anyone . . . help us to reconstruct what happened . . ."

"That's why I'm here."

"We've pulled the feeds from all the area vidcams and assembled them back at the station. Aryel?"

She shook her head. "I won't be able to see anything that Gaela can't see better. I need to deal with the press and get on top of the streams before the Conference gets under way."

They could just see around the corner of a nearby intersection, to where a ranked mass of media vans and shouting journalists pressed up against the barriers the police had erected a block away. The sturdy figure of Robert Trench stood with his back to them, facing the vidcams. He had, along with a police press officer, been keeping them at bay for a good twenty minutes, but even from this distance they could hear the clamor for Aryel Morningstar.

Gaela's lips twisted in distaste. "Better you than me." She stepped toward the car. "I'll see you later, then. Good luck."

"We're going to need a lot more than luck," Aryel said.

Several miles away, Mac's little group huddled in the basement of a disused building, much like the ones Masoud had described. But Mac had had the presence of mind to realize they needed to put as much distance as possible between themselves and the converging sirens, and as he ran had sent a gasping message over a ghost code to

the rest of the congregation to pick them up in the side streets that
led away from the Newhope traffic circle. The others on their way to
the meeting had responded immediately. While the police were still
counting the bodies, godgang members were being bundled into
cars and ferried away, by a variety of routes. They had been dropped
off at different locations close to this new safe house south of the
river and had made their way in on foot.

Now Mac and John were holding a whispered conference.

"You should go now, brother John," Mac said. "Make it so you
get there early. It'll make you seem more earnest-like."

"I don't think I should leave you all like this, after such a terrible
loss . . ."

"Loss! Brother John, you are mistaken."

Once the immediate danger was past and they were safely
indoors, Mac had gone through a surge of rage and hate that threatened to unhinge him completely. He had clenched his teeth and
prayed his way through it, and been rewarded by the descent of a
calm, detached clarity. It showed him what had happened, and why,
and how it was simply the next and inevitable step in the inexorable
unfolding of the Lord's great Plan.

This serenity, this insight, was another great and humbling gift,
one that he understood he needed to impart to others who might
be struggling as he had been. He felt the rightness of his words as he
spoke them.

"Simon and Zack are already in Heaven, seated at the right hand
of the Lord. They may have died at the hands of the Beast, but they
died glorious. And their deaths are a sign to us of the sacrifices that
must be made if we are to rid ourselves of the Beast. We are entering
another stage in this struggle, John, one that you were the first to
foresee. You made a grand start yesterday. You learned things that we
needed to know. Today is the time to build on that. While the rest of
us lie low, lick our wounds, and recover our strength, you will be the
one to guide us to the next battle in this war."

A shiver went through John. He was unclear as to whether it
signaled inspiration or uncertainty. He knew Mac would have no
such doubts.

They spent a few more minutes arranging logistics and exchanging new ghost codes. John wanted to stay and join the prayer for their fallen comrades.

"We'll be prayin' for you as well, brother John," Mac said sternly. "An' our prayers must not be wasted. Once you have received our blessings it'll be time for you to go."

He raised his voice. "My brothers, gather round." The twenty or so men in the room shuffled into a circle. Those who had been part of the morning's struggle limped or bore black eyes, or other signs of damage.

"We pray for the souls of brother Simon and brother Zack," intoned Mac. "They have fallen, and in falling have ended one chapter and begun another. We now know that we cannot continue to hunt the abominations one by one as we have been. We know that the next step is to step it up. And we thank brother Simon, and brother Zack, for sacrificing their lives to show the world the truth of the abominations, and to set our feet right on the path of the Lord."

He reached out, grabbed John by the shoulder, and gently pushed him into the middle of the circle.

"The first steps on this new part of our journey have already been taken by brother John here. Today he goes back into the lair of the Beast, into great danger, as a soldier of the Lord. His mission is to find us a path through their maze of deception, so we can strike right at the heart of the Evil One. The stronghold of the abominations must be broken, and their ambitions must be laid waste. And brother John will show us the way."

He raised his hand and brought it down to rest on John's head. His voice rose, a singsong cadence that the others caught and turned into a chant.

"I bless brother John. The blessings of the Lord be upon him, guide him and keep him so that he be a light unto us all."

Other hands came down on his shoulders, his back, his chest.

"I bless brother John. May he not falter."

"I bless brother John. The Lord keep him safe."

"I bless brother John, bravest of all of us."

John's doubts thinned and shredded like the morning mist. Mac was right; when the finger of the Lord came down and touched you, it felt like nothing else. It felt like this. He knew himself to be caught, and cradled, and catapulted toward a mighty destiny.

He clasped his hands and bowed his head for a moment, murmuring his own blessings back. Then he slipped free of the benedictions, wiping away tears of joy as he strode to the door, and out.

"But *why*?" Gabriel asked again.

"Gabe, I don't know how to explain it any better."

"But it doesn't make any *sense*."

"Gabe, how much of the stuff you see in other people's heads makes sense?"

Gabriel had to concede that a lot of what he picked up was pretty confused.

"But they don't go and *kill* people."

"Who doesn't?"

"We don't. I mean, the Squats people don't. Even though a lot of them don't like norms either."

"That doesn't mean that no gem has ever killed another person, Gabe. It just means that you haven't met any of the ones who have." Bal sighed. It always felt as if he was explaining things to Gabriel several years ahead of schedule, but there was nothing else for it. Dissimulation was a bad strategy to try on a mind reader. "Those gems this morning killed two of the norms, remember."

"But the norms were trying to kill them first."

"What's your point?"

"Well, doesn't that make it okay?"

Bal's hands were braced on the kitchen counter as he leaned forward. He looked down at them, noticing and then immediately, carefully, un-noticing the scars on his knuckles. It was a trick of mental self-distraction they had learned, a way of misdirecting Gabriel away from the things they did not want him to home in on.

"Killing someone is never *okay*," he said. "If someone is attacking you and the only way you can protect yourself is to fight back, fine. And if the person who's trying to hurt you gets killed by accident while you're defending yourself, then that's not quite as bad as if you killed them on purpose. But that doesn't make it *okay*."

"Why not?"

"Well, how would you feel if you killed someone? Even by accident?"

"That would be *terrible*," Gabriel said immediately, then frowned. "I don't know what it would really be *like*, though."

"What d'you mean?"

"Well, what happens when people die? Like Nelson and the people this morning? Where do they go?"

Bal was nonplussed. "They don't go anywhere, Gabe. That's it. They just end."

"But they can't. There's too much there." He spooned another mouthful of porridge and blinked up at his father. "What happens to all the stuff in their heads?"

"Oh *Gabe*." Bal dropped his head in his hands and scratched at his indigo hair. He wished mightily that Gaela were there for this conversation. "It just stops, baby. It disappears. People aren't like tablets, there's no backup for our brains. When we die it all fizzes away into nothing."

"Are you sure?" The frown deepened. "That doesn't seem right, Papa."

"I'm pretty sure, Gabe. No one's ever been able to prove that anything else happens."

He wondered whether to venture into this minefield and saw from the child's tilted head and sharpening gaze that it was too late to avoid it. He organized his thoughts as best he could, and plunged in. "Some people, religious people mostly, believe that there is some kind of life after death. They think there's a way of continuing on in some invisible form in some invisible place. But they don't know where it is or how it works, and if it's true no one's ever managed to send a message back to tell us about it."

Gabriel set his spoon down and pondered. Bal was grateful he had abandoned trying to understand the hatred of the godgangs but on reflection decided that might have been the easier line of questioning.

"If it's invisible maybe Mama can see it."

Bal barked a startled, delighted laugh. It was such an unexpected, such a *logical* thought.

"Maybe she can, baby boy. But don't you think she would have noticed by now?"

"Maybe you have to be there when someone dies, to notice where they go." Gabriel liked this notion and was clinging stubbornly to it. "I bet I could tell, if I were there when somebody died. When they were invisible, going to the invisible place, I'd hear what they were thinking."

Bal got his chortling under control. It was all getting a bit too macabre. "Maybe you could, Gabe. But you wouldn't want to have to prove it."

21

FROM HIS SEAT ON THE MEZZANINE LEVEL ELI COULD LOOK DOWN AT THE delegates as they approached the registration desk to slap passes onto identity scanners and slip tablets into docks. He was multitasking, checking the final running order and the dedicated links that had been coded to his tablet, flipping over from time to time to see what was happening on the external streams, and keeping an eye on the floor. The numbers were slowly increasing. He could hear a growing buzz of conversation from the lounge adjacent to the main hall as coffee was collected and colleagues located.

Every now and then a louder note punctuated the hum, an exclamation of greeting or surprise. He could not help wondering if any of the minor explosions of astonishment were due to his report. It was out there now, for better or worse, accessible on any tablet logged in to the Conference datastream; he would be presenting the key conclusions later that morning. It would be released to the press immediately afterward. He could see them gathering, a little knot of journalists and vidcam operators coalescing between the entry doors and the inner barrier beyond which they were not, as yet, permitted to go. They darted forward from time to time, coaxing reactions and predictions out of the new arrivals. They would, he knew, be on the lookout for him, and he was grateful to have escaped the gauntlet.

He had been the first delegate to register, arriving hard on the heels of the staff. Rob had been right to predict that he would find a return to sleep impossible. The confluence of the Conference, the second gem and the first norm deaths, and the seeming inability of the police to locate the godgang had fed the increasingly polarized vitriol on the socialstreams. He had read the early newstream reports and then started monitoring the exchanges, looking for patterns.

There were few, a development that troubled him. When Aryel Morningstar had first directed him to the growing online antag-onism, he had been sure that at least some of it was being quite deliberately seeded. There'd been a recurrence of themes and terms of abuse, a carefully casual precision to the damaging suggestions and embedded links. It was disturbing now to note that although this sense of organized malevolence had disappeared, there was no reduction in the volume of posts or the extremes of opinion. Despite the new randomness with which accusations and conclusions were delivered, the war of words was clearly escalating. Whoever had fueled this fire had backed off and bowed out, leaving the acrimony they had stoked to burn hotter and brighter without any need for further intervention.

The damage is done, he thought. *They've got what they want. A popular schism, on opposite sides of which people will feel a need to line up.*

Just as Aryel had said.

He glanced over the half-height mezzanine wall again. There was still no sign of her. The steady stream of anonymous faces was start-ing, however, to be punctuated by a few he recognized. There was a politician who had come to prominence by agitating for greater scrutiny of the gemtechs; supported the Declaration; continued to press for suffrage of competent gems; and expected to win their votes if successful. Her existing constituency was sufficiently lib-eral that she ran little risk of alienating one electorate by courting another. Hard on her heels came another representative, this time of an area struggling with long-term economic malaise, who had likewise criticized the gemtechs but had urged caution with respect to gems themselves.

He spotted fellow academics, Tobias next to an even more splendidly robed female cleric, the chief executive of Gempro in the center of a swarm of aides, and Robert Trench. The reporters who had clustered around the Gempro boss drifted away to collect around Rob as fast as decorum allowed. Eli suppressed a chuckle. Even from this distance the industry man's body language betrayed his irritation.

Attendants were on hand to help with equipment and answer questions. He could see four from where he sat. Powder-blue hair glimmered from the head of one of them.

Rob must've arranged that. Nice touch.

The Gempro contingent finished registering and swept out of view. Rob escaped the journalists and bustled up to the desk. The gem attendant clearly recognized him, and they exchanged a few words as he registered. He kept looking around, peering ahead into the lounge as though trying to spot someone. Eli mouthed "I'm here, on the balcony" into his earset and sent it as a message. Rob went still for a second, listening, then glanced up and nodded.

He appeared on the mezzanine a moment later. He had not stopped for a coffee, and Eli could tell that he needed one. They had barely said hello when a heightened murmur from the floor below made them both turn and look down.

Aryel Morningstar had arrived. Horace was with her, as were several other gems Eli did not recognize. He was surprised not to see Donal, but on reflection it made sense. Aryel would know that there would be people, among the press and the gemtechs in particular, who would make it their business to identify attending gems and their abilities. Donal's had the potential to cause embarrassment.

The press swarmed forward. Aryel's party stopped, and she gestured for the others to go ahead while she spoke to them. An array of vidcams were thrust in her face.

"What more can they possibly expect her to say?" Eli wondered aloud. He had watched the interviews from the latest crime scene that morning. She had been patient and thorough, somber and articulate. The newsstreams had gotten enough to keep their vidclips fresh until there was more actual news to report.

He glanced at Rob. "You were very good too, by the way."

"Thanks." He nodded down at the floor. "She's better."

Eli flicked his tablet over to the live newsstream feeds and found her. Rob adjusted his earset to pick up the tablet audio.

. . . hopes for this Conference?

"That it will affirm the fundamental equality of all human beings, and set us on the path to achieving an integrated and harmonious society."

Do you know anything more about the dreadful events in the City this morning? Have the missing gems been located?

"Not that I'm aware of, but that is a matter for the police. I would just like to repeat our appeal to them to come forward. Only then can they tell their side of the story; only then can we truly understand what happened. And of course the woman who survived this morning's attack may require medical treatment."

Aren't you concerned that they may be dangerous?

"Anyone may be dangerous. The capacity to do harm concerns me less than the willingness to use it."

They've been very willing, haven't they?

"What little we know about these people indicates that they've acted in self-defense. But," she held up a hand to forestall interruption, "I would absolutely agree that we do not have the full picture, and it will not be possible to make truly informed judgments until we do."

Aryel Morningstar, Newsbeat. I'm James Mudd, features editor. Would you please explain—

"Mr. Mudd, I'm very glad to meet you. We've been concerned about your reporter, George Brooks, who was attacked two nights ago. I trust he's getting better?"

On the feed Aryel's face, brow furrowed in concern, looked up and slightly to one side of what Eli surmised must be the Newsbeat vidcam. Beside him Rob chuckled softly. The image shifted and panned out to capture the man who had spoken. He was clearly taken aback. For a moment it seemed as if he might say something rude in reply, but a quick glance told him that the exchange had a broader audience. His mouth opened and closed a couple of times before he said gruffly, "He's doing very well."

"That's good news. We wish him a speedy recovery."

She smiled, catching him off guard again as he tried to recapture whatever he had been about to accuse her of, and turned away, her attention shifting to another questioner as she began to move slowly toward the registration desk. The press corps shuffled along with her. By the time James Mudd realized that the moment had gone, so had she.

Rob was still laughing quietly when Eli touched his shoulder and pointed over the mezzanine wall at a group that had entered behind Aryel's entourage. Their progress had been impeded by the throng of reporters. They were led by a man with the haughty, sharp-nosed features of a pre-Syndrome aristocrat. He wore a ferociously expensive suit and an expression of disdain that stopped barely short of disgust. A tall, blond woman with red lips stood beside him, her hand on his arm. She leaned toward his ear, whispering something. There was a tension about the pair that told them she was preventing him from striding forward, scattering the people in front of them.

Felix Carrington was evidently not used to waiting—certainly not, Eli thought, on gems. But Zavcka Klist held him back and, with a sharp glance at the rest of the Bel'Natur contingent, ensured that they held their places. As the crowd around Aryel elongated and thinned, they resumed their own progress toward the desk.

A few of the journalists, the ones to whom she had already spoken, shifted their attention to the newcomers. James Mudd had apparently recovered, and he approached Carrington and Klist. A few words were exchanged. Eli had the impression that Zavcka wanted to avoid catching up with Aryel.

She finished registering and maneuvered the bulk of her cloak through the access gate and into the Conference proper. As soon as she had gone, Zavcka said something that ended the Newsbeat interview. The Bel'Natur delegates moved briskly to register, Carrington pausing only to deliver what was apparently a stock sentence or two to the other reporters who had thrust vidcams forward.

"Interesting," Rob said. "No confrontation, then."

"Not out here, anyway."

Carrington appeared to be having some trouble registering his tablet. The blue-haired attendant came over to help. He ignored her, directing his question to her norm colleague who stood a bit farther away. She recoiled at the snub. The other threw her an apologetic look as he stepped forward to assist.

Even from this distance Eli could see the compression of Zavcka Klist's lips, the coiled anger in her body. She stood one station over from Carrington and was not, he suspected, having any problems at all. Nevertheless she looked up and said something to the gem woman, smiling graciously. The woman approached, the blue head bent over the equipment for a moment, then straightened up and nodded at Zavcka. Carrington appeared to be itching to go, but she made him wait while she thanked the attendant. The others clutched their tablets awkwardly. Then the entire group swept beneath them, and out of sight.

"Well," said Eli.

"Not exactly house-trained yet, is he?"

"You'd think he would at least have learned to fake it."

They descended. Rob muttered something about checking in with the events team and scurried off. Eli surveyed the crowded lounge, trying to plot a course that was least likely to intersect with anyone to whom he would have to speak.

The gemtech delegations were dotted around the room, on the fringes where there were chairs and tables at which one could sit and review the Conference documents. In most of their clusters it was a functionary, an aide to the most senior executive probably, who feverishly flipped through the links as they tried to assess what was coming. Except in the Bel'Natur group, where the blond head of Zavcka Klist was bent fixedly over her tablet. He had no doubt as to what she was reading, or what her reaction would be.

He was less certain about Aryel's, and felt a stab of guilt that it was not all as she might have wished. But then she had never said precisely what conclusions she hoped he would come to, nor suggested that his findings should be other than his own best judgment dictated. He spotted her, small hands wrapped around a steaming cup as she chatted with the pro-gem politician.

She was dressed as always, swathed throat to hump to toes in her charcoal-black cloak, in marked contrast to the crisp stylishness of the rest of the room. But they collected about her anyway, and the enveloping darkness of her garb seemed merely to underscore the strange gravitational pull she exerted. He watched for a moment, mentally sorting them out into those genuinely seeking an opportunity to join the conversation and those trying, and failing, to look as though they were doing something besides listening in. She stood easy and strangely elegant in the middle of it, sipping her coffee, for all the world as though she were a fashionable guest at a glamorous party and not a misshapen piece of former property.

The other gems were far less relaxed. They congregated near one of the entrances to the auditorium, hair glowing in every color of the rainbow. Aryel's companions had been joined by the few other gem delegates, and as soon as the doors were released they slipped inside.

Eli made to follow them but was delayed by Tobias wanting to introduce him to the bishop, then a fellow researcher from Prague saying hello, then the cautious politician waving his tablet.

"I've just read your introduction," he said. "This is—I don't understand. What you're suggesting—"

"I'll do my best to explain in the presentation."

"But don't you understand the implications? What it'll mean?"

"I believe so."

He left the man standing open-mouthed and strode toward the doors. Zavcka Klist looked up and saw him from the other side of the room. Her face was livid. He caught her eye and inclined his head, a cold greeting, and then he reached the exit and was out.

The gems had commandeered the center rows at the rear of the small auditorium. They sat three deep, backs to the door and faces forward.

Clever. They get to look down on everyone else for a change. It's tough to belittle someone you know is staring holes in the back of your head.

His own seat was reserved at the very front. He stopped to say hello to Horace, who had regained the self-possession he had lost on the night of Nelson's murder but was far more subdued than at their first meeting. As Eli glanced back he saw Gaela. She was standing next to a uniformed officer, tucked against the rear of the auditorium, where she could see everyone who entered but was unlikely to be noticed herself.

They've got her scanning the delegates. Good lord. He smiled a greeting and she nodded back.

When someone who was not Rob slid into Rob's seat beside him, he didn't need to look up. "Hello, Miss Klist. We're still on speaking terms?"

"Dr. Walker. This could have been such a beautiful friendship."

"I sincerely doubt that."

"I didn't realize you were this eager to be the center of attention. I suspect you'll find you don't like it."

"What I *would* like," he said evenly, "would be for people to stop expecting me to behave like a politician. I don't come to conclusions based on whose agenda suits me best. If the data—including the data you provided—supported a different result, that's what I'd be presenting. As for personal consequences, I didn't get into this to become rich, or famous, or popular. I took this job in order to tell the truth. In your world that might indicate a shocking lack of ambition, but I don't live in your world. And I don't want to."

"You may find us difficult to ignore."

"I hope not." He smiled as pleasantly as he could manage. "I understand that Gerin Provis is doing very well now, but doesn't like changes to his routine. I'd hate to have to disturb him."

He let himself enjoy it, the shocked widening of the smoke-dark eyes, the slackened jaw and stunned expression as she processed the name.

Gerin. An early interview, before the formal commission to produce the report, before the Declaration even. Later removed to a care home, under vehement Bel'Natur protest. Prototype retinal scanner in a human skin. Not that that's what his genetype file had recorded, or what anyone had guessed. Eli remembered only huge, pale eyes that took up half his face, over a harelip and a nose with the cartilage so undeveloped as to barely be noticeable, and the way he had thrust that grim head forward, grunting vapid, monosyllabic answers into the awkward space between questions, as he stared unblinking into Eli's eyes from a few inches away.

Now Eli looked deliberately up toward the back of the auditorium, searching for the glow of Gaela's fiery hair, and felt Zavcka Klist follow his gaze. It took a few seconds to sink in.

When she looked back at him again it was with pure, naked rage. He watched as she absorbed the realization that she had been outflanked; as she weighed alternatives, and judged this too dangerous a road to travel; and as she pulled back the anger, filing it away somewhere to grow hard and implacable. It lasted no more than a second. The harshly beautiful face composed itself. He kept his own still, even as he felt his insides shrink and go cold.

"Gerin," she said quietly. "Well. I'd almost forgotten about him."

"It's so easy to lose track of one's tools, once the task is complete." His voice was steady, a fact of which he felt unreasonably proud.

"And so easy to choose the wrong ones. It's surprising that a man so committed to veracity would ally himself with those who withhold so much."

She shifted in her chair, glancing up to where delegates were streaming in through the doors. A hint of viciousness crept back into her voice as she watched Aryel Morningstar make her way to a specially shaped seat. "Or maybe you do know more than you've said. I wonder. How far have they trusted you, Dr. Walker? With the deepest and darkest, the holy of holies?"

He thought immediately of Gabriel, and of the other secrets that Gabriel implied. "I don't know what you're talking about."

"Don't you? You should." She looked back at him. "What's she hiding under that cape, Dr. Walker? You want to reveal an important truth? How about that one?"

He had almost stopped noticing Aryel's deformity. The protrusion under the omnipresent cloak was as much a part of her as sky-blue eyes and a warm smile. He had, in the rush of events over the last few days, forgotten to be curious about it.

"What makes you think it's important?"

"Why else would she be at such pains to conceal it?"

He was baffled. "I don't understand what you mean by *conceal*. She's dysmorphic. It's winter. What do you expect her to do, run around in a bikini?"

Zavcka Klist smiled a frost-hard smile. "You really don't know?"

"Know what?"

"That the material is a military-grade electromagnetic reflector. Very expensive, very hard to come by, and virtually impervious to scans. I doubt even Gaela Provis could see through it." She stood up. "You think we have secrets, Dr. Walker? You think our agenda is the one you need to worry about? At least you know who we are. You might want to ask yourself what the famously frank Aryel Morningstar so desperately needs to hide."

22

John pushed open the front door of the UC outreach center and breathed a sigh of relief. It was empty, save for the boxes upon boxes of clothing, food, and other donations from citizens and corporations who would not, he was sure, have shown anywhere near the same charity to the deserving, human, poor. There was a case of brand-new tablets with linked earsets, balanced atop another of medicinal teas and tinctures, both half-buried under factory-packaged bed linen. Here was a basket of freshly baked bread, next to a crate of oranges. He stepped around them and continued through to the back office. It too was empty, and he leaned against the wall. It would be only a momentary reprieve, but he was grateful for it. His certainty of the morning was wavering, and he needed to regroup.

It had begun to diminish at check-in, when, without Tobias to mediate, he had had to deal directly with Mikal. He found the giant's face impossible to read, difficult even to look at, and Mikal had little to say, at least to him. He could therefore not be confident he remained unsuspected. His nervousness was matched only by his outrage when he realized that the adjacent office was occupied today not by the gem Gaela but by a pretty young female police officer with whom Mikal carried on an easy exchange that, to John's way of thinking, bordered on flirtation. That the police-woman responded in kind was a shock somehow more hurtful than he had been prepared for.

He had been trying to convince himself that the connection he thought he'd sensed had most likely been the product of an over-wrought imagination, or at the very worst a very rare perversion, when he arrived at a small block of apartments close to the quay-side with his first delivery of the day, a cartload of necessities for those who had arrived with little. Strains of lazy music stopped as he wrestled it inside, but there was no interruption in the conversation between a sleepy teenage couple and a shaggy-headed young man as they helped him unload. The trio's hair colors were as modest and matte as his own, but he had seen the young man on the late-night newstream, standing next to Aryel Morningstar, shouting at Tobias; and the seven fingers the other boy raked through his black locks confirmed his origins as well. John was surreptitiously trying to spot the girl's gemsign, already growing angry at whatever gemtech had spawned her for making it so obscure, when the talk turned to how they had met, her family's furious objections, and the degree to which she absolutely, positively did not care.

He'd barely made it out of there without betraying himself, caution returning in the nick of time, when the one called Donal turned to him, with every indication of concern, and asked if he was all right.

"Yer heartbeat's goin' a mile a minute there. John, was it? Sure luggin' this stuff in't too heavy fer yer?"

For a moment the shock had steadied him. He'd muttered some-thing about needing the exercise and excused himself, a cold tongue of fear lapping at his spine. He was too stunned even to wonder how the other had known.

The next two deliveries were uneventful, small parcels to obvi-ous grotesques who did not meet his eyes and thanked him with a far more acceptable level of nervous respect. He had recovered his composure somewhat by his fourth consignment, to a large residen-tial building in the middle of the Squats. He had been eager for an opportunity to get inside, knowing from Tobias's tour the day before that this was an important structure.

"Maryam House is the original heart of the community," the priest had said. "It can't hold everyone anymore, so there's an effort to make more use of the leisure center as a sort of social hub. And of course we hope the role of the church will grow, in time. But this is where the founders still live, along with most of the residents who need special care. The way they've been integrated is just remarkable. It's a special place." He'd sighed. "Nelson lived here."

John had clenched his teeth and nodded in pretend sympathy while a little spark of excitement lit within him. The ones they'd miss most, along with many others who'd simply accept the inevitable, who couldn't or wouldn't fight back. Mac had been similarly delighted last night, and after the terrifying predawn brawl, culminating in the loss of Simon and Zack, John was even more inclined to try to identify a soft target.

But when he had finally been admitted, groaning cart in tow, he'd been unprepared for the reality of the community room. The rocking, the twitching, the fixed stares at tablets and vacant looks elsewhere, all under a sea of radiant rainbow hair. The disfigured faces and disproportionate physiques and multiplicity or absence of features, limbs, digits. These were not, he realized, merely the intentional malformations or collateral damage that they had all become somewhat used to. This group included the accidents.

He was still standing awkward and open-mouthed when the middle-aged woman who'd met him at the door returned to tug gently at his sleeve and with a jerk of the head indicate that he should follow her through to the kitchen. Sally, her name was. Sally Trieve. Another big shot wasting time and money on a lost and unworthy cause.

"Try not to stare," she said quietly, as he negotiated the cart around the periphery of the room. "I know it's difficult. Most norms have become so unaccustomed to disability."

He had to respond. He tried to think of something obvious and inoffensive. "*They* must be accustomed to it. Being stared at, I mean."

"Doesn't mean they like it." She fixed him with a look that was too sharp for comfort. "Imagine if it was you, how you'd feel."

Now that was an utterly ridiculous thing to say. No decent human being could suffer such a fate. Only among the Remnants was there ever an occasional birth defect or developmental disorder, and even those fools were belatedly, but increasingly, coming forward to get their next generations fixed. But there was no hope of that with the gems, even without all the moral objections to the continuation of an unnatural race. They were too wrong, their modifications too intrinsic to be manipulated away. He didn't have a problem with putting the useful ones back to work, as long as no more were manufactured and they didn't breed. Get some value out of them. Maybe. This was a contentious issue within the godgang, but there would be no argument about the rest. Half the ones in this room didn't look like they'd ever been good for anything. What in God's name was the point of them?

But he'd had to bite his tongue and swallow his bile and studiously avoid looking at the creatures that arrived on either side of him to help unload the cart. He had never felt so exposed. He remembered that Donal had somehow spotted his disquiet, and tried to focus on remaining calm. Deep, even breaths, remember why you're here, what you've already achieved, how much more work there is to do.

They aim to make us forget who we are, Mac had said. *They aim to make us lose but they don't want to fight us outright. They are deceivers, remember. They aim to make us think there ain't no fight, so we give up without a struggle. An' that's our strength, my brothers, because with the help of the Lord we know the truth. We know we're in a fight, an' we know we can win.*

He needed a dose of Mac, a boost for his resolve before he had to head back out again. Too risky to pull out his tablet. He activated his earset and with a sinking heart listened to the tone flip instantly into message mode. He could not leave dead air; Mac would think something had gone wrong. He spoke quickly and quietly, a detailed message outlining what he had already learned that day. He hoped Mac would pick up on his deeper meaning and call him back.

He was just finishing up when a gust of cold wind pushed at the office door and told him someone had entered out front. He broke the connection and stuck his head around the door. Two more volunteers: his guide of yesterday and the woman who had been stationed here earlier. She looked surprised to see him emerging from the back, and he muttered something about checking for any updates to the deliveries list.

"Nothing's changed, I don't think. How're you getting on?"

"Couple more loads to Maryam House."

"Let's see if we can get it to them in one."

He felt better with the company, normal humans at least even if they were misbelievers. They formed enough of an obstacle to make gems step aside as they maneuvered two carts down the narrow lanes to the apartment building. His appreciation dimmed when he caught a glimpse of their progress past the dark glass of an entrance and realized what a spectacle they made, straining in shameful servitude. He put his head down and tried to distract himself by listening to the others.

"Any word from Tobias?"

"Just a quick post. It was about to start. He'd had a look at the Walker Report, says it goes a lot further than anyone expected."

"Further how?"

"He argues that gems are the same as us, basically. Any segregation or discrimination would be genetically unfounded, I think that was the line."

"Wow. That's . . . it actually says that? Is there a link?"

"Not yet. I guess they'll release it a bit later."

John kept his jaw firmly shut. They had arrived and he took the lead, hauling his cart up the shallow ramp that ran alongside the stairs. Donal was at the door, talking to a tall, powerfully built gem with short hair that glowed a deep bluish color. There was a child with the big man, a little boy with a clear, bright face under sandy-brown curls. It looked as though they had been going out and met Donal coming in.

The sight of the child startled John to a halt. He registered a similar hush from the two behind him and then caught their whispers.

"Is that Gabriel?"

"That's him."

Gabriel. Someone had mentioned the name. A special child, a blessed child. Ample justification for allowing gems to breed. He had had to move away at that point. Perhaps he should have stayed, learned more then and been less surprised now. He had not imagined a gem child could look so shockingly ordinary.

Donal broke off and turned toward the three norms with their carts.

"Here come the Good Samaritans," he said, and palmed the door open. John was sure there was a faintly mocking note in his voice. Anger rose up in him again, but he had a method now. He kept his face carefully bland, his breathing controlled, his mind focused. He moved forward with the cart. The big man stepped clear, holding the boy's hand.

Beside him the child turned suddenly and looked straight at John, head tilted, eyes wide with surprise. "What?" he said. His voice was clear and piping, and filled with horror. The man glanced down at him and then sharply over to John.

"Gabe?" said the father.

"He . . . you . . ." Suddenly the child was tugging on his hand, trying to pull him away. "Papa, don't go near him, he wants to hurt us. Papa, he's a bad man."

John stumbled and stopped, staring at the child. Behind him he heard the UC woman say, "No . . . no, this is John, he's here to help." There was an uncertainty in her voice that stunned him. "Isn't he?"

"No," said the boy. Panic squeaked in his voice. "He came here to find out about us, so he can come back with his friends."

The big man pushed the child behind him and stepped forward. Donal released the door, letting it slide shut. John felt as if the Squats were suddenly tightening around him, like a noose.

"Who are you?"

John's mouth opened but he could not force anything out. He was aware of the two carts and two people on the narrow ramp behind him, the breadth and height and strength of the gem in front. He looked a lot like the one this morning, the one who had killed

Zack and then fought all the way to the edge of the terrace, and over. John's ribs still ached from the encounter, but in the lifting and carrying and pulling of the day he was sure he had given nothing away. He tried desperately to think. He had sailed through the identity checks. They had no reason to suspect him. Stay calm, remember the mission.

"I'm John Senton," he managed. "I'm volunteering my time, like she said. I don't know what's got your kid so upset."

"You're a liar!" shouted the boy. Tears were streaming down his face. "You killed Nelson! You and someone named Simon and someone named Mac! You keep thinking about it!"

John recoiled, almost falling into the cart behind him. The mantra in his head, the clear memory from the night before last that had carried him through all the trials of the day, shuddered to a halt.

The child was shrieking now.

"And you killed that other man! And tried to kill that lady! And you want to hurt my papa!"

The big man turned and stooped suddenly, sweeping the child up into his arms.

"Gabe, that's enough. Stop. Get out of his head."

"But he did it, Papa, he did, and he hurt Callan too, and he hates us, he *hates* us . . ." The child was shaking like a leaf in a gale, trying to burrow into his father's chest.

"I believe you, baby. But you need to stop now. You're hurting yourself. Stop looking. Just stop."

He cradled the boy's sobbing head in a big, scarred hand and stared over it straight into John's eyes. John felt the world fold and collapse around him.

"Don?" the big man said quietly. "Please take Gabe inside." He handed the boy to Donal. As Bal pried the child's fingers loose, looking down for a moment, John felt a surge of power come back into his legs. He moved sideways, fast, vaulting the railing to land on the steps, leaping down them. He had taken no more than two sprinting strides along the pavement when a hand landed on his shoulder, stopping him dead and whipping him around.

The big man flipped him against the side of the building as though he were a fish landed on the quay. The air slammed out of John in a rush. He slid down to the ground. Behind he could see Donal, standing in the doorway, clutching Gabriel to him. His erstwhile companions stood beside the forgotten carts, faces blank with astonishment.

Bal stood in front of him, face impassive save for a flaring around the nostrils and a fury sparking deep in the brown eyes. John offered up a last, silent prayer.

From the doorway, Gabriel said, "Papa?" in a scared little voice.

"I know, baby," he replied. "Don't worry. I'm not actually going to do it." He raised a hand, flicked at his earset. "Mik? We need you. And your friend."

They had pulled him into a fenced square of frozen lawn at the side of Maryam House. Sergeant Varsi had planted herself in front of the closed gate and was trying to make sense of what she was being told. Her colleague stood to the side, tablet in hand, scanning no doubt for any inconsistencies in his story or recent history. Their transport sat out front, blue lights ominously flashing.

Gabriel was gone. As soon as Mikal and the female officer had arrived, racing over from the leisure center while the one on patrol screamed in from the far side of the Squats, Bal had left Donal to provide the initial explanations and disappeared with the boy inside the building. He was back now, though, flanked by the other two gems. John huddled against the fence, as far away from Bal as possible.

They had tried at first simply to insist that they had reason to believe he was a member of the godgang and needed to be arrested and investigated. But the two UC volunteers, who stood as far apart from him as they could get, had failed to understand and kept interjecting with explanations that involved Gabriel. John had clutched at a faint hope that the gems might back down rather than allow the child to be exposed, and had said over and over that he didn't know what they were talking about and he was sorry if he'd somehow scared the kid.

It hadn't worked. Once the police started to ask questions about Gabriel, once Bal had realized that he could not be kept out of it, he had taken a deep breath and raised his hands to shut the others up. He spat the words out into the bitter wind that blew across the icy grass.

"My son is psychic. He can perceive what people around him are thinking. As soon as he got close to this—John—he could tell who he really was, and why he is here."

"You're telling me your son can read minds?"

"Yes."

"Well," the policewoman shook her head in bewilderment, "I've never heard of such a thing." She glanced at Mikal, who nodded confirmation.

"Where is he then? Why isn't he here explaining this himself?"

"Because he's five years old and he's terrified."

Her frown deepened. "You expect me to make an arrest on the word of a five-year-old? Based on an unproven psychic ability?"

"It's not unproven." This from the UC man.

"You know about this child?"

The man nodded eagerly. "I saw him do it before. A couple of days ago. A poor suffering woman who couldn't speak. He looked right inside her head and pulled out what she wanted to say."

She stared at him. "That sounds very unlikely."

"It happened right in front of me. It was amazing. I felt privileged to witness it."

"Many people witnessed it," the woman put in. "He's a gift from God, he truly is."

The policewoman looked back at Bal.

"If this is true, why is it a secret? You didn't want to mention your son. Why not?"

"Because of this." He waved a disgusted hand at the UCs. "We're trying to give him as normal a childhood as we can, even though he has a unique ability. This kind of attention, all these people talking about him, doesn't help."

They looked aghast. Varsi took in their expressions, and Bal's, and sighed.

"No, I guess it doesn't. But look at it from where I'm standing. I've got nothing to go on besides your word. And his." She glanced at the other officer. "Anything?"

"No priors, good neighborhood, good job." He gestured at the tablet. "Hasn't shown up to work for a week or so, though."

"Really? Why's that, Mr. Senton?"

It caught him off guard. "I've been . . . been busy . . . other things . . ."

"Couldn' fi' it into yer gem-bashin' schedule?" Donal shot back. He had pulled out his tablet, was doing something with it.

"That's not it! I'm not . . . I'm here, aren't I?"

"Yer a liar." Donal raised the tablet at him. It flashed. "Which I can prove in jus' a mo', I think, wi'out bringin' the wee lad back into it." He flicked at his earset. "Wenda? Hi, darlin'. Callan awake?"

He listened to the response. Mikal rocked back on his heels, a sapling swaying over their heads, and chuckled. As a cold sense of finality settled over John, his earset started to vibrate.

It could only be Mac. He had one chance, maybe, to send a message. Warn them. Once he was arrested, his earset would be removed. If they realized who he was talking to, his earset would be removed. But if he was quick and careful and Donal kept them distracted, he might be able, finally, to deliver on his promise.

He was contained inside the fence. No one was looking at him. He shrugged to receive and spoke as quietly as he could.

"Hi, honey."

A moment of perplexed silence from the other end, then, "Brother John. You okay?"

"Just trying to sort out a bit of a mix-up." They all remained focused on Donal. Still, take no chances. Callan might not have seen him clearly. "Mistaken identity. There's a kid here who thinks I have something to do with those murders."

He could feel the tension ratchet up on the other end. "Why would they think that?"

"Kid's a mind reader, apparently. Claims to be looking right inside my head."

"Oh . . ." Mac caught himself. "Only the Lord can do that."

"Well they say he's got previous, so they have to give him the benefit of the doubt." He kept his voice as light as he could, but he could hear his own desperation. "Big to-do. Cops came racing in."

A beat as Mac processed the message.

"Are they going to hold you?"

"Yeah. It'll get sorted any second now, I expect."

"How?"

Across the lawn the three gems and two police officers peered into Donal's tablet. It seemed to be taking a while for them to get an answer. The UC pair stood with their backs to him.

"They've sent my picture to the one in hospital."

A deep breath, then, "I'm sorry, brother John." Mac's voice became quick, clipped. He had obviously decided to abandon subterfuge in favor of speed. "This the same child? The one the UCs were on about?"

"Yes."

"Is he there now?"

"No."

"Describe him."

"Little. Brown hair. Looks normal."

"How normal?"

"Completely."

"Dear God."

Something had changed with Donal. He still looked at the tablet, but there was a stillness and attention about him now that John somehow knew was aimed at him. He stopped listening to whatever Mac was saying and focused on Donal. A gust of wind whistled through the bars behind him and ruffled the young gem's hair. John saw his ear.

"Yes, I know you've got to go," he said to Mac.

"Now?"

"You wouldn't want to be late."

"Bless you, brother John."

23

Distinguishing Features: A Comparative Study of Social Behavior

Prepared for the European Conference on the Status of Genetically Modified Humans, London, December 131AS

INTRODUCTION

One year ago I was asked to examine the question of whether genetically modified humans are fundamentally different from unmodified humans; not in terms of their origin, to which the answer is obvious, but in terms of their ability to function in and to form social groups, to integrate and interact with other groups, and to become, in the context both of their individual and group identities, engaged and productive members of the wider human family. Or, as an eminent member of the cross-party committee which commissioned this report put it to me at the time, "Do gems have any chance of ever becoming normal?"

This last point is of particular significance because, despite what some may think, the variation in "normal" social structures and behaviors is enormous. What we think of as "normal" changes across cultures and over time. In most places, and in most times, "normal" has described the ethnicity, heritage and habits of powerful elites or demographic majorities. The correlative definition of the weak or the few as not-normal could historically be relied upon to coincide neatly with prevailing cultural and racial preferences.

So I asked the committee what they meant by "normal." You are the scientist, came the response. You tell us.

I should pause for a moment both to thank and to congratulate them for their courage in issuing so revolutionary an instruction.

I must also thank my team of researchers, interviewers and analysts, and the geneticists, social workers, physicians, psychiatrists and other dedicated professionals upon whose assistance and insight we have relied. And last but by no means least I must thank the hundreds of genetically modified humans who consented to be interviewed, and who in many cases allowed us into their homes, hospices and workplaces, enabling us to observe their progress as they adjusted to a drastically different set of surroundings, expectations and opportunities, and a fundamentally new way of life.

This report will examine in detail each of the issues upon which I wish merely to touch in this Introduction. The embedded links will lead to the analyses on which our conclusions are based, and to the source material for those studies. Except for the redaction of names and other identifying information to protect the privacy of individuals, we have withheld none of the data with which we have been provided, and upon which we have relied.

One of these resources requires special mention, and a particular caution. We are grateful to have received a report from a leading bioindustrialist conglomerate, detailing their internal investigation into an assault committed by a genetically modified male upon two norm females. Vidcam surveillance documented the assault, which resulted in the death of a minor and severe injuries to the surviving victim. Names, faces and other identifying features have been redacted as mentioned above, and the vidlinks have been restricted to prevent further distribution, copying or streaming. Nevertheless the images are extremely graphic and very distressing, and while included here for the sake of transparency are unlikely to add much to an understanding of the incident, which is discussed extensively in both the internal report and our external analysis.

The questions surrounding this dreadful event encapsulate many of the issues which we are attempting to understand, and with which this Conference intends to grapple: the unknowns of the genetic legacy to which gems are heir, the doubts about the ability of some gems to lead independent lives, and the implications of the sudden, unrestricted introduction of thousands of gems into the wider community. The assumption of the assailant's parent gemtech was that his actions were the result of an inadvertent genetic trigger, something unintended and unforeseen but possibly widely replicated throughout the gem population. Their search for this supposed engineering error, while thorough, was unsuccessful.

Our analysis has suggested a different explanation, one which requires us to revisit, however uncomfortably, our idea of "normal." While the assault constitutes a horrific aberration from what would have been considered acceptable in almost any culture at any point in time, it is by no means a unique event in the history of the human species. Such crimes, while thankfully always rare, were well known and documented in the centuries prior to the Syndrome. Then, as now, no convincing explanation could be found, although theories ranging from the existence of a metaphysical evil to the psychological damage inflicted by childhood abuse to, yes, a genetically encoded flaw were put forward, studied and debated.

Our survey of the historical record, coupled with the lack of any apparent differentiation in the attacker's genotype profile, has led us to the working hypothesis that, to the extent this gem's actions had a genetic link at all, it was less likely to be the result of an array that had been engineered *in* than of a heritage sequence that has never been engineered *out*. This makes his capacity for extreme violence in no essential respect any different from the potential that may exist within each and every one of us.

The fact that a gem may commit a horrific act does not, ipso facto, imply that the horrific act was committed because he or she is a gem.

We have become unaccustomed in the last century and a half to the levels of warfare and violent crime that used to sadly be commonplace. It would be both easy and reassuring to imagine that the shared crisis of the Syndrome, and the changes to which it gave rise, have somehow eliminated this capability; have jumped us up an evolutionary step, so that we no longer feel the need to harm each other. I have only to point to the recent, equally horrific assaults on and murders of gems on the streets of London, by those who claim to be "true" humans, to refute any suggestion that the genetic distinction between gems and norms makes one group intrinsically safer—or saner—than the other.

But what about the distinctions within groups? It is common parlance to say that not all gems are equal; it is certainly true to say that not all gems are the same. Again I will point out that this is also true of norms, and is not of itself a distinguishing factor between us. However there is no getting away from the reality that there exists within the gem population a vast gulf between those who are most intellectually gifted, socially competent and physically able, and their brethren who suffer from mental deficiency, physical deformity, or an inability to play well with others; far more so than amongst norms, where the latter imperfections have been almost completely engineered away.

And here we come to a secret which everyone knows, which is so ubiquitous a truth we seem somehow to have concluded it to be irrelevant—the fact that, apart from a few Remnants living remote from society, none of us are unmodified. We are all gems. Engineered characteristics aside, many of the illnesses and aberrations which we (and they) find so deviant and distressing are exclusively present in them *only because they were engineered out of us*.

Again we must ask the question: what is normal?

It is true that evolution would probably not, unaided, have thrown up a human with hyperspectral vision. It also would not have thrown up a population free from congenital defect. It would—and did—throw up a fair number of musical geniuses who happened to be blind, intellectual giants who happened to have neurological disorders and political leaders who happened to be crippled. In their coupling of extraordinary gifts with unfortunate limitations, gems represent the continuation of a truly human legacy.

Within the gem population, as within all populations throughout history, the almost infinite combinations of genetically encoded benefits and disadvantages form a continuum of incremental variation. Within this range the evidence shows that outcomes are mitigated—both positively and negatively—by environment. This has led us inescapably to the conclusion that any subdivision, any implicit and automatic categorization of gems by ability or disability, would be scientifically spurious.

Furthermore, if we rely exclusively on genome analysis (as opposed to the historical circumstance of conception and birth) it becomes clear that this continuum seamlessly merges those we classify as gems with those we think of as norms. There is no point of purely *genetic* variation that divides us. Crucially, there is also no evidence that the choices gems make, the ways in which they act and interact, are on the whole fundamentally different from what we would expect of norms under similar circumstances. Our study therefore concludes that, while genotype does influence the individual and social behavior of gems, it does so to no greater a degree and in no significantly different a manner than for norms.

The answer to the question asked by that member of the commissioning panel is a qualified yes—and the qualification simply is that *they already are normal.*

I expect to hear the cry *But they're different!* rising from many thousand throats when this report is made public. To which I can only reply: Yes they are. They are as different from us as the European conquistadores from the Aztec agriculturalists. They are

as different as the Pygmy tribes of sub-Saharan Africa from the
dynasties of Tang and Ming. They are as different as the Roma-
nian orphans of the Cold War from the intellectual elite of the
Ivy League. They are as different as the Indians of the American
plains, in their homes of hide and bark, from those of the Asian
sub-continent, in glittering and bejeweled palaces. They are as
different as that.

ELI WALKER, PH.D. (MIT) (EDIN.), FRAI, FIBMS

Eli came off the stage feeling battered. He dawdled, his back to it,
gazing up the terraced rows of seats as the rest of the room filed out
through the rear doors. There were only half as many people as at
the gem meeting a couple of days ago, but he felt as though he had
just had to face down ten times the number.

*Aryel was right. Again. What's happening out in the world is reflected
in here.*

"Penny for 'em." Rob, at his elbow.

"I was thinking how different this was from the other evening.
I expected to get raked over the coals then, but everyone was more
interested in pitching in to help solve the problem. Here I've done
exactly what I was asked to do, and you'd think I had personally
insulted everyone's grandmother."

"What you've done has made their job harder. A lot of them were
relying on having some kind of scientific excuse for the restrictions
they already know they want to put in place—and you've said nope,
this is a question of ethics, not genetics. Of course they're pissed off
at you."

"I didn't actually mention ethics. Not out loud anyway. And, this
doesn't prevent them from doing the wrong thing."

"It makes it harder," Rob said again. They began to move slowly
up the room, following the crowd out. A few people were pointedly
lingering along the aisle, waiting to talk to Eli. He scowled at them.

"Any news on this morning?"

"I think they've identified the dead. That's about it."

One man stood squarely in their path. He was portly and well
dressed, and Eli thought he looked familiar. Rob knew him: a lawyer,

one of the team of specialists hired to advise on constitutional and regulatory issues. His name was Jeremy Temple. It rang no bells.

"I thought your presentation was excellent," he said to Eli quietly. "And at the risk of making a lot less work for my profession, it occurs to me that you've validated the notion of having no separation at all between gems and norms."

"Well, yes," Eli said, puzzled. He was sure he'd seen the man before.

"Pardon me, Dr. Walker, but if you take that to its logical conclusion, it means we don't need an extensive legal framework to deal with 'the gem question.' It suggests a solution that is both practical and ethical." He made quotation marks with his fingers while Rob grinned. "We don't need new laws and regulations, we don't need special protections or restrictions. What struck me is how well the existing infrastructure has coped since the Declaration. It's been stretched, of course, but the fact that you have the data you have tells me the system works, even if it's creaking. It needs money and it needs personnel, but those would be required anyway."

"What are you suggesting?" Rob asked.

"That all we need the law to say is that there are no distinctions within the human species, and gems are the same as everyone else. Same rights, same responsibilities. No special treatment beyond dealing with each individual's needs. Think of it this way."

They had stopped just inside the doors. He was animated, excited. His voice had risen a bit. Eli knew now where he had seen Jeremy Temple before: at St. Pancras station, five days earlier, meeting a beautiful black-haired woman in a purple coat.

"Say we found, right now, today, a group of Remnants that we hadn't known about. They've been living off the grid for over a hundred years, they've got all sorts of problems—diseases, inbreeding, risk of the Syndrome, complete unfamiliarity with the modern world, you name it. And now they want to rejoin civilization. Would we institute a whole new set of laws and departments just for them? Would we require them to wear some kind of marker? No, we wouldn't. We'd absorb them. We'd treat their illnesses, we'd protect them from the Syndrome and make sure the children they had from now on were immune, we'd educate them, and in a generation or two you'd never know the difference."

"Okay—" Rob was thinking. "You're saying everything basically continues as it's been since the Declaration, and the unresolved stuff—like voting rights—defaults to the norm standard?"

Temple nodded.

"What about the gemtechs? At the moment it's not clear if gems should have the right to sue them . . ."

Temple frowned. "The courts are refusing to entertain any motions until the legal issue is resolved. For this to work it would have to be done in a way that didn't hang the gemtechs out to dry. I know a lot of gems might not like this, but I think the gemtechs would have to be granted an amnesty. Draw a line under the past. Maybe they have to pay for things that are reversible, like removing the contraceptive implants. And they get to develop their intellectual property in ways that are benign—medical research, voluntary adaptations for space travel." He shrugged. "Something useful."

"This is brilliant," Eli said quietly. The man looked at him.

"No, Dr. Walker, it isn't. It's obvious. But it wasn't three hours ago. It's become so because of what you just did up there." He swallowed and looked at the floor for a moment. "That's not to say it's what will happen. There will be serious opposition. Bel'Natur will fight for their proposal."

"I'll fight for this one," Rob said. Eli nodded.

"That's what I wanted to make sure of, that this idea would have your support. Both of you. I'll discuss it with colleagues over lunch." He hesitated. "It would be helpful to know how the gem community feels." Eli and Rob looked at each other.

"It's not my place to speak for them," Rob said. "But I'm as sure as I can be that it would be welcomed. Eli?"

"That's my feeling as well."

"We'll run it past Aryel Morningstar and get back to you. Where can we find you?"

"I'll be working with the legal team when I'm not in the main hall. Here's my comcode." He pulled out a tablet and tapped at it.

"This is pretty brave of you, Mr. Temple." The man looked up at Eli in surprise. "Bel'Natur has a long reach. As do the others."

"The gemtechs can—" He stopped himself, shook his head. "Fortunately I don't have to care what they think. This is an issue that my wife and I feel very strongly about."

"What a dark horse you're turning out to be, Jeremy." Rob chortled. "I hear you're newly hitched. *And* expecting."

"Yes, well." He was nervous suddenly but blushing and beaming nonetheless. "Once we knew the baby was coming we thought we'd better get a move on."

"Congratulations," said Eli.

They found Aryel having a hurried conversation with Gaela. She threw Eli a warning look and he put a hand on Rob's arm, stopping while they were still out of earshot. Gaela looked close to tears. She gave Aryel a brief hug and practically ran from the room. Aryel activated her earset immediately.

"Commander Masoud, I've heard. I can be reached for another hour." There was a strained anger in her face that Eli had not seen before, but her voice as she left the message was as level and musical as ever.

"What's happened?"

She told them about the apprehension of John Senton. "Callan identified him from a photo, which allowed the officers to run his DNA. It's tied him to all three scenes."

"You mean the godgang sent a spy to try and infiltrate the Squats?"

"That's what it looks like."

Rob swore quietly but forcefully for a good half minute. Eli glanced at the door Gaela had disappeared through, then back at Aryel. She gave him a tiny nod. He hoped that Rob would not think to ask the obvious question.

"How did they spot him?"

Aryel sighed. "Gaela's son figured it out."

"Her son?" Rob frowned. "How? I thought he was only little."

"He's five. He . . ." She shook her head. "Will you forgive me if I don't go into exactly how he knew? Gabriel has a unique ability. It means he often finds things out by accident. This one was a bit too much for a child his age, and he wants his mama."

"Okay . . ." Rob looked from Aryel to Eli, sensing, maybe, some shared knowledge. Eli hurried to change the subject.

"We've got some news for you too. On the back of my show this morning." He realized that he still did not know her reaction. "Umm. I'm not sure it was what you were expecting."

"I didn't anticipate you would make the case so forcefully." The smile she gave him punched a warm hole in his chest and did something very strange to his diaphragm. "It's official, by the way. You are definitely one of the good guys."

He remembered the exchange from their first meeting and chuckled. "I think we might have found another one."

She listened to Rob's account of the conversation with Jeremy Temple while they sat down to lunch.

"Who is he?"

"Solicitor. Top firm. He used to do work for the gemtechs back in the day. Stopped a few years ago—from what he told us I'm guessing when all the nasty stuff started coming out he decided he didn't want to be part of it."

"He sounds perfect." She broke off a piece of bread and nibbled at it. "I was hoping someone besides me would float this solution."

Rob stared. Eli laughed. "You had it in mind all along?"

"I've always thought that if the world were as it should be, there would be no categories, no divisions between or amongst us. But we are where we are, and that is not a notion most people are going to be able to accept very easily. I expected to have to fight a rearguard action. I still might. But the chances are better if it's someone else's proposal."

Rob pushed his chair back. "I'll go and tell him. And then I'm going to see what Conference security know about this guy at the Squats. If they tried it there . . ."

"I suspect Masoud's security planning is better than the UC's." Aryel shook her head ruefully. "Poor Tobias. He's going to be apologizing for a month."

Rob hurried off and they were left on their own. Eli caught the murmurs and sideways glances from the delegates at surrounding tables. The other gems were dotted around the room, one each at tables otherwise full of norms, in what he thought must have been a deliberate strategy.

A tacit demonstration of what integration might feel like. I bet they're all like Horace—articulate, polite, nonthreatening. He wondered if he should be finding the maneuver appalling instead of admirable.

He had never dined with Aryel before. He was surprised by how much she ate.

She caught him looking. "High metabolic rate."

"You don't need to explain to me."

"Yes I do." She smiled. "I eat like a gillung."

He glanced at the bulge under her cloak. "Is that why?"

"It's part of it." Again that sharp blue gaze. "What's bothering you, Eli?"

He told her what Zavcka Klist had said. "Is it true?"

"About my cloak? Yes."

She regarded him quietly for a moment as he pushed vegetables around his plate. "Look. I have work to do. I need people to listen to what I'm saying. My particular gemsign would be a distraction."

"If people knew you were using military camouflage to hide it, it would be even more so."

"True." Her brows creased as she mopped up the last of the sauce on her plate. "The implied threat, of course, being that Bel'Natur will leak that if they feel like they're losing ground. They haven't so far because they think if the world turns in their favor they might be able to get hold of me and find out if what's underneath has any commercial value. I understand they haven't got anywhere trying to parse my genome, which must be driving them crazy. But you've put them on the back foot now. They must realize the odds are against them getting me or anyone else back into a lab. Even if an unrestricted version of the murder vid mysteriously finds its way onto the streams, its impact will be reduced. And if your friend Mr. Temple's idea gains any traction, discrediting me will become that much more important."

She dispatched the final forkful, chewed and swallowed. Eli was staring open-mouthed.

"You *knew* all this?"

"Just thinking it through aloud." She dabbed at her lips with a napkin. "How very helpful of Miss Klist. I almost feel I should thank her for the advance warning."

"I'm sure that wasn't her intention."

"I'm sure you're right. But have you noticed? She has quite a temper."

24

rington and Zavcka Klist could just see Aryel Morningstar and Eli Walker deep in conversation. Felix had furiously instructed the rest of the Bel'Natur team to go out and mingle.

"And remember to be nice to the fucking gems. Since they're just the same as us now."

As soon as they were alone he turned on Zavcka.

"What did I tell you? What did I fucking tell you? He's a secret weapon all right. Just not fucking ours."

"I didn't—"

"What the hell is supposed to happen now? You said you had this under control. The right incentives, remember? We were going to present the optimum solution. Not so fucking optimum now, is it?"

"I disagree." She felt strangely calm. Maybe it was a reaction to Felix's hysterics. Or maybe the failure of grander schemes had simply cleared her vision. "You heard them. No one was expecting that from Walker. Trench and Morningstar might have known but I don't think the other gems did. Even the liberals don't know what to think."

"How exactly does that fucking help us?"

"Felix, stop swearing at me." She snapped it sharply enough to shut him up. He blinked at her in astonishment.

"The result of Dr. Walker's performance is that we are now the *only* ones who have a solution to present. Everyone else was waiting for him to outline sets of criteria for different classes of gems, onto which they could then map their preferred plan. We weren't. We started from a position that the only categories that make sense are ours."

"He's just said there aren't any!"

"He can *say* whatever he likes. There still needs to be a structure. People still want to know where gems fit into the world. We'll tell them. And if they say it's not in keeping with Dr. Walker's analysis, we'll say we don't agree with him but even if he's right, so what? We still have a mess to sort out. We still have gems who should be working for a living and aren't. We still have limited public money with which to support them. We still have companies that were deprived of their assets even though they never broke any laws. Are you listening to me, Felix?"

"I'm listening." He spat it out.

"Our plan is based on resources and functionality. We point out that we've already built in all the protections to make sure gems aren't taken advantage of, health and safety, all that crap. It can still work."

Oh it's our plan now, is it? He had gotten himself under control but he was seething.

"And how do you propose to manage that? Speaking as an expert?"

She ignored the sarcasm. "The press will have his report by now. Since it patently does not solve any real-life problems, I say we release our proposal as well. All channels, just go for it. Let's see which one the streams like better. Along the way a few other facts will emerge that the public will find relevant. At the end of the day the decision will be made by politicians, and they go where the votes are."

Much as he disliked admitting it, she did have a point. Maybe they could still pull it off. But she was not going to be calling the shots, not anymore. As soon as this was over he would find a way to get her out. Until then he needed to stay calm, take control of the situation, remind everyone who was really in charge here.

He entered a drink order on his tablet and tried to make his tone conversational. "So you think if we just ignore Walker everyone else will as well?"

"Felix, right now the majority of people at this Conference would *love* to ignore Eli Walker. We need to show them that they can."

Gaela sat on the floor with Gabriel, watching carefully. The electromagnetic signature flickering around his head, always stronger than anyone else's, pulsated in time with his breathing. She was looking for any change, any sign that the trauma of the day had inhibited his talent. Or enhanced it. It had seemed bigger than usual when she first got home, spiky and strange, and she wondered if the horror he had sensed had scarred him in ways beyond their reckoning.

He had been calmer by then but had still flown into her arms and clung on like a limpet while he told her about the bad man and his terrible, terrible thoughts. She had asked him to show her what they looked like, maybe see if they could take the images out of his head and put them somewhere less scary. He was working with his tablet now, little fingers tracing colored lines and shapes onto the screen. She glanced at what he was drawing and shuddered.

Bal reached down over her shoulder, handing her a steaming cup. He dropped a quiet kiss on her head and retreated back to where his tablet was propped up.

"Mama?"

"Yes?"

"Is Aunty Aryel okay?"

"She's fine. Why?"

"Because of the bad man."

"He's in jail, baby." She reached over and stroked his head. "Remember? The police took him away and they locked him up."

"But he has friends."

"Was the bad man thinking about Aryel?" asked Bal.

Gabriel nodded without looking up from his tablet. "Yes. Not out in front like with you and Uncle Donal. Deep down."

"Deep down, what?"

"Bal," said Gaela.

"Deep down she's who they hate the most."

Gaela scooted next to him and wrapped an arm around his shoulders. "I just left her at this big meeting where she's trying to fix things so everyone is safe. She said to give you her love and she'll come see us when she gets home tonight. There's lots of people there, lots of police. Dr. Walker's there. Nothing will happen."

"And, you know," Bal said, "it's Aunty Aryel. They'd have to catch her first."

Gabriel looked up. Bal raised an eyebrow at him. Gabriel smiled back. Gaela sighed and stretched her legs out, back propped against the sofa.

"You two. Honestly."

There was quiet for a few minutes then. Gaela sipped her tea and watched her son's aura slip all the way back to normal. He glanced up a moment before they heard a knock at the door.

"Sally," said Gaela and Gabriel together. Bal rolled his eyes at them and went to open it. Sally Trieve stepped inside, returning his and Gaela's greetings, drawn face relaxing slightly as she spotted Gabriel sitting cross-legged on the rug.

"Hi, Sally."

"Hey there, Gabe. How're you doing?"

"Better." He looked up. "Thanks for taking care of me today."

"Oh . . ." Gaela and Bal heard her voice catch in her throat. Only Gabriel heard her say, *Oh, sweetie. You don't have to thank me.*

"You're welcome," she managed aloud. Then to his parents, speaking softly but without secrecy, "I wanted to see how you were. What Gabriel went through today . . . obviously it's not quite like anything we've dealt with before, but there are things we can do to help children who've witnessed tragedies, violence . . ."

Gaela rolled to her feet and went over. Gabriel stayed where he was. The grown-ups spoke quietly for a while. Sally refused tea and pushed herself out of her chair.

"The Conference," she said, on her way to the door. "Someone told me Dr. Walker basically started it off with a hand grenade. I know you had to rush home, but did you hear anything . . . ?"

Gaela chuckled. "That's a good description. He was fantastic." She caught herself. "At least we thought so. I don't know if you'd agree."

"Yes she would." Gabriel looked up from the rug. "Sally's good."

"Gabe."

"What? She is."

Sally Trieve was laughing in spite of herself. "Coming from you, my lad, that is a high compliment. And yes, if what I heard is true, I'm very much a fan of Dr. Walker."

"His report's just out." Bal indicated his tablet. "What did you hear?"

"That he said gems and norms are the same, basically."

Gaela shook her head. "He didn't exactly say that. He said the ways in which we were different didn't mean we were abnormal, and that by and large our behavior is affected by environment more than engineering. And he said something else interesting, which a lot of people in the room didn't like. He said that since the Syndrome they had created a homogeneous society, where there weren't any more big disagreements around things like race and sex and religion, and everyone could expect to have good health and long life and strong kids and so on. And he said the reality of gems is a challenge to that, but a healthy challenge. Something the norms should be glad to get back."

"Wow." Sally shook her head. "I'm going to have to think about that."

"But the godgangs do disagree. With everything." Bal glanced at Gaela.

"The bishop who came with Tobias pointed that out. Eli said that's true, and one of the ways to understand the godgangs is as a reaction against the fact that there aren't really that many divisions anymore."

Gaela's gaze drifted over to Gabriel. He had discarded the tablet and was working instead on another tower-tree of blocks. This one had multiple trunks, connected via a network of branches. He was concentrating on it, ignoring the grown-ups. His mother's face was thoughtful. "He had a great line—he said we're in an arms race between intellect and instinct, and sometimes instinct wins."

GODGANG MEMBER CAUGHT BY GEMS

The police have confirmed that a 32-year-old man has been apprehended in connection with the murders of two genetically modified men in London this week. The men were killed in separate incidents on Wednesday night and in the early hours of this morning.

The suspect was arrested shortly before 11 a.m. in the neighborhood known as the Squats, where many gems have settled since the Declaration. His identity has not been released; however, witnesses at the scene have identified him as John Senton, formerly a member of a United Churches congregation in northwest London. Current UC members involved in providing relief to the gem community claim that Mr. Senton presented himself as a volunteer, and that they had no reason to doubt his sincerity. There is speculation that Mr. Senton's real motive for volunteering may have been to facilitate the activities of a group which has been engaging in violent attacks against gems.

The first of these occurred on Tuesday night with a brutal assault against a gem named Callan (*né* Bel'Natur), 23, who remains in hospital in a serious condition [UrbanNews.ldn/gem _patron_left_for_dead]. This was followed within 24 hours by the mutilation and murder of Nelson (*né* Modicomm), 27, who appeared to have been thrown from the roof of an office building in what observers say may have been an act of religious symbolism [UrbanNews.ldn/gem_murdered_by_godgang].

Hopes that an intensive police investigation and increased patrols would prevent further mayhem were dashed earlier today by a violent confrontation in the City between up to sixteen members of what the police have indicated may be an extremist religious sect and two gems wanted for questioning in connection with a disturbance at an employment center earlier in the week. This incident resulted in the deaths of the gem Burot (*né* Biomin), again due to a fall from the upper story of a building, and two members of the gang, apparently from injuries sustained in the fight [UrbanNews.ldn/two_norms_killed_in_attack_on_gems].

Police sources have indicated that DNA evidence has been secured linking John Senton to all three crime scenes, and that they are now attempting to determine the whereabouts of the other members of the group. They remain tight-lipped about what prompted the initial suspicion that Mr. Senton might in fact be a member of the anti-gem godgang. There have been confused reports that he was unmasked by a child resident of the Squats who is rumored to possess some form of psychic ability. While this explanation does not appear to be tenable, Urban-News has confirmed that Mr. Senton was initially apprehended by gems before being handed over to the police, and that a child was present.

The authorities remain confident that this latest development will have no impact on the security of the European Conference on the Status of Genetically Modified Humans, currently under way in London. The high-profile meeting was thrown into controversy earlier today by the startling conclusions of the Walker Report, intended to provide the basis for determining a permanent settlement for the various classes of genetically modified humans. UrbanNews live feed from the Conference can be accessed **here**.

James Mudd stabbed open the link on his tablet. George's battered face appeared on the screen, propped against pillows. The swelling had gone down, but he still looked like a refugee from a pre-Syndrome war vid. The bruises ranged in color from angry purple to a sickening yellowish tint. Mudd felt a pang of sympathy. But he'd said he was up for working, and work needed to be done.

"You finished? We have to move fast."

"Still going through the Bel'Natur thing. It's one hell of a scoop, boss."

"It isn't a fucking scoop."

"But you said . . ."

"They changed their minds. The Walker Report has the whole place in an uproar. All we've got now is a head start. We've been trailing an exclusive. We're going to look like muppets unless we can come up with a spin that no one else has. What I think is, you seen the latest from the Squats? About the guy they caught?"

"Yeah."

"It's the same kid, right? The one you heard about from the UC."

"Got to be. There's been a couple of posts about him on open streams already, I've been checking."

"Good man. Okay. So far no one really knows about this kid except you, but that won't last so we've got to use it while we can. Here's our angle: how the Bel'Natur Proposal would deal with the reality of a mind reader with no gemsign, versus the Walker Report pretending it's no big deal."

"You want us to spell out what they'd do with the kid?"

"Surmise, George. All we're doing is surmising. Let's just go through it. Key points. What's Bel'Natur saying should happen?"

"Okay, well, I haven't read all of it yet, but basically they're pitching it as a guardianship-type arrangement. All the gemtechs take legal responsibility for the gems they created. That includes education, therapy, health care. They're supposed to make sure they have meaningful and fulfilled lives, whatever the hell that means."

"Go on."

"Part of their job will be to make sure gems are productive, so they get them trained, find them work suited to their abilities, negotiate the terms, provide appropriate supervision."

"How's that different from indenture?"

"The gems get to keep what they earn, after the gemtechs deduct their fees. Those are supposed to cover the cost of caring for them of course, as well as the placement itself. My guess is there won't be a lot left over." George's eyes and bandaged fingers were moving, flipping through notes on the split screen of his tablet. "Gems can apply to be released from the legal protection of the gemtechs if they manage to build up enough of a balance, as long as they satisfy a committee that they can find work and housing, and they don't pose a risk to society. If they plan to keep on using their abilities to make a living, they'll have to pay a licensing fee."

"So the gemtechs would need to keep tabs on them."

"Yeah, the whole thing depends on a shared global database. Mandatory registration of all gems and any offspring, including genome provenance, abilities, gemsigns, everything you can think of. They'd have to stay current with it no matter where they are or what they're doing, so, a permanent geotag implant to ensure compliance. Kids with no gemsign, like this one we're talking about, would have to get one applied at birth. Simple gene surgery to get the glow into the hair."

"They'd allow them to have kids?"

"They're cagey about it, suggest the same kind of committee setup to review and advise, lots about the inherent dangers of unsupervised recombinations. But they're in a bind because they haven't come up with anything that gets them back into the business of high-volume manufacture—they say they would expect it to proceed mainly on a voluntary basis. Reading between the lines, I think gems who agree to give up reproductive material for engineering and to be surrogates would get bonuses or have an easier time getting past the release committee, something like that."

"So what would the situation be with a kid like this one?"

"The parent gemtech—or gemtechs—would have automatic guardianship over the children, but they wouldn't remove them from the biological parents. They're proposing a transfer mechanism to move gems between gemtechs in the interest of, quote, promoting and honoring family life."

James Mudd chewed his lip in thought. "So more natural kids means more new gems coming into the system, but less control over what abilities they have. If any."

"Yeah, but think about it, boss. If random mixing lands you a psychic, which the gemtechs always said they couldn't create, they're not exactly going to be complaining, are they?"

"Nope. And this way you know where your telepathic, telekinetic, what-have-you is and what they're up to. Not to mention being able to pick them out in a crowd."

"Exactly. As opposed to Walker, which says . . ." George shook his head. "What, exactly? I've been scanning through that as well. I can't figure out what he actually thinks should happen. It's like a kid who can read your mind is no different from a kid who can play Mozart."

"The guy's spent so much time with them he doesn't know which end is up anymore. Okay, George. Pull everything you can on the kid and start drafting."

Yet another safe house. Yet more dark, cold, unfurnished rooms, reached in a breathless semi-panic after another frantic scramble. And yet more brethren, talking, praying, checking weapons. Ready to stand, ready to fight. Every time they were hurt or threatened their numbers grew.

Losing John was a blow, leavened only somewhat by the arrival of so many reinforcements. He had been a good soldier, clever and brave, full of faith despite a tendency to tolerate some of the softheaded ideas that occasionally found their way even here, into the heart of the true Church. And yet he had been taken. Mac did not think it a coincidence that the news of his capture was intertwined with and diluted by the rumors seeping out of the cursed Conference. The Lord was sending a message about what was needed and what was not, about the direction of travel and the destination, showing them what could be accomplished and what must be abandoned, at least by them, at least for now. They were being refocused onto the right target.

Someone had brought a map, a huge antique paper thing over which the city sprawled like a harlot. Mac and two or three others crouched around it, tablets carefully oriented at key locations, magnifying the mazes of streets and alleyways that they would need to navigate. They measured distances, discussed traffic and times of day, checked for closures and diversions.

One of the men looked up at Mac. "Are you sure we can find it once we get in?"

"There's only the one, brother, and it ain't exactly hidden away. We'll find it."

"Might still take a while," another pointed out. "It's a big place. We need a plan B, in case we run out of time."

Mac nodded. This was good. This was serious, proper military thinking. No one was taking the mission lightly, or in any doubt about how it would end. "Plan B is, we ascend on the spot if we have to. A search might slow things up, that's true, and at least we'd be heading in the right direction. But we should aim to move fast enough so we can finish the job in the right and proper manner."

The men all nodded. The one who had spoken first said, "How many others?"

"As many as we can manage. God willing, we'll smite more than we can bring to witness."

"And the deceiver?"

"The deceiver comes with us."

DAY SIX

25

THE SECOND DAY OF THE CONFERENCE DAWNED CLEAR AND COLD AND bright. There was a diamond hardness to the air that made Eli want to throw open the windows, lean out and drink in the frost-gilded city; and at the same time to shrink away, slink back under the covers and hope the sparkling blue morning would pass him by unnoticed.

He did neither. Instead he buried himself in his tablet, surfing the streams, hunting for any hint of another overnight calamity. There was none. He noted in passing the further evolution of public opinion as the core findings of the Walker Report were arrayed against the key requirements of the Bel'Natur proposal. Much journalistic attention had been given to their incompatibility. The streams condemned both as equally distasteful; the Newsbeat analysis featuring Gabriel had generated at least as much outrage as approval. A sense of deadlocked recrimination pervaded the online dialogue, and he wondered, with mingled relief and foreboding, if it had seeped out into the streets, holding the proponents of violence and their potential victims in a tense equilibrium.

Finally he sent the same, single-worded message to Aryel and to Rob.

Anything?

She responded first. *All safe, I think.* And then Rob: *No reports.* Eli sighed, rubbed his face, and allowed himself to think about a shower and coffee.

He checked again later, compulsively, as he picked at breakfast and fantasized idly about taking off for the day, leaving them all to battle it out while he walked and thought of nothing. But in his brief absence the stalemate had become punctuated by hints of a possible exit, a third way that might cost less in cash or conscience than either of the presumed alternatives. There was no mention of Jeremy Temple, nor any official line on what was afoot—just the merest suggestion of another solution, attainable via a more palatable set of compromises. There was an inference in an editorial, a throwaway remark from a minor official, a much-reposted socialstream comment. His weariness slipped away as he read.

It is manipulation, he thought. *The whetting of appetites, the preparation of a way. Subtle, sophisticated, irrefutable, and untraceable. I should mind. I really should.*

Once again the circle, the prayers, the exhortations to stand for the Lord. Once again the butterflies, and the blessings, and the descent of a calm certainty. Mac took his time, looked each man in the face, called every name. He had made sure to know them all, though there were more now than ever before. He had hardly dared hope that so many would be prepared to trade words for deeds, but events of the past day had done more for their cause than if the abominations and blasphemers and misbelievers had all gathered together to dance on graves on the day of the Lord. His sermon had only consolidated what the streams had called forth. They were ready.

"This is a great day, my brothers," he said finally. "We don't know our fate but we know our mission, and we know today will see it through. In our trust we honor the Lord, in our faith we travel to meet Him. As kings and shepherds once were, so are we now."

A chorus of amens. There was no need to discuss where they were going, or what would happen when they got there. The plan had been honed and rehearsed in the long hours of the night, carefully calibrated for maximum impact. Tasks had been assigned according to ability; not all would face the ultimate trial. But despite Mac's portentous words, they knew full well that those spared combat faced almost certain capture.

So they were quiet and grim as they clustered by the door. There was but a moment's pause as the white glare of the morning flooded in. No gray skies to hide beneath, and more than one man felt a twinge of unease as he stepped forth into the cold blaze of midwinter sun.

Then they split into their groups and slipped away.

Felix Carrington was speaking. He gestured from his position at the end of a curved table, one of seven panelists arrayed for debate and inquisition. The other outlier was Aryel. He had come last to his chair, Eli suspected so that he could sit as far away from her as possible. He had apparently not anticipated that he would end up facing the diminutive gem and her outsize dysmorphia across an empty half-moon of stage. He had attempted to counteract this unfortunate juxtaposition by angling himself toward the audience instead, swiveled uncomfortably so that he presented her with only his profile. Aryel sat motionless, hands folded together on the table, and looked straight at him.

Her direct gaze and his studied avoidance emphasized that he had also, unwittingly, turned his back on the others: the secretary of state in charge of the health and social services portfolio, the European Federation's attorney general, the United Churches bishop, and Robert Trench. The discussion was being moderated from the center by an aging journalist, a sufficiently uncontroversial and beloved public figure to have satisfied the Conference that he would manage the proceedings without bias.

Supposedly. He had a huge following, and Eli thought that the stasis of the streams could easily swing on any hint from him of approval or reproach.

At the moment there was neither. He was allowing Felix to hold forth on the significance of the murder that had taken place at a Bel'Natur dormitory almost two years previously, an uncensored vid

record of which had mysteriously appeared online the previous evening just as Aryel had anticipated.

"Should it impact on the Conference's deliberations? Of course
it should," he said. "Dr. Walker may have decided it's of no consequence, but we can see from the streams that the public does not
share his opinion. The idea that we shouldn't do all we can to avoid
such a tragedy beggars belief."

Rob interjected wearily, pointing out once again that Eli had
minimized neither the horror of the child's death nor the importance of preventing future crimes. Felix waved him away.

"The point is, the public wants to know that someone who could
do such a thing is not going to be living next door to them."

"The point is, we can't tell by genetype *who* might do such a
thing. A psychopath could be living next door to any one of us."

"Does anyone here actually believe there's the same chance a
normal human being could commit such a crime? Anyone?" He
waved theatrically at the audience.

The room stayed quiet. Eli resisted the urge to put his hand up.
He was keeping an eye on Zavcka Klist, also seated near the front.
The panelists were free to bring members of the audience into the
discussion if their expertise was relevant; he had already been called
upon by Rob, Aryel, the secretary of state, and the cleric. Zavcka
looked poised and ready to be included. So far she had not been.

Felix thundered on. "Look, I've spent my life in this business.
I know more about gems than a bunch of academics, and I know
there are risks we should not be prepared to take. We've seen this
week how dangerous and secretive they can be; we are learning just how much they have to hide. People are beginning to
wake up to that reality, and this Conference needs to address their
concerns."

He sat back, arms folded in a show of righteous indignation, and
deliberately turned to bestow a withering glare on Aryel. He was
disconcerted to find her smiling back. The audience shifted and
murmured.

The moderator's face stayed impassive over steepled hands, but he
looked at Felix long and hard enough to make him turn around and

sit up straight. He then told the delegates that since online rumor and innuendo provided so much of the context for the day's discussion, they might as well deal with what it had thrown up.

"One of the matters to which I believe Mr. Carrington has alluded concerns you, Miss Morningstar."

Aryel nodded briskly. "I find the rumor less interesting than what it implies," she said. "The idea that someone has been trying, essentially, to look up my skirt"—she raised an amused eyebrow at Felix, to a chorus of titters—"is offensive, but not surprising. Nor is their petulance at having failed."

She paused to let the wave of chuckles finish washing around the room. Then she leaned forward, jaw set, eyes still on Felix. The movement accentuated the outline of her swollen back. Once again Eli noted how she took the audience with her, their mood returning to serious along with hers.

"I make no apologies for protecting my privacy, but I am concerned by the insinuation that privacy is somehow dangerous."

"There's a difference between privacy and secrecy," said the secretary of state.

"Indeed there is. How would you characterize a desire not to be illegally scanned by an unauthorized agent?"

He blinked in astonishment, cleared his throat, and allowed that that was not something the government would consider acceptable. Felix had gone rigid, eyes wide. The triumphalism of a moment ago was back in his body language. In the audience Eli could see Zavcka Klist mouth, *No. Don't.*

Up onstage, Felix could barely contain his excitement. "Excuse me, minister, but that is an *excellent* point, I'm so *glad* she brought it up." He actually slapped at the table. "Illegal scans by unauthorized agents. *Well.* What a *good* example." The moderator looked ready to interrupt this sudden flood of sarcasm. Aryel caught his eye. He paused for the briefest instant and then waved Felix on.

"You want to know what's wrong with allowing gems to carry on as though they were norms? Some of you don't see the problem with letting them go unregistered and unsupervised? Here's why. Everyone has heard, I'm sure, about the psychic gem."

Eli tensed. The muttering around him spiked, exclamations of *What?* and *Is he serious?* audible throughout the room. Many people, he thought, had not heard, or else had dismissed it as tabloid hyperbole. He saw Zavcka Klist ball her hands into fists as she leaned forward. On the stage Rob threw a quick look at Aryel. She was sitting as still and calm as before.

The moderator said, "I beg your pardon?"

"It's a juvenile who is able to read the minds of people nearby. An unregistered prototype, which we now know has been hiding in the Squats. I believe *Miss Morningstar* here is well aware of it."

He waved contemptuously at Aryel. The bishop frowned and interrupted.

"If you mean the very young child who was instrumental in capturing a violent criminal yesterday, yes I have heard of him," she said. She spoke loudly, and there was an angry edge to her voice. "I'm not clear what you mean by *hiding*. As I understand it he and his parents are well known in the community."

"His *parents*. Well if we had the database set up, you wouldn't need me to tell you those gems are not his parents. *I* know that," he stabbed a finger at her, "because the female is Bel'Natur and *we* know she cannot *possibly* have had a child. All the people who worry about gem juveniles might want to concern themselves with how she got hold of this one. And by the way, any electromagnetic scanning *she* does when she's not assisting the police is also *unauthorized*. But the main point is this." He drew himself up and addressed the audience.

"Suppose this gem were to be treated as the Walker Report suggests. Not to mention this other crazy idea I hear is making the rounds. As though he were a normal kid. They would allow him to grow up, maybe even go to school, with *ordinary* kids. *Your* kids. He'd know what they were thinking. Imagine if you allowed him into your home. He'd know what *you* were thinking. That's bad enough, but what happens when he grows up? If he could go where he wanted and do as he pleased? What do you think he would end up involved in? Spying and stealing, that's what!"

Eli had a moment of déjà vu then, taken back to the meeting at the Squats and the sense of an audience taking a single, deep breath as they listened and listened, and then exploding into the silence at the end of a speaker's flourish. This time it was not Aryel's place to marshal and calm them, and the shouts of disbelief, condemnation, and anger sloshed back and forth. He could not tell whether Felix had registered that a fair amount of the outrage was directed at him. He sat back, apparently proud of having delivered such a stunning coup de grace. The moderator thumped the table and called ineffectually for calm.

Finally, though, Aryel did flick a sideways glance at the crowd. Then she pushed herself to her feet, an incongruously graceful movement, eyes front on Felix. The room went quiet. As the last calls died away she sat back down again and spoke.

"What would he end up doing if he were in your custody?"

"What?"

"I've read your proposal. Let's assume, for the sake of argument, that this child does have this ability. You're going to ensure that all gems put their talents to good use. So tell us, to what use would you put his?"

"We could make sure it was only used for legitimate purposes."

"If you could, I wonder why you think he couldn't. Or wouldn't. Let's face it, Mr. Carrington, for all you know there might be quite a few anonymous mind readers around, minding their own business and not troubling a soul."

"No there aren't."

"What makes you so sure? History is full of stories of people with psychic abilities."

"There's no evidence that any of those stories are true."

"But you're sure the story of this child is true. Why?"

He sensed something, maybe, and tried to backpedal. "I've read the reports."

"What reports would those be? The ones on the streams?"

"Of . . . of course."

"I've read those as well. They are journalistic hearsay, no more proof than the old tales you've just dismissed. Less in fact, since some of the historical psychics were tested quite rigorously."

Eli found he was holding his breath, stunned at how dangerous a game she was playing. Zavcka Klist had gone still and cold, face impassive. Felix sensed a final victory in the silence of the audience, the acquiescence of the moderator, Aryel's lack of denial.

"Rigorous testing is exactly what's needed."

A quarter of a mile away, on a corner where a main road was bisected by a smaller street, three men emerged from the Underground. They strolled toward a food kiosk that had for several years been festooned with hand-printed signs proclaiming that gems were welcome. Its business had increased in the last few days, with messages of support for the injured and beleaguered. A banner fluttered above, streaked into a rainbow with a dozen colors meant to represent the most common hues of phosphorescent hair. The proprietor was a plump, jolly woman who changed her own hair color weekly in a further expression of solidarity. Today it was a vibrant pink. She had never been able to get it to glow properly and had long since given up.

She realized, as she set out cups and swung into a practiced banter, that these customers were among what she called the sourpusses—no smiles or repartee, glares at her hair and the signs. Usually they went elsewhere, or launched immediately into abuse. She was puzzling over this when she noticed one of them slide in behind her and another come crowding up at the side.

And then she was shouting at the top of her lungs as they dragged her out from behind the counter and into the road, vehicles screeching to a stop, feet slipping on the icy pavement as she tried and failed to find purchase, her breath billowing out in a fog. Toward the towering monument in the plaza opposite, one of them breaking away to swing something into the skull of the attendant that sent him crashing to the ground, and all the while the other two were hitting and pulling and cursing her, and then the third man had hold of her again, and she was shrieking and shrieking, she could see the stairs winding up inside and *Oh my god* they were dragging her to the top . . .

She had been hauled halfway up the first flight, clothes torn and face bloodied and out of her mind with terror, before the other vendors and passersby were able to pull them off her and the first police patrol came screaming up.

Five minutes later another call came in, echoing into the earsets of
the officers at the scene as well as those guarding the Conference hall
and on patrol in the area. Three more men, masked and hooded this
time, had been spotted in a service alley that ran behind the building.
They had disabled the security vidcam, but not before the operator
had seen them start to attack an environmental systems exhaust hatch.

By the time the police arrived the hatch had been wrenched open.
There was no sign of the men. The first officer on the scene peered
into the gaping hole and declared the conduits too narrow for anyone
to have entered. But there was doubt in his voice, for the men had
not yet reappeared on any other vidcam feeds. He asked the building manager to run a diagnostic on all systems and sent for the bomb
squad.

There had been just enough time for a second cluster of patrol vehicles to gather at the mouth of the alley, and for the officers on foot
to be deployed throughout the building to double-check internal
hatches and secondary means of ingress, when a man wearing an
old-style greatcoat walked up to the desk in the lobby. He gave his
name as a delegate who had already checked in the day before and
explained that he had lost his tablet and identity pass and needed
to have the new ones registered. The senior attendant immediately
excused himself to alert the police, for the supposedly mislaid pass
had been used to enter the Conference that morning. His blue-
haired colleague busied herself trying to link the delegate's replace-
ment pass and tablet.

When she looked up to tell him that his biometrics were not
syncing properly with the Conference's datastream records, he
pulled an antique electronic stunner from the pocket of his coat and
shot her in the face. Then he strode toward the access gate. A second
stunner had appeared in his other hand and he used it on the senior
attendant, who screamed an alarm into his earset as he ran forward.

Without a valid pass the gates would not open, and with a
weapon in each hand the man could not vault them. So he stuck
them back in his pockets to launch himself over the barrier and had
only managed to pull one out again when the security guards and

police officers who had been dispatched to listen at air vents came tearing back into the lobby. This time he missed, but as they scattered to avoid the charge he dodged away into a corridor and disappeared.

It took them several minutes to find him, and several more to eliminate the threat of the stunners. All the while he barked a continuous series of situation updates and confirmations into his earset, while they shouted at him to give up and tell them who he was talking to. Finally they brought him down, at the cost of two stunned officers joining the injured attendants in a hospital transport. It was only later, when they broke his tablet encryption and tried to trace his uplink pathways, that they realized he had been speaking to no one at all.

From her post in the old leisure center at the Squats, Sergeant Varsi listened with growing disbelief to the emergency calls and urgent reports that poured into her earset. Mikal stood just inside the door. She kept her input muted so she could brief him without adding to the confusion.

"They're attacking the Conference?"

She shook her head, frowning as she tried to understand what she was hearing. "It sounds that way, but what's happening doesn't make sense. None of it is big enough, there aren't enough of them, it doesn't seem coordinated . . . unless it's *so* big that these are just small parts of it . . ."

"A distraction?"

She looked up at him. His strange eyes blinked back at her; his strange hands opened and closed. She liked him enormously.

"I don't know. Maybe. That's already occurred to Masoud; he's pulled everyone in close to protect the delegates."

"Do you have to go?"

"Don't think so. We're not going to leave the Squats without a patrol. They've already diverted one of our units, but the others have been taken from the financial district."

"You're sure Aryel and the others are safe?"

"So far they're fine. Don't worry, we—" She stopped, suddenly rigid, as a new series of communications were barked into her ear.

These were for her, and they came from the remaining unit, close to half a mile away. She flicked the sound input back on and grabbed for her jacket and utility belt.

"Varsi responding. En route, I repeat, en route. Emergency services confirmed. Mikal," as she shrugged into the jacket and clipped her tablet in place, "how many people in the Tyler block? Over near the park?"

He ducked back through the door as she rushed toward him, moving his giant bulk with considerable speed and dexterity. "Should be seven, spread over four apartments. They're all new, came in this week. What's happening?"

"There's a fire. Patrol rounded the corner and spotted hooded men running in with lit cocktails. Door is smashed. Doesn't that building have an alarm?"

"No."

"Suppression system? Sprinklers?"

"No. Hasn't been retrofitted yet."

"Shit." She spoke into the earset. "There are potentially seven occupants, I repeat seven occupants, on floors . . ."

"One and two."

"Floors one and two, I repeat first and second stories are occupied." She listened again. "Got it. Get them out, I'll go after the bastards."

She was almost at the double doors when Mikal grabbed her shoulder. "Sharon, *wait*. You're going after them alone? You can't. Let me help."

"*No*." She pushed his hand away, a shock like electricity at the feel of the double thumbs against her palm, not bad but *strange*. "I'm armed, I'll be fine. You stay inside, lock the door, contact the other blocks and tell them to do the same. Get everyone indoors. Fuckers aren't just targeting the Conference, they're here in the Squats."

Mikal did as he was told. Three minutes went by. Then five. People checked in from the firebombed building. Everyone was out, no one was hurt, fire units were on the scene, it was under control. The minutes were creeping up to ten. He decided to hell with playing it cool; ten was a good number and he'd call her then if he hadn't heard.

Her comcode buzzed once and flicked straight over into message mode. He was leaving something that he hoped sounded witty as well as worried when he heard a beeping behind the desk. He checked the systems monitor. It was coming from home, a fire alarm in the community room of Maryam House. He hurriedly tacked the news onto his message.

"It's not a smoke alarm. One of those you have to activate, like a panic button. Outer doors are fine, though. I'll find out what's going on."

He called Bal first, knowing he would be down there. With Gaela and Gabriel, probably. It was his day to organize lunch and keep an eye on whoever showed up in need of company or a meal, as was the regular habit of many of the more vulnerable residents. He had said, grim-faced as they perused the streams last night, that he would neither duck the obligation nor let his family out of his sight. Gabe was a little quiet and a little sad after the trauma of encountering John Senton, but he'd said he didn't want to be kept cooped up in the apartment. Bal thought he was looking for the reassurance of kinder minds.

But there was no answer. None from Gaela either, nor Wenda. Half a minute had ticked by. He called in the emergency, unlocked the door, and ran.

There were two vans parked in front of Maryam House. One was the United Churches transport that had brought so many to safety over the past days, and as he skidded around the corner and saw it his initial feeling was one of relief. But he knew all the UC volunteers, and the man who leapt into the front and gunned the engine was not one of them. Nor were the two who shoved something in through the side access door—something that kicked and struggled—known to him.

They dived in after whoever it was and slammed the door shut. He was moving fast with fifty yards still to go when he saw Bal. The

big man's face was covered with the blood that matted his glowing indigo hair. More poured from half a dozen wounds. One leg
dragged behind him, and he staggered and fell on the threshold of
the undamaged front door, roaring his fury and his loss as the vehicles accelerated away.

26

THE ATTORNEY GENERAL HAD BEEN SPEAKING, EXPLAINING THAT WHILE the Temple solution might prove politically impractical it was legally really quite straightforward, when proceedings were interrupted by the moderator with the news that violence had erupted not only nearby but within the Conference building itself.

"Commander Masoud has asked everyone to stay calm and remain in their seats. This room is secure, and we don't want anyone to get mixed up in what's going on outside."

An uproar, naturally, people on their feet regardless. Security guards appeared inside the hall. A police officer hurried in, looking for the delegate whose pass had allegedly been lost. His identity was confirmed. She hurried out again with him in tow. Rob and the attorney general conferred quietly, as did Aryel and the bishop. The secretary of state was speaking into his earset, back to the room. Eli at first assumed he was being briefed, but from where he sat could see that the man was doing most of the talking. Zavcka Klist walked to the edge of the stage and stood there, arms folded, until Felix Carrington came over to speak to her.

Finally Masoud strode in, spoke to the moderator for a few seconds, then gave the audience a clipped summary of what had taken place in and around the building.

"We don't believe there is any danger to you. However, I'm going to ask you to stay here for a few minutes longer while we complete our sweep of the building. We are maintaining a very heavy police presence in the area—"

He broke off and turned away, frowning at something coming into his earset. The moderator jumped into the breach, suggesting the panel be adjourned until the organizers decided how or whether the rest of the day could proceed. Eli stopped listening to him, because Aryel was also on her earset now, her chair screeching back as she surged to her feet, all color drained from her face. She met Masoud's eyes. Were it not for his darker pigment, Eli thought the policeman would have been as pale as she.

He found himself on his feet as well, moving without thought toward her as she rushed from the stage. Masoud made to leap down, then caught himself and readdressed the audience. "Ladies and gentlemen, I've just been made aware of another incident. It's in a different part of the city; what I said just now still applies to you . . ." He came off still speaking, striding after Aryel as she made for the door. "Please stay here. Stay here."

He did not mean her, though, for he wrapped an arm gently around the huge lump of her cloak to help her along, just as Eli caught up with them. Rob was scrambling after. His calls of "What's going on? What's happened?" were picked up and echoed back from a dozen throats as the delegates stood and stared, already aghast at the latest, unknown tragedy. Eli reached over and grabbed Aryel's hand. She was still listening to her earset, and for the first time her sky-blue eyes seemed to look at him without seeing.

"Aryel. What is it?"

"Home," she replied, and he could hear the shock in her voice, the anger and something that sounded like fear. The word seemed to bring her back and she paused, taking in his face and the calls from the crowd beyond. When she spoke again her tone carried like a shout, although it seemed she spoke quietly.

"They've attacked our home. *My* home. This was just a diversion. They've set fires, they've—" She drew a deep, ragged breath. "People have been killed. And taken. It seems they came planning . . . planning to take some of us . . ."

A general intake of breath, soft cries of dismay. Eli saw Rob behind her, open-mouthed. Farther back, even Zavcka Klist looked stunned.

"Who?" he said, and as he asked the question he knew, with a sinking horror, what the answer could not possibly be but was going to be. "Aryel, who did they take?"

"Donal, and Gaela." Her eyes squeezed shut, as though if she could just hold it back for another instant it might somehow be less real. The name came out in an exhalation that sounded like despair. "And Gabriel."

In the end it had been easier than he expected. *Planning*, thought Mac. *Can't beat a good plan.*

They had avoided the risk of any direct communications being intercepted by simply hacking into the police voicestreams. It told them who was being sent where, and when. The advance teams had done brilliantly. His own, much larger group waited until the closer of the two units on patrol peeled off in the direction of the Conference. They knew where the other was, far away on the opposite edge of the Squats, and about to stay there.

Once the Tyler blaze was under way, they had simply to drive in, directing the stolen delivery van, loaded now with the Lord's army, up to the front door of the UC center while they listened with approval to Sergeant Varsi's exchange with her colleagues. When she tore off after the brethren who had drawn firebomb duty, the coast was clear.

He himself had stepped inside to deal with the misbeliever who came forward, all smiles, asking what goodies they had brought today. When he stepped back out, knife wiped clean on her jumper and safely stowed, the hijacked UC transport was also purring away. He

jumped into it and they moved in convoy over to Maryam House.
The street seemed to have cleared before them, and when they got
there the Lord favored them once again. A straggler perhaps, a small,
twisted, saffron-haired creature hurrying along and focused only on
his earset, not noticing them crowding up behind until he was at the
door. And then it was too late; he was held rigid with a palm over his
mouth while his hand was slammed against the identipad. The door
hissed open. They dragged his body inside.

The community room was just as John had described it in that
last, long message, like one of the ancient paintings of a scene from
the Pit. These gems were not like the ones they had caught out
on the street, not all of them anyway. These stared blankly and sat
still or gibbered and screamed and tried to run. He had counted
on being able to force the information they needed out of someone here, and for a moment wondered if any of the abominations
would prove sufficiently capable. And then he heard it, like a gift
from the Lord, the cry of a child.

There was no need to go hunting. He was sitting at a table,
between a large woman with turquoise hair and a younger, smaller
one with too many noses and not enough chin. The woman shoved
the boy behind her and surged forward, while the girl shrieked and
scrambled away on hands and knees. In a doorway at the back a big
man with short, bluish hair had appeared at the child's first call, and
now he ran forward too.

But he was checked by the mayhem that was erupting all around
them as Mac's men descended on the abominations with knives and
clubs. Mac could see him out of the corner of his eye, battling bare-
handed with Rich and Pavel while he shouted at the boy to get
back. The turquoise woman loomed in front, catching him a sharp
one to the jaw before he slashed out with the knife, ripping a line
across her chest.

She and the boy screamed together.

And then it went a bit mad, a bit confusing, the shrieks of the
child and the woman and all the others, the shouts of the man and
the other men, the red haze of combat finally lifting enough for him
to see another red, the hair of a woman who grabbed the boy and

ran for the door. He leapt over the body in its pool of blood and matted turquoise and sprinted after her, catching up as she stumbled out of the carnage into the lobby. As he clutched at her she spun away and kicked out, crouching to protect the child in her arms, and he lost the knife. But he had her and the boy, and the others had seen and come after, and together they wrestled her up and out toward the waiting transports.

He shouted for anyone left inside to follow. Three came behind, dragging a fourth, a young man with shaggy brown hair who kicked and cursed and struggled. He nodded approval and left them to it, leaping into the back of the delivery van that now held the woman and child. Most of the men who remained piled in with them. As the doors swung closed he glimpsed, skidding around the corner at the far end of the street, a giant.

Then they were moving and he leaned forward to remind Dirk not to go too fast. The point was to get there as quickly as they could without attracting attention. He dropped back to a steady pace and Mac had a chance to sit back, catch his breath, review events, and contemplate the captives. They were huddled into a ball, the woman trying to wrap herself as much around the child as possible. He thought he saw her lips move and he reached forward and slapped her, hard, and then wrenched the earset away.

She gasped at the blow and clutched the boy even closer. He flinched as though it had been he who was struck, and whimpered. She turned a red, tearstained face to Mac. The glow from her hair was demonic.

"Please, please let him go. You can do whatever you want to me, but he's just a baby, please . . ."

"No."

"Please! We can stop, put him out through the back, keep going. He's a child! Please!"

Mac was pleased to see that the boy was feebly shaking his head. He leaned forward, deliberately, and slapped the woman again.

"He's the one we came for. You and the other one, you're just a bonus."

She screamed at that, a despairing wail that bounced around the inside of the van. The boy whimpered again, tugging at her shirt, and then a small hand fumbled up to try and cover her mouth.

"Another sound from either of you and I'll cut out your tongues." They went as silent as they could. He thought about doing it anyway. But it was different here, crammed into the locked van in the dark, five men staring through the racing gloom at a woman who shook with muffled sobs and a strangely limp and quiescent child. He decided it was better to deliver them whole unto the judgment of the Lord.

It occurred to him that the same view might not prevail in the other transport, and he thought for a moment about calling over. Best not, though. The alarm must have been raised by now, no telling what kind of surveillance the agents of the Beast might be using to try to find them. It didn't really matter if the other one got damaged. The Lord would understand.

They had done so well. Not just the one deceiver, the dangerous infant, but three. And almost the best three. The ones whose powers were sacrilege, who could sense things that should not be sensed and know things that should not be known, and tell lies that the world would believe. Almost the best.

There was only one who would have been an even greater triumph than these, and he had prayed hard and thought long to find a path to her. But it was impossible. She was too well guarded, too perpetually surrounded by press and police and politicians for them to get close. He had finally had to concede defeat, turn the assault on the Conference into the ruse that would give them a broader, though not a deeper, victory.

Still, it was a shame they had not been able to get her. Such a shame.

Aryel bent over her tablet, as though she were trying to physically reach through it and into the grief and terror and chaos of Maryam House. She sat crouched on a low stool and had kept tight hold of Eli's hand, drawing him down so that he knelt beside her. He peered at the screen, over the mass that was her right shoulder. Horace crouched to her left, face slack with horror. Rob and Masoud hovered, listening and looking, muttering into earsets.

Mikal was covered in blood, none of which, he assured them, was his. In the background they could see that the front steps leading into the building were spattered with pools of red. Police and paramedics raced through it. Bal had finally been pressed down onto a stretcher, although he kept pushing the medics away, shouting at them to go and help the people inside, and at the police to find the others. His desperate pleas echoed through their earsets, in time with the bloodstained face that kept jerking up into view. It was all Mikal could do to hold him in place.

"He doesn't know how many there were, maybe ten or twelve," Mikal managed. "Three are still here . . ."

"Alive?"

"Not sure, at least one of them is, I think, but . . ."

"Make him tell you!" Bal again, the shout a little weaker now.

Mikal shifted in their view, holding the big man down as gently as he could. "They can't, mate. He's unconscious. And even if he weren't . . ."

He looked back out of the screen at them, his shoulders moving in a bleak shrug. A hand fell onto one of them and Sharon Varsi's face crowded into view beside his. "Is Masoud there? I'm queued up on channels."

Aryel pulled back and Masoud took Horace's place. "You have something?"

"Another body in the UC center, sir. Norm female. We're trying to get tracker codes for the vehicles but it's going to take a few more minutes and I think we'll find they've been disabled anyway. They wouldn't have put together an operation this thorough and not thought of that."

A sound like a sob from Bal, faint and desperate. Her lips pursed in sympathy and her hand shifted from Mikal's shoulder to rest, it seemed, on his stretcher. "I tried to question one of the assailants, sir. He regained consciousness briefly, but all he would say was 'judgment.' He said that over and over. I pressed him and he tried to say something else but I couldn't make it out. Something like 'home'?

Or 'hole'?" She shook her head. "I don't know what it was. The medics say he's not going to be waking up again anytime soon."

Masoud nodded. "We've got all available units looking for them, and more heading to you." His fingers were already moving over his own tablet. "I'll run those words through the profile apps, see if they give us any probables." He looked back at her. "Anything else?"

"Just that everyone we've been able to speak to agrees their leader went straight for the child, sir. One of the victims, a turquoise-haired lady, I don't know her name . . ."

"Wenda," said Mikal. They could hear Bal crying now.

"She was killed trying to protect him. Along with three others, plus the UC victim. Six more seriously injured, including Bal here. One of the assailants was dead when we arrived, another has died since, and the one I was questioning is in a serious condition."

She glanced down at Bal and sighed. "It seems Gaela was in a back room, an office of some sort, when it started. She grabbed her son and tried to get the hell out of there and they followed her. The ones that were left in the room swamped the young man and took off after them straightaway. He was close to the door, and as far as I can tell that's the only reason they chose him."

"What about the fire? You went after that group, didn't you?"

"Yes, sir, that's where I was when this happened. I spotted them but they kept dodging into alleys where my unit couldn't fit. I was coordinating with the other unit and I figured we'd get them cornered in a dead end eventually, but all the while they were just leading me further away." Under the professional crispness she sounded desolate. "When we got this call I realized what they were doing so I abandoned the chase and came here. I should have stayed, caught the bastards, found out where they were going."

"You couldn't have known," Aryel said. Beside her, Masoud grunted agreement and reared up to his feet. "Varsi, I'm prioritizing your comcode. Anybody remembers anything else, or the one you've got does wake up, you get back to me. I'm on my way, and I don't mind if he's still there when I arrive. He gets no priority for transport, is that clear?"

"No danger, sir."

Varsi slipped out of view. Aryel said, "Mik, take care of Bal. I'll be back in a minute." She broke the connection and just sat, staring at the blank screen.

Masoud reached down and gently touched her shoulder. She looked up.

"Aryel, I'm heading over there. I don't think you should come, not yet." Eli was surprised to see her bow her head in agreement. Masoud seemed to be too, but he only nodded briskly and left.

Aryel said quietly, "Horace, would you go and find the others, please? Tell them what's happened, and make sure they stay together and stay here." The request seemed to bring the green-haired gem back to himself and he slipped away, wiping at his face as he went. Eli heard an increased murmur from behind them as the press, kept back by a grim-faced security guard, parted to let him through.

She went back to staring, chin on hands, at a point somewhere in the space between her nose and the empty screen. Rob said tentatively, "I think I should go and find the secretary of state. He needs to know what's going on."

She nodded.

"And the press . . ."

"Yes, please. I can't just yet."

"Eli?"

"I'll stay with her."

Rob departed, most of the press in tow. Eli pushed himself off his aching knees and onto a neighboring seat. He looked around. They were in a strange bubble of quiet, a damper field that shrouded this little seating area just outside the lounge from which they had entered the main hall. In there he could hear a distant hubbub of voices, diminishing every time a new bit of news came online and then rising again as faces poked out to stare across the floor at them.

He had no doubt that everything Varsi and Mikal had just told them would be streamed live within minutes, either from witnesses at the scene or some impromptu press conference Rob would hold once he had briefed the politicians. Only the Newsbeat vidcam operator remained, a young man who kept his equipment pointed resolutely in their direction. Eli wondered why he bothered. There was nothing to see besides Aryel's bowed back as she sat and stared into empty space.

"Hope," she said finally, so quietly he could barely hear her.

"What?"

"Hope. That's it. How ironic."

She reached for her tablet and he thought she was going to get back to Mikal, but she activated a different interface and leaned forward for a retinal scan. Her fingers slipped over the surface as she spoke. There was a harsh note to her voice he had never heard before. "Masoud's gone, isn't he? Just as well, he'd try to stop—But we need transport. *Now*."

"You want to go home after all? We can find a car, I'll borrow Rob's."

She was on her feet, moving fast as the tablet slid back inside her cloak, turning to survey the room. The sense of purpose and swift action was back, leavened now by some grim and ruthless decision.

"No. Much closer. But we need to get there quickly: they've had what, fifteen, twenty minutes . . . they'll almost be there . . . we need to make it in five."

Her gaze swept past the guard and found James Mudd, hurrying back from the direction of the restrooms, already starting to berate his young colleague with the vidcam for having waited instead of following the others. Aryel strode forward.

"Mr. Mudd. You have a press vehicle with global uplink capability out front, yes?"

"What? Why?"

"Yes or no?"

"Yes."

"Excellent. I need to get somewhere, and I need to get there fast."

She headed toward the main entrance, not waiting for a response. Mudd stared at her in bewilderment and then trotted to catch up, jerking his head at the vidcam operator to keep up and keep shooting.

"You expect me to *help* you?" he said as he fell into step beside her. "Why?"

"You're going to want to help me. You get me . . . us . . ." She glanced at Eli, who nodded. "Get us there and in exchange I will tell you exactly what has happened. You'll be able to broadcast details of the Maryam House Massacre ahead of everyone else." Her voice had gone from harsh to bitter, acrid. "Not to mention the rest of it."

"The rest of what?"

"What happens next. Mr. Mudd, yesterday you tried to question me and I avoided you. Bel'Natur promised you an exclusive and failed to deliver. Your reporter tried to do an exposé on us and almost got killed. I will give you a scoop that makes up for all of that, but we need to get there *now*."

"Get where?" They were almost at the doors.

"Newhope Tower."

27

He swore and spun his car around to rendezvous with them there. She kept the link open as she explained, and they could faintly hear him barking orders to the search units over the background wail of his siren. Still, it was clear they were going to arrive first.

"They'd need more than a few people to pull off what you're suggesting. Why would they take such a risk? In broad daylight? Even if they made it up there, they'd never be able to get away again." James Mudd was voicing ready-for-streaming objections, all of which were being recorded.

Aryel's hurried review of what had happened at the Squats, delivered while they piled into the transport, had already been released. Masoud had then screamed at them to hold any further live streaming until they knew for sure where the godgang was.

"My guess is, whoever still can will meet them there. They may already be waiting. This will be a last stand. People forget," she shook her head in frustration, "they forget what today means. I hinted at it after Nelson was killed, but I couldn't be explicit . . ."

"Why not?"

"Because I felt certain organs of the press would have spun it that it was me who was giving people ideas and stirring up conflict."

Mudd had the grace to look sheepish. She sighed.

"Anyway, few understood because the old holidays aren't observed anymore. Today is Christmas Eve. It used to be a day for the declaration of allegiance to god and the giving of gifts in his honor. The Conference is supposed to deliver its preliminary conclusions tomorrow, a date which also commemorates the birth of the Christian prophet, a man who was believed to be the son of god and to know more than other men. I think they've gone from simply being whipped up by that coincidence to believing Gabriel is somehow his antithesis. An evil incarnation."

"Why would they think that?"

"As you know they believe all gems are man-made abominations of nature, but for some reason they have fixated on this particular child. Now the UC members have recently been buzzing about him as well, but they think just the opposite, that Gabriel is a child to be celebrated. A blessing, not unlike the child whose birth they revere. The way the godgangs see the world, any interpretation the UC have is going to be completely wrong and probably influenced by the devil, what they call the Beast. We know from the John Senton case that some godgang members are ex-UC and still have links to them, including, I would imagine, access to their streams."

Eli was nodding as the picture she described came clear to him. "Allowing them to see all the posts about Gabriel and focus on him as a target of great symbolic significance. One they could actually acquire."

"As opposed to me, you mean. Yes."

"Along with the means to capture and transport him."

"Yes."

"If they were after the kid, why take the other two?" James Mudd jumped back in. He was cueing up as they spoke, itching to upload.

"It may have just been opportunistic, or there may be some symbolism there too. The prophet Christ had two saintly parents. He was executed as a criminal, along with two other criminals.

Their theology is based on the idea of a holy trinity, a single god
with three identities. There are a lot of threes in it." She glanced out
of the transport's side window as they veered into the traffic circle
around Newhope Tower. "We need to get as close to the apartments
as we can. The outside ones, for the viewing terrace."

Masoud's voice came in, thin and tinny through the press van's
ancient speakers. "They won't be able to use them, Aryel. I asked
for all exterior elevators to be shut down two days ago. I spoke to
Newhope services personally."

"I'm sure you did, Commander, but I suspect these people will
have a way around that."

The way was a kid named Rollo, who had a low-grade job in building services and a talent for quietly accessing systems well above his
clearance level. When the signal came in, he had sent the elevators
down to the street and messaged back with a newly programmed
security code that needed to be entered before they would move
again. The risk of anyone else attempting to access them was obvi-
ated by the four men in coveralls who strolled up just as they hissed
down and set up bright orange barricades.

The people hurrying in and out of the building's main entrance
gave them not a second glance. Most were already distracted by the
large public screens that lined the lower windows, where a top-of-
the-line trending algorithm had replaced advertising and newstream
bulletins first with the incidents at the nearby Conference venue,
then with the confused reports coming out of the Squats, and now
with Aryel's concise summary of events there, bracketed by Mudd's
promise of further live and exclusive coverage.

Mac noticed only that the attention of the public was elsewhere
as the vans stopped on the delivery ramp that led down into the
bowels of the building. The elevator doors were little more than
thirty yards away, and no one was looking in their direction.

The police chatter had disappeared from the hacked stream ten
minutes or so ago, but that was expected. He heard sirens wailing in
the distance, too far away to be a worry. He jumped down from the
van and turned to help pull the woman out. She seemed dazed, not

quite aware of her surroundings, and she stumbled at the long step down to the ground. The child still clung silently to her.

They were all out, and he looked over to the other transport. The driver and the two others who had ridden with the prisoner now held him upright between them. His hands had been bound behind his back, and his mouth taped shut. The sides of his face were drenched in blood. Mac hissed a warning, but one of the brethren was already shrugging out of his coat to drape it over the young gem's damaged head, hiding his bloody face and pinioned arms.

The woman was wearing a hooded jumper, and they pulled it up to cover her hair. No more could be done in the way of disguise. The two groups merged and moved toward the elevators, the men closing ranks in a tight cordon to hold and hide the prisoners in the middle. Behind them a line of vehicles began to pile up, blocked by the abandoned vans. Shouts and blaring horns erupted in their wake. He heard a door slam and footsteps, and glanced back to see that a couple of drivers had gotten out. But they were reluctant to leave their own vehicles, and he ignored the calls and curses that followed them as they crossed the plaza.

Harder to deal with was the woman, who staggered and swayed as she moved. He had a hand ready to clamp over her mouth should she try to scream, but she was breathing raggedly through it, eyes down to slits as though facing into a glare. He wondered if it was the weight of the child, but her arms were like iron bands around him. Her pace kept dropping, though. The young man was trying to stop entirely, eyes wide with fear as he saw where they were headed. It took four brethren to keep him moving, his feet scraping across the ground. The woman was down to a shuffle, and Mac swore and cuffed her.

Out of the corner of his eye he could see that people around them were turning to look. A sound reached his ears, cries of surprise and excitement rippling across the plaza. The sirens sounded much louder. They were more than halfway there. The men in coveralls were opening the barricades, creating a channel for them to walk through and into the elevators, entering the code. But the woman stumbled, and he cursed at her again as they yanked her forward.

"She can't help it, Mac."

The voice, clear and musical, not loud but a tone that carried. He spun around as though stung.

Aryel Morningstar was walking toward him. Off to the side a vidcam operator kept pace, next to a man with a press badge who muttered rapidly into an oversize earset. In the distance he could see the public screens refresh. A new scene flickered into life: this scene, here and now in the plaza at the foot of Newhope Tower, streaming live under a Newsbeat banner. Exclamations of recognition from viewers, and then they turned away from the screens, looking for the source.

She stopped. There was barely ten feet between them.

"You've hurt her, haven't you? You couldn't have known, but pain makes her ill. She can hardly see, or think, or move."

It's not that bad, Gaela thought. The sting of the slaps had triggered her synesthesia and she was fighting back the waves of purple and puce, but fear and the cold and most of all the feel of Gabriel clinging to her, silent and trembling, was enough to keep it from escalating. She never became completely incapacitated. Aryel must want her to play it worse than it was, and she let her knees buckle. The men holding her rocked and then pulled her upright.

"You can't get any further with them, Mac. This is it."

The other captive jerked forward suddenly, throwing off the coat. A cry went up from the puzzled witnesses on the plaza, comprehension dawning as they saw the bloody head and taped mouth. Mac glanced over at Dirk. A knife appeared, pricking the young gem's neck.

"Anyone gets in our way and it ends right here. Right here! The day of the Lord!"

Screams now, people shrinking back at the sight of the knife and then edging forward again. The vidcam team took advantage of the momentary space to find a better angle. They were in front of the fringe of onlookers now, almost at the barricades, shooting back at the nine men, their three captives, and the small, lone gem who challenged them. The godgang had surged a few feet closer to the elevators. The crowd, still thin but building, formed an arc of faces, gaping mouths and waving hands and shouts of protest.

Aryel Morningstar moved forward a few steps, keeping the distance constant.

"Wait, Mac! You don't have what you want. You think the Lord wants them? Are you going to settle for this?"

"The Lord will witness our victory!"

"Oh, it's *your* victory now, is it?" Her voice blazed with contempt. "I thought you were acting for the glory of God. But no, all you want to offer up are foot soldiers and children. Is that the limit of your ambition, Mac?"

Mac was aware that she was delaying them. There were sirens all around the plaza now. But her scorn rankled.

"God will not be deceived by you! Or by him!" He yanked roughly at Gabriel. Gaela lost her balance as she jerked instinctively away. One of her arms came loose, and the men who kept hold of her grabbed it as they hauled her up and held her still. Gabriel's little legs were still wrapped around her hips and she clutched him one-handed. Another knife appeared, held now to her throat.

"God knows that he is a deceiver and an abomination! God calls us to deliver him to judgment!"

"Why him?" The shout came from behind, in the direction of the elevators, and Mac swiveled. James Mudd and the vidcam operator stood within the channel of the barricades, backs to the brethren in coveralls.

"The world is watching you, sir!" Mudd called. There was a tremble in his voice that he was unable to entirely control, and it felt as though his heart was trying to batter its way out through his chest. This was far, far more than he had bargained for. "Thousands of people will want to know why!"

"Especially when you have a choice." Aryel again, and he spun back.

"It's me that you want, Mac. On today of all days, you want me. You know it and I know it. You want a real victory? Let them go, and I will come with you. No tricks, no struggle. Release them and you get me."

If he had known, Eli would have tried to stop her. When they swung around the perimeter of the plaza and spotted the two vans on the service ramp, she had shouted at them to pull in and let her out, *now*. Then, as James Mudd relayed the sighting to Masoud and released the recorded interview to the streams, and as the driver cut across traffic to the screeching of tires and honking of horns, she handed Eli her tablet.

"I've accessed a file and made it ready for immediate upload. I have to go ahead, but I want you, and Kate there"—she nodded at the uplink technician in the driver's seat—"to cue it up for release to the streams."

"What is it?" asked Mudd, patting himself to make sure he had everything as Kate pulled in at a pedestrian crossing and stopped.

"The truth about who and what Gabriel is. I'm going to try to end this on the ground, but if I fail it might just be enough to stop them. Which means it has to be on the streams if he gets taken into the elevator." She turned and stared at Mudd, blue eyes intense. "Someone needs to be there who can bring it to their attention. On the way up. Someone they're more likely to believe than me. Do you understand?"

So Eli should have known, really. Should have realized that she would have thought it through, understood what would be required, and been prepared to deliver. But she was one step ahead again, as always.

Kate crouched beside him, keeping the feed from the vidcam locked and live. They watched the monitor, tense and silent, Eli's fingers poised over the release icon on the screen of the tablet. When Mac wrenched at Gabriel, as though he were a thing and not a child, he knew he could not risk waiting any longer. He flicked the icon and watched it spin the data up to the streams. Another banner appeared on the live feed, the new headline flowing past, an inset window there for anyone to tap into life on their tablet and access the full file.

Police sirens screamed in on either side of them, angling through the jammed traffic. On the monitor she offered herself in exchange, and his heart nearly stopped. He grabbed the tablet and leapt from the van. Masoud, racing past, saw him and jerked to a halt.

"Where is she?"

"There. Trying to stop it. Alone."

Mac was dumbstruck. It had to be a trick. She stood just too far away for them to grab her without splitting their ranks and risking the intervention of the crowd, but close enough for him to almost

taste the deeper victory. She held her hands up in a gesture of sur-
render. Behind her the first police officers pushed through the circle
of onlookers and stopped at the sight of the knives.

He backed away and shouted to the men who still guarded
the doors of the elevators. James Mudd felt himself grabbed and
pulled backward. He did not resist. The boy with the vidcam was
hauled into the elevator beside him. The picture being streamed to
the screens around the foot of the building, and to the hundreds of
thousands of other screens and tablets around the world, jerked sick-
eningly and then steadied again.

"You want to know what we're about?" hissed a voice in Mudd's
ear. "Come with us and see." He nodded, mouth dry.

Aryel stepped forward again, enough to be out of reach of the
police, still well clear of Mac's itching fingers and the safer bottleneck of the barricades.

"Come on, Mac. Them for me. Are you going to deny the Lord
on His day?"

"No." He pointed a trembling finger at her. "You just want us to
release the child."

She shook her head. A note of disdain crept into her voice. "Not
especially. I want you to release the man and the woman. You can
keep me and the boy."

Gaela cried out at that, a wail of protest. One arm was twisted
painfully behind her now, and the other, trembling under Gabriel's
weight, was starting to slip. He still clung to her torso, silent and
unmoving.

"No," Mac said again. He was backing toward the elevators, the
need to get out of there an urgent coiling sensation in his belly,
but he felt there was an opportunity here. Something that should
not be missed. "One of them. Just one of them for you, and not
the boy."

"The woman." Her answer was immediate, autocratic. "She's
almost done for anyway. Take the boy from her, bring her halfway
here, and I'll come to meet you."

Mac stared. Then he nodded to his men. One of them wrenched
Gabriel away from Gaela, and she screamed again, reaching for him

as Mac wrapped a hand in her hair. He held the knife now, but she struggled anyway.

"Gaela!" Aryel's voice cracked out like a whip. "Stop fighting. Let me get to him."

Gaela jerked as though stung and looked up, green eyes burning into blue out of a bruised, tearstained face. Then she stumbled forward, almost pulling Mac along. Aryel went to meet them. As they reached each other Mac shoved Gaela hard, sending her staggering forward. When he made as if to grab Aryel she checked him with a look of cold contempt and swept on. He kept the knife close to her face as he walked backward, watching the tall police commander and the traitor Walker break through the crowd to take hold of the weeping, red-haired gem woman. The policeman shouted something, racing forward, and there was a sudden panic and tumult, and then they were in the lifts and sweeping skyward.

28

He was a fall child, born a day after the equinox, into an autumn of revolution.

In the high Himalayas that year, purple- and blue-haired miners fought pitched battles against imported mercenaries, bringing the works to a standstill, sending commodity prices crashing, and hacking the trade streams that usually carried productivity data so they transmitted instead images of poisoned bodies, frozen and stacked like cordwood against the walls of the tunnels that had killed them.

In America, a new underground railroad came suddenly overground, citizen groups coordinating to flood the streams with suppressed reports and smuggled vidlinks. Mass protests on the streets of every major city brought transport and trading to a halt. The gems and their supporters took advantage of the chaos to occupy tracts of prime land, even whole towns, and demand that they be designated for their exclusive use in a new, more equitable system of reservations.

In Australia it emerged that the genestock used for intense modification had, for close to a century, been almost exclusively aboriginal. The remaining norm aborigines rose up in fury, declaring the racism of past centuries far from dead, breaking gems out of their dormitories, and attacking their handlers. In Thailand a stunning young woman with glowing lavender eyes negotiated her way past security and onto a live lifestyle stream and revealed that in Southeast Asia, Sweden, and the countries of the Gulf, her parent gemtech did a roaring trade in engineering and selling gems for sex.

And in the Home Counties of England, around the same time that a hugely valuable hyperspectral prototype disappeared while on assignment, slipping her guards to join the growing escapee ghettoes in the crumbling backstreets of London, a baby boy was born.

His parents had dithered about whether they wanted a child. They both worked in the bioservices industry, he as an accountant and she for an equipment supplier. So when they decided it was better to go ahead than wait too late and risk regret, they naturally selected in vitro to ensure that absolutely nothing would be left to chance. Everything was briskly planned and tightly scheduled: the conception, the gestation, the delivery. They never fell in love with family life, but he was almost two years old before they realized that something was wrong.

When pediatricians and child psychologists told them their claims could not possibly be true, they turned to the gemtechs. The firm responsible for producing the fertilized egg indignantly denied any error. The parents demanded a genome analysis to prove that the child was not theirs. It proved the opposite. They accused the company of falsifying the results and looked elsewhere for confirmation that they had, somehow, been implanted with a radically engineered embryo.

Their conviction that they were at best victims of a mix-up and a cover-up, and at worst of a full-blown conspiracy, was made sharper by their firmly held view that gems were a subnormal subspecies to whom few ethical boundaries should apply. They had been active campaigners against increased regulation of the gemtech industry and had drawn much ire as a consequence. They became convinced that there existed a double agent, some insidious enemy at whose identity they could only guess, who had inflicted a gem child upon them in a twisted scheme of sabotage and revenge.

This outlandish tale gained little traction, especially since embarrassment and suspicion made them reluctant to share it widely. Plus the child's alleged abnormality was inconsistent, unpredictable, and generally held to be impossible. They knew better. They found their way, eventually, to GenPhen.

Henderson found no traces of proximate engineering in the genome either but spotted evidence of the boy's ability almost immediately. It made their story far more believable. The most sensational prototype he had ever heard of had fallen inexplicably into his lap. He suggested that all the parents' problems, including any lingering taint from the unfortunate affair, could be made to disappear from their lives along with the child. They would have to disappear themselves, of course, change their identities and start again elsewhere. There was money for that, a massive transfer from the Bel'Natur conglomerate for whom he acted as proxy. The firm would become the boy's legal guardian and would never trouble them again. They took the deal and fled.

By the time Henderson looked up from a careful, weeks-long examination of his latest subject, the world had changed. The Declaration took him completely by surprise. His interim report had generated an enthusiastic instruction to proceed; now no one at the head office would acknowledge his existence. His staff had gone. He found he had few remaining contacts in the crèches, and they advised him to run. The gravity of the situation became suddenly, chillingly clear to him. But he had resources of his own, homes in different countries, funds in myriad accounts. All he had to do first was get rid of the child.

Exactly how the boy came to be left on the doorstep of the Squats was never clear. The most charitable interpretation was that it was Henderson's attempt to anonymously hand him over to his own kind. But the condition in which he was found, wrapped up, drugged, and dehydrated, meant he had been far more likely to suffocate than survive.

The gems took him in, hid him for fear that Bel'Natur could use the release from his norm parents to reclaim him from the authorities, rehabilitated and reared and loved him. It was also they who figured him out. Through means left unclear they retrieved the entire datastream of his previous history, recognized the thoroughness of the earlier work, and went looking for an answer that fit the evidence. Aryel Morningstar herself narrated a brief summation.

"Gabriel carries a heritage sequence that used to be associated with a high risk of schizophrenia. Thanks to the gene surgery performed on the pre-embryonic cells of his great-great-grandparents, this is no longer the case. The junk code that might have made it difficult for him to distinguish his own consciousness from others' has been stripped out, and the core sequence has been freed to express itself. His ability to perceive the thoughts of people around him is a naturally evolved trait, but it was the Syndrome-safety engineering of the past century that has enabled it to be expressed beyond infancy."

She had attached her own study as proof, different elements commissioned from a series of black-market labs, correlated and compared with archive databases from mental hospitals and paranormal research units. But that was not all she included.

His original genome analysis was also there, along with the Gen-Phen report addressed to Bel'Natur. Henderson's recorded summary was there, directed to Felix Carrington, with the timestamp proving delivery. The vid that Eli had already seen was there: the child without voice or memory, the burns and bruises and trash bag wrapper. And finally his birth parents, their norm lineage confirmed by genetype, accepting the offer and signing him away.

All of this Aryel Morningstar gave to Eli Walker. And Eli Walker gave to the world.

Aryel stood, her back to the glass wall beyond which the city slipped away, Gabriel in her arms. She had ignored Mac's knife, and there before the doors had simply plucked him away from the man who had taken him from Gaela. The boy had clamped on to her as he had to his mother, arms and legs wrapped around the folds of her cloak. Every now and then she glanced up, her gaze sweeping the crowded pod, catching James Mudd's eye, looking across to the other elevator, where Donal had slumped to the floor, checking the display that counted off the levels as they ascended. But mostly she kept her attention on the child.

Now that they had their prize and were on their way, now that there was no more chance of being stopped, the godgang had gone surprisingly quiet. There was no shouting, no bluster, no abuse. They ranged around the perimeter of the pod, looking from Aryel and Gabriel to the Newsbeat team as though they could not quite believe what they had accomplished. Mudd wondered if their presence there, the knowledge that they were being streamed live to the planet, was what kept them in check.

His young colleague with the vidcam, a young man only just past his apprenticeship, was trembling and Mudd took hold of the equipment to help steady it, muttering a reassurance. Based on what, he did not know. Newsbeat's generally negative stance on gems was not nearly radical enough for the godgang; there was no guarantee they would get out of this alive either. Aryel Morningstar caught his eye again, and he glanced down at the vidcam's monitor, tapped it, then slid his tablet out of his pocket.

"What are you doing?" Mac. Edgy.

"That"—he pointed at the monitor—"it's not working properly. I need to make sure the picture they're getting is clear."

He babbled on as he pulled up the stream, asking questions that Mac did not answer. The headline flowed past. He did not have to feign surprise. He looked up at Mac and cleared his throat. "E-excuse me."

"What? We're not live?"

"Yes we are. It's fine. There's just something else that's come in on our feed . . . about this boy . . ." He held the tablet out to Mac. The godgang leader glanced at it for a moment, then pushed it away.

"Lies. All lies."

"How do you know? It says there's proof—"

"Shut up."

The other men shifted and muttered to each other. One of them said, "What is it, Mac?"

"Says this abomination is really a norm kid." Mac snorted.

The men looked at Gabriel, noting once more his lack of gem-sign. Aryel Morningstar met their eyes levelly over his small, sandy-brown head.

"They say he doesn't really have powers?" another man asked. He sounded uncertain.

"Oh, he does. A norm *with* powers, 'parently. *Natural* ones." He shook his head at the idiocy of such a claim while the other men added their own sounds of derision. James Mudd tried again.

"How . . . how can you be sure it isn't true?"

"How? *How?*" Mac brandished the knife. "'Cos humans don't *have* powers. Only the children of God and the spawn of the Beast. And if you want to know which one this is, there's your proof right there." The knife waved at Gabriel. "No child of the Lord would cling to an abomination. No human child neither."

"But—"

Mac pointed the knife at him. "You are here to witness. Not to speak."

Aryel Morningstar made a sound that could have been a sigh, or a gust of silent laughter. Her blue eyes closed for a moment in acknowledgment, or resignation, and she shifted Gabriel's weight slightly. Then her eyes opened again, and she did sigh now, and look at the display, as though they could not arrive soon enough.

Eli and Gaela stood in front of the window-size screens on the plaza. He had grabbed an emergency blanket and wrapped it and his arm around her shoulders, trying to lend comfort and support, but he felt he might be leaning as much on her as she on him. She was shaking, hands clenched beneath her chin, her breath coming in sobs. Masoud was nearby, pacing in a tight circle, growling into his earset as he tried to get the elevators halted. All around them police and paramedics milled, keeping the crowd back, everyone staring impotently at the screens. Teams had already run inside, but there was no hope of getting to the terrace in time.

They watched James Mudd's exchange with Mac. Eli found he was not surprised at the outcome. He knew he was terrified, panicked, and powerless, and in that strange paralysis he found himself noticing things with an acute, almost painful intensity that was new to him.

The moment they got into the elevator Aryel had started doing something with her hands. It was a subtle, small movement. She had clasped her wrists, forming a sling for Gabriel to sit in. Her fingers moved carefully, first the right hand doing something to the sleeve of the left. Then she stopped, shifted her grip, and began on the other side. He saw that she must have undone some hidden fastening, for the fabric gaped open around her left wrist.

His earset buzzed. For an insane moment he hoped it was her, but on the screen she silently checked the display again and brushed her lips across the top of Gabriel's head.

Mikal's voice came into his ear.

"Where's Gaela?"

"She's here. She's right here with me. Are you seeing this?"

"Yes. I'm with Bal."

He pulled the 'set off and slid it over Gaela's ear. He caught a snatch of Bal's voice, weak but steady, as she pushed it into place.

"Gaela? She can do it. Aryel can do it."

Do what? he wondered, and watched her right hand slip out of view, unhurried and unnoticed, the sleeve withdrawn into the black density of cloak. There was a bunching of the fabric beneath Gabriel's seat, and the hand reappeared through a slit, a center seam he had barely noticed before. The entire garment seemed bigger, wider, the huge lump of her shoulders more swollen and tumorous than ever. She was breathing deeply and evenly, like a diver preparing for descent.

There were only a few floors to go. She murmured to Gabriel and crouched suddenly, as though he was slipping from her grasp. She was back up before the men could react, grip once more secure, but now both sleeves were gone; both hands emerged from the lengthening slit in the cloak. Gabriel's legs were tucked under it and the fabric billowed loose around her own. Mac stared at her, frowning, as though aware of a change but unable to pinpoint it. He was opening his mouth for a challenge when the elevator slid smoothly to a halt. The doors pinged open, and the cold wind of the terrace blasted inside.

Over at the Bel'Natur building, Zavcka Klist stepped out of her own elevator and ran for the perimeter walkway. Her eyes still scanned the tablet in her hand, and she barely managed to dodge the people and furniture in her way. Startled looks followed her. A few called out. She ignored them.

She had left the others behind at the Conference, had already half-decided to burn her files and simply walk out, disappear, watch from a distance while Felix dug himself into a deeper and deeper hole. She could see that the plan was doomed. Bel'Natur could survive its failure; in all likelihood she would not.

What had flashed onto the streams in the last ten minutes looked set to change her prospects. Exactly how depended on what happened in the next two. She skidded into the corridor and slammed up against the glass, staring across the gulf at Newhope Tower.

Rollo had been thorough. The doors leading into the building from the terrace had been locked using a command program no one had ever seen before. Faces pressed up against the glass, service staff and office workers shouting soundlessly, hands slapping and fists pounding. To no effect. Mac cast a cool glance over them and turned away.

They had intended to shove Aryel out of the pod but found it unnecessary. She sidestepped them and strode ahead as if she owned the place, into the biting cold and clear blue and crunching frost underfoot. The godgang crowded after, the men who had ridden up with him dragging Donal from the other elevator. James Mudd was seized by the elbow and prodded forward. The vidcam kept pace beside him. The operator had stopped trembling but his lips were bitten hard together to keep himself from crying out.

She reached the center of the terrace and spun to face them, the cloak swirling around her braced legs. The sudden movement checked the men and they shuffled to a stop. There seemed to be nothing but sky behind her, arcing up into the infinity above their heads, an azure amphitheater fit only for gods.

On the ground Masoud stepped in close on Gaela's other side, teeth bared at the screen, growling, "The barrier's mostly clear, for viewing, but it's nine feet high, they won't be able to—Oh *shit*."

Because they had thought of that, of course, and two-thirds of its height had been cut away, down to the metal railing fronting the glass, the gap barely hip high and wide enough for two.

The men moved forward, slowly but deliberately, as though testing her, and she moved back, once more keeping the distance constant. They were holding Donal just in front and to the side of the vidcam. Eli could see his bound and bloody hands in the foreground corner of the frame. Ahead of him Aryel was getting perilously close to the gap. She seemed to be murmuring something to Gabriel. But then she glanced up without raising her head, a sharp blue flicker from under smooth bronze brows, and Donal's hands clenched.

The image on the screen began to tremble again. For the first time there was a sound from the operator, a sobbing intake of breath. James Mudd said, "You can't expect us to . . . we can't . . ."

"Keep shooting." That whiplash voice, and the image steadied. The men stopped, looking at each other and at her, muttering their confusion.

Mac stepped into the arena between them, knife glinting in the sun, and she took a long stride back. The cloak billowed toward him, the center seam open almost all the way now, only Gabriel's small arms wrapped around her neck keeping it in place. As the heavy fabric fell back Eli glimpsed a strange unevenness against its inner surface, as though it was lined with something that had a life of its own, something that whispered and moved and had expanded in the last few minutes. There was a hint of textured brown against the black, a massed rustling in the darkness.

And then, suddenly, he knew.

Her face was fierce and proud, but her voice as she spoke to Gabriel was as gentle as a lullaby. "Gabe? Tuck your hands under my coat. It's cold." She rubbed his back to encourage him, tugging lightly at his arm, and he did as he was told. The cloak hung loose on her shoulders now, and she tightened her grip on his torso.

"Cold?" Mac's voice was loud and harsh, a note of hysteria in the sarcasm, his bewilderment finally boiling over into rage. "You're worried he's *cold*? He's going to be colder in a second."

"Yes," she said quietly. "He is. I'm sorry, baby. It won't last long."

They laughed at that, and Mac leapt forward. She spun away from him, graceful as a dancer, and ran for the gap. The cloak was half-gone in one stride, left behind in two, a black shroud that entangled Mac and sent him sprawling. He had just a glimpse of her back, the impossible limbs sweeping up above her shoulders, a flash of creamy down underside, bronze-bright flight feathers drawn sharp against a searing blue sky.

Her third step drove her up, into the breach and the clear air. She spread her wings, and jumped.

29

Screams on the plaza, watchers recoiling in shock from the screens, where the image jerked and fell sideways and blurred anyway. Amid the pandemonium, a rippling, reverent astonishment. For the second time that week Eli's legs threatened to collapse under him.

Gaela was already sprinting away from the building, head craned back to look. She spotted them instantly, bronze against blue. Eli recovered himself and was beside her a moment later. So was everyone else, dozens and dozens of them now, hundreds, ringing the building, every face pointed at the sky. Aryel Morningstar was high up but descending, sweeping down in a wide spiral, holding the little boy tight against her chest.

"She can fly," came a disbelieving whisper from somewhere nearby, and Eli glanced over to the speaker, a man tipped so far back he looked as unsteady as he sounded. He staggered a little as Eli watched, arms flapping for balance. His gaze did not shift from the tiny figure high up against the tower, a fixed point, a sky anchor beneath which he swayed and turned. The strange dance swept through the crowd, along with the phrase, a murmuration

caught and echoed and thrown up like a prayer from a hundred
throats, as though to say it out loud might make sense of what
they saw.

"She can fly. She has wings. It's *wings*. She can *fly*."

And here and there, begun and bitten off, because that was wrong,
ridiculous, had to be, the notion was archaic and impossible, "She's—
She's a—"

But still it presented itself, rising phoenix-like, rampant now and
sweeping up and over the barriers of history and logic. Eli heard it
not said in the trailing exclamations, the mouths stopped by clasped
hands.

A new image flashed up on the screens of Newhope Tower, a
view from below, one of the vidcam crews on the plaza zooming in.
It caught her as she appeared to say something to the child in her
arms, her dark hair loose now and blown back from her face. They
were more than halfway down, and the crowd fell silent. Seconds
that felt like years ticked past, and then there was the dark shadow
of her wings over the plaza, and more cries as people shrank back,
stumbling out of the way.

Her feet hit the top of an ambulance first, driven onto the sidewalk
in a show of feeble readiness, and she took a long stride across it to lose
speed. Then off, wings spilling the wind of her passage as she dropped,
and she stepped out of the air and onto the ground as lightly as she
had left it.

She dropped another kiss onto Gabriel's head and looked up, eyes
sweeping the plaza, wings sweeping the air as she turned. A pile of
blankets was stacked in the open bay of the vehicle, next to a para-
medic whose knees really had gone. She picked one up and wrapped
it around the boy, murmuring something to the medic, stepping
clear to look around again.

And then Gaela reached them and Aryel stepped into her embrace,
returning it and relinquishing Gabriel. He looked back at her then,
from the safety of his mother's arms, and it seemed as though he
might be starting to come back to himself.

Eli Walker slid to a stop and found himself unable to speak. Next
to him Masoud appeared to have suffered the same affliction. She

turned to them. Her wings were still half-open, sunlight glinting off soft bronze feathers limned in gold. Her eyes were the color of sky.

"Eli." The voice still musical, still carrying, no longer incongruous. "Take care of them. Get them to Bal. Masoud, you need to get up there."

She was backing away as she spoke, wings arcing up to catch the air. "I have to go. I told Donal what to do but I don't know if he could hear me."

"He heard you," Eli managed, and Gabriel added a tiny nod of confirmation. But she was already gone, flying fast up the gleaming gray skin of the tower.

The shouts were unending now, people jumping up and down and pointing and screaming in exhilaration at the sight of her, as though this departure had broken some sort of spell. She changed direction, cutting a sharp angle close to the building, and they saw that the small silver pod of an elevator was descending.

Donal and James Mudd and the boy with the vidcam were slumped inside the pod. Mudd had already ripped the tape away from the young gem's mouth and was stripping it off his hands. The operator wearily adjusted his kit, knocked askew when Donal had spun away from his distracted captors and body-checked him toward the elevators. He centered the vidcam on them and brought it back into focus. When the bronze shadow flashed below them, he swung it around and caught her circling to look again.

Donal crawled over to the rail and dragged himself upright. He pressed a bloody hand to the glass. She soared past, fingers outstretched to brush against it. Then she blew him a kiss, curved away from the elevator, and flew straight up.

Zavcka Klist watched the tiny figure of the winged woman pause beside the pod and then resume her swift ascent. She drew a deep, deep breath, maybe the deepest of her long life, and felt it shudder on the way out. She stepped back smoothly and quietly, acutely aware of the floor beneath her feet, the hard feel of the tablet in her hand, the cold that wrapped around her spine and braced it.

The ones who had followed her stayed, buzzing with excitement, eyes flickering from tablets to the miracle of Newhope Tower, while she slipped away.

Some moments begin a cycle and some moments end them, and some remain forever mysterious.

No one ever knew what Aryel Morningstar said to Mac and his men, back up there on the terrace of Newhope Tower. They saw what she *did*, all those faces pressed up against the glass, all those tablet feeds hacked and streamed live. They saw how she drove them back, huge wings like judgment beating down out of a sparkling sky, until they crowded against the doors to the elevators. They saw her face clouded in wrath, her lips shaping strange words as she shouted, and they saw the men cower and weep in fear. They saw how she kicked away their knives and clubs but never touched them, and how she stood guard, wings spread wide, between the men and the edge until Masoud and his officers arrived to take them away.

For all the recordings of that moment, all the apps and analysis, they never could decipher what the words were.

Aryel Morningstar would only smile sadly and say that it was a moment, and it was necessary, and it was gone. Few of the godgang ever spoke again, and never about the terrace of Newhope Tower. For the rest of his days Mac would blanch and shudder and turn away when asked. If they pressed him too hard his bladder would go, and after a while they stopped.

AFTERMATH

30

Seizing the Moment

GREAT BRITAIN'S ACTING COMMISSIONER FOR GEM AFFAIRS DR. ROBERT TRENCH SPEAKS OUT

Autofeed   @Observer.eu/commentary/GMH_crisis_Trench_post/ 2512131AS

To say that what happened yesterday was amazing would be the understatement of this and probably several other centuries. The pundits are already picking our shared experience apart, asking whether those few minutes of horror and revelation and sheer, gut-swooping wonder was the most globally witnessed moment ever. The more thoughtful—or perhaps just the more cynical—among them are questioning what, if anything, we should take away from this week's events.

They've asked my opinion, and I am expected, I suppose, to be politely neutral. To not read too much into things, not get carried away. To publicly play down the significance of what we learned, while privately the government scrambles to work out what to do about it. But if there was ever a time to be brave, to do the unexpected, this is it.

So let me be blunt. What happened yesterday was a seminal moment in the history of the human race.

Oh, we've seen courage and calm in the face of danger before. Also mindless hatred and brutality, and self-sacrifice, and sorrow. This is not the first time we've learned deeply kept secrets, and had to face hard truths. But it may be the first time we've had the reality of the worst and the best that human beings can be slapped in our faces quite so hard. It may be the first time the choices that we have to make, as a society and as a species, are quite so stark.

I spoke with Aryel Morningstar late last night. You may find this difficult to believe—I did, and I was there—but in the midst of her grief for five more murdered friends, her worry for those wounded in both mind and body, having to deal with the chaos left behind in the Squats and the personal consequences of revealing her unique gemsign and ability: she was also profoundly concerned about the effect these events would have on the gems of Europe, and perhaps the world.

Anyone who has been following the politics of the post-Declaration era will understand her anxiety. Quite apart from the crass commercial priorities of the gemtechs, and the widespread economic pain of their near-collapse, most of us have remained profoundly uncomfortable with *difference*. We're too ready to believe that people who don't look just like us can't possibly *be* just like us. We think if they can do things we can't, they'll inevitably use that power against us. And now we've got a six-limbed woman who can *fly*, for god's sake. If anything was ever going to fuel the fire of our paranoia that's it, right?

Wrong. At least that's what I told her. Look at the streams, I said. Look at what's actually happened since you stepped inside that elevator. Look at the condemnation of the godgang and the gemtechs and Nicholas Henderson and Gabriel's birth parents. Look at the sympathy and support and admiration and sheer *love* pouring in, from all over the world. Look at the demand for justice.

Look at how happy we are to know that a human can fly.

She waved that one away with typically Aryel-ian grace, and asked me to pass on the gems' deep gratitude for the outpouring of goodwill. "The public have been amazing," she said. "Their reaction gives us so much comfort—but it's up to the politicians to make sure that the lives that were saved today are worth living. And that the deaths were not in vain."

She's right, of course. Politicians are a cautious lot. They prefer incremental shifts to bold action. They like studies and inquiries and retrospective reviews. Money talks, and they listen. It took close to three *decades* of constant campaigning to get even the partial gem suffrage of the Declaration of the Principles of Human Fraternity, and that scraped through by a pretty narrow margin. Politicians respond quickly to the electorate, and not much else.

So let's consider the question, electorate. We have an opportunity to do the right thing and to do it *now*. What has emerged as the Temple Solution is simple, practical, efficient, and above all it is *just*. The realization that the norm child Gabriel is no less remarkable than his adoptive gem mother should be all the proof we need. The rejection and abuse that child suffered should never again be visited on any child, gem or norm. The sooner we get rid of the distinction, the sooner we can make certain of it.

We can do it. We have the evidence of the Walker Report and of Gabriel and of Aryel Morningstar herself, perhaps the most profoundly engineered person on the planet. She is also the most *human* being I have ever met.

We should not wait. We should claim her and the other gems, just as we claim Gabriel, just as we claim every other extraordinary person who has graced us. We should do it proudly and we should do it now. We need to stop floundering in suspicion or, even worse, being paralyzed by guilt. We need to think about history—both the past about which we can do nothing, and the legacy of the present which is unfolding right now. We need to ensure that we are not among the generations forever condemned by our children. We need to stop being scared.

You want to see different? Take a look at Aryel Morningstar.

Do you really want to see her put in a cage?

"He's really le' them have it, eh?" Donal's voice was rough with pain and drugs, and, Eli thought, barely concealed emotion. He swallowed past the lump in his own throat and looked up from the tablet feed he'd been reading aloud to where the young gem lay propped up on pillows in the hospital bed. His head was swathed in bandages to twice its normal size, holding in place the biogels to maintain stasis in the wounds until the scaffolding on which new ears would grow was ready to be grafted in place.

"He says he doesn't care if he gets the sack. He's had to be circumspect a lot in his job, and he's sick of it." Eli shifted his position a little, glancing over to the other young man who sat in a wheelchair next to the adjacent bed, listening keenly. Callan's head was tightly covered by a skullcap-like dressing, and one leg and both arms were encased in bone splints, but his face was clear of bandages. Beneath the swollen, bruised skin, crisscrossed by the faint purple lines of plastic surgery, Eli could see vestiges of the beauty Sally had spoken of.

"I also think he feels guilty. It was his responsibility to make sure you were all taken care of, that the right resources were in place, and, well . . ." Eli gestured up and down the length of the ward, where the gems who were not in intensive care lay in a neat row of partitioned cubicles, mostly still in drugged sleep at this hour of the morning. The sound-damping field around Donal's bed had been expanded to take in his neighbors on either side, and the partition walls between them had been pushed back. "He's trying to make up for it."

"He's succeeding," said Gaela quietly from the other side, and Eli swiveled to look at her. "Not that I blame him for anything that's happened. Dr. Trench always did his best by us. But this," she waved a hand at the tablet, "it's gone viral like nothing I've ever seen. It's the top post in every country, in just about every language . . ." She glanced over at Callan, who nodded. "He's hit a nerve, bless him. People seem convinced."

She looked down, stroking Gabriel's hair. She was perched at the foot of Bal's bed with the boy stretched out between them, apparently half-asleep. Bal curled a bandaged hand around his son's feet.

"Th' question is," said Donal, "how long they *stay* convinced. I mean we're all the rage this mornin', bu' I was gettin' spat on in Edinburgh not much more'n a year ago . . ."

Gabriel shifted in Gaela's lap, and she threw a warning look at Donal. Bal cleared his throat.

"Aryel," he said, and left it at that for so long that Donal said, "Wha' abou' her? Apart from her bein' the second bloomin' comin' o' course."

"Just that. That's the nerve he hit. They *want* her. They want to claim her, like he said, they want what she is to be part of what they are. She means something else to them, something more . . ." He shook his head. "And we're the price. That's what she engineered, that's the bargain. They don't get her, they don't get to be part of her world, unless they take all of us."

"It's not what *she* wanted," said Eli. The realization had been ebbing and flowing from him in waves all night, and now it settled into a cold, stunned clarity as he listened to Bal speak. "She wanted us to get there on our own. There was something in her face when she knew they were taking you to the tower, when she knew what she'd have to do. She didn't want to be a bribe, she didn't want . . ."

She didn't want to have to manipulate us quite this much. The thought came and went like a flicker of lightning, but not before he saw Gabriel's brown eyes blink open at him and slowly close again.

"No, she didn't," said Bal quietly. "But when the moment came she had to make it count. We—most of us—have known Aryel's gemsign for some time. She knew it would mean something different from norms, that she would have an . . . impact. She said it would be better in the end if she never had to use it." He sighed. "But."

"We are where we are," said Gaela.

"Exactly."

The silence stretched out for a long time, until Gabriel stirred and pushed himself up, rubbing his eyes. He glanced nervously toward the door at the end of the ward. Gaela followed the motion, squinted at it, and cuddled him close.

"It's just the nurse, Gabe. We saw her before, remember? She's okay."

The boy nodded hesitantly, and sure enough the door swung open to admit a white-smocked woman bustling efficiently toward them. She frowned as she saw the figures perched on the end of the bed, but her face cleared immediately as she registered the woman and child.

"You all right there, dears?" she said kindly as she entered the damper field. "You'll let us know if you need anything, won't you? I just came to let Mr. Donal know, the grafts should be ready by around lunchtime. It's a quick procedure, only we didn't think to ask . . ."

She had stopped beside Donal's bed and looked confused and a bit embarrassed. The gems stared back at her, nonplussed.

"Is everything all right?" asked Eli.

"Yes of course, right as rain, we just . . ." She faced Donal and took a deep breath. "We've set them up to grow exactly the same shape and size as before, it's what we would normally do, I just thought we should make sure that's what you wanted." She gave him a pleading look.

Eli felt his eyebrows shoot up and caught the glance that flew between Gaela and Bal. Between the bandages, Donal's face was turning red. He spluttered.

"Wha' the—O' *course* tha's wha' I want! Why wouldn' I?"

The nurse's relief did battle with her increasing embarrassment.

"That's what we thought. Just checking. Right, well. That's all sorted then." She was backing hastily away toward the edge of the field. "I'll let them know it's fine, shall I? And I'll be back to take you down in a couple of hours. In the meantime, if you need anything, anything at all, just lean on the call buttons, someone will be in directly." She turned and fled.

Bal let out a long breath. "Wow."

"Well," said Eli.

Donal was still livid. "Can you *b'lieve* she asked me tha'? Wha' kin' of a blooady question is *tha'?*"

"An important one," said Eli. He glanced over at Callan. "When they did your grafts did they ask about your hair? Whether you wanted to change it?"

The man in the wheelchair shook his head. Eli looked back at Donal. "She gave you a choice," he said. It took a minute to sink in. Donal's face slowly cleared.

"Oh."

"A life without gemsign. It's not a small thing, my friend."

"I guess I shouldna bin so testy abou' it." Now it was his turn to look embarrassed. "I'll make it up to her later."

He looked around for a change of subject and settled on Gabriel. The little boy was drawn and pale, far less animated than usual, but he appeared to have emerged from the nearly catatonic state of the day before. He stayed attached to Gaela as though glued. "How're you doin' then, mate? Feelin' a little better?"

The child nodded. "A little better." His voice was slow, barely above a whisper, and he glanced toward the door through which the nurse had retreated. "Everyone's trying to think nice thoughts around me."

"Does it help?"

He nodded again. "It's still bad though." His eyes squeezed tight shut, as if he was fighting back tears, or trying to block out an image. "Aunty Wenda," he said, and the faint voice trembled.

"What happened, Gabe?" asked Bal. "Could you tell?" Gabriel's little face crumpled for a moment and Eli and Donal stared at Bal as though he had gone mad. Gaela's lips tightened, but it seemed she understood something they had not.

"No," the child replied. "It was like you said, Papa. She just went . . . out. She wasn't there anymore." He looked over at Callan and seemed to gain a little strength. "She thought about you. She was thinking about you the whole time."

A spasm of pain passed over the damaged face and he slumped, staring into his lap, head bowed in acknowledgment.

"Callan?" said Gaela. "Was she . . . ?"

"We didn't know," he replied quietly. His voice was warm and husky, and Eli thought he heard tears in it. "It's possible. We talked about trying to find out. Seeing if we could get the records." He looked away, up and out as though he could see through the screened windows set high in the wall.

"You could still do that. Aryel would help."

Callan nodded listlessly. This time the silence stretched out like an ache, low and unbearable. Eli longed suddenly for Aryel, wanting to be soothed by her presence, craving the beauty that clothed her every look and step and fluttering feather. It was like craving a drug. He looked around, elaborately and ridiculously casual, as though she might at any moment push through the swinging doors or appear outside the windows. He was sure he fooled no one. "Where is she anyway?"

"It's as you say, Eli," said Bal. "The world's changing. It's going to roll right over us before we know it. She has some things to take care of first."

Far down the sweep of the great river, where the new finger of forest stretched through abandoned industrial neighborhoods to kiss its shore, Aryel Morningstar stepped softly under leafless boughs and thought about another forest, a long long time ago. She could not shake the sensation that she was being hunted, again, as though this moment were just a brief respite before she must break cover; and the bleak awareness that this time instead of fleeing she must break toward her pursuers and be caught. She wondered if the tinge of despair was linked to the distant sound of a helicopter, no doubt a press drone sent up on the news that she had been spotted.

Her companion walked close beside her, unawed by the wings she had fluffed up around herself for warmth and seemingly unaware of her mood. He was an old man, tall but beginning to stoop a little, dressed in an ancient, ragged coat that she thought she remembered from their first meeting at the foot of that mountain gorge a lifetime ago. For a while there was a peaceful quiet between them. He was the first to break it.

"Well," he said, "I think you did as well as you possibly could have under the circumstances. But did you underestimate them, Aryel?"

"I underestimated *her*. But then she didn't do so well herself. She lost control of her own plan."

"Though the consequences will fall on others, I understand."

"As ever. Not that Felix Carrington is an innocent. I can't find it in myself to have any regrets for him."

Once the crime scenes at the Squats and Newhope Tower were under control and Masoud had had a chance to glance through the Gabriel file, he had invited Felix to assist the police in their inquiries. The Bel'Natur chief executive had brusquely declined, whereupon Masoud had made clear the nature of the request by arresting him. For an hour or so last night the streams had been alive with pictures of him being bundled out of the Bel'Natur offices and into the back of a police transport. Aryel had looked for the standard, strident denials from press officers and corporate counsel. She found instead a cautious statement of surprise, concern, and an unqualified commitment to assist the authorities with their investigation, and had known who was now in charge.

"Ah, your redoubtable Commander Masoud of the Met. He's quite sharp, you said. Any chance he might reach the right conclusion?"

"I doubt it. Zavcka knows how to cover her tracks. Even Henderson didn't know about her, did he?"

"Not according to our contact." The man's lips twisted in distaste. Aryel caught the look.

"I didn't ask for him to be killed, Reginald."

"No, Aryel, you did not." It was neither criticism nor praise, just a statement of fact.

"You know there's going to be a lot of attention on you now. A *lot*. The whole Remnant angle is going to be scrutinized closely. There's nothing I can do to prevent that."

"I know. It's fine, we're prepared. The only thing we can be accused of is giving you refuge, and I think they're unlikely to give us a hard time about that at this point." He shot her a wry smile. "We can honestly say we know very little about where you came from, which will only make you even more glamorous."

Aryel made a face. "Don't rub it in."

"Sorry. What happens now?"

"Now I have to play the game. Be what they want me to be. I can't see a way out of it, not if we want to secure our future."

"You've led such a lonely life, Aryel," he said gently. "What you risked coming to this city, forcing yourself to live in a straitjacket . . . might this new situation not have its compensations?"

"I haven't been lonely these past few years. Not much. And they've worked so hard to make things easier for me. Gaela mapped the surveillance so I could fly a little at night, not to mention nicking the fabric for my cloak. Bal and Mikal knocked a whole floor through to give me an apartment I could stretch in. I thought, if I could just make it happen without becoming the focus myself maybe I'd be able to slip away quietly afterward, go back to Brecon—" She broke off, shaking her head. "Some of them might even have come with me. Bal and I talked about it."

"You could still come back to Brecon. So could Bal and his family."

"I'll be traveling with a bit more of an entourage from now on, I think." Again the buzz of the helicopter intruded and this time he seemed to register it, and to understand.

Bells began to ring somewhere far away, high and clear in the cold air. Aryel stopped and cocked an ear to listen.

"Christmas morning. Feels wrong somehow." She started moving again, heading back toward the river. "We'd better go."

"Yes. No point wasting the moment."

They walked in silence for a minute or two before Reginald said, "She'll be watching of course."

"Of course." Aryel sighed it out, resigned, bitter.

"Aryel. You know you did the right thing."

"Yes, I know. Ask me how much it helps to know that."

The old man sighed in his turn and said nothing. They walked side by side under the barren trees, feet crunching softly on a deep, frost-rimed carpet of leaves, until they came to a sudden widening of the tributary, a little above where it met the main channel. Centuries-old buildings crumbled along the edge. One of them looked to have been a warehouse, built right over the water.

Aryel and Reginald stepped inside, through a gaping hole where part of a wall had fallen away. Two gillungs lounged at the edge of the pool. Eli, had he been there, would have recognized one of them as the woman Lapsa, and the other as the outspoken man from the community meeting. They were having a quiet conversation with several norms who sat or crouched near the water and who wore the same rough, patched, outmoded clothing as Reginald.

"All set?" asked Aryel.

"Just waiting on you," said the man. He pushed himself half out of the water with one brawny arm, reaching up to clasp hands with the norm closest to him and waving farewell to the others. He and Lapsa slipped quietly below the surface. They would wait until the watchers above were fully focused on Aryel, and then shadow her home.

Aryel said her own good-byes, and Reginald pulled her into a rough embrace. She stepped clear, blue eyes blinking a little, and they watched from the shelter of the old warehouse as she walked out from under the trees and sprang skyward.

They were gathering on the quayside, the service originally intended for Nelson expanded now to mourn the six gems and one norm lost to the godgang's rampage. The sweet, sad notes of a guitharp rippled over the growing crowd as the residents of the Squats drifted down the main street, others joining them from the alleys and passages that led back to the boulevard. It was choked with uplink vans, and reporters with vidcams wove through the slowly moving stream of people. They appeared not to be intruding on anyone, but Mikal was keeping an eye on them nonetheless. Looking out over the patchwork sea of glowing and dull heads, he saw Eli Walker and Robert Trench arrive, flanked by the secretary of state and a squadron of aides.

He waded through the growing crowd to where Tobias stood, black-robed and somber, clutching his book. He was surrounded by what seemed like the entire contingent of UC faithful, not just the local congregation but from across the city as well. He craned back to look up at the giant gem. Mikal answered the question he could see in the priest's eyes.

"She's on her way. You're okay with it not being quite what you'd planned, right? All the others . . ."

Tobias was nodding vigorously. "Of course. This is so much bigger now."

Mikal agreed with a small smile and turned away, privately wondering if Tobias's estimate of *bigger* had more to do with Aryel's gem-sign than with the preponderance of the dead who had not shared his faith. He found that Sharon Varsi had appeared beside him, and his battered heart lifted a little.

"I wanted to come. Is that okay?"

"It's better than okay."

They stepped onto the quay itself, close to where the young musician sat with his instrument. A loose circle was gathered around him, listening to the lament that flowed from his fourteen fingers. His blond girlfriend stood nearby, among a cluster of gem youths. She seemed easy enough with most of them, but Mikal noted how she glanced askance at Jora's warped features and edged away.

Across the circle he saw that Eli was also watching, and caught the scientist's eye. Eli nodded grimly in acknowledgment. Beside him Sharon sighed.

"It's funny, but I feel bad for him too. Seems he was really trying to be rational and balanced, get the right decisions made for the right reasons . . ." She shook her head.

"He'll get over it. He knows Aryel, and Gabriel too. He's going to be in too much demand to spend time worrying about what went wrong."

Beyond the sound of the music he began to hear faintly the whir of a helicopter, and he looked downstream. He spotted the machine well before he saw her and bit back a surge of anger as it edged up the river, at the noise now starting to overtake the sound of the guitharp. Whatever press organ was controlling it must have realized, though, because the drone banked high and retreated.

Aryel came into view, wingtips flicking up droplets of water as she soared out from under the arches of a bridge whose span was lined with staring faces and pointing arms. Mikal saw the vidcams swing as one toward her, the clasped hands and hungry stares of the norms, heard the sudden hum of prayer. He saw how his own people looked up with a sigh of relief but without reverence at her return, felt their quiet ripple of welcome that was so far from worship, and felt a pang of sorrow and regret that had nothing to do with the dead.

Sharon's gaze swung slowly around the gathered throng and back up to rest on him. There was a new, sober understanding in her face, but all she said was, "I hope she's ready for this."

He gazed steadily down at her. His strange eyes blinked once.

"Love lies less in awe than in acceptance, I think. Though neither is all that one might hope for."

She smiled, though in truth she looked closer to crying, and took his hand.

ACKNOWLEDGMENTS

MY FIRST AND FOREVER THANKS TO ANNA AND ALISON, WHO READ FIVE rough chapters and said to keep going, and to the rest of the ®Evolution Readers: Cherryl, Joad, Pete, Jon, Matt, Betty Ann, Alf, Rachel, and Enrique. Your comments and critiques were invaluable.

I'm deeply grateful to Jo Fletcher, Nicola Budd, and everyone else at Jo Fletcher Books and Quercus, and to Ian Drury and his colleagues at Sheil Land Associates, for making it better and making it happen.

And to Millie, for the accompaniment.